Praise for

"A first-class first _____ is
George's grasp of t_____ovel
such a pleasure. . . . A thinking person's thriller, written
with skill, self-confidence and sensitivity—a fine piece of
work." —*The Washington Post*

"*Taken* is a tough and tender thriller by a writer who
knows the world of the heart as well as the world of
crime. . . . This is a moving, gripping and multilayered
story in which the search for love touches everything,
even grief for a lost baby." —Perri O'Shaughnessy,
author of *Writ of Execution*

"Gripping . . . You'll pant with every plot turn as you revel
in George's sensual, often profound prose." —*Glamour*

"A gripping thriller with real emotional power and
remarkably subtle characterization." —*Kirkus Reviews*

"*Taken* is that rare thriller that gives as much weight to
its characters and prose as it does to its ticking-time-bomb
plot. The story drew me in, but it was the author's fallible,
very human cast that kept me coming back for more.
I look forward to reading anything that Kathleen George
writes." —George P. Pelecanos, author of *Right as Rain*

"[An] offbeat thriller . . . *Taken* boasts three ingredients
too often missing from the suspense genre: irony, humor,
and plausibly flawed, cliché-free characters."
—*Entertainment Weekly*

"[An] engrossing thriller . . . A lyrically
written and fascinating tale." —*Booklist*

FALLEN

KATHLEEN GEORGE

A DELL BOOK

FALLEN

A Dell Book / July 2004

Published by
Bantam Dell
A Division of Random House, Inc.
New York, New York

This is a work of fiction. No characters are meant to represent real people. The author has rearranged the Steelers' schedule and invented a few businesses and streets; she has altered Pittsburgh geography when necessary—for instance, the Pocusset Street of the novel is a combination of three Squirrel Hill streets. However, much of the real Pittsburgh is here as well.

ISBN 0-440-23664-9

44270691   7/10

Manufactured in the United States of America
Published simultaneously in Canada

OPM   10   9   8   7   6   5   4   3   2

For Hilary

ACKNOWLEDGMENTS

This book owes a great deal to the generous people who were willing to consult with me and teach me along the way. I acknowledge gratefully: Ronald B. Freeman, retired Commander in charge of Major Crimes, Pittsburgh Police; Carl Kurlander, screenwriter; Tom Smith, filmmaker; Frederick Fochtman, Director and Chief Toxicologist, Allegheny County Coroner's Office; David Hairhoger, pharmacist; Richard Moriarty, physician; Fran and David Fall for information about Squirrel Hill; Joyce Barlow Dodd for information about Athens, Ohio; Sandra Driscoll for details about the Wayne State Medical School; Tammy Brokaw for computer processes. I would like to thank Ann Rittenberg, agent, and Jackie Cantor, editor, for their good services. Space, time, and funding—invaluable supports—came from the MacDowell Colony, the University of Pittsburgh, and the Pennsylvania Council of the Arts. To all, my deepest thanks.

FALLEN

1

TO SAY IT WAS ALL GRIEF, ALL ALONG, WAS STRETCHING IT maybe, but not by much, Richard Christie thought. Evil, mistakes of the heart, cold-bloodedness were only the disguises, the inky shapes and cloaks. Sketching itself at the back of his mind, when the case drew to a close, were snatches of "Nowhere Man," the sweet young voices of the Beatles conjuring his own boyhood. The song would have been playing on the radio as he raced into the house and out, hopped into his mother's car and dashed out moments later, eager for the next game or distraction. He tried to remember who he was then, what he felt, what sadnesses tugged at him. He supposed, in retrospect, he was lucky to be so ordinary.

INSIDE THE HOUSE ON BEECHWOOD BOULEVARD, ELIZABETH IS waiting for the detective. Eight times, eight visits, one week. She watches and waits. He's told her he won't be bothering her so regularly anymore.

The person who killed her husband has not been found, that's the bare-rock truth.

Seven days, eight meetings ago, Commander Christie said the usual tough things about finding the killer—his sentences might have been spoken by any detective in any film—but his eyes were soft, full of feeling, and she never doubted his sincerity. He knew her husband a little, that was part of it, and anybody who knew Daniel loved him.

And here she is, a week later, the funeral over by several days, the children back at college—a difficult decision but if her work has taught her anything it's that people need to take up their lives again—here she is, alone. Yesterday brought a glimpse of what real desolation is and today she got the whole blank canvas as she wandered through the house, almost dizzy with the space and silence. People called, of course, but less frequently now that the funeral was over. They'd expended their store of philosophy in those first three days of mourning. There was nothing left to say but "Anything new? Have they found anything?" She turned the machine off because it was hard to keep saying, "No, no, nothing."

The house is empty, the larder bare. The funeral meats are gone, unthriftily given to anyone who would accept cold cuts, pastries, roasts, hams, salads. Even the children took some of the surfeit. Elizabeth wanted the food and flowers *out* of the house. She wanted to *throw away*—same as when she was spring cleaning or tackling the base-ment—anything, everything.

Now there is nothing. She wonders, should she fill a pitcher of water, put out two glasses? The detective never takes anything. She walks back and forth inside her own house as if it belongs to a stranger.

OUTSIDE THE HOUSE AND ACROSS THE STREET, AT THE EN-trance to Frick Park, a man in navy jogging clothes stretches and appears to look nowhere in particular except possibly at his well-clad ankles; yet, between this reach and that—done awkwardly, he is not an athlete—he manages to watch Elizabeth's house. He wonders if she is alone in there. Runners run by. Children chase one another with shrill ecstatic threats while their mothers attempt to herd them to the playground section, yelling, "Don't run, watch where you're going." The man is only a shadow in their peripheral vision, not noticeable or memorable.

■   ■   ■

THERE'S A REASON FOR EVERYTHING; SOMETHING GOOD WILL COME of it, a composite invisible someone murmurs to Elizabeth. She identifies the composite: minister and neighbor and wife of colleague.

Reason? she answers. What about just desserts? Dan didn't deserve to be cut off so young.

His short good life was better than many long lives, the little chorus offers, trying to help.

Elizabeth opens the refrigerator. A quart of milk, a chunk of cheese.

At least the detective doesn't sermonize. In his silences are simple meanings: This is tragic, this is sad.

There is a tap at the door. Elizabeth hurries to it and lets in her guest, her almost-friend, the homicide commander with the sympathetic eyes.

He asks, "How are you holding up?"

"People have been very good to me."

The detective, Commander Christie, nods seriously. "I would hope so."

She leans forward to close the door.

OUTSIDE, THE MAN IN THE PARK STRETCHES, TRYING TO IMAGINE the conversation in the house. What do they *say?* He tells himself, *I should go,* but he doesn't. How strange that life has handed him circumstances that put him here, now.

COMMANDER CHRISTIE REFUSES ELIZABETH'S OFFER OF WATER.

"Ice cream?" she tries with just the smallest hint of self-mockery. "I gave just about everything else away. I couldn't deal with real food."

"I'm fine." He sits down across from her and says, "Nothing, really."

When she's seated, he says, "I thought maybe you could help me think. Just possibly there's something we're not understanding in the way of motive. A twist. A surprise."

But she has already thought of every cross word her husband ever reported, every cross word sent in her direction, every patient her husband found troublesome, every client she couldn't make a connection with, and she has not come up with reason, motive.

"Daniel had a way better than average life. It didn't have many ugly spots. He never hurt anyone." *Wonderful marriage, good kids doing well in school, respect of the community, a great benefactor* . . . said the minister.

"Jealousy, then?" It's almost a statement.

"If people felt it, I don't think it lasted all that long," she says tartly. "Not if they got to know him."

"Then my mind goes back to the Pocusset Safe House."

Her husband had just founded a home for troubled teens, and one of Christie's earliest ideas, his second idea, actually, was that people in the neighborhood weren't happy about it. "The kids might be rough kids, drugs, crime. Had your husband heard any flap like that?" he asked eagerly. No, she told him. The neighbors were amazingly accepting and everywhere else her husband was being thanked and honored for this community service.

"I have one of my men nosing around still," he says now.

This does not strike her as a productive line of inquiry. Even though some of the residents might not like the idea of the house, it was a stretch to imagine one of them shooting her husband over it. And why take his wallet?

It seems to her his first idea was right—a drunk, a criminal, an addict probably, shot him in his car in his parking lot for his wallet. Nobody saw, nobody knew. A strange freak randomness took Daniel from her. Senselessness is the only thing that makes any sense. That's her theory.

ACROSS THE STREET, THE MAN STARTS TOWARD HIS CAR, WHICH is parked several blocks away, but changes his mind when, about fifty feet away from where he exercised, he turns back for a last look and sees a large moving truck has pulled up, nearly obscuring his view of Elizabeth's house.

■ ■ ■

THE DETECTIVE IS PATIENT. HE IS ABLE TO SIT FOR A LONG TIME. Elizabeth feels as if she's at work—she's a therapist, a detective of sorts—but that the roles are reversed. She's the struggling one. He sits calmly holding the large basket of woes. He says, "I'm worried about you. Are you going to be all right?"

She thinks the word *terrible,* the phrase *I feel terrible.* Life is precious. She must find a way to feel kindness, generosity again soon.

The detective nods as if she's spoken.

She does not have to tell him how there's an echo in her thoughts, the living room seems cavernous, the high ceilings oppressive rather than splendid. Or that she's embarrassed to practice in the field of mental health when she's afraid she's losing her precious marbles.

He knows.

She will miss him when he's not "bothering her so regularly anymore." That simple. He's decent. He's company. He has the trick of waiting before speaking, good trick, not to fill every silence with nonsense. There will be an erasure mark where he once was. Each time he comes, he sits across from her in the chair with the big arms, she sits in the middle of the sofa. He leans back and then forward over his knees. She offers food, or as today, water and ice cream, he refuses. Already they have their little dance. Wonderful, the way this happens between people, routine beginning.

She allows herself to say, "What I feel is pretty frightening."

"Violent crime makes people scared and bitter," he says.

She turns the word around, considering it. *Bitter.* Most people say *angry.* "I feel dangerous. Furious."

"Of course," he says. "You had a life with him. That alone. And then he was . . . everybody says he was exceptional."

"He was." Between them on the table is the newspaper clipping with Dan's picture, the one she chose, a snapshot of him standing in the yard—tall, angular, even a little awkward in his largeness, his head canted slightly to the left. A big man with a shock of hair that didn't always stay calm, simple clothes, not flashy. Wonderful eyes. He wore glasses, which couldn't disguise or hide those eyes that held so much thought, compassion. She loves that photo. He was real, he was human.

Christie takes it up and looks at it, then puts it down carefully, shaking his head.

She says, "Daniel had faults, everyone does, but his were minor."

"What were they? His faults?" Christie asks, alert.

"The hairs that come with selfless dogs."

Christie laughs.

"He worked too hard, put strangers first."

"Rough on you, then."

"Sometimes." Petty complaints, weren't they? That Dan didn't always hear when she said she wanted something, needed something—a vacation, time with him. Time at their cottage, only an hour and a half away. "Why do we keep it," she would ask, "if we never get there and other people use it most of the time?"

"His fault was not being able to clone himself so that everyone could have a piece of him."

Christie nods, watching her. "You're letting things go forward with the . . . the opening, the dinner, all that?"

"Yes. All that. Official opening in ten days."

"I want to ask a favor. Could you find a way to include me in the dinner?" Christie asks. "Believe me, I hope something breaks by then, and if it does, I won't intrude. But if not, it could be helpful to see some of the people he worked with, in that setting. Just in case."

She nods. "That's easy. Consider it done." The Pocusset Safe House was founded in cooperation with the police, so why not have one of them there? But, how strange to think of Daniel's colleagues and associates and other pillars of the community being scrutinized. "At the beginning—at the beginning, you said it was a bum, an addict you were looking for."

"We're not dropping any possibility. It's just . . ."

"Nothing's surfaced yet," she supplies.

"Right. And someone was very direct. No witnesses. It looks purposeful."

Everything freezes up in her at the thought of that kind of anger directed at anyone in her family.

Christie waits until she looks at him. "If you're keeping something from me, the slimmest idea, all I can say is, don't." The trail is getting cold and they have nothing, nothing. "It's been a week already, people forget things," he presses. "So even if it's something we need to keep more or less quiet . . ."

It's the wrong tree by far. She answers levelly, "Nothing like that. Honestly."

"I'm not here to torture you. I'm trying to solve it, understand? It's puzzling and so we have to look at everything."

Elizabeth nods.

He's restless and yet he sits in silence for a while longer with only the telltale jiggling of his leg to betray him.

October, gorgeous weather, the air is clear and dry. The sun streams into her house in low slanting shafts. Late-afternoon sun makes for longing in her, always has, a physical feeling of loss, the dropping of the heart and stomach. Add autumn to that. Add grief to that.

"You're back to work?"

"I saw two clients this morning. I skipped a meeting this afternoon. After today, I'm back full-time."

"It can help."

"I know. I believe in work. Dan did, too. He loved work. He . . ." Something happens before she can stop it, a flash, a series of images. Suddenly she's crying. "I'm sorry," she says to Christie. "I can't get control of the crying yet."

"No need to."

"Oh, but there is. I'm seeing patients tomorrow."

"Your work is 'other-directed.'"

The detective's phrases sometimes surprise her. "Well . . . yes." Her task is to compartmentalize—be with her grief at home; be objective, selfless, at work.

"That's hard."

Commander Christie is twitching his leg again. Wanting to wrap this up. A police detective, after all. To him, a decent clue would be: another woman in her husband's life, financial difficulties, chemical habits not under control. She knows what things would make the case easier. In a quick move, Christie stands to go and fumbles to give her another card—funny, since she already has three from him. One at work, one on the kitchen counter, one in the bedroom. She will put this one in her purse. "Call me if you have even the slightest urge to say something. It may seem very small, insignificant. That's okay. Call me."

If only detective work could bring a man back. If knowing a thing could undo it.

The detective leaves, looking back once over his shoulder. She nods and watches him make his way to the car. She does not notice the people across the street in the park, not a one of them.

FRANK RAZZI'S LIFE WAS ALL SURPRISE THESE DAYS. TURN A PAGE, turn around, *bam, bam*. He had the feeling of being catapulted onto and off one of those dizzying disks children ride at amusement parks. Blood pressure was surely off the charts. His head throbbed, he could feel blood pumping to his neck, his eyes; he was all raw nerve endings, alert; his mind whizzed like a planet in a cartoon—sizzling firecracker circles of light. He had never felt more alive.

The last thing he expected four months ago was to lose his job in the entertainment industry. Funny phrase, that. The last thing he expected two months later was to leave L.A. or to patch together a temporary life as a peripatetic academic, teaching scriptwriting in two places—a little town, Athens, Ohio, and a city, Pittsburgh. Never in all those years had he thought he would come back to Pittsburgh. Yet here he was, again, having taught his one shorter Tuesday course in Athens, ready to do his seminar at the university tonight.

Before this, he'd breathed on the city twice, once ten years ago, once on a weekend before starting the new job. Then he'd done this commuting routine seven Tuesdays in a row—at first he was scared, but it turned out to be easy—drove in, did his gig, drove out, back to his rented house in Athens. Six times, easy. Last week was different. He hadn't planned last week either. It had happened. He hadn't planned it, yet there was a certain coming together in his life. As if there were a plan.

He had followed the dots and now he stood at the entrance to the park and looked across the street to the handsome house where Elizabeth Shepherd had come to the door twice, once to let in the man who drove up in the blue car and the other time to let him out. In between, a big moving truck pulled up. The driver got out and went into the house next door. Then moments later, that same man and a woman opened the front door and started carrying things out to the truck. Frank figured the house was sold, since there was no sign out, but something happened in his heart, the tumbling of a lock. In a reckless mood, just following the dots, he crossed the street and approached them as they got to the truck with their boxes. He was breathless with the craziness of what he was doing.

"Excuse me. Is this place by any chance for rent?"

"Nope. For sale." The man supported a box on his knee and said irritably, "The agent is supposed to come by tomorrow with some signs. The signs should have been up by now. It's for sale."

Hardly able to contain himself, Frank said, "I might be interested in buying around here in a couple of months . . . if certain things work out." In that split second, as he spoke, he pitched to a new place. He fantasized his seedling job in Pittsburgh blossoming to something full, long term. Other wild things, too, zipped through his mind. "Looks like a nice house."

"Too bad," the woman said, shrugging. "The agent says it'll go fast. Couple of people are already lined up to look."

Frank thought she was bluffing. He caught a whiff of loss, bankruptcy, maybe September 11 fallout. "Too bad," he agreed. He turned and began to walk away, but turned back. The husband wore a sweat suit, the wife wore jeans and a long-sleeve T-shirt. They were moving the boxes themselves, after all. They had just put down a couple of them on the patch of lawn in front of the curb and were starting back toward the house when Frank said, "I'm curious. What would a place like this rent for if you *were* renting it?"

The husband turned and said, "I don't know. We're selling." The wife, having turned, too, looked at Frank more closely, taking in his hair, his clothes.

"I'm thinking as I speak here, but if I paid you, say, two thousand a month rent, on a month-by-month basis, kept the place up, put in some nice furniture. First off, it looks better for selling. But also, if things work out for me, if I sell another property I have . . ."

He was going too fast. They looked more defeated, beaten down, than curious.

He forced himself to speak more slowly. "I know a little about real estate," he said. "It's a wise way to go. Renting a property out. I've done it myself. 'Cash cow,' my accountant calls it."

The man said, "You have a card? We'll call you if . . . if for some reason we change our minds."

The woman tipped her head back to the house. "Card is a good idea. We have a lot of work to do. We can't just chat." Frank patted his pockets and made a show of looking through his wallet for a card. She watched him curiously and said, "You don't even know what it looks like inside. Well, never mind, we're not renting it. We need to sell."

Frank Razzi scratched his head and gave a bemused smile. "Out of cards. You're right," he said. "I got so excited, I didn't give you any background. I have that problem of leaping ahead sometimes. The thing is, I've been looking at houses along this whole row. I know I'm going to end up in this city one way or the other. I have a son lives with his mother a couple of streets over and I want to be close to him. I know *what* I want. It's just a matter of finding it and getting the other place sold and working out a couple of other things. Well," he said, "there's a chunk of my life story." Then he paused and smiled. "It just seemed right. Still does."

"Well, maybe things will work out for you," the woman said, frowning.

"I'd like to see inside. If you can spare a couple of minutes."

The woman looked toward her husband and made a "why not?" gesture with her hands open. "Couple of minutes. That's all. In case in a couple of months . . ." Then she and Frank started slowly toward the house. "It's a mess now," she said. "We're all in boxes."

"I can handle it, even though I'm one of the orderly types," he teased. "Everything in its place."

"Oh, well, hold on, then," she said, softening a little.

Frank was aware of the husband, pattering behind. Listening. It didn't matter. The wife was in charge and she was starting to like him.

"You seem very decisive," the wife said, "or maybe it's impulsive."

"I'm coming from L.A. To a guy from L.A., the houses here are extraordinary. Graceful buildings, with history. If I were renting this one, I'd get a landscaper in," he said offhandedly, crossing the threshold and pointing backward. "Fix up that front yard."

"We always tended the yard ourselves," the husband muttered. "Landscapers cost too much."

"I'd pay. A good yard . . . I'd want it for my son, but it raises the value, too."

He was standing in the living room. They'd let him in. It was a sign. He began to turn this way and that, pretending to look about. It couldn't be a more ordinary house, but they didn't know that. They waited expectantly as if he'd be impressed. He struggled for something to say. "I'd put some sort of blinds up there, maybe the vertical louvers."

The woman looked at her husband. Her look might have meant "*This* is good. They cost more than horizontals." She turned back to him. "You'd pay for the blinds?"

Frank tried to slow himself down. Things always went better when he withdrew, tamped down the intensity. "Then, as I said, I'd buy it, or someone else would. A little polish helps to sell a place. That, and bread in the oven, as everyone now knows." He smiled. They watched him as he made a show of measuring cabinets and floors by pacing off the distances.

"You an architect?" the husband asked.

"No." Frank shook his head. "I'm an attorney, Author's Guild right now. Mainly computer and phone and fax work. I can keep working wherever I am, if that's what you're worried about. But when I was in my twenties, I worked in real estate for a while. . . . Could I see upstairs?"

The woman lifted a box and said, "There's a master suite in the middle, then a room that's good for a den or study or exercise room or even like a dressing room to your right, and then two choices for your kid's room or a home office or whatever. You'll figure it out. We're going to keep moving."

Frank went upstairs. He didn't really need to look; it was ordinary, and *like* one he'd lived in and ten others he had once been in. Walls, tiles, the usual. It was the windows and their prospects that interested him. The house on his left, the one he'd been studying, could be seen clearly from the small bedroom.

When Frank got back down to the living room, he hoisted one of the smaller moving boxes and carried it to the truck outside. He handed it over to the husband, saying, "I couldn't walk out empty-handed. You're going to be at this all night. Just with the boxes alone."

"Thanks."

"Who moves the furniture, the big stuff?"

"We have some people coming over tomorrow."

"Well. You're busy and I just appeared out of the blue. So. The short answer is, I like it. Thought I would and I do. You'll want to talk to each other. Think it over. Talk to your realtor. Maybe renting isn't right for you. Okay. I'll keep looking, anyway, in the neighborhood. I'll call your realtor, talk, see what else he might have." He took out a notebook and wrote down his phone number.

"Would you go as high as twenty-five hundred?" the man asked. "For rental?"

"No, no, I'm afraid not." He handed the woman the notebook and asked her to write her name and the realtor's name. Could they see his hand? Could they tell he was drenched, that his heart was exploding? No. Mind, heart, and guts in an uproar and people never knew.

Outside, he wrote in the notebook what he had told the Bunsens. Guild lawyer, L.A., real estate in his twenties. Son (not daughter). Hard to remember which script he was writing and he didn't want to get tripped up. Had he said the son's age? He didn't think so. Seven sounded good. Seven tugged at the heartstrings. A boy. He'd name him Matt. He wrote that down, *Matt. Seven years old.*

Frank walked to his car, which he'd parked on a side street three blocks away, and drove to Pitt, where he would be teaching a class in a few minutes. Nothing to do with law. That's all right, he told himself, keep it fluid. Truth is fluid. Tumbling off the amusement park ride, still giddy, he drove and parked in the lot on Forbes. He felt more visible than usual. Speech had made him visible. As in Shakespeare. He sobered a little even though a feeling of queasiness remained when his heart stopped pounding.

The Bunsens might not pursue the idea at all. A relief in its way. Calming. And also disappointing. He was struck by how he didn't know himself, could surprise himself. He had never thought to come back, yet now it seemed it was exactly what he'd had in mind all along, all along.

WHEN HE LEFT ELIZABETH'S HOUSE, CHRISTIE GOT INTO HIS CAR, deep in thought. In his peripheral vision were fifteen or sixteen people jogging past him or doing their thing, exercise-wise, in the park. A warm October, so people were taking advantage. He had no reason and not enough time to study them.

He was thinking about Elizabeth. She'd tried to be cooperative from the start, but she was stuck, shattered, and not able to add anything. For now it was going to have to be fibers and footprints and luck. Luck meant somebody talking, somebody using the credit cards in the wallet, that kind of thing. They'd done the usual: dusted Dr. Ross's office, the outside doors, the parking lot behind the building where the murder had happened. They'd interviewed the nurses and patients and cleaning people and the other doctors who shared the practice.

He didn't feel hopeful.

The gun had been pointed right at Daniel Ross's heart, close range. The bullet went straight through the body, into the car seats, front and back. The only good prints inside the car were Daniel's and Elizabeth's. The wallet, which would have had a hard-enough surface to take a print, was gone. The door handle wasn't telling them anything; the killer had used gloves or wiped the door or Daniel Ross had opened the car door for him (or her) or never closed the door to begin with. Of the shoe prints, maybe the hard loafer, size ten, maybe the running shoe, size eleven, maybe the moccasin, size twelve, belonged to the killer.

The sense of it was not coming clear.

The wallet, he didn't buy it as the main motive. A bullet straight to the heart, no evidence of a scuffle. The man was adored by everyone except maybe some one person who hated him.

Now in a little under two weeks there was going to be the dedication of the building over on Pocusset Street, practically in the park, a little bit of country in the city, a completely renovated old house that had once been derelict. The money Daniel Ross had used for it was what he'd inherited from his father, a doctor; he'd used the whole lump sum for the project. Quite a statement.

"His own home was abusive?" Christie had asked Elizabeth.

"Subtly so. There are all kinds of abuse."

The Pocusset Safe House was pretty fantastic. Counselors and social workers volunteered their time. Kids could stay for a couple days when it was inadvisable for them to go home. The place looked like a classy bed-and-breakfast. Ross had made sure it was run by a board of professionals in cooperation with the Pittsburgh Police Department and the Parent and Child Guidance Center. Safe haven, intervention was the idea.

Elizabeth would volunteer three hours a week, free counseling, once her life straightened out.

"Are these people good or what?" Artie Dolan, Christie's best detective, exclaimed when they first looked at the place.

"They seem so," Christie answered.

Artie Dolan had nodded, saying, "Sometimes people hate the people who save them. Or try to."

Christie joked, "So you're saying it's somebody who doesn't like nice beds, quilts, good food, kind people. . . ."

"Doesn't want to be talked to nice and fed and stuffed into pure cotton sheets," Dolan continued.

Not featherlight humor, but they clunked along as best they could.

Christie now headed back to the office, where he still had a whole crate of files from Ross's home office sitting beside his desk. The least he could do was carry a few folders home with him, try to do a little bit after dinner.

Wednesday. He and Marina had his kids tonight.

No, no, it was Tuesday. Man, where was his head? Tuesday. Tonight he was supposed to meet up with Darnell Flowers, the sixteen-year-old boy he befriended once a week, kind of like the Big Brother Program without the program. Darnell always liked to come to the Investigative Branch because he wanted to learn about detective work. The boy usually got there around four. By now, he'd have been hanging around for a while.

Darnell once saved the life of the woman Christie intended to marry. Neither Christie nor Marina would ever forget the boy or his courage. Yet, back a year ago, when Darnell called him, the boy began with "I don't know if you remember me? You took me to identify that house where the men shot that woman and—" Funny. Most people thought they were the center of the universe. This kid had no father and his mother was a ball of fury. Yet somehow he was still a good kid.

In the last year, they managed a few ball games, but mostly they met at the office on Tuesdays and often went home for dinner with Marina. Tonight she had a meeting, so they were on their own.

Christie jogged up the steps to the second floor. Darnell was sitting on a chair outside his office door. He wore jeans and a brightly colored warm-up jacket, pink and blue with yellow piping. His blue cap pointed backward. His hair was getting a bit long, but altogether he looked good, as if he cared about himself.

"I got worried you forgot," Darnell said.

"Nah. I had an interview. Come on in with me. I just have to gather up some files I need to take home." He felt the boy move into the office behind him.

"You work at night?"

"Yep. When there's a case."

"You still on that Dr. Ross case? I been reading about it." Reading. Reading was good. "You have a lead at all?"

"Why? You hear anything on the street?"

Darnell shook his head. "Nothing like that. I was just thinking about it."

Christie decided on two file folders. Why take home more than he could do? "How you doing in school?"

"Tomorrow I have two tests."

"You going to study?"

"Yeah. Later tonight."

"Good." Christie carried the folders loose, made sure he had his car keys. "Where do you want to eat?"

"Minutello's."

"Good choice."

On the way to dinner, Christie said, "I'm going to drive by the place I told you about. The Pocusset Safe House. They have counselors there, good people."

"Counseling, I can't do that. It's weak."

"I think when it's done right, it's the complete opposite of weak."

They drove for a while. The boy tapped his foot. His shoes were very clean, new. "That's that place the doctor put together, huh?"

"Founded it, yes."

When they were in front of the building Ross had worked to build, Christie said, "If things get bad at home, even if they don't . . ."

"Just go in there?"

"Yep."

They looked at the building for a while. Darnell shook his head. "Right in his heart, huh? How come he let somebody get that close? In a parking lot. At night. Start up the engine, drive away, that's what he should have done. He wasn't too street smart."

"Maybe not."

"Somebody knew him, that's what I say."

See, it was that clear.

ELIZABETH WANDERED TO THE KITCHEN WINDOW AND LOOKED out at the backyard, thinking how amazing it was, how crazy, with all this unseasonably warm weather, the dahlias were still coming in. The phone rang, but she let it go, listening to the clicking sounds the answering machine made while the tape got into position. The volume was turned down, but she could just hear enough to know it was one of her husband's colleagues. Christie and her kids, that was about all she could handle. She had tried to call Jeff, but he wasn't in. She had just talked to Lauren, who thought maybe she should come home.

And Elizabeth had stood at the counter, tracing the tile, chipping off a piece of something—icing? glazing?—with her fingernail, thinking of the order that Lauren's presence would bring. Talk, cooking, the news, supper at seven. Instead she tried to be unselfish. She said, "If you can, if you can, give it a little more time. You'll be coming ten days from now—we could see how you feel then. You'll know you gave it a fair try."

Dan had died on a Tuesday, the funeral was on Friday.

Saturday and Sunday felt like the longest days ever. . . . They had decided, all of them, to try to take up their lives again.

She'd wanted to say, Yes, come home. But there was noise in the background—the chaos of the dorm with its endless prospect of rescue from isolation—and she hoped simple routines would lift her daughter, carry her along.

It was not even six o'clock now, but she got a sudden wild pang of hunger. Meals were spotty. She kept forgetting to eat.

She removed a carton of ice cream from the freezer. Calcium, anyway. She put three scoops in a bowl and put the carton away. In her imagination, Daniel stood at the doorway, chuckling. "Well . . . " he said. "It's sort of supper."

She wanted to reach out and touch him. "The kids are having a rough time. Jeff is restless. Lauren cried in class today."

He nodded. "How did you manage at work? How many people did you see?"

"Two kids. A sixteen-year-old girl, a fourteen-year-old boy. I thought about you the whole time."

"I thought about you, too," he said in her imagined scene. This took her aback. Could the ghost made up of her own thoughts have feelings? She was afraid to breathe lest she lose the voice. Then he surprised her by apologizing. "You wanted a vacation and I put it off, didn't I? If I could take you to France tomorrow, I would. I didn't do right by you. I didn't make love to you often enough. Too tired, too old, too distracted . . ."

Elizabeth put down her spoon of ice cream. "Not old, handsome, but distracted, yes, you were," she said. It was quiet, no noise in the house. For a few minutes she couldn't find his voice, then he was back. "What will you do tonight?" he asked.

"Read maybe."

"Good." And with that, he seemed to retreat.

Elizabeth left the ice-cream bowl in the sink with water in it. She stacked the mail in piles. The last few days she barely looked at it, only separated the bills from the junk mail from the sympathy cards, took the bills to her study, and put them in a drawer. All her life she'd paid on time. What did sixty-seven dollars here or a hundred and thirty there matter?

A life gone, a man gone forever . . . for working late . . . for his wallet. Some things you couldn't get your mind around.

If they caught the man, if, a big if, and if she attended the trial, how would she react? Would she fall into place behind others of a liberal persuasion, wanting most to influence the consciousness of the killer, to say, "This is what you did, to him, to me, to my children. This is what you took away. Look at me. Make me know you understand *what you did.*"

She would not be able to ask for the death penalty, even in her anger she knew that. Life in prison, yes, but what if she came face-to-face in court with a skinny, desperate boy, someone her husband would have wanted to help?

She moved through the house, expecting Dan to be there, in the flesh, at every turn. You could know all about grief, but living it was something else.

She would call Jeff around nine if he didn't call. One phone call per day per kid. Like parceling out pills.

Out front, the moving truck was still parked at the curb. The owners of the house next door—she hardly knew them, they'd only been there a year—were carrying things out of the house. She hadn't known they were going. They'd sent a card, some cookies.

She would live again, she was smart enough to know that, but how and when? Ten years, twelve, before she's sitting in a little café in Italy, feeling joy? Springing toward life, other people.

Finally, sitting at Daniel's side of the bed, she picked up the book he had been reading. Tears welled up again as if she could feel his touch, still, on the book. *Stones for Ibarra.* A very good book, the back cover told her. As she opened it, she had no idea it was going to be about deep grief. Or

that she would read until one in the morning, with only a
phone call from her son, Jeff, to break the silence.

CHRISTIE WOKE WITH A JOLT. HE'D FALLEN ASLEEP SITTING UP
in his living room, reading the files. The folders had
thumped to the floor, waking him. He heaved the file folders he'd brought home onto his lap again and reached up
to raise the wattage of the floor lamp next to his chair. In
his peripheral vision, he saw Marina look at him worriedly
as she passed to go down to the basement. Laundry.
Seemed it never got finished.

Time together, real time, hard to find. That's what Elizabeth was trying to say. Daniel Ross had been a busy man
and had put her second.

Old bank statements, charge statements, phone bills.
He'd been through the most recent ones before, but now
that the case was a week old and looking bad, he thought
he'd better start on the old stuff. He began jotting down
phone numbers. Good God, he didn't have the patience.
He wasn't that kind of a cop.

Paper and lists, he hated. People, he loved.

It was from people he got his clues, his gut feelings. But
all the interviews last week had led to nothing. The colleagues were fat or thin, sour or pleasant, puzzled or
philosophical, and all of them sad, but they didn't, even if
you put every irritation into one pot, make up much of a
motivation to kill.

Elizabeth says it was a stranger.

A street punk or an addict would have used the credit
cards by now, no doubt about it, and the cards were still
clean. This was a weird case.

His gut told him the person who killed Doc Ross was
something special.

Now, even though one of his men had been through
Ross's home computer and these files once, Christie was
going through them again himself. Homicide investigation wasn't an exact science. Who knew what small entry,
virtual or real, would give a hint?

But bills. He groaned. Maybe he could ask Marina to go through the financial records for him. She had more patience than he did. His inability to concentrate on printed matter for long periods of time embarrassed him. Maybe it meant he wasn't very smart.

"Don't throw anything away," he'd told Elizabeth. Yet the idea of wading through more paper killed him.

And Elizabeth had said, "Of course not." He could see her clearly—tense, soft, vulnerable. She had a soft look, light curly hair, pale skin, clothes that flowed when she moved. He got afterimages of her sadness.

People, yes. Faces. Emotions. Give him people every time. He picked up his main folder on the case. The current stuff.

He turned to the newspaper articles, more his style.

In the *Tribune-Review* was an article from a month ago, titled *Native Son Buys Home for Troubled Teens*.

He's been a classic papa-doc, a favorite pediatrician in the Pittsburgh area for nearly a quarter century. He's Daniel Ross, who grew up here in the Squirrel Hill section of town, went to medical school at Pitt, and stayed here to practice. He opened three offices in the area, one in Shadyside, his original, one in the North Hills, and one in the South Hills. Some patients whisper that they've never received a bill from him. And he's no stranger to community service. But when the police announced they wanted to establish a "rescue home" for troubled teens, Dr. Ross came forward with more than a contribution. He purchased the property for them, worked on renovations, gave advice, organized volunteers. They asked him to be president of the board and he took on this task. As president, he persuaded some of the city's best physicians, social workers, and psychologists to give their time to the endeavor. The original task force suggested naming the home for Dr. Ross, but he modestly declined. He asked if it might be called the Pocusset Safe House. That is now its official name.

Asked why he became so interested in this project, Ross explained he has had the opportunity to heal many children of many physical ailments, but that there were other kinds of ills that visited some children, social wounds that were hard to cure. "I'd like to make a small move toward soothing troubled children."

What will happen at the Pocusset Safe House? 1. Counseling, both individual and group. 2. Intervention when parents and children have reached an impasse. 3. Rescue. There will be made available, on occasion, overnight stays in an innlike setting. The project began as a joint effort of the Police Task Force for Child Safety and the Parent and Child Guidance Center, explained Michael Gilden, director of the Guidance Center, but everybody agrees Dr. Ross should be honored at the opening of the rescue house for his contributions, both financial and visionary.

Simple enough. One photo shows one of the bedrooms at the Pocusset Street house, a second is of a grandmotherly woman in a kitchen there, a third bears the caption "group meeting room."

From the *Post-Gazette*, a similar article of two weeks ago, titled *Retreat for Children and Teens Gets Boost from Local Pediatrician*. This writer got Ross to talk a bit more. He was quoted as saying, "When I was a boy, I became aware of a couple of kids in trouble. The parents didn't care for them in the ways they needed. They felt neglected and alone. I thought, even then, someone has to step in, someone has to help. Two boys I knew well died young. One, at any rate, might have had a chance at a stellar life. He was resilient and positive. Another was abandoned and I don't know that he ever got over it. He didn't have much of a chance."

Who were these boys? Christie wondered. Did they have parents, brothers who might have seen the article and taken offense? Pah, he chided himself. A long, long, long shot, but so much more interesting than the charge-card receipts and canceled checks, which, from all he'd seen so far, were charitable contributions, college tuition, subscriptions, clothing, equipment for the office, utilities paid, the usual.

Finally he read the obit. One week ago. There was that

friendly picture of Daniel Ross in his yard. A listing of honors from high school on through college and medical school. More paragraphs on his work with the Pocusset Safe House. Survived by his wife, Elizabeth, his son, Jeffrey, his daughter, Lauren.

IT WAS EIGHT-THIRTY, CLASS FINISHED. HE CARRIED A SATCHEL with the sweats and running shoes stuffed in, lecture notes, class papers. He'd changed to jeans and a sweater for class. He walked to the lot on Forbes where he'd parked.

He hadn't been very good tonight. Kept losing his place as he spoke. Would there be complaints?

He started up the car. He was hungry, tired. A three-and-a-half-hour drive ahead of him.

Up Forbes, down Murray, onto the Parkway and west.

He drove in a dream.

He passed into West Virginia, then Ohio.

What had he done? What was he doing?

Thirty-some years of waiting to get what he wanted and needed, Frank told himself. Thirty-three years of feeling no matter what he accomplished, he was a zero, a cipher, in the shadow of another who thought of him as a boy who never had a chance. Stories of late blooming had always gotten to him, as if all along he knew he was putting in time, waiting to live. He felt like the old guy, Kizer, who worked at Paramount the first year he was there. "Something is *in the way*," Kizer kept saying, irritably waving a hand in front of his face, trying to get rid of the constant nagging spider's web that kept everything out of focus. Old Kizer, it turned out, had cataracts. Frank felt like that. Something in the way.

People thought he had been living a real life all along, they did. He managed to have relationships of one sort or another but he knew himself well enough to know he chose the cool acquisitive types for brief liaisons and he messed around with the desperate ones, women broken down by something, when he became overcome by a need for connection. He could do it eight times a day so long as the woman was cracked and broken. She started getting ideas she could put herself together, he began losing his dick; she started feeling pity for him, he told one lie after another until she lost herself again and he could love her again. Then— by then—having been seen too much, too nakedly, so to speak, he dumped her. He knew himself, anyway.

Even had a wife for a while up until six months ago (officially). It was actually over six years ago, and she was one of the acquisitive ones, easy to lose. No kid, though. Invented the kid.

Never been a lawyer. Invented that.

He'd been in a lot of cities: Cleveland, Detroit, Philadelphia, Denver, New York. Real estate, no, he hadn't done that. Made that up.

L.A. scriptwriter and script doctor. That was the true tag until Paramount TV "let him go" last year. He had an IQ of 165, way up there, but it didn't solve everything. He got nervous. He hated to get nervous, he hated the suddenly flagging confidence. If he could fix the world, he would make sure nobody ever got "let go." They'd keep you on until you calmed down and got right again or you found yourself another job.

Blather. He was lying to himself. He didn't really care what happened to anyone else. He'd been held down all his life from being all he could be.

Never had a chance, eh?

And no wonder, no wonder. Too much interference.

It didn't matter how capable he was, he couldn't even own his own name, had to keep moving from one place to another, changing everything, and making do. Forty-eight years old and he had no past. He was a made-up man, every day new again. His chest cavity was empty, no heart. Just the outside. The hair, the skin, the clothes. But damn if the mind didn't keep working. The will.

WELCOME TO OHIO. Highway signs were so friendly! His phone rang. He kept driving and didn't answer.

Drove in a dream. An hour collapsed and felt like a minute, just as thirty years had collapsed to a day.

He slowed down just before Pleasant City, then went into the town, just stopped the car on a small street and walked. He knew that behind all those darkened windows, and the ones with little reading lights on, or more likely the television going, were people with huge problems. Many of them had done terrible things, had terrible things done to them, most had taken the pummeling without much fight. Dazed was better, they thought. Dignity down the gutter. Repress, repress. He was not like that. He knew every dirty thing he had done and why. He could catalog every vengeance that had been required of him and why. People who didn't know their true natures were people who feared moral ambiguity. They were driven by fear and weakness to try to fit. He was not. He'd made his own way for a long time and he'd done it by being conscious, knowing everything. He lived on the very edge of impulse. In a way, he was pure, more pure than most men. He acted on the moment. Accident and will were one in him. That was some sort of alchemy, wasn't it? To be guilty and innocent at the same moment. Consciousness, yes, but also—what?—an instrument of the gods. Ha. Shakespeare knew. Thinking and passion, *not* opposites. You could know and know and know and know but it didn't stop the explosions.

He got into his car again. He drove slowly, and it made him think of that joke about the marijuana smoker getting pulled over, the officer saying, "You're a danger on the road, man." The smoker saying, "Sorry, Officer, what was I doing, eighty?" Being told, "No, buddy, you were doing five miles an hour." Don't be too fast, don't be too slow, he reminded himself. Dangers either way.

Just before Marietta, the phone rang again. The idea of renting the house was magical, calculation and accident both, but it threw him off balance just now. He must be tired, dog-tired, for he was gripped by indecision, *even though* he felt it had all been decided hours ago, and he looked at the phone sitting on the passenger seat, but couldn't answer just yet, couldn't speak.

2

HARRY VITTLES, THE TEN O'CLOCK THIS MORNING, SAT STIFFLY in the chair he always chooses, afraid to talk about his own problems at first because he was worried about her. He's sweet, a gentle sort, round face, large eyes, glasses a bit askew, a body that's going pudgy, and hands that want to cover it. He always wears hard shoes. Elizabeth wonders every time if his feet hurt and found herself this morning noticing the way he tucked them under his chair. Harry's wife left him, and he spent a good eight months on the why and how, but now he's turning the corner, looking at women, joining a choir to boost his social life.

"Choirs are a hotbed," she said before she edited the remark. The more pure the music, the more the arousal, for some reason. Among the people she's seen, that is. Handel. Hot. Harry laughed and then she did. "I'm going to sing," he said, an ant-bumping-into-a-crumb moment.

They bring in love, newness, as well as loss. The teenagers she's seeing this afternoon will choose the couch, going for comfort. They're tricky, bored, smart, and sometimes she's inclined to think they *do* know almost everything about everything and are only about to begin the process of not knowing.

Daniel. Gone. The idea is like an explosion. Too big to be true, then true. When will she get used to it?

Because some of the time, he's not dead. He is hovering

on the edge of this dream, alive again. About to phone her, about to get home before she does tonight and put some cheese out to tide them over before dinner is ready.

Then the phone rings and it's Christie saying he wants to pop in and see her at the office, some more questions he wants to ask her.

"I have a cancellation at two."

"I'll be there."

Elizabeth sits forward at her desk after hanging up the phone. Then she gets up and walks to the window. Outside it's gorgeous again, sunny and warm, that golden wash coming over everything. She takes the one soft chair near the desk, waiting.

"HOW AM I DOING?" FRANK RAZZI ASKS HIS WEDNESDAY SEMINAR in Athens, Ohio. Today has been a strain. He's not much in the mood to talk smart.

One boy salutes, a couple of students shrug. Two girls titter.

He never thought he would end up teaching and he's just beginning to realize there's a knack to it. Ask a lot, be rigorous and demanding, keep talking as if it's fun. Right. He has them reading three screenplays a week and writing ten pages a week, and so far they haven't lynched him.

"I think the only thing worth making a film about is the threat of death," one boy says.

The girls roll their eyes toward the boy. Who wants to get *this* serious?

Frank makes an effort to concentrate. "Explain yourself. What?"

"I like to be scared. Everybody does. But what does it all boil down to? Death. Fear of death. Everything boils down to that."

"I'm listening," Frank says.

"That's all," the boy says.

One of the girls giggles.

One of the theories of film is that it acts out death, past-tenseness, every time.

Frank says, "You mean, a kid falls out of a tree, or he can't find his mommy and daddy in a mall, he experiences something strong, powerful. He survives. Terrifying but exhilarating." He has their attention. "Annihilation and freedom in one whiff. The little kid is having a premonition that death lies in wait—ha, he might not be here tomorrow. The big bear, the boogeyman will get him. Goes to the movies. Wants the same experience. Facing death and getting past it. Am I understanding?"

The boy twitches a shoulder. "Sort of, yeah. *Minority Report, Private Ryan.* Something to be afraid of."

"*High Noon,*" Frank adds. "*Casablanca, The Pawnbroker.*" His titles don't do anything for the kids. "Well, do the rest of you agree?"

The tough, dirty-looking girl in the back row says, "Yeah. Death. Murder. That stuff."

"Fear is what drives a script," the first boy asserts. "Maybe not always murder, but fear, death."

Frank feels his eyes close for a second in an overwhelming fatigue. The class ends and he is not at all sorry. He could keep them a few minutes longer, but he has other things on his mind. Like. How to calm down, how to get a breath. They don't know, can't see, he's physically shot, can they? Dopey little runts. Wanting to talk about *all scripts,* as if they know anything in depth yet. And he has to answer about that house in Pittsburgh. It's decided, of course, it's decided. So why can't he say the words?

It could be he's stymied by dumb practical matters, like what is he to do for furniture? He's already bought a set of remaindered furniture for the house in Athens and for the time being he needs to be there three days a week at least, classes Tuesdays, Wednesdays, and Thursdays, office hours Wednesdays. The Tuesday night class in Pittsburgh goes until eight-thirty, so it's reasonable to expect he will want to sleep there instead of driving back at night. And then weekends, Thursday night through Monday, if he spends them in Pittsburgh, that's five nights there and he can't do that without furniture. He'll need *some.* Move the

Ohio furniture to Pennsylvania or buy more? If he had any sense of humor he would laugh at the ridiculousness of his dilemma. He decides. Buy. A couch, a chair, a lamp, a bed, two rugs. A coffeemaker, a toaster.

Tomorrow he has to teach his Tuesday/Thursday introductory class in media writing. He's having them read scripts and come up with an outline for a television series episode and then do proposals for a public television documentary. They'll be almost ready to land jobs by the time he's done with them . . . let them spin out of control in L.A. if that's what they want. He's tried it, he's kept pace, eaten well, looked at people whose eyes move as fast as pinballs bobbing on their way down the maze. Now that he's left the City of Angels, his internal speed is down from five hundred miles an hour to four hundred.

He has his own eighty-five somethings he's pitching to producers, agents, networks, but from afar. Ouchless from Athens. Shouldn't have fired his agent, but he did, and so don't look back. Thanks to the departmental budget for copying, he's keeping copies of all eighty-five circulating out there all the time. Well, not eighty-five . . . okay, forty. Okay, twenty, but if it's a lottery, he's bought quite a few tickets.

Cleaning house. Sweeping things clean. A new start. He knows with a dead certainty he's going to get a bite on at least one of his proposals, because everything is connected and he has a strange feeling of luck. When the machinery begins to work, the whir and hum is palpable, a vibration.

In the Xerox room, where he has to pick up three of his twenty lottery tickets, the kid who works there is hunched over one of his screenplays. Reading it? Her cropped shirt rides up and he sees the round softness of her upper butt.

She looks delectable.

Slow down. Slow down, he tells himself. Hunger shows. The well-fed get whatever they want.

He will call his PCP and make an appointment if necessary, and it will probably be necessary, because he knows himself and Valium is in order. One week of Valium—or

Xanax, even better—followed by a round of antidepressants and that oldest of remedies, the one they used to give to a sick old king to stave off death or a crazy young prince to knock his eyes back into his head. A girl, a young girl to drain off the fury.

CHRISTIE HAS ASKED HIS FIRST QUESTION AND GOT A CLEAR answer.

Elizabeth has told him the two people referred to in the article about her husband—the two young people whose lives were not saved—were his high school friend Theodore Luckey, an African American boy, brilliant, promising, who died in his senior year of a combination of pills and alcohol, and Daniel's half brother, Gerald Paul LaBeau, who had lived with the family only a short time, in his teens. The half brother went by his middle name, Paul, and the LaBeau name was his mother's maiden name. He died at age twenty-four of a drug overdose, in Atlantic City.

"In what way did these deaths haunt your husband?"

"He found them both devastating. He never forgot. He adored Theodore, Ted, especially, and he was distressed about that death all of his life," Elizabeth explained. "It was a bit less usual thirty years ago than today for blacks and whites in high school to be good friends, you know, there were terrific racial tensions then, but he and Theodore were best friends."

"I see."

"Daniel was first in the class, Theodore was a close second, and Paul was third or fourth. Their spitting contests had to do with literature and physics."

Elizabeth speaks as if she is on a witness stand, the way she answers each question, not embroidering much. Something about her tone makes Christie feel prosecutorial, formal.

"Your husband talked to you about his friend? In what way? When?"

"Many times. He was impressed by the fact that Ted—

who had an abusive father—somehow managed to leap over the barriers. Dan used to tell me Ted had a wild intelligence. Apparently the boy read everything, he was hungry for life. Just . . . very special. An extraordinary spirit."

"Sad."

"Very sad."

Silence. Is there a clock ticking?

Christie wonders why he didn't become a shrink. Sit in a comfy chair and get people to tell you things. He does the latter most days of the week, but rarely in such comfort. This is the life, he thinks, as a kind of inner joke, even as he admits to himself that not all stories told in a room like this are his cup of tea. Elizabeth Shepherd's life, Daniel Ross's death, on the other hand—he wants the whole scoop, childhood on up.

"How did Luckey die exactly?"

"A fall, a broken neck, actually, but he had so much junk in his system at the time, it would have killed him anyway. At first the police thought there was foul play. Then they decided not. Dan thought there was. He always thought there was. He said Ted Luckey was special and maybe he got hurt, killed, on account of it."

"That idea would be a lot to carry, wouldn't it?"

"It was. The death was ruled an accident, but Dan felt an injustice had been done."

"Did he talk to people about his feeling?"

"Yes, he did at the time."

"Did your husband know Luckey took drugs?"

"He knew there was an episode when the boy was thirteen or so, but Dan kind of peer-counseled him and he thought Ted was completely clean after that. He was surprised when drugs were involved in the death."

"Did you think he was being naïve?"

Elizabeth's eyes glitter. She comes close to smiling. "Only when he wasn't talking to me about it. When he talked, I believed him."

"Tell me about your husband's father." They've already talked about how it was the old doc's money, his savings, that went into the Pocusset Safe House. "He died how recently?"

A tilt of the head. She surveys him. "Two years ago. He was not doing too well. He had moderate senile dementia and even though my husband researched everything on the market, nothing much helped to reverse the effects. The last couple of years were rough because his father was the kind of person who was used to being in control, you know, the sort of doctor who didn't tell his patients much, just dictated. It's harder for that kind of person, someone who's been authoritative."

"How did they get along, your husband and his father?"

She pauses for a long time. "Daniel was dutiful. His father was never easy. The teenage years were especially bad. Dan's father was cold by nature and even mean-spirited a lot of the time, but *mostly* cold, remote."

Christie nods. "How was the old man to the half brother?"

"I guess he got worse when the second son showed up. It's a weird story." She winces.

Showed up alerts his interest. He asks levelly, "We're talking about the boy who died at twenty-four? Paul LaBeau?"

"Yes. Long story. I'll try to make it clear. You see, Paul was dumped on the family. And it was soon after Dan's mother had died. She died very young of breast cancer. She was only in her thirties. So there was *a lot* of trauma. Dan's father—and Dan—had a lot to get used to. This other boy was with them for four years. I think Dan dealt with things a lot better than his father did. His father never got over the embarrassment of the second son showing up."

"Which boy was older?"

"Dan, but only by three months. The boys were the same age basically, so it was clear to all of them that my father-in-law had been involved with this other woman when his wife was pregnant. The other mother, Paul's mother, had worked in the office at the crucial time. Then she left town. Then one day fourteen years later, this was about a year after Dan's mother died, she just showed up. She didn't want to move in or marry his father or anything like that. She wanted to get on with her life, she told them. She wanted to dump her kid. Dan heard some of it because Paul's mother just came in and yelled a bit and did her thing. And she *did* go off without the boy. So Daniel's father put out the word that he had adopted a boy who he said was a distant relative and he enrolled him in the same high school as Daniel, same year because, well, they were the same age. Thirteen, almost fourteen."

"Messy."

"Very. The boys knew they were half brothers, but they didn't leak it since their father had put out this other story."

"Sounds hard for any kid."

"Right."

"How did Paul take it?"

"He had a lot of anger. He tended to take it out on Dan. But Dan tried to be supportive. He felt for the kid."

"He told you all this when?"

"The first time he told me was right after we met, when he was in med school and I was in grad school. I think it was one of the reasons I fell in love with him. He was a kind of miracle of acceptance. He'd had a couple of really rough things happen and yet he was the sweetest-tempered guy."

"How did he take Paul's death?"

"He took it hard, even though there had been a complete estrangement by that time. Very hard. See, nobody had heard from Paul after high school. He must have decided he didn't like his second family and he simply disappeared. My father-in-law was perfectly happy with that, I'm sorry to say. They assumed Paul went to his mother, but since she didn't answer their letters or take their phone calls, they didn't know differently for a long time. Later my husband persisted and found out that Paul wasn't with his mother. It turned out he had earned enough money somehow to put himself through both college and med school, so I suppose the old guy *had* had an effect on him even though they never seemed fond of each other. He was almost a doctor, too."

"Where did he go to school?"

"In Michigan."

"Why Michigan?"

"I don't know."

What Christie notices in this room, apart from the comfortable chair, the vacuum marks on the rug, the orderliness of it, is the silence. Between words there is a silence so large, it puts him into slow motion. Perhaps it's some sort of Zen thing she does, slowing a person down.

"Mother? Other relatives there?"

"It didn't seem so. He just seemed to pick Michigan."

"When did your husband track down the story? Before or after the death?"

"Before, and then after. It's complicated. Communications never went the other way. I mean, Paul never got in touch, just like his mother. Dan actually put a detective on it. He found Paul and tried to reestablish a relationship. That's when Paul was in med school. Then when there was another long silence, phone disconnected and that sort of thing, he went up there looking for Paul and learned he'd died. Nobody had notified him because nobody knew Paul *had* a brother or father."

"He died at school?"

"No, in Atlantic City, on a vacation. He seems to have stopped off at a bar in a really seedy end of town. He got drunk. Someone helped him shoot up. He never made it."

"There was a history of drugs?"

"Yeah. It came out after. The people in Michigan weren't saying much about it, but Dan called the police in Atlantic City and Paul was apparently found near his car. Drug overdose."

"Your husband tried to keep up a relationship."

"Yes. We never would have found out Paul died except that Dan had this . . . worry. This need to be in touch. Apparently after the death, the mother was contacted and the body was cremated and sent to her. But she never even contacted my husband or his father. Dan visited her anyway because she had the ashes buried under a tree in the backyard where she lived then."

"She was difficult?"

"Difficult," Elizabeth seems to say without vocalizing the sound. "She said the adoption hadn't 'taken' and Paul never belonged to the Pittsburgh family anyway, so why bother them? She said her son was an independent sort, *she* never could keep track of him, he'd made his own way, paid his own schooling, and she hadn't heard from him for seven years, hadn't seen him for eleven years. Didn't know he was in med school. Dan tried to get some emotion out of her. Dead was dead, she said. Dan remembered the way she said it. 'Crazy's crazy, dead's dead.' "

"You think the old doc was embarrassed about his thing with her, being reminded of it?"

"That's what my husband thought. He never asked his father anything directly. I think he sensed there was too much mortification there."

"Tell me," Christie asks levelly, "how did your husband become so warmhearted when he didn't have that in his background? Forgive me if I sound rude. I'm fascinated by how some people come to their feelings and some don't."

"I am, too. Always. I think he was always sympathetic, even as a child. His mother was pretty good, I think. She was quiet and intellectual and straightforward. Apparently she read all the time, about ten hours a day. Some of it was work, editing, but some not."

"Ten hours a day is a lot."

"She might have been a quiet unsung genius. Maybe she wanted to write, and somehow never did. She loved books."

"You think maybe she didn't pay much attention to her husband?"

"I'd guess that. I never knew her, only heard about her and saw pictures. She died when my husband was only a boy. Twelve."

"Did *you* get along with your father-in law?"

"He liked me well enough. I was always trying to soften him so he and Dan would have a few good moments."

"Did it work?"

"Sometimes."

"Did he talk about his other son?"

"Never."

"Do you have any idea how he reacted to Paul's death?"

She shrugs. "Quietly, is all I know. No fanfare. Relieved, probably, I hate to say."

"A blocked-up man."

"You've got it. Yes. Commander? Do I get one question?"

"Sure."

"Why are you asking about all this?"

Christie again speaks carefully. "I don't know. I go by my gut. And the newspaper interview with your husband prickled my skin. He was mourning two deaths—well, no, that's not the word, he was . . ."

"Memorializing," she says thoughtfully.

"That's it. Memorializing."

"Does it help you to find his killer?"

"Not so far. Who did your husband think killed Ted Luckey?"

"He thought Paul did it. That's partly why he went looking for him. But only partly. He was worried about Paul, too. Anyway, Paul never admitted to anything like that, but Dan thought maybe Paul's death was a confession of sorts. So the Pocusset Safe House memorializes both of them. It was where Ted Luckey used to go to study. It was Ted's secret hideout, and it was where he died."

"Wow. Same house?"

"That was Dan's idea. See, it was just an old derelict house all those years, before Ted and after."

"I see. Did Dan stay in touch with Paul's mother?"

"He lost track of her. She was a drinker. She could easily be dead by now."

"Would you write down her name for me, just for my

records? Maybe when I go through the files, I'll see something with her most recent address."

"So you still need my husband's papers?"

"Oh, yes, just for a little while. I'll be as efficient as I can," he promises.

Elizabeth reaches for a pad of paper and writes, *Michelle LaBeau. Bellingham, Washington.* After a long silence, she says, "I keep picturing some punk kid on the street with his wallet."

That's her favorite theory. Still. Gun to the heart. No struggle.

"We're still monitoring credit-card use," he says.

She nods and looks at her watch.

He looks at his and stands to go.

"Do you know anything you didn't know before?" she asks him.

"Yes . . . a different kind of thing."

"Will it help?"

"No promises."

He leaves, climbs into his Taurus, and puts a call in to Records to pull up the case of Theodore Luckey. "You have it?"

"Yeah," he's told. "Started out as an accident case, then became a murder case, but after nothing was found in the first week, it was ruled an accidental death caused by drinking and pills combined. Kid was eighteen."

"Oh."

"I'm reading, reading. Immediate cause of death, broken neck. Hmm. There were some whispers of suicide along the way. The word comes up here and there, but that wasn't the ruling."

"Can you have the file sent over?"

"Sure."

Wednesday. They will have the kids tonight. Right. Today is Wednesday.

AFTER WORK, ELIZABETH DRIVES TO HER HUSBAND'S OFFICE. SHE has not come to the site before, where it happened. It's an ordinary parking lot, two cars leaving, nobody noticing her. She parks near where she knows it happened. They talked on the phone—that night, that Tuesday night, only eight days ago, before he died. Again she tries to remember each word.

At the office, late at night, he'd been doing letters to people he hoped would take up the funding in future for the Pocusset Safe House. Obsessed. Finding his brother had been like that, years ago. Now it seemed—even though this made no sense—he *knew* he was going to die and was hurrying to leave a legacy—but no, that makes no sense. Because. Autopsy report said this was the case of a healthy man, in his prime, cut off by a violent act.

And he couldn't have had a premonition, because in his talk the day before, the week before, there was still romance and a future for the two of them, the recurring promise that they would spend more time at the cottage, travel, find time to make love like youngsters; they would also fix up the house, stay healthy, hope for grandchildren, spoil them.

It had been a quick phone call, about nine. He said he was almost finished with his work. She said, "That usually means another two hours." She asked him if he'd eaten and he said he'd had a salad ordered in at seven, might be hungry again when he got home. She told him there was leftover pasta.

"Just a couple of things I want to finish up."

"Seems like I'm always reheating something that was better fresh," she grumbled.

Nothing more. No "I love you" that night. She knows better than to feel guilt over a bout of common bickering, but she feels it anyway.

What if? What if she had insisted he come home? Would the timing have been different? Would some other person have been the target?

His blood was here, right here, scrubbed away now, but . . . Foolish to come, maybe, but she has to work through it her way, she has to make herself know it.

The talk on the car radio, the news, intrudes on her thoughts. She turns the radio off and listens only to herself. Those times he couldn't go away with her? She'd get brief fantasies of freedom that began with "If he weren't here, I'd . . ." Sell this place and move to something smaller, travel, get to know more people.

Why hadn't she gone to the cottage by herself? Traveled to Europe without him, taken the kids? Dependent?

She wanted to be with him. That simple.

Now what? Nothing. It's only ten minutes to the Safe House even in traffic. She drives there. The least she can do is make sure the project he cared about is exactly what he would have wanted. She pulls into one of the seven parking places, thinking they'll have to arrange for extra street parking for the dedication dinner.

Inside, everything smells new. Wood, carpeting, paint. She tells the woman who is on duty, Mrs. Taylor, a grandmotherly figure, "I just felt like coming by, checking on things."

"Everything is okay here."

"Just so you know, I told the caterers they could bring their own tables and set them up. I thought that was easiest."

"Tell me anything I can do. I don't know how you can pay attention to this. . . ."

"It helps. It helps a little."

And then she leaves for home, thinking about what will fill her evenings now. For a long time, she will be figuring out what to save, what to pitch, which policies he had, who to call, what to transfer to the kids. His clothing. His books. The work will help, yes, because she'll still be with him. In a way. And each thing she gives up will seem a betrayal. She can predict that much.

When Elizabeth gets into the house, she slips off her blazer and hangs it over the dining room chair. She sorts through the mail. Electric bill, estimate from the contractor who is supposed to fix the back deck, flyers, appeals for money, chance to buy concert tickets, sympathy cards. She drops them on the table and moves to the kitchen. Eggs. Eggs are healthy.

Making an omelet and a cup of tea, she feels the quiet punctuated by her single plate hitting the counter, the hiss of the boiling water.

"Trying to eat," she says, "to live."

Almost a voice, a hum, a murmured "Good."

With a plate and mug in hand, she walks back to the dining room, where she sees the mail. Home is harder. Home is tricky. There is a temptation toward suspension, with its own rules and rhythm; if she doesn't move forward, doesn't answer the contractor, he's still here.

But the silence.

Her heart beats, her body continues to function. She doesn't feel old yet, not widow material.

She moves the mail aside to put her plate down, sees her blazer hanging on the back of a dining room chair, lifts it off, and carries it to the hall closet. When she opens the door, which has a mirror on the back of it, she's startled to see herself. Angry. It's in her eyes, the set of her shoulders.

Her body is ripe, mature. It knows how to serve her. Anger lights the fire. She knows it's normal, the body's insistence on being alive. It's all competition—plants for the light of the sun, people for more days, more minutes. Not me, I made it, you're down, but I'm still here.

Her body needs to be used. Walking. Running? Yard work? Will that do it? Does it have to be love?

She returns to the kitchen and eats standing at the counter. She is not old yet, she will be faced in time with choosing companions for this theatre event or that dinner, she will pretend to be in the flow again one day, someone will take her elbow, say something kind. There will be temptations. The machinery of living. Her heart beats with fury, wanting him back, wanting the last eight days to disappear.

■ ■ ■

SITTING IN THE CLINIC, FRANK FEELS LIKE A WASHUP, BUT IT'S
the only way to get Valium tonight. He will have to go
back to stockpiling. Across from him is a young African
American father, holding his son of about a year old, looking worried. It's just a cold, Frank wants to say, just a cold.
Fathers who worry over their children interest him. He
will put one into a screenplay someday, he knows. People
who are warm, good, are tricky to write, risk being dull,
but he will put a young father in something, just because
he wants to explore that kind of person. Who knows, who
knows.

He would like to make a movie with someone like a
young Denzel Washington, someone so beautiful you
can't get over it. He's written one screenplay with a young
Denzel-type. The man isn't a father, though, just a
teenager who wants to be a doctor. Oh, he knows what
he's doing, all right, he knows where the impulses come
from, he stays conscious, he is transforming the grit and
scum and mess of reality, he is making something admirable of his own darkness. He knows how to take a
snatch of memory, a pinch of fact, a dose of imagination,
and—Denzel, *c'est moi.*

"Hey, fella," the young man says to his son, "smile for
me, huh? Big smile, huh?"

"We should go have a few drinks," Heinz Ersicher said,
when Frank came out of his classroom earlier. "Have a
talk. How's it going?"

"Okay. I'm giving them a lot of work."

"Good, good. I'm hearing wonderful things. We should
get together soon, talk. Clarify."

Adjunct, only for one quarter, Ersicher told him at the
beginning. And like a boy, he thought, But if I'm good, it
will turn out to be more than that. And Heinz, reading him
correctly, has been explaining repeatedly how universities
are run. "Can't be helped. We're replacing a quarter leave-
of-absence, so that's all we have." His neediness shows and
he feels embarrassed around Heinz, who got him this gig
and the one in Pittsburgh (a semester, a few weeks beyond

the Athens job) and now also looks embarrassed at his empty-handedness. Do bad clouds follow Frank around, the bastard brother, the Don John, the Edmund, getting only the scraps? Frank knows it's all attitude. You expect glory, you get it. You interpret things badly, your one black cloud attracts a couple of thunderheads, and pretty soon they're joining up like a chorus, getting ready to rain big-time.

What he's done. He can't think about it. Can't. His hands shake uncontrollably if he lets the thought in. It must have been meant. He didn't plan it. And so . . .

The things that are unplanned are . . . pure in a way. From conception on down the line. It's true, there is more life in bastard brothers. True. More grit, more life, more groin.

When he gets in to see the doctor, he sits across from her, wondering what's the best way to make her like him and therefore get what he needs. She's angular, shy, has long hair in a single braid. She will want to be smiled at, he decides, and he has a dazzling smile. Dazzling Razzi, one woman told him. California white teeth and a bit of a tan and the good sort of eye-wrinkles. Now the new beard coming in. If he decides to keep it.

"I'm new in town," he says, engaging her eyes. "You'd think after twenty years in L.A. I'd be calm in Athens, Ohio, but I'm not. I'm new at the university. Teaching is new to me and I'm feeling a lot of stress. I guess part of it is the public speaking. I mean, I've had nervous periods before, I just didn't think it was going to happen again."

She consults the chart. "You teach media writing?"

"Yeah. I do. I get embarrassed because—" He holds out his hands, which shake on cue for her. He smiles his best smile. "I've had this happen a couple of times before. I hate it. It's as if I get one scare and the body just can't stop reacting."

"Oh. That's a pretty standard description of a panic attack. Now, if standing before a group is the problem, there's something some people call the public speaking pill—" she begins.

Cripes, he's way beyond all that. "Oh, I know," he says, but he keeps smiling at her. "It never really helped me. Inderol. Propanolol. Well, it's okay, but it doesn't turn it around, you know? I might—if you trust me on what my history is—need an antidepressant again. I thought I was done with them. Four years ago I had a combination of Xanax and Zoloft and it did the trick. In four weeks I was improved. Then I felt great in about three months. Then I stayed on Zoloft for a while after that, about a year, I think."

"Hmmm," she says. "There's an antianxiety pill we're having a lot of success with. BuSpar."

No. No. He doesn't want BuSpar. "I had that once. It had a reverse effect on me, some sort of kickback."

"How do you mean?"

"More anxious. I'm overly sensitive to some drugs, I guess."

"You tried BuSpar when?"

"A short bout, a year ago. After BuSpar juiced me up, I took three days of Xanax and I was okay again."

"So you had a recurrence?"

"A short one." He keeps smiling. "I fought my way out of it."

He has the names of several other doctors. He will just keep going, if he has to, until he has enough.

"I'll give it a try," she says. "Your magic combination. But I use Valium instead of Xanax. It's safer."

Typical, typical.

"I'd want to see you again in a week."

That means seven Valium. No way.

"I have to go out of the country for a couple of weeks."

"Oh. How can you do that when you're teaching?"

God save him from these responsible types. He needs one of those old guys who just wants to get you in and out.

"They allow for this trip because it's related to what I'm doing. I have a couple of meetings with some financial backers in France. I double up on classes, make some up, give in-class assignments." He's heard of people doing this sort of thing, so invention comes easy. "I let the students in on it all—the financial end of producing films. That's part of their learning, too."

"Does the trip by any chance have you especially nervous?"

"Maybe. Could be."

"And you're a writer. Any title I'd recognize?"

"No. Small things mostly. A couple of documentaries. Two full-length indies. I worked as a scriptwriter for public TV for a couple of years. I assisted on the Civil War series. I started out writing jingles for radio."

Would have liked to work on the Civil War series. Never did jingles for radio, except in his head. But she seems to like these two little tidbits, nods imagining them. And for him, it feels better to make something up.

"You know Ken Burns?"

"Yes."

"I'm sure it's an amazingly high-stress business. I can imagine."

"You can't," he says. "Trust me." He smiles.

"I have a pretty good imagination."

Ha, she shows some spirit. Watch the quiet ones with the long braids.

He says, "You've written a scene thirty-seven times, no exaggeration, some actress who's been out boozing can't deliver the lines, everybody decides to save her ass by asking you for number thirty-eight."

"I get it."

"Or film. You're on location, all cast, cameras rolling, food tents are up, the director eats his eggs and bacon, takes a phone call. The backer just pulled out. The money. The whole thing collapses."

Her eyes are bright, listening. "Nothing to depend on, at any stage of it. You're up one day, down the next."

"Mostly down." And calculated by hours. He keeps spinning. "I'm usually strong, but just lately, I think with the teaching preparations, I'm not getting enough sleep.

It's always for me just a matter of turning it around. Anyway, anything I start on, I should probably have enough for three weeks, till I get back to the States and get myself un-jet-lagged."

"Okay," she says. "I'll see you in three weeks, then, when you're back from France." She begins to write on her little pad.

Twenty-one Valium. A month of Zoloft. It will help.

When he leaves, the young father who reminds him of Denzel Washington is still sitting there, his son asleep in his arms.

LAUREN SOUNDS BETTER, SOMETHING MORE FORCEFUL IN HER voice "Mom? Hi. You okay?"

"I'm okay, just out of breath from sweeping the back porch."

"Good. Movement is good. I started back to running this morning."

Her daughter is doing better.

"Mom? I got a ride this weekend. I mean, I know I'm coming in next weekend for the dinner. But. This other guy is coming in late late Saturday and coming back here late Sunday. So I'd have basically all of Sunday with you."

"Only one day? Because I could come get you—"

"Well, some people asked me out for Friday and Saturday. I thought you might think that was a good thing to do. But still, I feel like I have to see you, so if I come home this Saturday and again next weekend . . ."

"Honey, anything you want. . . . I'm glad you're trying to go out. Try to have a good time. What time would you get in, then?"

"We'd start out after the football game."

Football.

"So, I'd get in ten, eleven. Late."

"Is he a careful driver?"

"I think he is. I could jump out and hitch if he isn't."

"Jump out and call me."

Her first thought upon hanging up, before she could

edit it out, was to tell Dan their daughter was coming for a visit.

She wanders to the front door, as if by some magic Lauren will be there already. Outside, she sees people running, walking, using the park, the neighbors next door locking up, carrying clothes on hangers over their arms.

IN HIS CAR, GOING TOWARD THE PHARMACY, HE FEELS A SURGE of courage and calls the realtor in Pittsburgh. Of course no one will be there, it's six o'clock already, but just in case. . . . The phone rings ten times, and just as he's about to hang up, he gets a message telling him his man may be reached at home! He can't write anything down as he drives, but he memorizes the number and calls it. "Charles Schulties?"

"Yes. Here. Speaking," the man fumbles.

"Frank Razzi. I left a message for you earlier."

"Yes."

"Got a message from the Bunsens late last night that they were willing to rent. I took today to think about it. I want to rent the place on Beechwood."

"Right. They told me they were willing to do a month-at-a-time lease, but I'd be more comfortable with a sixty-day."

"That's fine."

Another surge of courage lifts him. "They said it could be immediate. You know, I said in my message I could come in on Friday to sign the papers and get the key?"

"Yes . . ."

"Well, it turns out I have some time tonight. I'm on the road anyway, and I got this idea I might as well come in and do all that tonight. Would that be all right?"

"Tonight? What time?"

"I could be there at . . ." Frank consults the dashboard. "Nine-thirty, ten tonight. Is there any way I could look at the place again? I was just about to order some carpets."

"I can't turn over the key, not until it's official. I could meet you at the house, let you get a quick measure."

"If it's not out of your way, I'd be very grateful."

Papers crackle in the background. "Heck, we work all hours in this business. I'm meeting a couple at another place at eight-thirty. Everything I work on is a mile from everything else. Should be okay." Frank could hear more noise of movement and crackling of papers. "Let's see, I'm talking to myself here, I'll need rental agreement forms, credit history forms, the key. . . . You won't be much later than nine-thirty?"

"Right. The measuring will take me under five minutes."

"But just so you know, no key until it's official. Tomorrow, I do a routine credit search, so you're clear by Friday."

Frank skips the pharmacy. Tomorrow is soon enough to get rid of the shakes. He passes his own house—the other rented one, in Athens—and is onto Route 50 and, before he knows it, Route 70. He has to get something to eat but that can be from a drive-thru. If he does seventy-five, eighty, he will be there in three hours and fifteen minutes.

Even though he knows he'll be hungry soon, he pulls over to fuel up and ignores the plastic sandwiches and candy bars, buying only a bottle of Coke. Then he's in the car again, with people pulling out of the malls everywhere on the way home, the light completely gone out of the sky. Oldies on the radio.

He stops for food at nine, just a Whopper and a shake, and gets onto Route 79 where he bypasses Morgantown. He's getting mighty used to this road. It'll be a couple of times a week from now on. Once, on a Friday night, right after he was hired at both Athens and Pittsburgh, but before the teaching had begun, he'd driven in on a muggy summer night, late at night then, too. He'd parked downtown at a meter, walked around, couldn't get a feeling for anything. Nothing much was the same, only Kaufmann's Department Store and a few of the municipal buildings. Then he'd driven the Parkway straight up to Squirrel Hill and taken Pocusset to Schenley Park. For a while, he just drove around the park. Simple. Just to see the place again. Then he went to Aiken Avenue, where the doctor's office was, thinking just to look at the building, and he saw Dan himself, driving out, at ten o'clock. At first he didn't recognize him, then he did. Surprise and fear ballooned in his heart. Late hours, he thought. He wondered how often Dan kept these hours.

Then he came in for the class the week after and drove to the office and parked across the street again, but he didn't see anyone. He felt almost soft, sentimental.

Then there were those newspaper articles and the phone call he made that froze his soul.

Then.

A wasp is in a room, the room isn't yours. You get rid of the wasp, it's yours again.

This time he goes straight to the Squirrel Hill exit and parks on Murray Avenue for a moment, just catching his breath. Nine-forty. He hopes the guy, Schulties, is still there, but he needs to screw his head on first. Things are pretty quiet. He gets out of the car and stands in front of where Silberberg's Bakery used to be. He's almost crying. Silberberg's is gone. The place is now a fancy bread store with contemporary prices. Things change. How they change. People pass him, in cars, on foot. Nobody notices him, nobody can see through who he is now to who he was then.

After only five or six minutes on Murray Avenue, he gets back into his car, sucks in a deep breath, and drives up to Beacon and over to Beechwood. He parks his car behind the realtor's car and summons his easygoing personality.

Schulties gets out of his car.

". . . so good of you," Frank is saying.

"Not a problem. We can sign the papers in there at the kitchen counter or in my car. Either way, we'll need a flashlight. There are no lamps and they took the bulbs out of most of the ceiling lights. Actually, my car is more comfortable."

"Sure. The car," Frank says.

The flashlight is helpful for reading the fine print. No surprises, so far as he can see.

"You'll need to call tomorrow to switch gas and electric to your name. Telephone, cable, all that. Here. I have a sheet with all the numbers on for you."

Frank takes the sheet of paper, for which he's grateful.

"You still want to do the measuring?" Schulties asks doubtfully when the papers are signed and he has two checks in hand, one for rent, one for security deposit. "Basically, you can't see in there."

"Just a quick look, then."

Schulties laughs a little. "You're eager, like a kid getting his first place."

What Frank has in mind is borrowing the key, while the agent sits in his car, but Schulties says, "Maybe I'll just come in and use the john while you're at it."

The two men go inside. Schulties directs the flashlight beam from wall to wall and while Frank makes a show of pacing off the living room, Schulties locates the first-floor bathroom and goes in. When Frank hears noise in the bathroom, he quickly opens the kitchen door, switches the lock off, and closes it again.

Schulties doesn't check the kitchen door before they leave. They walk outside, with Schulties making a big show of locking the front door.

Finally the realtor waves and drives off, powering his window down and saying Frank has his number if he needs anything else.

Frank sits in his car until he is sure Schulties is gone. For five minutes he looks at the nicer house next door, wondering which lights belong to which rooms and how long it will be before he sets foot in that house. Finally, he walks around to the back door of the house he has rented and he slips in. In the dark, he makes his way up to the bedroom on the left that looks out on the house he wants to watch.

Luck! He's ecstatic! He can see her plainly. She lies on top of the bed, fully dressed, reading. He watches her turn a page, turn another. In the square of window she's like a figure on a movie screen, lovely, not that he can see her close up, but surface loveliness is not what he means anyway. *Something in the way she moves.* The phone rings and she picks it up. Ordinary and normal. Quiet and sad. She sits up, leans forward, puts a forefinger to her eye (tears? thought?), pulls into herself. He watches for a long time, slack-jawed as a teenager. Her hair is soft. He wonders how long until he can see her close up. She's been hurt, thrown off guard, stunned, the way people are most beautiful, in grief; already he's fallen a little in love with her.

When he leaves, he goes only a few blocks and parks along the golf course in Schenley Park. It seems nobody is around anywhere at all. He gets out and walks, nobody to bother him, thinking he will get home at four, sleep for four hours, go to his meetings, pick up his pills. He walks up and down for five minutes, thinking, becoming the boy he once was, becoming the other name, not Frank.

Over on the road, a patrol car stops. Two policeman come toward him. "Everything okay?"

"Everything's fine."

"Is that your car parked over there? The beamer?"

"That's mine."

"Well, we don't like people hanging around after hours in the park. Could breed trouble. You meeting anyone here?"

"Not a soul."

"Better if you left, then. You have someplace to go?"

"I was just going home."

"You have ID?"

"Sure." He shows them he is Frank Razzi. Faculty member at Ohio University. He gets back into his car and drives to Athens, digesting his strange cocktail of emotions: fear, anger, remorse, survival ecstasy. So some of the time, as he drives, he's up high, his spirit way up above the sunroof, flying way up high where he can look down and feel sorry for his tiny sorry self and most of the other minuscule sorry people bopping around the world.

AT ONE IN THE MORNING, MARINA WAS ASLEEP BESIDE CHRISTIE, and while her breathing was calm, regular, he was not at all sleepy yet. He was exhausted, but wired up, because once they got the children to bed, he began reading the new files he brought home. He put aside the Ross papers and got himself into a state over the death, thirty years ago, of Theodore Lucky. The boy's high school photo flashed in his memory still, a hopeful, even joyful boy. Faces, people, that's what he loved. And he loved Ted Luckey's face.

Strange. A broken home, an alcoholic father, and a level of poverty that usually didn't produce star students. But there Luckey was, second in his class at Taylor Allderdice, which was a smart school, the most difficult school in the city system. Headlines screamed, *Scholarship Student Found Dead,* and *Suspicion Surrounds Death of Taylor Allderdice Youth.*

Police reported that alcohol and drugs were found in his system at the autopsy, enough to account for the fall. He was found slumped, dead, on the hillside off Pocusset, broken neck. Daniel Ross explained to the detectives it was where Ted Luckey went to study, in a house that he "borrowed." Sneaked into. The detective wrote, *Strange house, not a residence for a long time. Locked up and the owner gone for years. The house is filled with books, floor to ceiling, with only enough room to walk between the piles. Must be hundreds of thousands, no exaggerating. There's all kinds of stuff—history, fiction, philosophy—even on the stairway. Books stacked twenty, thirty high on every step. People who could remember owner said he was "eccentric." Owner died and his son (strange, too, nobody ever sees him) pays the taxes and keeps the house as a storage place for his father's books.*

The boy's body had been found off behind the house, down a steep hill, between a ditch and a tree.

There was a fairly big investigation. Canvassing, interviews with teachers, students, neighbors. Daniel Ross was far from the only kid interviewed, but in all the transcripts Christie read, people either liked Ted Luckey or didn't know him that well. Even playing the race card, the police had not been able to come up with a motive. Had he had a white girlfriend, angered some white boy with that? No, it appeared not. He had *friends,* but no big romance anybody knew about. He worked as a dishwasher after school, and when the restaurant closed for the night, he apparently sneaked into the "safe house" and did his schoolwork.

Maybe he went there other times of day, too. Apparently, being around his father only got him a beating. That's what the neighbors said. Then, poor Ted Luckey. Following in the family pattern, it looked like, letting drink and drugs get hold of him. *The boy may have intended suicide,* the detective wrote, *because what else could he have been about, taking in all those pills. Seconal. The drugs were not found at scene, but two empty bottles and one partly filled bottle were found in his mother's medicine cabinet.*

Finally, everybody caved in and called it an accidental death.

Christie had seen enough suicides in his time to be unsurprised. Often people didn't know, didn't suspect. Successful suicides were clever liars up until the moment they decided to make a sign to the world that said, See, you haven't been looking, I haven't been okay all along.

He liked the boy's face.

Daniel Ross had mourned the boy, even managed, thirty years later, to buy the property where the thing had happened and turn it into a home for kids who had nowhere to go. A beautiful gesture, and yet . . . Christie's first thought was a cop's thought: Maybe Ross had met his friend that night, pushed him over the edge, then lived with the guilt for half a lifetime. It *could* have happened that way. Christie read the police reports, the alibis. Apparently, Daniel Ross was doing work on the lighting system of the school play until ten that night, then he took a long walk through Schenley Park with a classmate, Nadine Broton, who lived in the other direction, then the walk back home, through the park again. Nobody saw Dan Ross on the way home, nobody who was sure.

The brother, Paul LaBeau, was interviewed, too. He'd watched television all evening in the finished basement of their house, he said, and his father supported that statement.

Ted Luckey's father was a suspect for a while, but an airtight alibi established he was drinking all night, around the corner from where he lived. Thirteen people had seen him in the Homewood bar.

Ted Luckey had played basketball. He played well, of course. Everything he did, he did well. He held down a job, washing dishes, never complained. He had A's in almost everything, honors courses, too.

Gave the police a bit of a ride before he got buried. Probably never could have guessed that thirty years later, his death would affect a different policeman who couldn't get to sleep.

Wednesday night crept toward Thursday morning. Christie thought he had better soon haul himself off to dreamland.

Paul LaBeau did it. Old Doc Ross lied. Young Daniel Ross suspected but didn't know for sure, carried it as a burden into his adulthood.

That's what he'd guess if *guessing* solved anything. And he was still nowheresville with what had happened to Doc Ross, forty-eight years old, in a parking lot outside his office late one Tuesday night, a little over a week ago.

3

AT SUPPERTIME ON THURSDAY AFTERNOON, AFTER HE'D FIN-
ished with some appointments at the office, Frank put his
shaving kit and some clothes on hangers in the backseat
of his car, along with a case of wine and the student papers
he needed to grade; then he headed for Pittsburgh again.
He had one Valium in him and that meant he was feeling a
little more steady.

On the way into Pittsburgh he detoured to Ikea, thinking he would buy basics: couch, table, lamp, bed. But wan-
dering the brightly painted warehouse, he couldn't bring
himself to be so slapdash in the matter of furnishings, and
decided to take more time, get better things. He purchased
only a couple of cups, glasses, a coffeemaker, two down
pillows, and an egg-crate foam thing that was supposed to
lift the sleeping body up over a too-hard mattress. Folded
over, it would make a temporary bed. He was a little old to
be sleeping on the floor, but he would have to do so for a
night or two. He wouldn't be sleeping much, he guessed,
and that was nothing new. He got lightbulbs.

When he stopped before the house, then began to edge
the car into the driveway, he thought, What have I done,
how can I do this? For a wonderful, brief moment, he saw
some humor in the pose he'd created. Lawns, he'd never
thought about them; he didn't tinker with broken toilets;
he didn't call people to do seasonal checks on heating and

cooling. In L.A. he'd owned a condo with its ready-made repair staff. He was not handy. Cranky disposals and the care of deck furniture he had left to Lisa when she was with him. When she left six years ago, he realized how little he knew about running the place. Other than that, he didn't miss her, exactly. She was cool and that didn't interest him much. She'd wanted someplace to live, someone to buy her things; he'd wanted someone on his arm at this and that event. Six years together, hardly a treat, and six years apart, until he could hardly remember her. Then the paperwork last year. Not the kind of marriage his brother would have had—oh, no—more like his mother's pathetic brief liaisons. So, you learn from your elders.

He drove up the driveway and parked. The garage-door opener was somewhere in the house. He hadn't been able to find it in the dark last night.

He's not supposed to be in there until Friday. If Schulties has come by and locked the back door, he's going to have to go to a hotel. He sits for a moment thinking about that. Blood swells in him. Fury. Whatever the medical fact of it, blood does actually boil.

He has not liked most of his life, that's the truth. No, to be specific, he has never felt his life was *his* life. Instead he seemed to have put in a good forty years not being who he was. Who would understand that? Inside he was a boy who could feel joy, a man who did things comfortably, in the company of others.

Alone much of the time. Alone in his mind the rest of the time.

Elizabeth.

He said her name to himself. Man, you could put her right into a film, the way she moved, fluidly, in that economical way, as if dancing. He knows completely, without any hesitation, he must get to know her.

He climbs out of the car quietly and tries the back door. Ah, good, still open.

Yes. A kitchen. One socket over the sink. He screws in a lightbulb. Light switch near the door, on, off again, he'd better not use it now. He walks about, still feeling the glare, feeling exposed, as if someone had snapped a picture. His eyes adjust to the dark. He can see the rectangle on the kitchen counter that is the garage-door opener.

He slips out, careful to leave the door ajar, powers the garage door up, and parks, hiding his car. Then carrying the few clothes he's brought and the small purchases, he repeats his entry into the house. Standing in the kitchen until his eyes adjust, he wonders if anyone noticed him enter the house. Who would care?

He moves into the next room, an eating alcove, then the next, a proper dining room, then the living room and the small room off it that the owners said they used as a reading room.

All this space, crazy, but he wants this, exactly this. He allows himself to climb the stairs, look at the bedrooms again. All this, three bedrooms, and the place in Athens, too. His breathing becomes jagged.

He goes to the small room, just stands at the window. There she is, reading again. A different book, it looks like. She looks toward the phone—ha, he can almost hear it ring—and lifts the receiver. She shakes her head, sits at the edge of the bed, leaning forward, shaking her head. Stands. Walks. He can almost hear her voice. Almost. In his mind.

When she draws the blinds, he feels shut out, angry. Did she see the light moments ago? Does she always shut the blinds at night? Or did she sense his presence?

After a couple of hours of quiet and stillness, he goes out to get the egg-crate bedroll and the pillows.

"WE FOUND THE WALLET," CHRISTIE TOLD ELIZABETH IN THAT phone call late Thursday night. "We're going over it for prints now."

"Who did it?"

"That's a little harder."

He told her what he knew, backwards, as it were: A. That night, a few hours earlier, a fifteen-year-old boy on the

North Side tried to buy a computer by phone with her husband's credit card. When the police arrived, the young man
was routed out of his basement, and he turned over the wallet. The wallet was *given to him,* he kept explaining. It seemed
like luck. B. The boy told a story. He had an uncle who
sometimes slept at Light of Life Ministries, sometimes slept
out in West Park. Every three days or so, the uncle came by
the house for something to eat. The uncle told the boy he
had found the wallet almost a week before and that it had
had some cash in it. He'd used most of the cash for food and
drink, but he handed five dollars over to the nephew on
Sunday. He said he didn't feel confident about trying to use
the credit cards himself since he didn't look like a person
who owned such things, but maybe the boy would know
what to do with them. The boy sat on his hands for four
days, then finally, Thursday, used one of the cards, trying to
make a purchase by phone. Alarms went off. The police
went and got the kid from his basement and started questioning him and whoever else might know something
about his story. C. Some homeless men at Light of Life Ministries confirmed that a man named Jones showed them the
wallet early last week. A few assumed he'd stolen it, but
most believed he'd found it. He was excited by his luck.

The kid's alibi for the Tuesday night of the Ross murder was hard to verify. He'd been home, hanging out, he
said, with his younger brother. The brother, of course, said
he was there, and Christie had to make the kid write out
everything he'd seen on TV that night. He was a channel
surfer, not particularly articulate, so it was hard going.

That was all Christie knew when he talked to Elizabeth
by phone that night.

"You don't think he did it? The boy?"

"It doesn't look likely, but it's some kind of lead. We
need for you to look at the wallet after forensics is finished, tell us if anything else is missing."

"Of course. You mean tonight?"

"No, no, tomorrow."

"What about the uncle?"

"We're looking. We've talked to people who've talked to him. The portrait is consistent. He drinks. He's on the dole in various ways. He appears nonviolent. Nobody's ever seen him with a gun. It might take a little time. I'll let you know as soon as we find him."

Christie took the wallet to her at her office at noon on Friday. She sat at her desk and looked at it for a moment without touching. Then she began to look through it, opening each compartment carefully.

"Any credit cards missing?"

"All the ones I remember are still here. There were usually a few receipts. They're gone. Thrown away, I guess. Pictures of me and the kids." She looked up. "In the park or in a trash basket somewhere. He had a couple of ID cards, one from the hospital, one for car insurance. Those are gone. And the . . . the driver's license is gone."

"We noticed that."

"Someone's going to use the license."

"We hope so."

"Do you think whoever did it did it for the license? Someone who hangs around that park?"

"It's hard to know just yet."

The sun streamed in through the slatted blinds, striping her and the wallet. Her fist tightened over the wallet. "Do I get to keep this now?"

"If we could have it for just a while longer," he said gently. "It's evidence." She handed it over. He took her hand and held it for a moment, but he could see that his comfort was going to make her cry, so he released her hand.

FRIDAY AFTERNOON, FRANK WENT TO LAZARUS.

At Lazarus he paid an extra hundred to have the bed, bedclothes, nightstand, dresser, sofa, table lamp, end table, two rugs, table, and chairs delivered in twenty-four hours. It was a start.

"Just a little purchase," the clerk said whimsically. Then she added, "I like your choices. I can actually picture your little apartment."

Right. He'd only bought enough furniture for the efficiency she was imagining, but he couldn't rush into any more yet. He wanted to do it right. Needed a decorator, really, had no skill at arranging things in the physical world. He didn't have patience for details. Still, bare bones as his place would be, the furniture was a good-enough quality; he could function as of tomorrow: sleep, eat, read.

Lazarus, done. Check. Next he gets himself to Pottery Barn and buys cups and plates and a few utensils from the sale table. Enough to get by. Peeler, spatula, can opener. Now he's got to get in some groceries.

There are markets near the house in Squirrel Hill, but . . . He tilts the rearview mirror to look at himself. He is one of those people who looks nothing in middle age as he looked as a youth. He was once narrow, he is now full, solid. His teeth were crooked, they are straight. His ears stuck out, they've been tucked back. His face has aged. His hair, which was long, unruly, and *light*, is tightly trimmed and darker now, except for the gray. He's improved with age. Two of his colleagues out in L.A. talked about going to a high school reunion and not recognizing anyone and not *being* recognized even when everyone knew who they were looking for. They showed before-and-after pictures, chortling at the ravages of age. Frank takes a hard look at himself and concludes that out of context he is not recognizable. Yet there was that time in Florida last summer a woman thought she knew him, so he plans to take very few chances. He'll do his one course at Pitt, not go out much.

He stops at a Kuhn's market far from home, closer to Lazarus. Coffee, bread, eggs, sausage, pasta, olive oil, garlic, potatoes, salad vegetables, steaks, toilet paper, paper towels, soap. That ought to do it.

He stops at the realty office and picks up a key. Official now.

The day is beautiful, again beautiful.

As he pulls into the driveway, he sees her outside, just standing, looking at the yard. Fear grips him. His hands begin to shake uncontrollably again. Why had he thought he would speak to her at a moment like this? Impossible. He fumbles for the garage-door opener, which he now has on the passenger seat, and drives into the garage, trying to pull himself together. He almost forgets to turn off the engine. God! He gathers the grocery bags and carries them all at once, allowing him to look preoccupied as he walks from the garage to the kitchen door. He doesn't look up or to his right. When he settles himself and peers out the window of the kitchen, she is not there anymore and he doesn't know if she was there when he went from the garage to the house. Later, he checks again, and she is weeding slowly. He can almost hear her sighing, every third tug.

IT TOOK CHRISTIE THE REST OF FRIDAY TO TRACK DOWN THE uncle of the boy who had Daniel Ross's wallet. They finally caught up with him in West Park on Friday night. He was cooperative. He showed them where he slept and demonstrated how he had found the wallet among his bed rags. Forensics came back positive for the uncle's prints and the two nephews' prints and three other sets, including Daniel Ross's. The police set out to find and print the people at Light of Life that John William Jones had talked to.

Jones seemed willing to sit for questioning by the police all Saturday. He was in a good mood, content to eat police provisions in place of whatever stew was being served over at Light of Life. "It's nice and warm in here," he chuckled, even though it was ridiculously warm out for October, and Christie got a boyish pang of nostalgia to imagine sleeping under a bush.

On Saturday afternoon, he and Marina took the kids to the Science Center, which was really only a couple of blocks from West Park and the spot where the homeless man had slept on a tangle of brightly colored rags under a bush. Christie ended up telling Marina about it as they walked around an exhibit of shapes—trapezoids, triangles, octagons. The arrangement of clothes Jones had slept on had looked haphazard at first, but underneath was a layer of paper bags and under that a layer of plastic supermarket bags. Clever. Still, he couldn't imagine that poor boozer getting the whole way to Shadyside and to the back parking lot of a doctor's office, then hopping a bus back to the North Side. The homeless in each area of town stayed put. They didn't get on buses or hitch rides. No. Someone had either handed over the wallet or discarded it, and Uncle Jones was insisting it was the latter.

FOR LUNCH ON SATURDAY, FRANK MADE HIMSELF AN OMELET filled with cheese and tomato, very buttery, not bad. He stood at the kitchen counter eating out of the pan. He wore his reading glasses and toted around a stack of papers he was half through grading—a regular guy, who could doubt it? Even he didn't doubt it that day. The work, the waiting for furniture, made him feel rooted. He thought, This is what lives are made up of: getting dressed, eating, putting the usual strings and things into the nest, tiring out, sleeping. Today it seems the extraordinary moments in his life, his brushes with acts perceived as evil, have not happened. Amazing, how some days he can carve it away and simply live the meat of his life. Why is that? How is it? The Valium, maybe, the Zoloft. Repression in a couple of pills.

He watched the house next door last night until about two. She didn't go to sleep until one or later, since the lights didn't go off until then. He's not sure when she woke. She might have been lying there in the dark, like he was.

Patience.

When he gets back to Athens, he will call that woman Sandra from the History Department or play a few moves with that kid in the Xerox room, dissipate some of the energies. Didn't those polygamists know it? More than one is needed. One is like a glaring spotlight. Reflected light enchants.

Patience.

The doorbell rings. Through the glass he can see a large Lazarus truck. Amen. Something to sit on, sleep on.

"Nice house," the beefy delivery man says. He looks happy to be doing his job. Imagine being happy to heave all that stuff for other people.

Frank points the mattress and box spring and frame up the stairs, the sofa and dining table to the right spots.

When the men leave, he sees he has made three little islands of normalcy in the midst of echoing empty space. Sit, dine, sleep. He will need a lot more *stuff*.

Carefully placing his work on the dining table, which still has tags dangling, he begins to work. At first it doesn't feel natural, but then it does. A glass of water. The tags cut. Just a man, working.

IT SEEMS FOREVER UNTIL LAUREN WILL GET HERE. ELIZABETH goes to the door, goes to the window, as if this will change the clock. Outside she sees a Lazarus truck. New neighbors already and she doesn't have a civil impulse in her. Maybe next summer, a Sunday brunch or something like that.

She has work to do.

It seems wrong to her that her husband's papers are in the hands of the police. She wants them back. Her job for the next months will be to read everything he wrote, did, paid, jotted down. It will be a tedious job, but she doesn't mind. After the papers, the clothes. Then the medical books, given to someone who needs them. She will keep his other books.

On impulse, she dials Christie's number to ask how long her husband's things will be out of her hands, but it's Saturday, and the phone rings for a long time up at the Investigative Branch. Finally, somebody who doesn't sound very official picks up.

"Is this the desk sergeant?" she asks.

"No, ma'am, they're all away from their desks. Is there a message?"

"Never mind. I have Commander Christie's cell-phone number. I just thought I'd try the office first."

"Yes, ma'am. I think they said he's off with his kids. We're supposed to use his cell phone if there's anything, you know."

After hanging up, Elizabeth spins a few wheels and does not dial Christie's cell, but she considers letting him know the civilian receptionist is hardly professional. Three hours later Christie calls her back, explaining he had to spend a few hours with his family and asking if there is a particular something she called the Branch about.

"I didn't leave my name or a message."

"Ah, we have our methods." After a gentle pause, he asks, "What is it?"

"His papers. You said to call and check if you're done."

"We're working long hours, honestly," he tells her, "and right now we are a bit caught up in the wallet—what that will tell us. I need a little more time."

"Of course. I understand." The clock tells her she has five hours until her daughter arrives.

Before Christie hangs up, he tells her the police are trying to find out if any of the homeless saw a stranger hanging around their things in the park.

It will not be solved, it will not be solved. She must move on.

ON SATURDAY NIGHT, CHRISTIE SITS WITH ROSS'S FILE FOLDERS again.

He feels like the ghost of Dan Ross, looking into this old case, and wondering, after the fact, what the seventeen-year-old boy known as Paul had to do with the death of Ted Luckey. But *something* feels unsolved. Lots of vapors. Things seeming real and then floating off into the ozone.

He called the lab earlier today with a few questions. "In 1972, how common was suicide from Seconal and alcohol? How well was it known, say, among kids then, as a way of doing it?"

"Plenty of people knew about it," he was told by the woman in the lab. "Kids, you never know what kind of information they're going to pick up. Could your kid lay hold of Seconal is the question."

Christie explained that the boy's mother had had several prescriptions.

"Ah, that explains it, then. He might have tried one or two before the big dose. Look up Seconal on the Web, you'll see plenty of stories."

Poor Ted Luckey falling, falling backwards over the hill, body twisted. And then lying there in the rain. What a way to die. The storm, branches falling on him.

Pah. What is he doing? Case full of ghosts.

He comes upon the thick file folder he wants—marked "Gerald Paul LaBeau." It's organized, chronological, with birthday cards from Daniel to Paul in a young hand. School report cards. The boy must have left all this behind when he left the Ross house. Paul was a smart kid. Lots of A's. Letter of commendation from one teacher. Small drugstore-style picture of a woman—the boy's mother, presumably, with short pixie hair and beads, a knowing look in the eye. Christie studies the photo, trying to get a sense of her.

School newspaper article with pictures about the "foster" brothers being among the top students in their class.

A sheet of paper with four phone numbers, one checked. Johnson Investigations. No date. The paper is brittle. Johnson Investigations would have been the detective agency Ross hired to find his brother. About 1978 or so? A news article from the Detroit paper, brief.

A Wayne State University medical student, Gerald Paul, died Saturday of an apparent drug overdose in Atlantic City, New Jersey, while on vacation. Classmates and teachers expressed shock and sadness at the death. Paul graduated summa cum laude in pre-med from Wayne State and was ranked among the top in his medical school class. A memorial service will be held in University Center in September.

Gerald Paul is survived by his mother, Michelle LaBeau, of Bellingham, Washington.

Altered his name. Dropped LaBeau in Michigan.

And an obituary from the Seattle paper, which did not mention either of the Rosses, father or son. Simply:

Gerald Paul LaBeau, 1955 to 1979. Mr. LaBeau is a graduate of Wayne State University. He lived in Detroit and was scheduled to begin his third year of medical studies at Wayne State School of Medicine. He is survived by his mother, Michelle LaBeau, of Bellingham, Washington.

No written report from the P.I. Nothing else in the folder other than a single phone number on a single sheet of paper.

Christie closed the folder and then something struck him about the phone number he had just seen and he opened it again and took out the single sheet of paper. A 724 area code added in a different pen. That meant the number—the entry in the folder—was recent, since 724 was a newly instituted area code. He leafed back to the detective agency phone number mid-folder. It was the same except for the new area code. That meant Ross had recently looked into the folder.

Christie felt a little shot of excitement. He took up the slip of paper with the number and even though it was late on a Saturday evening he tried to call Derek Johnson. A mechanical voice told him the number was no longer in service. Damn. Had to have been in service not all that long ago. He looked in the phone book and saw just a plain old Derek Johnson out in the north suburbs, in Gibsonia. Another 724 number.

A hearty voice answered the phone. Christie explained who he was and what he was calling about.

"Oh, that was my father! He's out of the business. Eight months ago."

"Does he live with you?"

"No, no, he's got a new wife. He's in Florida."

"His number down there? Can you give it to me?"

The son gave it. "At the moment he's not there. You'll get his machine. He went on a four-day cruise. Just to Freeport, I think."

"His files are where?"

The man groaned. "Some here in my basement. Unfortunately. I told him I didn't want to keep them, but he was worried someone might call. Just like you did. The older ones are in storage, most I'd say are in storage. The recent ones are here, my headache."

"Well, let me talk to him first. When does he get back?"

"Monday night. Late."

"I can wait that long. He's happy in Florida?"

"Very happy. Very very happy."

"Good," Christie said. Nice to know some lives turned out okay.

He stared at the paper with the phone number. He looked at his watch again and dialed Elizabeth Shepherd. She answered the phone on the first ring. She sounded a bit better. "My daughter's here," she said. "A quick trip, just for a day."

"I'm sorry to call so late."

"It's okay. We're just going to sit down to eat. Terrible hour to eat, but they do it all the time in Greece and Italy."

Twenty past ten. It gave him indigestion to think of it. He'd indulged at this time of night himself in the days before his life became more regular, before Marina. He said, "I just have a quick question. Do you know if your husband recently made contact with the detective he used to try to find his brother?"

"No," she said. She sounded puzzled. "Recently? Why would he?"

"Just a phone number I found," he said carefully. "Just curious if you knew of any need he had for a detective."

"No," she said again, but he could hear she was unsettled.

"If you think of anything, give a call. I'm sorry I called so late."

"Anytime. We're always up early, too."

So. She was either lying or she was not in the loop.

She called him back at eight on Sunday morning. "It isn't anything that's going to help you now but I think I know what it was."

"What?"

"Recently—I didn't know he did anything about it, and maybe he didn't—he talked about finding Paul's mother again. He wanted to know what things of her son's she had kept. Notebooks or anything. He wanted to see them."

Christie whistled silently. Ross was a bit of a detective himself. Obsessed. Taking on a cold case like that.

"Had something happened recently that got your husband stirred up?"

"The Pocusset house, I guess. Stirred up memories."

Christie thanked her and hung up. Maybe, he thought. Maybe. He decided not to bother her anymore with the bee in his bonnet. He called and left a message with the Sunday desk sergeant for the head of Homicide in Atlantic City, saying a Pittsburgh detective needed to look at the files on Gerald Paul's death.

What was Ross after? Schoolbooks, notebooks?

More here than the ordinary, if one only knew how to see it.

FRANK LAY ON THE BED, TRYING TO GET USED TO HIS NEW PLACE, thinking. The new mattress was soft, the way he liked it. It made him think of the bed he slept in as a teenager—that one soft because it was old, this one because it was expensive.

Memory. True? Accurate? You never knew, when you made a business of images, if you'd been revising, polishing, even inventing.

Just as last night, sleeping on the floor with only egg-crate foam between him and the wood had reminded him of the couple of times he and his brother slept outside in summer when it was too hot to stay indoors. The way the mind works, leaping to make connections, analogs. The floor became the hard ground; he remembered the pinch in the small of his back, the smell of the grass and the honeysuckle vines that tangled on the fence to his right. For a moment last night, the memory was so sharp, he thought he smelled the pungent summer perfume.

Accurate? Yes, he decided. Other people, regular people, didn't know for sure whether the red ball they threw to Fido was six inches in diameter or twelve. Whether there were three windows in the bedroom or two. Other people's memories were fuzzier, he was sure, because at the time they were living the life that was to become memory, they weren't watching, while he was. His recalled images—smells, looks, words, sounds—were . . . pristine, etched, as the expression has it. He was a detective all along, putting it together.

Somewhere in the depths of his belongings, among other photos, are three of a shy woman he never even knew. Filched and carried with him; at a later point, packed up and sent to his mother; at another point, packed and sent to him by ordinary post. In every photo this shy woman is cloaked in a cardigan, carrying a book or curled over a book. Had she ever taken the cardigan off, put the books down, assumed other positions?

"What was she like when you were young?" he asked, plucking the odd blade of grass, pretending casualness. He and his half brother had set up a camp in the yard because it was a hot summer night and they didn't yet have air-conditioning. What was Dan's magic? Dan once smiled and said magic came from mothers.

His brother was fourteen at the time, he was still thirteen, and the word *young* meant seven, eight years old. Dan answered thoughtfully: "She wasn't one of those mothers who ran off with friends or played tennis or tossed me and my friends baseballs in the backyard. She was off doing her own thing, quiet, maybe some people would think *too* quiet, shy, I guess. She read me to sleep, I used to like that.

She had eye strain sometimes. She was a freelance editor. I know I told you that. Very into books. She gave me books for every gift. She was, I don't know, a nice person."

Elizabeth curls around a book, too. Interesting. Oedipal, for sure, never done with that old stuff. Frank gets a flash of a moment in a bar in Detroit, Dan saying, "She's wonderful. Her name is Elizabeth."

Because he has the window open a crack, Frank hears Elizabeth coming out of her house with the visitor who arrived last night—daughter, no doubt. He couldn't see her well, but he felt irritated at her presence, which meant to him that he would not be able to make an approach just yet. Now he hurries to the window (weren't the moving men curious that he put his bed in the smallest room!) and watched them get into the car and go. A daughter, surely. And they are going out to breakfast? He slips downstairs, makes coffee where he can watch the house and driveway for activity.

Once more he sits at the dining table, reading student papers. His mind won't hold on to their words. He's itemizing the furniture he must move here from Athens eventually to fill out the place. Desk, for certain, and file cabinet, other bed, dresser, assorted tables, easy chair. The sofa he has in Athens can go in the small room with his desk. Beds moved to the two larger rooms. Four more weeks, four and a half, and he's done with the Athens gig.

A student is writing about love, a scene in a park. Other memories stab at him. Call them up, he tells himself, Don't be afraid. What are the details? he asks, as if he is teacher and student both.

Springtime. Sixteen years old. The ground wet, the earth softening, the trees in Schenley Park—everywhere, in fact—a glimmering light green, abundant with new leaves. His brother carried yesterday's *Post-Gazette* to sit on, not thinking, probably, that in time the wet ground would seep through the paper. His brother carried books in his arms, too, a large stack of them.

The spring, the growth, the earth, a crazy mixture of

feelings. Sadness and rage. Something about whatever his brother felt, did, had, was the right thing. The thing desired.

Breathing in the smell of wet earth and fallen blossoms, he followed his brother. He stayed way behind and was not seen. His brother veered off the cement and walked into the park. Eventually he did, too. There had been a lot of rain and so the earth squished beneath his sneakers and a rim of mud came up around the sides of them.

Then Dan walked down the road where the golf course meets it on both sides. Purposeful. Walking fast. Carrying the bag with the four sandwiches he'd made in the morning and the two apples he'd put in.

The sun came and went, teasing.

His destination became clear.

Nadine sat on a boulder. She had an old red sweater around her shoulders and a blanket over her knees. The sweater was nubby, wool? She read and made a note, read and made a note, very intense. Oedipal. Pre-Elizabeth, this girl who was fourth or fifth in the class, from a poor family, and somehow she held down two jobs, too.

Nadine did not look like the popular girls. Their hair was molded, styled; they wore lipstick and mascara. Her wavy chestnut brown hair fell around her face, loose.

A branch must have crackled. She looked up, smiled, wrote something hurriedly, and then put her notebook aside as his brother approached.

They both looked happy.

Lit textbook. He saw them pointing and leafing through pages and talking.

A wind blew up. He slid down behind a tree, watching. He rocked back and looked upward. The sun returned briefly. The trees were beautiful, everything was, as beautiful as he'd ever seen. There was that little bit of sun dancing in and out of the clouds, and giving the leaves a glaze of light.

Dan and Nadine looked serious now, something had happened, one of them had said something wrong.

They both opened their texts dutifully. After a while his brother said something. She looked straight at him and answered. He nodded soberly.

Eventually they studied. Eventually the sun stopped dancing in and out and the rain began. At first it was a comic spattering, something that suggested it might go away.

His brother offered Nadine a sandwich. She seemed to refuse it but finally took it and ate. Suddenly everything between them was all right again. How had it happened? The rain came harder and she put the blanket over their heads. Their laughs wafted up.

There he was, in the rain, hunkered down by a tree, no lunch for him.

Frank goes back to the student's work in front of him, trying again to concentrate. The work thuds, moment to moment. The boy in the screenplay says, "Hey, you know Pete and Jim? They're having a party. I thought you might want to go."

"Okay," his love interest says.

He writes in the margin, *An invitation isn't interesting on its own. What is unique here, what is happening?*

The student won't make any sense of that. He sighs, considers what else to say. Is the student too young to have sharp memories? The kind that twinge? Pain?

Like: Nadine's hair was shaping around her face in strands; cartoonlike sections of bangs came almost to her eyebrows. His brother leaned forward and kissed her.

Did they smell like corned beef and mustard? he'd wondered. His brother kissed Nadine again and slipped an arm around her. She didn't resist. The blanket went over their heads. Smell of wet wool, blanket and sweater both. Finally the rain came so hard, they had to come out from under the blanket.

In and out of reverie, he writes notes to the student, automatically does the assignment he gave to the student: finding details.

His brother looked up and saw him, the half brother,

the Don John, the Edmund, the wrong one, the bastard, watching.

He slogs through the student paper.

When he hears the car pull in next door, he's grateful for the new focus for his attention.

The mother and the girl go into the house with their arms around each other.

Damn. He can't see them anymore now, not in daylight. He walks restlessly from living room to dining room to kitchen, up the stairs, down again. He forgot to buy a television, a radio. It's too quiet here.

He forces himself to grade one more paper, and as a reward, he takes himself out for a drive. Which way? He chooses north again, Ross Park Mall.

A television and a radio later, he sits in thick traffic, having forgotten there's a Steelers game. There's nothing for it but to listen to the pre-game warm-up on the car radio, switching back and forth to news. In the midst of the frustration, he gets a small pleasure from thinking this might be exactly what he'd be doing if he'd never left. His life went on without him and he's walking fast to catch up to it. Can't be done, some would say. How can you walk into thirty years of alternative videotape, or film, all those hours of the not-lived life? Yet he's doing it. Some have walked on water. He walks on the surface of time.

Drives in a dream.

Gets to the house.

Touchdown.

That voice. Myron Cope was announcing football thirty years ago in that same cracked-glass, stridently joyful voice!

Struggling to get the TV in, he imagines her seeing and offering him a beer, but this does not happen. He's breathing heavily and plops the box on the living room floor. Classless, he thinks, television in the living room. But that's where the couch is. Eventually he'll put it downstairs in the basement room, and the other big one from

Athens upstairs in one of the bedrooms, and he'll put his older, smaller one in the kitchen.

It takes him two hours to get the TV up and running with all the menu preparations he has to punch in. Without cable, the reception is so bad as to be laughable. Gray figures with zigzaggy lines across their bodies play football in slow-motion replays while he waits on hold with the cable people. After the Steelers lose, he makes himself a small steak and a salad. He eats watching the local news.

Then he goes back to the dining room table and his work, letting the television drone a monologue. It's like having the company of a senile old man who can't stop talking, better than having no one in the house.

Grit, grit, grit gets it done.

Oh, how he remembers. A miracle mind. The details are so vivid, you might think the things that come to him happened yesterday.

The thick rain that day. He remembers the feel of it. By the time he got to the road that cut through the golf course, all the golfers were gone except one, a man who looked sort of insane, trying to hit a ball he could hardly see. In the rain! It was laughable. The man wanted to hit his wife, probably.

The rain beat down harder. His brother and Nadine ran while he stood there, soaked, and while the angry man kept swinging at a golf ball he couldn't possibly see in the rain. Later, working his way slowly to Bartlett to Murray Avenue, then Silberberg's Bakery, a little Saturday routine, he saw Nadine go to the left, up the hill, his brother straight ahead toward home.

He jingled the change in his pocket, winked, and said to the clerk, "The usual," while he dripped rain all over the bakery floor.

The clerk laughed, blushed, and handed him a cheese Danish. "You're soaked," she said.

"The things we do for love." He could tell the comment intrigued her.

It was still very dark out as he went home. Clouds of deep gray rolled above him; thunder rumbled.

For a while he stood outside the kitchen window, looking in. The kitchen light was on because it was so dark out.

His brother had just emerged from the basement stairway with a bath towel. He was drying his hair and trying to sop up the water from his dripping shirt. Finally he gave up and peeled it off. He poured water into a saucepan and lit the burner under it. There were unwashed dishes in the sink, things all over the counter—bread, newspapers, containers from food brought in. Dan began to straighten the place. The woman their father hired came only every other Tuesday and the three of them could get way ahead of her in making work. Suddenly, his brother looked up and saw him, then after a moment's surprise, opened the door and let him in. "Did you forget your keys?" Dan asked.

"Yeah."

"Why didn't you knock?"

"I did." He pulled out a chair and sat, rainwater dripping from his face and hair and clothes, all over the floor.

His brother tossed the towel to him. "You should probably take your clothes off. You'll get sick."

Instead of using the towel, he let it fall to his lap.

"I didn't hear you knock."

"Well, I knocked. Your mind was elsewhere."

His brother didn't challenge him, but reached for a change of subject. "Get your cheese Danish?"

"I did."

The water began to boil. His brother turned off the water, wrapped a pot holder around the handle of the pan, and poured boiling water into the green mug with the Tetley tea bag in it. "Why don't you dry yourself off?" he asked.

"Don't want to."

"Oh. Well. All right. Hey, you want a cup of tea?"

"Okay. Thanks."

A second mug, a second Tetley tea bag. Attempted

buddy-buddiness: "I wonder if anything good is on television," Dan offered.

"I thought you'd be studying, being the worm," he said, peering through his dripping glasses. He felt very ugly.

"I ought to. Maybe I will." Dan put sugar in his own tea and pushed the sugar toward him. He went to the refrigerator for milk and began to open the carton over his cup.

"I hear she's had everyone in the school."

Dan jumped and the milk spilled. He put the carton down hard. "Do you have to make everything wrong or bad? What's the matter with you? Here." He shoved the milk toward him.

Paul. Paul then. Frank sees himself as if seeing a boy he knew, a classmate, someone else. He had laughed, saying, "I'm just looking out for your best interests."

"I don't need your help. Why don't you pull yourself together?"

Paul ran his fingers through his hair, which stood up stiffly. "Maybe you have a thing about waifs," the boy, Paul, said. "A savior complex. A guilt thing. Same thing with Ted Luckey. Makes you feel superior."

His brother shoved him.

There. Good. A reaction. He is Paul for a moment and can feel the aluminum of the chair on his shoulder, digging in, hurting him. Good. He can remember how he made a comic face and didn't break. "Poor little Dan," he said.

THE DAUGHTER DIDN'T LEAVE UNTIL TEN THAT NIGHT, SUNDAY. It was too late to ring the doorbell. He couldn't think of a reason. He watched Elizabeth drift, talk on the phone, read. Already he knew her rhythms. He could predict how she would move before she did.

Tomorrow morning, he promised himself.

When her lights went out, he slipped out of the house and into her backyard, looking for something that would make the right reason for conversation. . . . If he put on the garden hose, let it trickle, the sound of the open tap might waken her now. If he tipped over her garbage can, she might come to the window and see him before he got away. He couldn't find anything to mess up. He got worried he'd already stood there too long and so he sneaked back into his place, wondering how to approach her.

He woke at six. He watched her lights go on.

He dressed and packed up his work, ready.

When she went to her car, he left by the back door and started for his. He turned, walked straight to her, put out a hand, and said, "Hello. I just moved in next door. Frank Razzi."

He couldn't stop looking at her. It wasn't because of physical beauty, although she was nice-enough looking, just something about her, the expression in her eyes, so full of light it hurt.

"Elizabeth Shepherd." After a moment, she asked, "Is everything all right with the house?"

"I keep thinking of things I need to get."

"That's the usual way. It takes forever to put it all together."

"Right," he was saying. She had the door open and was sliding into the driver's seat. She didn't really seem to notice him. "You're going to work?" he asked, chastising himself immediately for pushing beyond the boundary she'd set up and with such a dumb question.

"I am. It looks like you are, too." She seemed almost amused.

"Oh. Right. I have to fly out to New York. Then back and to L.A. for a couple of days."

"Good," she said abstractedly.

"Well, it was good to meet you."

"Good to meet you, too." Form. She only meant it as form. She wanted to close her car door and so he let her.

He waved. A good subtle small casual wave.

Nothing. Nothing in return.

Slow down, he told himself. Slow.

4

ARTIE DOLAN WAS CARRYING A CUP OF COFFEE FROM ONE END of the floor at the Branch to the other when he heard the particular ring of his phone, and tried to walk faster.

Coleson saw him, said, "I'll get it," and a second later said into the phone, "He's coming."

The caller was the newish receptionist from downstairs. "Commander Christie is still in court, right?" she began. "I didn't see him come in."

"Yep."

"He always asks me to call you if he's not in."

"Okay."

"Young fellow says he was here before and" —she took a break to confirm and came back to the phone— "wants to talk to someone about the Ross murder."

"Give his name?"

"He signed in," she said. "Jones, it says on the sign-in."

"First name?"

"Tyrell."

"You bet," said Artie. "I'll be down for him." He abandoned his coffee and asked Coleson, who didn't look heavily occupied, to come with him. These were two clean detectives clip-clopping down the stairs. They bristled. They smelled good. In fact, Coleson was a fan of Binaca, and everyone was sure he never farted in his life or got fuzz in his belly button. Must wash his hair a couple of times a day, the way it flew away. Dolan was more normal, a fan of crisp white shirts and a good deodorant. Coleson stood sway-backed, a good-boy posture. Dolan was a small fellow, but straight and muscular, fit, swelled with pride.

They didn't often work together but on this day they happened to go downstairs together to frisk the boy Jones and bring him upstairs for questioning. It was helpful to have one white, one black listener to push different buttons if buttons were pushable, and they generally were.

At first when Dolan heard *Jones,* he thought it was going to be the little brother or the father come to add something to the story, but no, it was Tyrell himself, the boy who'd tried to use the credit card.

He let Coleson move forward and do the frisking, which he did with his butt way the hell out in space, so there would be no accidental hip to hip, dick to butt. His own style was different, he got closer, partly because it was the way he got people to spill beans, so close, Christie teased him, "You make them feel the pangs of love." Damned straight. A loved guy wants to tell you things.

"You want to come on up with us?" Coleson stood back and made a gesture of invitation.

"Yeah."

"Hi, Tyrell," Dolan said. "They treat you okay in the court hearing?"

"I guess."

"Okay. Good. You let me know if you get any kind of treatment from anybody that seems wrong."

"I will."

"How's your little brother?"

"He's the same."

"Means what?"

"Can't get him away from the TV. Not even to eat."

"Depressed."

"What? You saying that about him, or what?"

"Yes," Dolan said forcefully. "Maybe you, too."

By then, they were upstairs. Coleson, who'd been left out of the chitchat, walked ahead and made a show of getting the key to the interview room, then unlocking it, using lots of gesture, lots of space.

They all sat down.

There was a long silence. Dolan had to make wild grimaces to keep Coleson from talking, but he managed to get the message through that this boy was his job, his interrogation.

When he felt Tyrell was sufficiently worked up, Dolan said quietly, "So, Tyrell, what is it? Go on. We're listening."

"This dude came rapping on my door, and when I opened, he asked me a bunch of questions."

"One of our men?"

"No, from the neighborhood."

"Somebody from your neighborhood asking you questions?"

"Yeah."

"You know him?"

"I know him kinda, from school."

"Your age, then?"

Jones nodded.

Is it going to fall right in our laps? Dolan wondered. He took a deep breath. "What kind of questions, then? About the wallet?"

"No, trying to get around to murder. That doctor."

"Ross? The guy knew something?"

"No, but he acted like *I* did. Who'd I see? What cars was around? Where could he find my uncle to ask him about strangers, cars, all that. I told you guys what shit I knew. My uncle handed the wallet over to me. That's all. I put me an order in for some stuff, then it all come down on my head."

Dolan shook his head. "*Why'd* it come down on you?"

Jones looked at him for a moment, until he understood. "Not my wallet."

"Right. Something I want you to learn here. Never forget it. Something looks free, it looks like luck, you get nervous. You get that? Nobody's going to pluck you out of there. You do it yourself. Inch by inch. No, quarter inch by quarter inch. Now tell me what this guy was trying to get you to say."

"Where the wallet come from before . . . before my uncle get it."

"Why'd he want to know that?"

"I don't know. He said he was friends with the police and doing a little job. I got worried he was going to frame my uncle. My uncle didn't do nothing. I found out next day he *found* my uncle and started asking *him* questions, like he's somebody, so what's the deal with that? Police already asked my uncle."

"Who was the brother bugging you?"

"Some guy named Flowers. Says he's friends with the Homicide commander."

Dolan started to laugh, and once he got started, he couldn't stop. There it went, the luck, like a bird turning back into a handkerchief. "It's true. He is. What was he doing, then, just helping out us poor old detectives?"

"Seemed like it."

"Did it seem like he knew anything on his own? About the murder?"

Jones shrugged elaborately.

"How did you get here?"

"Got on a bus."

"You ever go to Shadyside?"

"No, never been. Look, I answered all this before."

"It's just one neighborhood over. You know anything about it?"

"I know it's fancy."

Dolan laughed. "Hard to believe, huh, when you see our digs in here."

Jones looked uncertain. Was he supposed to laugh?

"You friends with Darnell Flowers?"

"No way."

"Why is that?"

"White boy. He treat me like he's somebody and I ain't."

Dolan knew this deal well enough. You start to pluck yourself up and it gets real bad, people calling you white. He said, "Fair enough. Was he always like that?"

"I don't know."

"Think."

"No. Because he used to be just . . ." Jones made a smooth gesture with his hands that Dolan interpreted as *plain, straight, regular.*

"We'll talk to Darnell, get him off your back. What made you come in here, though?"

"He said he came over here all the time. Every week. I didn't want him spreading lies about me. I have things I got to do."

"What things?"

"My little brother."

Jones couldn't have said much that would get to Dolan's heart like that did. "You take care of him?"

No answer.

Dolan let out a large breath. Shit. He was going to carry Jones's burden now, for a day, a week, he didn't know how long.

Coleson was looking bored.

Dolan said, "We're going to get you a ride home. Tell me how you ought to feel when something looks to be free? Free or easy?"

Jones didn't remember.

"Nervous," Dolan said. "Real nervous. Look at the trouble you got into looking for a free lunch."

On the way out of the interview room, Dolan felt Jones jump. When he looked up, he saw why. It was a Tuesday. Darnell Flowers was sitting there in his chair outside Christie's office. The boy's eyes widened when he saw Jones walking beside Dolan.

"It's okay," Dolan told Jones, but it was loud enough for Flowers to hear, and Flowers jumped, probably thought for a moment he was the one being addressed. "He's up here to see his friend."

FRANK DROVE AS FAST AS HE COULD THAT TUESDAY, FOUR o'clock, nothing better in his stomach than fast-food take-out. He drove the car into the garage, powered down the door, and walked to the back door, studying the other house. Nobody home yet.

He went into his own place even though he would have to go out to teach again in an hour, little more. He thought, What have I done? What have I done?

His stomach was churning. He was tired. He dropped everything, climbed the stairs to the second floor, and lay down. He almost fell into a deep well of sleep and had to force himself up from it. What if he missed class? From oversleeping? He chortled at the absurdity of it. A grown man sleeping through an evening class. The teacher, no less. That would win him a place in the students' hearts.

In the fridge he found a piece of cheese and some bread. Enough. He poured a glass of wine from a bottle that was already open, sat in front of the television, nibbling his little French snack.

TUESDAYS. WHY WERE THEY SO CRAZY? DARNELL WAS SITTING outside Christie's office waiting for him while Christie tried again to connect with the P.I. in Florida. Bingo. Success. And Derek Johnson turned out to have exactly the same hearty voice his son did. Or vice versa, of course, the son having learned, imitated. "I've been expecting to hear from you," he told Christie. "I had to go out around noon today. Worried you'd call then."

"I did, in fact. Then I was in court."

"Damn. Always the way."

Outside in the main office, Dolan made a gesture to him, a "need a few minutes of your time" point of the finger, a nod toward Darnell. Christie nodded, puzzled.

"Which one is this about?" Derek Johnson was asking.

"What Daniel Ross hired you for."

"Wow. That's an old one. That's twenty-five years ago."

"Did you know Ross was killed?"

"No, get out."

"Yes. Two weeks ago now."

"Dr. Ross? You're talking about the son?" Johnson's

surprise sounded genuine, but he might be lying. "What was it, an accident?"

"A shooting."

"Shit. Well, I wouldn't have guessed that in a million years."

"Your son didn't tell you?"

"No, I never talked about my cases with him. And this was an old one anyway."

"So you didn't talk to Ross recently?"

"Well, I did, but only to tell him I was retired. He called me down here and I said I was really done with it. These were my years in the sun."

"Did he tell you what he wanted you for?"

"Not very specifically."

"Generally, then?"

"He wanted me to tie up what I started twenty-five years ago, he said. Just some facts."

Johnson was not the unfriendliest P.I. Christie had run into; he just hoarded information, like all of them did. Info was their bread and butter.

"When did you get this call?"

"August. Late August."

"You didn't do any work for him?"

"Not a jot."

"So Ross was looking for something about his brother," Christie said carefully.

"Well, relatives of."

"What did he want with the relatives?"

"I don't . . . know that he told me everything in a way that made sense. He was putting a lot of money he'd inherited into a home and he said he ought to know for sure it was the right thing to do. That there was nobody else who should get some of it."

"Sounds generous."

"It does."

"Know anybody who might want to kill Ross?" Christie asked as simply as he could. The detectives had already asked the questions about who stood to benefit, but the man's life was so tidy, he'd accounted for all that, and the simple answer was: wife and kids. Ross's colleagues had shares of the practice and his own portion was up for sale to a buyer the combined colleagues approved of.

Christie looked up. Artie Dolan had just walked in.

"No. I don't. I never saw anything like that in my dealings with him."

Christie pointed to the phone and mouthed, "Derek Johnson." Dolan nodded.

"I need to know what were those dealings, how are they filed, where are they filed, and can I take a look? That's it in a nutshell. This is a murder investigation."

Johnson whistled, a soft sound. "From twenty-five years ago."

"And anything in between."

"There was nothing in between."

"Even a phone call."

"Nothing until just recently."

From Johnson's voice, Christie extrapolated. A wiry guy, brown with sun, wearing shorts and sandals, wife slapping barefoot over the tiles with his late-afternoon iced tea or beer. Condo meeting at night, something like that. He'd made it to retirement and he was enjoying himself, best he knew how.

"I'll cooperate, of course. It's a puzzling thing, that a guy like that would be killed."

"You got it. So?"

"Right. First time I talked to Dan Ross was way back, let me think, 1979, no '78, I think it was."

"You have a good memory, or you have files handy."

"I have an amazing memory. The recent phone call just brought it all back. I never looked up a file—they're all in Pittsburgh in storage. I just let the old conversations come back to me. It was a sort of missing-persons case. He wanted to know about his brother, who went by a different name. . . ."

"Gerald Paul LaBeau."

"That's it. Well, I found the guy for him. He'd been in school, medical school. Paid his own way. I had to monkey around with names to find him. I tried the usual tricks, as I recall. Tried a different spelling of the last name, use of the middle name. Finally got him. He'd dropped the last name. He went to school as Gerald Paul."

"And."

"That was that. Ross paid me well, thanked me, told me he was going to get in touch with the brother. He said he'd get back to me if he needed me again."

"And twenty-five years later, he called you again."

"Right. Last August. I was already retired. Down here. He asked me could I look into things again. He said he was having dreams, funny dreams."

Dreams, that was something new. Christie waited, bit his lip. "Are you able to tell me anything about these dreams?"

"Well. That the death wasn't for real and could I look into it. See if it was possible somebody in Atlantic City had messed up."

"What did you think?"

"I thought he was kind of nuts. But then, I wasn't in the business anymore. . . . How did he put it? 'Haunted by a worry.' "

"Did he think his brother somehow faked the death?"

"He never said, but I got the impression that was one of the ideas bugging him. Maybe some trouble in Gerald Paul's background. Maybe something in med school."

"Did you make any guesses as to what the crime was, what Gerald Paul was running from?"

"I didn't. I considered the lot. Rape, murder, blackmail, theft."

"What sort of state would you say Ross was in when he called you?"

"Sad. Not angry. Thoughtful and sad."

"Did he say what had precipitated his inquiry? Other than dreams?"

"He . . . Well, it was a funny story. He heard from the mother of one of the little kids he treated. She and her cousin went to the same high school Ross did. And the brother did. And the *cousin* who had moved away thought she had run into his brother at an airport in Florida. The cousin talked to this man in the airport and the man said he didn't know her, didn't recognize her at all. He said he was a lawyer for the auto industry in Detroit."

"Detroit? Hmmm. What did you think?"

"I thought, Funny it was Detroit, but I kept an open mind. Ross was overworked, tired. Even he said so."

"No doubt you made a phone call or two to A.C. just out of plain curiosity."

"One call. Plain curiosity, as you say."

Christie jotted down, *Pulling teeth,* and Dolan came over to read the notepad. "Did you find any evidence that Ross was right, that the brother wasn't dead?"

"No. He came up pretty dead. Dead in Atlantic City."

"You called him and told him?"

"I didn't. I didn't want the hassle of refusing work or charging Ross a fee for my time or any of that. I just wanted to be retired."

"What did Ross say when you refused the case?"

"He said it was fine, he had other ways of checking into things."

"Where would the files be for the job you did twenty-five years ago?" He caught Dolan's sympathetic smile.

"In storage. In a bin. My son has a key and the combination at the house."

"Would you ask your son to let me look through them?"

"I'd want him to go with you. Just those files. The confidentiality of other people, other cases, has to be preserved."

"Agreed."

When he hung up, Dolan pointed to Darnell. "Tough love time."

"I HAVE SOME LEFTOVER STEW, SOME NICE CRUSTY BREAD," Margot says on the phone. "It would be nothing to bring it over and toss a salad."

Elizabeth must say yes although still, oddly, she does not want company as she's been told she will. Margot is a friend, another therapist, and she must say yes. What she wants instead of sound is silence in which to hear something—Dan's voice, his revelations from the other coast, something, maybe only the hum of silence, the truth of it.

She sets the table, noting the blue pleated place mats she's grabbed for the table. He'd called them handsome. She supposes they are. Dishes, silverware. She is functioning.

With five, ten minutes to spare, she goes into her study with no purpose whatsoever, and finds herself staring at the photo she keeps on her desk of her and Dan when they first met—oh, maybe three weekends after they began seeing each other. Who took it? She can't remember. His arm is around her; her body fits into his; they are merging, not wanting to be parted for a second. They forgot to eat for the first twenty-four hours, his one weekend off. They must have made love eight times in that first day. Then, just like that, they were a couple, as headed toward the future as if they had had a long and fruitful past together, with battles won and affections measured.

Because the camera was invented, there they are, young and glowing forever. Touching the picture, she feels the surprise of cold glass resisting her, because her memory, helped along by the photo, has conjured his big, warm body.

The doorbell rings. Margot wants to help and she must let her.

There is Margot, motherly, round, salt-and-pepper hair, carrying a pot and a bag of groceries. Immediately Margot puts the pot and the bag down on the porch floor and comes in to hug Elizabeth, a good long hug, strong, deep. Margot wants to help. She needs to do *something*.

"Work? Still okay?" Margot asks. She opens the door again to get the pot, which is fairly large and clearly heavy.

"Well, I worry I need them more than they need me, but I don't think I'm doing harm."

Margot laughs. "Good."

"Needy folks." Elizabeth smiles. "Retire us and we jump off bridges."

Margot says, "Watch it. You're outing the whole profession." She leans down and hoists the pot.

"God, how much did you bring?"

"Some for you to have for leftovers, too."

"And what's this?" Elizabeth reaches for the bag.

"Salad stuff."

"Ah. Thanks."

They move into the kitchen, where Margot puts the pot on the stove, finds a bowl, and begins to dump already-cleaned greens in. Just the sight of Margot working away in her kitchen, trying to be brisk, upbeat, moves her.

"The salad is only going to take a sec," Margot says. "I need to heat the stew a little."

Elizabeth tries to talk and can't. It's the kindness of Margot's intentions that gets to her. Suddenly Elizabeth is crying. "I'm sorry. Sometimes I can't . . . talk."

Margot leaves lighting the burner and embraces Elizabeth again. "It's okay. Anything is okay. Just tell me. I'll leave now if you want."

Elizabeth lights the burner—the thing has tricky timing—and she looks around, wondering what else she can do. "No, stay." It's hard to look at Margot. Her face is so concerned, it hurts. "I went to the cemetery this morning. I think I'll go again tomorrow."

"How was it?"

"Hard. Very real. Everybody assumed he'd want . . . have wanted . . . cremation. But he told me once, he'd rather the slow than the fast, rather be chilled than burned. Odd, huh, even men of science get these ideas. That you feel something after." Margot nodded. "He wasn't always predictable. I might not be able to talk about him just now."

"That's okay."

"Should I stir the stew or dress the salad?"

"Dress, if you don't mind. I'll watch the stew. I just wanted to be sure you were eating."

"I'll eat." Elizabeth dressed the salad and tried to be a good companion. She asked Margot about her ongoing battle with the man she shared an office with. Great shrink, but didn't pay his bills. Wouldn't agree to fix the faulty plumbing. Margot told of the last few incidents with sanity and humor. She kept the ball if not exactly bouncing, then off the floor. When dinner and dishes were done, forty-five minutes later, she exited gently, talking about how much she had to do.

When she left, Elizabeth felt relieved and almost light-headed, as if she'd imagined the evening.

HE TOOK UP HIS POST.

She was reading again, reading. Watching is a form of Valium, slow.

For a long time, nothing happens. He watches stillness, almost stillness, film slowing down to photograph. Flicker of breath. She turns a page of the book. Nothing. Looks up at the ceiling, pauses, back to the book. Nothing. He is mesmerized. She draws the shade. His mouth fills so fast, he cannot swallow.

5

BRIDGET STEVENS TUCKS A STRAND OF HAIR, WHICH IS AN eighth of an inch too long to wear over her forehead (it goes straight into her left eye), back under the edge of a butterfly clip, but she does it mainly to keep her hands in front of her face. She's crying. Even so, and while trying to hide that fact, she leans on one of the Xerox machines and leafs, in a practiced way, through the pages she's just copied to make sure none were skipped. Stop it, she tells herself. Sniffling, sniveling, snuffling, none of it appealing. A tear drops onto one of the pages; she brushes it off. Sometimes it's worse when you try not to. She could cry for eight years, it feels like.

She knows about deep breathing, but doesn't feel like doing it, or her body doesn't. Her breath comes in sharp, short intakes—seven in before she breathes one out. It doesn't matter, she tries to tell herself, what strangers think of her. Yet for some odd reason it does. What's next? Walk the streets, work at some fast-food joint. Borrow money. Take a bus back to St. Louis. No, not that. She got herself out of there; she will stay out. She'll figure something.

Wipes her eyes. Plunks the copies down. Leafs through the next copy to come off the machine. Hot paper.

There are nice people in the world somewhere. She just doesn't meet them.

Her father used to call universities "think tanks." Well,

this particular tank has a lot of bespectacled old fish in it and a couple of lean, nerdy ones trying to be mean sharks. The older people look tired and wear glasses; they fuss and mumble and read things most of the day. The young ones dart unathletically, trying to look cool.

One of the older men, who is an exception—in that he doesn't look pale and beaten down—comes in and stands, watching her. He's done this before. Frank Razzi. "So," he says, "you're a speed reader and that's a very moving story? What is this?"

She doesn't know him as well as she knows some of the others, but she's seen him around the place. He's growing a beard now. Frank Razzi. She always thinks, *jazzy*, because she has this little system she uses to remember names, has had it for years, long before she saw *Bridget Jones's Diary*, in which a character with her name does the same thing, sort of. "I'm sorry," she says, wiping her eyes.

"Maybe it's really bad and that's why you're crying?" He smiles. "I wrote it, you know."

"I haven't read it. There's no time to read anything in here," she says, trying her best to smile back, while a large tear rolls down her cheek to her chin, wobbles, and falls.

"Why don't we go downstairs and get a cup of coffee?"

When she answers him with only a shake of the head, he adds, "Tea, Coke, orange juice, whatever." He dips his head down to try to look into her eyes. "Get you to stop crying," he says, vaguely, looking at one of the bound manuscripts in a pile near the door.

"I'm supposed to stay here. There are a half-dozen more thingies"—she points—"to do." The room is rectangular and claustrophobic, painted recently, that eggshell color, and the smell gives her a headache. Friday they told her she was terminated as of the end of this week. Monday they told her they were docking her pay; this morning, the bitch in the main office told her, work two more "makeup days" and she gets her check for *last* week's work. Well, that's four more hours today and eight tomorrow. Friday they don't want her at all. She can't walk out now because she needs the check for last week's work. It's all she has.

"I never knew anyone to stand so valiantly by the machines. You get breaks, don't you?"

"Nobody ever told me about breaks."

"Did you ask?"

"No. Maybe the minimum-wagers don't get breaks."

"Are you kidding me?"

"Well, I get a half-hour lunch. It doesn't matter. I won't be here after tomorrow."

"Why not?"

"I can't seem to get here on time in the morning is the main thing. Which isn't my fault, believe it or not. I made up for it by never taking a break, not even for lunch, but—" She waved her hands to mean, "It doesn't matter."

"You're fired, then?"

She nods. Lots of people get fired from big jobs in their lives, yet she feels a hot shame anyway, partly because other things have gone so badly for her. If Razzi would only go away and leave her alone to cry in the hot, stuffy machine room, that would be better.

"You're fired and you still won't take a break?" His mouth turns down in a mock frown and he reaches for her hand and says, "I'll make sure you get your check. For now, coffee."

Tears spring to her eyes again. It's been so long since anyone has noticed her, she lets him tug her toward the elevators. The big blond woman who is in charge of her paycheck is out in the hall and sees her leaving her post. Fear fills her. The woman's face remains granite. Frank Razzi continues to tug her along past the woman, whose face registers disapproval, but who says nothing. The elevator doors open and the two of them get in. Safe. For a minute. Or so it seems.

"It's not as if a dumb little job like that matters," he's saying. He seems amazingly angry on her behalf. He's different from the others, except for the beard he's growing in the last couple of weeks, which makes him look like an academic. Otherwise, nice shirt and pants, no flab, no pallor, a cool look, like somebody who's been out in the real world. He must be quite a success. She makes copies of screenplays, treatments, something every day for him.

Does he notice her miserable five-dollar shoes?

Being pulled along and distracted has stoppered her tears. That's a good thing. She hates to cry, hates it.

Hardly anybody is in the coffee shop downstairs. A solitary man, reading. What look to be two Hispanics and one Asian man in university grounds-and-buildings polo shirts, sitting in a corner booth, smoking. The boy behind the counter is about Bridget's age, probably another college dropout wannabe-something minimum-wager running away from Nebraska or somewhere else a person needs to get away from. Maybe there is work in the coffee shop, moving a dirty wet rag over various surfaces. If she can get the boy's attention, she will check that out, but Razzi is still at her side, asking her, "Do you want one of those sandwiches in the case? Bread and something and sprouts?" He laughs. "They call it a California sandwich. It looks like old cheese, margarine, and a few dead twigs. I'm here to tell you this is not a California sandwich."

She says, "No, thank you, Mr. Razzi," thinking immediately it would have been wiser to take one, since that would save money for dinner tonight. "Or is it Dr. Razzi?"

"It's Frank."

"Frank."

Seated, with their coffees, she looks at her watch.

"How long have we been gone?" he asks. He seems surprisingly respectful when he asks this.

"Three and a half minutes, I think. I didn't notice the time until we were on the elevator."

Frank Razzi has rapidly moving eyes, just a little hard to get a bead on behind his glasses. Maybe it's the trendy invisible glasses that throw her off, because she's trying to see his eyes, but focusing on the clever way the specs are made.

Frankly Jazzy.

She has names for all the people she works for. Israel Olds: "Is Old." Herb Needlemyer, she thinks of as "Needs

Herbs" because he looks sickly. This distinguishes Herb
from Heinz Ersicher, whom she thinks of as "Heinz Is
Sicker." What else can she do, hauling reams of paper and
opening cartridges of ink and pulling crackled paper out
of jammed machines, but think of everything as slightly
different from what it is?

Frank's lips have a slightly pouty look. His graying hair is
trimmed tight, neat, an expensive cut. She herself is a complete mess, but she can tell when a person has worked at
cleaning himself up. He takes a sip of coffee from the paper
cup and grimaces. Too much caffeine in his life, maybe. His
hands have a tremor. He wears some sort of ring, but on his
right hand, not a wedding ring. He's . . . interesting.

"What is it?" he asks, tracing her gaze.

"Nothing," she says, but she's thinking he's nervous.

Suddenly something dark comes over his eyes. A screen
door over his eyes, making them darker. Then, as suddenly, the screen door opens and he says, "Tell me about
yourself."

"Nothing to tell."

"You're a student here?"

"No. I was trying to get work in the system so I could
eventually be a student, get my tuition paid for. I'm a university hanger-on. Just . . . just came to be around here."

"Boyfriend?"

She shakes her head.

"Not interested?"

She feels herself flush and shakes her head. "No friends,
that's about it."

"Oh, come on, now. Who managed to persuade you you
have no friends?"

"Some people I thought *were* going to be my friends.
One of them is my cousin. I never knew people could be so
awful."

"They can. That I know about. Like how? What particular brand of awful?"

"About money and stuff." Tears threaten at the memory of things done, things said.

"Money is nothing."

"Oh, yeah?" Easy for him to say is what she means.

"In the big picture, it's nothing. What? They took your money?"

"Not exactly. In a way they did. It's complicated." Her cousin and the others have made fun of her, called her boring, treated her with contempt, and she does not want to tell these things, nor to cry again, but somehow she finds herself talking.

"I was late to work every day. I could never get to sleep at night because of them, then I couldn't get up in the morning. See, the house is way out on the highway. I don't have a car and I don't have that much money. One or the other of them was always promising to wake me up and drive me in. Even when I got up I couldn't wake anyone else up. Finally, I'd run for that one dumb bus and it wouldn't come and I'd be late."

"Who are these people? Your age?"

"My cousin is one. The funny thing is, she's why I was allowed to come out here instead of going to New York, which is what I wanted to do—New York or L.A. She's two years older. My stepmom has no idea."

"Stepmom?"

"My cousin is my real mother's sister's kid."

"So, your cousin and who else?"

"I never know who's living there, really, it's kind of fluid. We're supposed to split the rent four ways, but there are always more than four people there. I don't know what the deal is. But when I got canned—I mean, Friday I got the notice—my cousin told me she'd been meaning to tell me I had to give up my room anyway. She said she had other plans for it. I told her I'd find another job, but she said I didn't quite fit with the crowd and this was a natural break and that there was somebody else who could pay a third and he was moving in on the first and needed my room. She said it was just a sign that we should both move on."

"She sounds charming, your cousin. Were you close at one time?"

"No. It's all so dumb. I got a Christmas card from her mother asking me to keep in touch with Jess. Last summer I got the idea I could come here, get out of the house, away from one bad situation."

"I get it. Into a worse."

Bridget is surprised Razzi can patiently listen to her woes. He is probably planning to write about hapless teenagers. She doesn't much like the idea of being used, and yet it feels good to vent. "Her friends are all drug-heads. I didn't understand at first. There was never any food in the house because the money in the kitty went for blow or whatever."

"When do you have to be out?"

"Tonight, they said. They're all very keen on that guy moving in. I don't care. I'll sleep on the floor. They'll have to bodily throw me out."

"What if they do?"

This she doesn't answer. Sleep in the yard? Sneak back in? Something demeaning. What can she do? She couldn't come to work today and also be apartment-hunting. She'll look tonight and on the weekend. Cheap is what she needs. Probably have to find another share with another five people.

He is chewing his lip. "People," he says. "Makes you want to give up on them."

"I want to."

"What do they expect you to do?"

She considers this carefully. "They expect me to give up and go back home. To get on a bus and go live with my stepmother."

"Where's your real mother?"

"Dead. Five years ago."

"Oh. I'm sorry. Stepmom is where?"

"Forget it."

"Why?"

"St. Louis. God, this is like therapy, the way everything comes pouring out of me."

He smiles. "St. Louis doesn't suit you? Sports, music, beer?"

"St. Louis, Mo." She pronounces it *mow* for him and gives it all the attitude she can and is gratified when he laughs.

"So, Stepmom and Pop are a bad deal as parents?"

"I'm not even sure who I'm calling my parents these days. There are about eight of them."

And, elaborate please . . . ? his look seems to say.

"My real mother, Mother's second ex, Mother's boyfriend before . . . dying. Father, Father's second ex-wife—i.e., the evil stepmother—Father's current squeeze. Six."

He appears to consider. "Lots of recoupling."

"You could call it that. I don't blame the evil step-mother for wanting to be rid of me. We have no reason to care for each other. Are you going to put all this in one of your works?"

"No."

She looks at her watch again. "Twelve minutes. I have to get back. I'm worried she won't give me my check."

"Who? Alice?"

"Mrs. Platt." She indicates a strongly geometric haircut line and makes a stony face.

He's delighted with her air-drawing. "Alice! Don't worry. I can get around Alice."

"You can?"

Bridget is standing to go and he's saying, "Poor old Alice." He tries to make the gesture she did to indicate the haircut. "Let me talk to her."

"So what is your specialty exactly?" she asks. "I mean, I know you kill more trees than anyone else around here. Are you just really prolific?"

"Sometimes. When I'm lucky. I spent most of my years as an unfamous script doctor. They came to me for fix-its. There were a lot of fix-its. All the while I was writing my own. This teaching gig—I don't know, I did it on a lark. Just for this one term. Poor old us, trying to get out of one bad situation and ending up lonely in Athens, O."

"So you're going back to L.A. after this?"

"Right. I fired my agent. I went a little nuts. I needed a break, I knew that much."

The boy behind the counter sighs loudly as they pass, puts a new tape in the machine, and begins to sweep the floor.

She can't remember all the steps in between, but she and the man who produces piles of paper are already at the elevator when she realizes he seems to think she has agreed to something. He's saying, "So, here's the plan. *After* we get your check from Alice, after you put in your unfair hours today, we hop into my car, I drive you back to your place, you get your things out of there—and we're off."

"I'm not going home."

"I agree."

"I'm not packed."

"I can wait. I'll sit in a bar somewhere or a coffee shop. I always have work with me. Always. You get your things, I take you to my house—"

"Oh, no. That's kind, but—"

"Wait, listen. You get the second bedroom. You put your stuff in there. I make something for dinner. No, let me think. I don't have any food in the house. We'll go out somewhere."

"No, no, no. I'm sorry I bothered you with all that—" How dumb does he think she is?

Hands up, his hands are up halting her speech as the elevator doors open. "Now, now, don't get uptight about this. I'll be away for nearly a week starting tomorrow. You can just *use* the place. Don't bring anybody else in, certainly not those bums you live with. Students house-sit all the time for teachers. Think of it as a job while you find a job. You're keeping the place occupied. Just sit around and paint your toenails if you want. I don't care."

The elevator doors close without their having gotten in. Bridget pushes the button repeatedly. The door opens again. "I couldn't. It's not the right solution," she murmurs.

The look on his face is all scorn. "Let's not be silly. You want to feel square, clean up the place, put some food in the fridge. Better yet, I have work you could do. I was thinking of—I was going to hire somebody, a personal assistant for a week, a month, to help me catch up. But I'll bet you could do it. I can tell you're smart; I've watched you working. *I'm* liking this idea a lot. I might have just solved myself about eight problems by taking a weeping maiden for a cup of coffee." He's looking at the buttons for the floors as if he does not remember where to go.

She reaches over and pushes 3. Weeping maiden. She doesn't want to be anything that old-fashioned.

She hasn't said yes, yet he's talking as if she has, and something tells her that if she resists, she won't get back to her station for some time. She'll tell him later she can't take his offer. He'll be miffed, but the truth is, she would rather sleep on the living room floor for two nights, let Jess's friends stomp over her. He could be dangerous. He doesn't seem dangerous, but . . . still. He might expect favors, certain thank-yous.

She'll find a place to live right away, whatever it costs, get a job—coffee-shop schlepper or something.

In spite of herself, imagination puts her at Frank's place for a second, in another part of the city, stocking his refrigerator, looking for the cleaning fluids. Being secretarial, filing or whatever. Taking his offer at face value.

The doors of the elevator open, he does a strange sort of bow and goes off, presumably to look for Alice. Bridget hurries to the Xerox machines and triples her usual pace. For a moment, her cousin's face comes back to her, full of contempt for all the things that are wrong with her: her unsuccessfully neon hair (it's not the idea of it, for Jess approves of *some* neon hair, it's just that hers isn't wild enough); her all-wrong body (Jess is almost anorexic); her inexperience in things sexual (Jess is notching up experiences as if she's about to write a book on the subject). But it's more than the specifics of hair, clothes, speech that make Jess hate her, because the truth is, Jess accepts plenty of people who are far less together than she is. Far less funny, far less interesting . . .

It's something deeper, the way her cousin marshals the others against her. It's the very fact of her ambition, her seriousness, that Jess can't bear. Thinking of the sheer size of Jess's contempt makes her recapitulate the shamed, angry tears of thirty minutes ago. So she *is* a weeping maiden in the Xerox room when Frank Razzi comes by, brandishing the check he says he "snatched from the hands of Alice, keeper of the books."

Bridget wipes her eyes. "I'm still supposed to come in tomorrow."

"You'll come in tomorrow. You'll be honorable."

This is one of those times, she tells herself, when you just have to let fate take over. This apparently successful guy with money to spare wants to buy her dinner. He wants to let her have a decent bed for a week or so while she pulls her life together. It feels like a *giant* move to say yes to it all, but that's only because it's unfamiliar and because, as Jess would say, she has this need to be in control, even if it means she's orchestrating her own suffering. Saying yes is like what Jess would call, with a shrug, "opening your legs and letting the strangers in."

AT FIRST WHEN ARNOLD KARHAKIAN SUGGESTED LUNCH AT Bruscetta's, Elizabeth said no, she didn't feel like being out in public just yet.

He said, "Is there someplace you like better—"

"No, not really."

"—near your office, maybe?"

She held her breath. He didn't understand. He was dense. "Lucca, then," she said.

When she got to Lucca, Arnold Karhakian was already there, making such a fuss about a private back table that everyone at lunch looked up from breaking off crusts of bread to watch him. Dan had stepped around his colleague's faults, his thick obtuseness, and handled him gently. She determined to try to do the same.

"There," he said, when they were seated. "Pretty quiet back here. We can talk."

Elizabeth looked at the wine list, put it down. No, not wine at lunch, for wine would be just another impediment to thought, connection, and she was already on the reserve battery. She studied the menu. Soup, bread, salad, all right.

Karhakian ordered wine and a salmon appetizer and the Country Stew entrée. He was a large man and the luncheon combo he ordered came with a dessert, flan or pear tarte, so she would not be getting out of here in forty-five minutes. She took a breath. Live through it.

He brought his thick hands together and pressed the index fingers to his lips. His eyes looked upward at her.

"You said there was something you wanted to go over about the dinner," she said.

He asked, "Well, just, how are we going to handle it? One of us has to say something. Or . . . we could still cancel if you think people will find it strange."

She was incensed. He was trying to take it from her, as if the thing were his. "I was planning to make a speech, a short one," she said levelly.

"Ah. Saying . . . ?"

She gritted her teeth and answered, "How much Dan appreciated everyone's support of the Pocusset Safe House. I intend to let them know it's to continue as he wanted it to, that I am in touch with his lawyers to make sure the paperwork is in order, and that the dinner marks the official opening of the house."

Karhakian looked approving. "Very strong."

She had considered canceling, but now the date of the dinner was close upon her, and Commander Christie wanted to use it for his own purposes. For her, too, it could provide a way of dealing with a host of obligations swiftly, people who needed something beyond the funeral. She would let it happen, and then the great thing was, it would be over.

The waitress brought Karhakian's wine. He sipped. Approved. "Do you think we ought to have another speaker? Your remarks will be brief. Do you think people will want more?"

"I doubt it."

"I was supposed to introduce him and he was going to

speak, a pretty serious gung-ho speech-length thing. Now, what I wanted to say is, if you need for someone to speak after you, to do the gung-ho part, I could step in. Not that I'm asking. I'm offering. If you're stuck."

An idea hit her. She felt perverse. She said, "If only I'd known. I already made an invitation to the police commander who is investigating the . . ." She couldn't say the word *murder* and getting stuck momentarily deflated her.

"I thought you said it was just you speaking."

"Well, Commander Christie needs to get back to me with his answer. If he can't do it, perhaps you could just extend some of the material of your introduction speech? My son and daughter are going to say a few words. I think maybe Lauren is going to read something."

"Oh, I didn't realize. I . . . I have to get the program to the printer by tomorrow at the very latest. I . . . didn't know you had decided all these things. They're not on the program."

In her solo efficiency at making the last-minute arrangements, she had forgotten about the printed program. It was this *problem* she had of not wanting to talk to people outside of her immediate family. "I'll call you this afternoon," she said, "with all the details."

"This afternoon, then," he said, and he dug into the bread basket with one hand, pulled at the plate of curled butter balls with the other.

People had fed off Dan when he was alive and now, of course, they would continue to. Of course. Karhakian still wanted a piece of him. Communion.

The soup was good, a creamy chicken potato leek combination, substantial. She followed Karhakian's lead and ate bread with butter. She'd eaten Margot's big supper, but awakened feeling thin and hollow.

Karhakian continued to come up with questions—about table arrangements, flowers, memorial ribbons at the banquet. Should he order different flowers, different ribbons? Again she had to tell him she'd dealt with this. The ribbons would be white rather than red and there would be a memorial wreath at the podium.

Maybe it's a form of grief. Help him, she thought. Find some kindness. Find some. "Do you think one wreath is enough?" she asked, even though she feared his answer. Karhakian appeared to mull this over. She thought, Please say yes. Gaudy was not Dan's style. You know it.

He got her message and concluded one wreath was most appropriate.

Before his dessert arrived, he shifted uncomfortably and asked, "Are you doing okay?"

"I'm trying."

"People have said you don't call them back."

"I'm not ready."

"This may be none of my business, but you're a lovely, young, vital woman still. What I mean is, it's important that you go on to have a rich, full life. Dan would want that for you, I know he would."

Flushing, she asked as lightly as she could, "Are you talking about men?"

"Men, dating, social life, friends, whatever. Not being bitter."

Bitter. That word again. "If I need to mourn for ten years, that's what I need."

"Ten years is a long time."

Granted.

"Well, you're lovely and appealing. Everybody wants to be with you. I hope you know that."

"Thank you." She tried to soften toward him.

"Can you laugh about things a little if they don't have to do with you?" he asked.

She wasn't sure, but her look must have given him the go-ahead.

"Mary tells me if I were out of the picture, she would finally have a good time. Men weigh women down, I know they do."

She didn't want to touch that.

"And the cure, funnily enough, seems to be more of the same."

Nor that.

He squirms in his seat, but then uncomfortable is Karhakian's middle name.

In Elizabeth's imagination, she is on a desert island with Arnold Karhakian, nobody else. How long, how many years or decades until she is able to make love to him, if ever? Never, she concludes. A back massage, perhaps. A wiping of the brow. Kindness, yes, she'd come around to that in time.

FRANK RAZZI NOTICED THE CLOCK ON HIS COMPUTER SCREEN. A little past four-thirty. Normally he would have headed home by now, but there was no chance he'd get responsible Bridget out of there early, so he had his face in his computer.

His small office was one of some seventy like it in this building, which several departments shared, so that hundreds of people passed through, using the classrooms, the cafeteria snack bar downstairs, the copy room.

The habits he'd formed in L.A.—writing stories, fixing the stories of others, finding stories—didn't die easily. On his computer he kept track of the online versions of more than a half-dozen dailies. Clicking and scrolling took longer than skimming a hard copy, so sometimes he got frustrated. He preferred the actual paper and ink, the surprises of things in corners, in small boxes—you could cover a real newspaper fast, and more thoroughly at the same time.

The *Chicago Tribune,* the *Detroit Free Press,* the *San Francisco Chronicle, The Des Moines Register,* and *The Seattle Times.* He'd done these this afternoon, almost as an exercise in self-control.

For many years in L.A., before computers made it easy, he had the *Pittsburgh Post-Gazette* sent to him, print version. He kept track. Read it in his office stealthily, felt like a cat treading across paper a step at a time so it didn't crackle noisily.

Now he turns to the online version, clicking, skimming,

but his looking is still more careful than with the other papers.

Local crime news.

Nothing pertaining to.

Because, if necessary, he is prepared to change his name again. It makes him almost whimsical to think it. Next time, Europe, he jokes to himself. Next name: Russell something or other. He has buried himself deep for thirty years. A jail term. A harsh sentence. Vengeful judge.

When he had that layover in Pittsburgh, ten years ago, he took a cab into Oakland and walked around near the universities, trying to rid himself of the terror that someone would call out to him. It didn't happen then, but it did in Florida, of all places, last summer, a woman asking didn't she know him from *somewhere*, handing him her card, but he didn't recognize her or her name. He'd been stunned, though, so frightened, he couldn't speak for seconds, but eventually he did. Detroit, he'd told her. Auto industry attorney.

That time, ten years ago, he walked around the city as if he were a stranger, perhaps someone *like* the later-imagined attorney from Detroit. Nobody called out to him or noticed him. Even then, he was no longer the ridiculous skinny boy—shaggy light hair, thick glasses, black heart. His hair had darkened naturally, then begun to gray; his body filled out. Braces his early years in college and then the "ear tuck" in L.A. when a woman he was seeing persuaded him he ought to.

He's one of the lucky ones! Age has disguised and improved him. Now the glasses, the beard coming in. No one would know him. Most people think they stay the same, and it takes others to see the changes, but he, he has watched himself objectively. He looks different, nothing like.

The call he made a month ago with a prepaid phone card—always careful, even though he hadn't guessed how much caution was needed—was what started the jitters in earnest. *She* answered in the cracked, strained voice, from all those years of cigarettes, the unmistakable voice. "Well, I'll be," she said. "I had the feeling it was somebody from my past." But she had something to tell him and it made her skip the preliminaries. "There's something you better know. I got a call from Bill Tuttle in Bellingham. Old Bill, I don't know if you remember him? He was always a friend to me. He was all agitated. He'd had a call from some guy in Atlantic City trying to find me. Bill knew I didn't want to be contacted, so he didn't say. But he got the number—it was a hotel—and he called back, and guess what? Your brother. Don't know what he was doing in Atlantic City, but under the circumstances . . . thought you might want a warning."

He stood in the phone booth, stunned.

"Are you still there?" she asked.

"Why now?" But he thought of the woman in the Florida airport with a certain misgiving. He should have said more, spun more.

"I don't know. Somehow you're not dead enough," she said ironically. "You should give me an address and a phone number. What if I have to call you someday?"

He cut her off with a question: "Did he find you?"

"He didn't find me. If he ever does, I might ask him to find out where the hell you are." After a silence, she said wearily, "Never mind. I'm not doing so well lately."

He didn't give her his number. Safer that way. Athens, Ohio, why would she ever in a million years guess that? She didn't even know his name. He'd managed to keep that from her over the years. Told her to send a package of photos and clippings she didn't know what to do with to Paul Ross in L.A. For all she knew he was recycling the old names, even though Paul Ross was not a combination he'd used after that.

Why was Daniel looking for him so intently again?

He tried to figure it. He read the papers even more religiously. He saw the interview. *One of them never had much of a chance.* He saw where Dan's mind was and how the Pocusset Safe House was stirring it all up.

No, he wasn't dead enough yet. The old anxiety invaded him. He felt watched, dissected, the blackness of his heart examined, a kind of moral surgery being done on him.

When Frank went into Pittsburgh the week before last and drove around and saw what he saw, he almost made a phone call. Leave me alone, that was what he wanted to say. He didn't have a plan. On the other hand, he wanted to ask about the newspaper interview, the "never had a chance" line, and to say he'd suffered all his life. He wanted to be dead again, safe, but also the opposite. Not dead.

There was a gun. That he will never be able to explain away. *Why did you have a gun if you had no plan? Why?*

I don't know.

It must never come to that.

Nothing in today's paper to feed his particular lust, nothing, nothing.

He turns to his Internet history, scrolls down to the date, nearly two weeks ago now.

The obit and the photo. It's true. He did it.

For eight minutes, he does not move. Only looks at the smiling face of the doctor. Daniel. Dead.

Israel Olds pops a head in, saying, "I wondered where all the files of the new majors were."

Frank jumps up, bumping into his desk, then his wastebasket, hastening to gather them up.

When Israel Olds leaves, Frank goes back to the article, which he knows almost by heart, but there's a fresh noise and he looks up to see Bridget, who has come into his office without knocking. She looks miserable and sounds a little breathless. "I just came to tell you I can't take your offer. I mean, I don't know you, I don't know your circumstances."

"You're right to be careful. I'm recently widowed."

"Oh. I'm sorry. About your wife dying."

"I stay at the house of a woman I'm seeing pretty often. Some nights she stays with me, but while you're there, I'll go to her place. That's the lay of the land. I'll call her. I'll stay over there tonight so you don't feel awkward. You can't sleep in the yard."

"I don't want to put you out."

"It's fine for me to stay at her place. Really. She does want me."

"Well, maybe a night or two, then."

He's been bumbling around, stacking this and that in order to block her view of his screen, and finally barks, "Wait for me out there." When she has left, he clicks off and shuts down.

But just then, Heinz Ersicher bops in, saying, "I keep missing you. Sit? A few minutes? I just want you to know I think it's a crying shame this is only a one-quarter job. So I've been agitating—"

"My misunderstanding. Sorry about that."

"Just so you know it's how things are. It wouldn't matter if you were Spielberg, not with this administration. They won't give us another slot no matter how we beg and plead. It's just the one-quarter leave replacement for Lilly Vanda."

"You told me last time we talked. It's okay." What does he look like? A guy who needs a handout?

"Because I saw your face drop when I told you there was no way there'd be a permanent job here and I've been worried about you ever since."

He wished Heinz would leave. It was no good to keep saying a thing over and over again.

"You didn't buy the house you're in, did you?"

For a moment, he thinks of the Pittsburgh house, but what Heinz means is the Athens house, the little piece of junk he lives in. "No, no. Rent. Just a simple place."

"It's okay?"

"Yeah, the owners got most of their stuff out, left some junk around, the odd tennis racket, some pretty hopeless tables and chairs, no bookcases, unfortunately. So I bought one wall system, left the books there, and brought most of my boxes of videotapes up here. It's okay. It's just for a few more weeks."

"Good. Anything you need in the way of a recommendation for another visiting gig like this, you can depend on me. Okay? Is there any chance the Pittsburgh thing might extend?"

"It seems to be just one term. Same deal."

"Well, you're a hell of a script doctor. There will always be work for you fixing other people up if you want it."

He nods. "I just got burned out."

Heinz hesitates. "Time for a drink?"

Inside Frank laughs to imagine disappointing old Heinz by saying, "Yes!" But he plays at regret, with "No, can't, have a few obligations."

SHE'S NEVER BEEN IN A BMW, SO BRIDGET IS WONDERING, WILL she notice the difference in the ride? The seats are nice enough, but the car doesn't seem new at all. Maybe he's had it forever. She straps herself into the front seat as he starts up the engine and cool air blows on her knees, kissing them just where her skirt rides up; she feels very vulnerable.

She's thinking she might just stay up all night, get out of there in the morning, find another place while he's away. Nothing she can't handle.

"Tell me where I'm going," he says in a voice that is clipped and irritable.

If only he would have a consistent tone of voice, she would not be afraid. "Coates Ferry Road. The down-and-dirty part."

"All seven of them want you out?" he asks. Now the question seems to mean not "Why are seven of them so uniformly cruel?" but "What is it about you, Bridget, that is so despicable?"

She doesn't know, that's just it.

And the seven are not *uniformly* cruel. There's her cousin, Jess, who is beautiful and definitely cruel and who wants her out. There are the two really big heavy girls who, if they were all performers, would be backup singers to Jess—echoers and harmonizers. There is one sullen, glowering, intelligent boy who has headphones on all the time and has begun to deal drugs in a modest way. One really passive guy with a lot of money. And one tall Indian grad student who looks confused most of the time but seems to need little space and is willing to cook for everyone every day. Assorted strangers in and out. And now some new shithead moving in and wanting her gone.

She watches out of the side of her eye as Razzi aims his car and drives absentmindedly to the place she has given him directions to. She doesn't talk because he seems to be very much somewhere else. When they arrive at their destination, she can't tell what he thinks of the frame house that's clearly falling apart. There are two upholstered chairs in the backyard and music is blaring from inside the place. She turns to him, but he's poking around in his pockets. Does he think it's so awful he can't look? She says, "This will take a little while."

"I know. It's okay."

He sits in the car out front with the engine running, so in spite of what he says, she feels she ought to hurry. How will she find all her things? she wonders as she's slipping in the back way.

No problem. Ha. A plastic trash bag and four boxes are stacked in the kitchen. Her heart beats so hard, she can hardly breathe. They meant it, they really want her out. But to pack her things for her, that's ugly, that's going too far. She peels back the lid of the first box. Yes, her things. Voices waft in from the other room.

Bridget, shaking, examines the contents of the boxes. Only half her CDs are here. It appears all of her books have been packed, since most of the first two boxes are books. The other carton holds miscellaneous things. Her CD player. Jewelry carelessly tangled together in a sign of dismissal. This and that. Shoes. She takes one earring out of a shoe and puts it back in, feeling hopeless. A photo of her with the others.

The big plastic bag is all clothing.

The confused-looking Indian boy comes into the kitchen. "I heard you in here. Is it all there?" he asks.

"I don't know. I had a duffel bag."

"It's around somewhere. Something happened between you and Jess, I guess."

"Nothing specific. She just had other plans for my bed."

"She is very hard on you. I never do see all the reasons."

Bridget can't help noticing his face turning soft toward her, not hateful. And yet he also appears to be nervous about staying too long or being discovered talking to her. "Are you hungry?"

"No. Thanks. I had some CDs that aren't here in the box either."

"You want me to look for them? What titles are they?"

"I don't know if I care enough to bother."

"But if they are your things . . ."

"You're right." She summons all her strength and enters the main room, where people look up from whatever they're doing, which isn't much—flicking ashes, turning magazine pages. Bridget can feel herself burning as she passes through to the other rooms, opening drawers and closets, finding the folded empty duffel bag, taking her toothbrush from the bathroom and, what the hell, the toothpaste she bought.

Somebody turns the music off. There is a growing hush as the others stop speaking. Even before she reenters, she knows the group is becoming unified, looking to Jess— who tells them what to think—for a cue. Apparently Jess has pronounced her cousin from Missouri too young, too square, too not-hot, too judgmental to live with them. And the others have caught the drift and defined her Jess's way: an eighteen-year-old without any experience of life. An immature baby who rains on parades.

Jess smiles and sits back on the cushions, watching Bridget's efficient tour of the corners and drawers. Efficiency is a bad thing, her cousin's face says. But Bridget knows by now it could be sleeping or dancing that's wrong, undesirable. It's whatever she's doing, this or its 180-degree opposite. That simple.

Bridget sees six hazy people, moldable people. The new guy is not there yet. For a moment she sees sweetness in them, who they *could* be, and in that flash, creating them, she almost misses them, almost loves them. In that moment, she sees uncertainty under Jess's smirk. Tears spring to her eyes in spite of her resolve to show no emotion.

"I know you can't get in at the dorms," Jess says. "But there's the Catholic Heritage House. Till you find friends your age."

The tears are hot enough to make tea with, full of shame that she is not older, wiser, looser, more charming. It doesn't matter. She's almost gone. It's almost done.

"Don't be a stranger," Jess says in a honeyed whisper.

Bridget just looks for a moment, shakes her head, and leaves by way of the kitchen, taking the trash bag, the duffel, and one box out the door.

Some people can't be explained, she thinks, trudging to the car with the box slipping out of balance and her fighting to keep it on her left arm and clamped down by her chin. What drives Jess? She pretends always, every day, about something or other, but why does she need to lie? And those others—needing to be in the orbit of someone who acts on meanness, but *why* do they need to be near a volcano? Jess has the big *it*, charisma and beauty. They like to be around physical beauty, the best coin of all, no matter that it's volcanic.

She sees what's happening as if it's a strange, dark film. The man in the car looks dazed and hardly seems to notice the person putting things in the backseat. He doesn't even think to help her. Figures. That's who she is, a dumb, unhot drudge.

"Pop the trunk," she says. "I have two more boxes to get."

At the house the blinds go up (a position they are almost never in) and several of Jess's acolytes peer out at the scene, wondering, no doubt, where the unmarked taxi came from and which part of all this they should be reporting.

CHRISTIE FIGURED HE WAS PROBABLY RIGHT ABOUT DEREK JOHNson, Sr., being a wiry guy when he met the P.I.'s son at the North Hills Storage Unit that Wednesday—for Derek, Jr., who sounded like his father, was an energetic 130-pounder.

As he fitted his key into the lock of the storage bin,

Johnson explained, "I haven't come over here since my dad moved his stuff in. I hate to see what condition everything is in. These places say they're not responsible for insects or water damage. It's hard to know what the hell we're paying for, then, but houses just don't have room for things like this."

Tin shacks on the landscape, Christie thought. To hold what we don't think we can throw away.

Johnson slid the corrugated door open.

Christie liked what he saw inside. Four neat black four-drawer file cabinets all in a row. One bed frame. Four new tires. That was it. The man did not keep junk.

It took some time for the younger Johnson to find the correct key for the right-most cabinet. The one I want will be on the left, he thought, dating to when the P.I. was new to the game. But he waited. Johnson pulled the top drawer open.

"What's it look like?"

Christie patiently looked at one file after another—1997, 1998, 1999. . . . Out of curiosity, he flipped open one of the manila folders and held it up to get the most light from the single bare ceiling bulb. The man who had let him in didn't stop him, but stood nervously, watching. Sad case. A father tracing his son's spending and his friends and not finding anything a father might want to hear. Debts. Arrests. Landlords kicking him out of places. Depressing.

Christie put the folder back. "Try the one on the left," he ordered Johnson. "Your pop was orderly, probably goes left to right."

The bottom drawer on the left yielded what he was looking for. Several folders from 1979, including one marked Ross. He removed it and began to hold it up to the light. "I'd like to take this," he said.

Johnson's body tensed, his face furrowed. "My father requested you read the folder here. All due respect, but he never let these things out of his sight without a warrant. A court order."

Christie nodded curtly. He found he could place the

folder on top of the file cabinet and read it well enough if he got out of the way of the light. He took out his notebook.

There was a report sheet, typed, of the P.I.'s work and how long each job had taken. A long time. He'd run the Social Security number through all kinds of banks and credit-card agencies. All he found was a restaurant job in Cleveland, then nothing else. Trail ended. Finally, he talked to the high school guidance counselor, who mentioned several schools Paul LaBeau had asked about. He focused on those cities and checked those schools and others in their vicinity. Rutgers. Cornell. Brown. Wayne State. He went to each of the schools, looking for a sympathetic person to get into the registrar's lists. He tried different combinations and spellings of the name. Gerald Paul LaBeau, Jerry LaBeau, Jerrold LaBeau, as well as LeBeau. He finally got it at Wayne State, under Gerald Paul. University degree and medical school. Social Security number matched. Patient man, Derek, Sr.

Christie wrote all this down and turned the pages over impatiently. A picture. A high school snapshot. Goofy kid, a little anxious-looking. Big smile, crooked teeth. Long hair. Impossible to tell anything. The boy looked happy enough, normal enough.

He put the picture back and thought of Ted Luckey's high school photo. Two highly strung boys. The ones Dan memorialized.

There was another couple of pages. Christie read about the search for the young man's apartment, phone number. Johnson had asked around cleverly and found that Detroit's Gerald Paul had a girlfriend named Mary Riley, whom he spent a certain amount of time with. He lived a couple of doors from a bar that served hamburgers and he went in there often enough when he was too tired to get anything else to eat.

Has in past worked for Detroit restaurant called The Duck, but not for years and no soc. sec. shows up. Two yrs. mostly school, two yrs. mostly work, next yr. finished undergrad, next yr. med school. In response to client's request for personal information, including movement patterns, he wrote, *there is a good chance of finding subject going from studio apartment on Vickers Street where girlfriend lives to classes at medical school to home apartment (1212 Enfield, Apartment 3) to Vincent's (bar on corner). But note, Mary Riley comes to his place much more often than he goes to hers.*

Seedy, prying this way, watching someone live a life. Christie asked Jr. to open the other file cabinets. He skimmed them before leaving, just in case there was another job for Ross. He didn't find anything. The whole time, the son paced, worried, no doubt feeling he'd betrayed the old man.

When Christie finished, it was past quitting time. He was late getting home. His kids would be there by now, being cared for by Marina.

FRANK LOOKED UP AT THE KID SITTING ACROSS FROM HIM, studying the menu. She would order modestly, he knew that much. Behind the menu, her eyes moved restlessly, checking out prices, working out how much she should order for dinner. She took up a third hunk of bread and chewed it hungrily. Squeezed her knees together. Well, he couldn't quite see that, but he knew she did.

"Bring on the real food," she said playfully, and they both laughed a little.

Laughter, the best medicine, as the little magazine used to say.

He tried to do that comic's thing, making his eyebrows go upward in teasing, but his internal electricity faltered and he didn't pull it off. "Now that I got your check for you, you really could skip out of work tomorrow."

"No. Even if Platt's a vengeful bitch."

He studied her. She reminded him of a dumpling. Apple. Of a child. Peaches and cream. It was why children were compared to food, that malleable fresh quality. She wasn't fat, only a tad more fleshy than was fashionable today when success was measured in minus pounds.

"I'll drive you in to work in the morning. I'll get you there on time." Her face fell. "What? What's the problem?"

"Nothing."

"What? Being seen with me? Am I that embarrassing?"

"No, it's just . . ." She took a sip of her Coke and looked around for the waitress.

"What?"

"I thought you were staying somewhere else." She shook her head and readjusted her fork and knife to make room for a large plate.

"I am, but I could still come over and drive you."

She nodded slowly. "But I could take a bus, too. Provided I get to sleep and wake up."

"You're embarrassed to be seen with me?"

"What people will think is . . . is part of it. You know."

"Who? Alice Platt?"

"Maybe."

"And what will she think of you? If she thinks you've been boffing your rescuer, doing a favor for a paycheck, so what? Right? It isn't true."

Bridget got very still and she stared at him. "Yes."

"Is that right?"

She nodded.

The waitress came toward them juggling two large plates and a new basket of bread. The plates of pasta steamed up into their faces, hers a hearty, low-cost, meatball version, his a rapini special.

They began to eat.

"Good spaghetti?"

"It's wonderful."

"Slow down. Don't inhale it." He caught himself being too paternal. Not the right note.

She allowed a little silence to go by. Then she surprised him with "You seem kind of down. I thought so earlier, even though you were trying to cheer me."

"I get preoccupied sometimes," he said, alert.

"I got the impression you were reading something that

bothered you. On the computer. When I came into your office."

He watched her. She had a brave, blundering quality. "I don't remember what I was reading. Could have been an ad for a men's suit sale."

"No," she scoffed. "I doubt it. You're not a suit kind of person."

"How do you know?"

"I don't," she said soberly.

"Well, I don't remember what I was reading. I read all kinds of things, though. I try not to limit or second guess. You never know where the next idea is coming from. You never know. The best ideas always kind of loop around. Or leap. Maybe a men's suit sale becomes a story of a would-be president."

"It's how my mind works. That's why I think I'd be good at film or television. I still don't know which. But I pay attention to all kinds of things. I notice things. And they become other things." She cut into a meatball and took a large bite, closing her eyes.

"You ought to be a student."

"I'm going to get in somewhere soon as I have enough . . ." She rubbed her fingers together to show *dough*, Italian style.

"How old are you?"

"Almost twenty."

"How almost?"

"A year. Pretty much."

So. Eighteen. He allowed himself to chuckle. She softened toward him when he laughed, he saw that. Even though her knees were still tight, tight together.

"Did it ever occur to you your cousin was jealous of you?"

"There's nothing to be jealous of." She looked seriously sad. "The color in the hair," she said, pointing to her head, "is misleading. My manner is . . . an act. I'm incredibly square."

"Everybody is incredibly square. When you think about it, square tends to be a good thing—construction, beauty, huh?"

He lifted his wineglass and saluted the square.

■   ■   ■

WHEN RICHARD CHRISTIE GOT HOME AT NIGHT, HE SPENT TWO hours with his kids. Quality. Hugging, stories, homework, nine and a half yards. As soon as they were asleep, he came downstairs to talk to Marina. She'd slipped out to the Giant Eagle while he was getting Eric and Julia to bed, so he found her putting the groceries away and he began to help her, guessing what she would want next. As he handed her lettuce and carrots, he fretted about the fact that with three current unsolved homicides on his desk, he had to somehow find the time to open up what Dan Ross thought was a possible fake death from almost twenty-five years ago and a possible murder from more than thirty years ago. Possible.

"Wow," she said. "Think of it."

He had. He was a kid then, a couple of years younger than Ross or LaBeau, playing baseball, watching cats catch birds, watching younger kids cut worms in half. Cataloging death. Beginning to notice girls. Marina wouldn't even have been in kindergarten. It was old stuff, going to be hard to make his men care about something that old when there was fresh blood on the streets, cases already open. And it wasn't even clear how to start working the cold, cold case until he chased down the notion that Gerald Paul, or Paul LaBeau, might still be alive.

He pulled Marina away from the refrigerator, which she was rearranging. She let him hold her tight. He wanted to say, "How do groceries and laundry keep us from each other?" even though he knew perfectly well their situation was common.

They stood and swayed for a while. She eased the refrigerator door shut with her foot.

"Are you unhappy?" he asked.

"Not unhappy, no. Tired. Missing you."

"Too busy," Elizabeth Shepherd had said of her husband, of the both of them. "Missing each other."

He felt so badly for the widow. He hoped if ever he got

killed he wouldn't leave Marina with the feeling of months of having missed each other. He snaked his hands into her hair. Marina had amazing masses of dark curly hair that reached the whole way to her shoulder blades. It made a person think she had a lot of everything—brains, feeling, passion—which was true.

She trotted back from wherever far away she had been, said, "You're spooked by something. Talk. Tell me."

He felt surprisingly grateful. He broke apart from her a little, leaned against the refrigerator, and said, "Right now, I'm just mucking around in the possibility of a long history between what happened to Doc Ross two weeks ago and old events." Both the way she slowed herself down to smile at him and the feeling he had about Ross and his gentlemanliness, all of it at once gave him that feeling of falling in love, of having already been captured.

"Mucking around," she said. "I love that phrase, mucking around."

THE EVENING HAD BEEN STRANGE FROM THE START. BRIDGET had assumed they'd go to Casa Nueva or Seven Sauces, but he'd driven to a place the whole way out in Nelsonville.

At one point, he took out a cell phone to dial this woman named Sally, but shook his head, saying the volume was too low. He got up and went to a pay phone on the way to the rest rooms. It didn't seem much better, from what she could see. He held one finger to an ear and just listened.

She found herself wondering where the Catholic House was and why she didn't just go there so everybody didn't have to do all this jumping around. Sally, she figured, either was saying no, not tonight, or something else he didn't much want to hear. He was trying to rebound too quickly, she thought, from the death of his wife. Rebounds were full of trouble, she'd always heard. He looked distracted again, disgusted maybe. "She wasn't home," he said.

"Who were you listening to, then?"

Behind his glasses, his eyes went still, then came to life

again. "The machine." He smiled. "You want to know everything. I'll call her again later. Wednesday nights, I usually go over there."

The world was a place of couples. All kinds, serious and not.

She was thinking, suddenly, all her possessions were in his car, not that they amounted to much, but still, they were about the only proof that she existed, so she was attached to them and wanted to see that they were safe.

He stood and patted his pockets, then reexamined his wallet. "Hmmm. Let me think. Twenty-some-odd dollars. I'd better use a card. Unless you have—"

"I have a ten," she said. It was all she had in the world, outside the final paycheck.

She had the feeling he was testing her, her honesty.

"Never mind," he said. "I'll use a card."

"It's up to you."

"Well, if you don't mind . . . I can pay you back tomorrow. I hate to use a card when I don't have to."

She handed over the ten. It occurred to her the money pretty much covered her meal, so if he didn't give it back, she would have to be okay with that.

Her things were still in the car, she was relieved to see. He drove her to where he lived, which, it turned out, was kind of far from the university. Why had she thought she could get a bus in? He pulled off the paved road and down a small dirt road of several hundred feet. "Woodsy," he said. "Looks very appealing to a guy from L.A."

The house itself was small and not fancy, which surprised Bridget a little. When she got inside, she saw it had an L-shaped living-dining room, a small Pullman kitchen, two bedrooms, but one of them, the one she was to sleep in, was mostly fitted out as a study with a single bed in it. The big main room was nice, but her father would have scoffed at the poor construction, the hollow-core doors.

"I think I'm very tired. The food. The day," Frank said, going into his bedroom. Bridget sat on the sofa, waiting. Was he on the phone? Charging up his cell? She couldn't hear his voice. He came back, saying, "I'll just go over there. There's no answer."

"Do you have a key to her place?"

"Yes." But he sat in one of the living room chairs, not moving.

"Do you have to pack some clothes?"

"What? No, no, I can come back here to dress."

Then he had left, but at nearly midnight, just about when she thought she might be able to sleep, he had come back, saying he didn't know where his key to Sal's place was, and he couldn't spend the night on the street, so why didn't they work a little harder on their arrangement, get her comfortable.

So at midnight, they had moved furniture. Bridget felt a large nudge of worry, both that the thing with Sally was going kaput and that moving furniture felt more permanent than she wanted. Yet she also had a curiosity about how it would all work out, even the part with him and Sally. She felt slightly more at home once they moved the desk and the computer to his bedroom. "This way, you have space to move your elbows and if I get inspired and you're asleep, I can work all night."

She was stuck for a reply.

"Sleep tight." With that, he had gone to bed—or to his bedroom, at least.

Her door had a lock, which she used. Lights clicked on, off, on, she saw from under her door. There were the sounds of drawers opening, hangers moving in a closet. Bridget was certain she would not sleep, and yet she fell asleep.

On Thursday morning at seven she tiptoed to the bathroom, where she washed her hair as fast as she could, hoping she wasn't using all the hot water. She had no cash at all left, not enough to get on the bus. He would have to drive her in.

She dried herself and put on a pair of sweats before leaving the bathroom. In a way, she was ridiculous, being so careful. He showed no particular interest in her. *Saving it for what?* Jess's voice asked.

Maybe because it was morning and she was alone for a moment, she noticed more than she had the night before. The little house had sand-colored wall-to-wall carpet. There was nothing on the walls except a calender in the kitchen. He wasn't *very* moved in yet. But then, single men tended not to have *things*. Still, he'd been married, and surely his wife had had lots of stuff. Where was it now?

She looked out her bedroom window and saw a huge yard and then woods. At first the trees were scraggly, but the woods thickened in the distance. She supposed people who came from L.A. rented a place with land simply because they could.

Shame it wasn't summer. She would set up the sprinkler. On a hot sunny day, a person could lie around in her nothings because there was nobody around to see.

She listened. Was he up yet? She thought she heard snuffling sounds. People were like cows and horses, weren't they, so animal. Remove the shampoo and deodorant, who's to tell the difference?

She chose pants and a long-sleeve T-shirt, one of her four outfits, which reminded her, she would need to see if he had a washer and dryer somewhere. When she finished dressing, she went to the kitchen and made coffee. For a moment she got stalled, wondering how much of a to-do she should make of breakfast. Would it be too pushy to prepare a whole egg-and-bacon thing? The refrigerator held no bacon or sausage, but she found two eggs and the better part of a quart of orange juice.

Juice, at least. She poured two glasses.

He came out in a robe, peering about, scratching his head, looking surprised to see her. Her stomach tightened as he observed her.

"I could make breakfast," she said. "You have eggs here. And bread for toast."

"Okay," he said sleepily.

"Would you like soft-boiled or fried? I'm not great at fried, but—"

"Just juice and coffee," he said. "Maybe skip the coffee and have it at work."

"I've already made it."

"Okay, then. We'll have coffee. I'll give you some money today to get some food in. No, let me think. This is Thursday. We'd better go shopping after my class and before I leave town. Take a lunch break. I'll drive you."

"Okay," she said, wondering if she should buy the food in exchange for utilities. Half the food? How long would she want to stay? Two days, twenty?

She hated herself when she was indecisive, which was pretty often. She felt like a thirteen-year-old runaway, not like someone her own age. The truth was, she was both less mature and more mature than others her age, somehow both at the same time, and even she, dicing herself all the time, knew it.

She put the eggs back, then quickly ate a piece of untoasted bread. It felt like stealing. Then suddenly, alarmingly, she was in danger of crying again. For without knowing she was going toward it—the fact of her loneliness—it was clear, when she allowed the truth in, that nobody cared what happened to her, not her father or her stepmother or Jess or any of the people at the house.

She put the cups out, waiting for him.

HE HAS NOT SLEPT MUCH, ONLY TWO HOURS, AND THAT SINCE five-thirty. He plugged in his computer and went back to the Pittsburgh paper, as if he would find something new there, some small item of information he had not noticed before.

The shower water hits him.

The ends of Bridget's hair remind him of so many paintbrushes with their bottom inch of color, a light wine-red that doesn't exist in nature. He can smell the shampoo she used. Her hair bothers her. Punky, the brand was called, she explained when they moved furniture. It was some teen product, a step up from Kool-Aid, but not many steps up. Her skin is a silver-white, so white it takes his breath away to think of it, and her cheeks are round with what used to be called baby fat. She's soft and young, hardly formed yet as a human being, and the idea of her openness exhausts him, nearly disgusts him, but not quite.

There is no Sally. No Maggie, either, a name he sometimes uses, no dead wife named Carol. There is a Lisa and a divorce. But better to invent things, choose them and juggle them.

"Are you a decent cook at all?" he asked last night as they drove toward his place.

"I can do some ordinary things."

"That doesn't sound promising somehow. There's always takeout."

"It's too expensive. I can function in the kitchen. I just have to see what ingredients you have around."

Modest. Indecisive. Wanting to run, wanting to help. And all the while, of course, it's already been decided.

He stands in the shower remembering snatches of conversation. It gives him a small thrill, defenses collapsing before him. Vulnerability. He has a nose for it. Ass, dick, everything comes alive.

Love, love. He's been searching for it for as long as he can remember. He knows it's not here—not a question in the world—she's only somebody who's been sent to him. A small help, a small comfort. A baby aspirin to set against a migraine. Hardly a cure for what ails him.

6

CHRISTIE HAD TO START SOMEWHERE, SCATTERSHOT THOUGH IT might be. Phone calls. He dialed a lot of Rileys on Thursday without finding anybody who admitted to being the Mary who hung out with Gerald Paul. When he talked to the chief, he reported on the Pittsburgh searches only, keeping Dan Ross's obsession to himself.

He rapped his fingers and dialed the Wayne State School of Medicine. He asked the woman who answered to identify some people he might speak to who had worked at the medical school twenty-five years ago. She put him on hold, he got cut off and had to dial twice and start all over. Finally, an hour later, he talked to a different woman on the staff, who had worked there thirty-seven years altogether, but the woman didn't know anything helpful about the death of the student named Gerald Paul. "It's dim," she said. "I can recall a fuss in the office and then reading about it in the newspapers later. What do you need to know?"

"Were there any rumors of drug usage at the time?"

"I didn't hear anything like that, but then, I was never in the loop, as they say. My *impression*—and that's all it is— was he was a nice guy who did his work and had had a tragic . . . accident on vacation. The problem is, I'm about the only one who goes back that far."

"Did you know his girlfriend?"

"No."

"Okay. Let's think," he said, trying to enlist her. "How about the names of people who taught there, maybe retired, but still live in the vicinity? There must be a few?"

"There are two I can think of that I heard bought places up north, but you could probably find them." She gave the names of doctors who had been professors there. "Teachers come and go. This place is completely different now."

Christie went to the computer and battled with the keys until it was time to go home. He didn't want to be late again, so he decided to work at home. Not so secretly, he wanted Marina's help. She was so much quicker than he at the computer. More patient and therefore more efficient. He cursed every time he got a pop-up. And he was easily distracted by the possibilities outside his line of inquiry.

She was spinning lettuce when he asked her if she felt like helping with a people search on the home computer. "I've got the names of some doctors who might know something, but 'up north' is a big area," he said. She finished rinsing the lettuce and put the spinner aside. "Let's do it now," she said.

At the end of an hour, she had found him the addresses and phone numbers of the two doctors retired to places up north and one more that she got by her own creative means—reading about publications and then tracing the name back to the med school faculty and then doing a people search. She told him the writer of the article was now in Cleveland. She was a wiz. So three possibles.

Christie spent between six and seven o'clock calling these people from the phone in the kitchen while he watched her put dinner together. For the first doctor he called, he had to leave a message. The others he got right away. They remembered Gerald Paul, all right.

Meanwhile Marina stood at the counter, listening and chopping broccoli and slicing chicken breasts into cubes. When that was finished, she fetched a basket of laundry from the basement and began folding while he talked.

One former teacher, an Irwin Steiner, said in a loud cocktail voice that he'd been shocked by the death of such a good student. He called it a tragedy. When asked about the drugs found in the system of the deceased, he got mumbly and said simply that he had not known the young man well enough to know there was a drug problem.

"Anything else you can tell me?"

"He was very bright. Got dreamy sometimes, but he could always pull out a good grade on just about anything. Seemed he had all sorts of references for things; he'd give you that instead of what you asked for, but he somehow got at the answer. Oblique. I think he read a lot. He was good in the hard medical, but he was even better in the other aspects of the work. But why are you asking?"

"I'm doing this in my off hours as a favor to his family. We're trying to put together a portrait for a memorial."

"Oh. Kind of long after the fact."

"It is. Some things take a long time to heal," he said just before he hung up.

"Wow," Marina said, tucking one sock into another. Her eyes were bright with interest. "You sure can lie convincingly. It's scary."

"In a good cause."

She folded his T-shirts, first in threes, with the sleeves neatly tucked, then in half, such a lot of fuss. He found this touching. He was still surprised that she loved him. He got scared sometimes that they weren't going to make it. One day she'd wake up and decide she wanted a more exciting life.

The second teacher, an endocrinologist named Sam Folino, said he had been shocked to hear there was any drug usage and that he had tried his best to keep that information quiet for the sake of the school. He'd been angry it made it into the obit. He had nothing to add about the man himself.

"Tight-lipped," Christie said, when that call ended.

"Hmmm. Let me think." Marina put the laundry basket aside and started the heat under the oil. "You gave up on the girlfriend?"

"I called an awful lot of Rileys, but nobody knew a Mary who hung out then."

Just as she began tossing the chicken and broccoli in the pan, the phone rang and it was the third teacher, Robert Saul, returning the call Christie had made earlier. Saul answered quickly that he had once worked closely with Gerald Paul, who did some research for him and even house-sat when he went away. "Personality? I thought he knew how to look out for a good deal. He came to me about house-sitting. I wouldn't say opportunistic, in that that has a negative connotation. Just clever. With an eye out."

"Would he have made a good doctor?"

"He would have made a good anything, I think. He was clever."

Marina stopped stirring and wrote something on the outside of the file folder and handed it over. *Name, married status, current residence of any girlfriends.*

Christie asked this question.

"Mary something in the time I knew him. It was an Irish last name."

"Riley," Christie said. "We can't find her. Know where she is and if her name changed?"

"It did. I think it did. See, she left town right after he died, but she came back a couple of years later. She took up with another medical student. They got married, so she would be Mary Connelly if she took his name. Connelly stayed here to work after he finished med school, but I heard they divorced, so I really can't say what happened to her. I don't know. I can't keep track of all of them."

"Right. Thanks. You've been helpful."

Marina looked at him expectantly.

"Thanks for pushing. Mary Connelly is the name we're looking for now. I'll have to try after dinner."

"We'll find her. She's who you need to talk to."

I. We. Marina bailed him out gently. He watched her finish what she called her mock stir-fry and toss a salad. He set some places at the kitchen table and they sat to eat.

He hated computers. People, people he liked.

■　　■　　■

"HIT YOU AGAIN?" THE WAITRESS ASKS.

"Yes," Frank answers, sliding the glass toward her.

The idea of simply bolting from his life in Michigan had occurred to him, that was the truth, even before Daniel found him. He was doing fine in school, he had friends, he had a girlfriend, Mary Riley, but none of it thrilled him. This feeling of floating, of being able to leave things behind, it was anything but new. When he was eight, twelve, the thought *running away from home* was a familiar friend, his closest friend. At fourteen, living with Dan and his father, he fantasized about skipping out—wanting to be shut of them, also wanting to surprise them with his disappearance. A pleasurable, vengeful thought, it got to be a habit. After his senior year in high school he'd done it, gone. Disappeared. Made a new life. He was free.

Medicine. He had a talent, but . . .

Even before Dan found him, he had been flirting with the idea of running again.

Then Dan came.

With his guesses and suppositions.

It was summer. He'll never forget. There he was, sitting one day in a bar in his neighborhood, horse-tired from his hours at the hospital, half watching baseball on TV, the poor old Tigers, struggling. It was bright outside, sunny, but dark inside the bar. He thought he was going nuts, having visions, because he looked up, and who walked in, silhouetted in the doorway, but his brother, Daniel. It didn't seem real. Dan looked at him, came over, waited a second, and sat down.

The life drained out of him. The man across from him made him feel small, ridiculous. Instantly, all his accomplishments came to nothing; he was a failure, just a bum drinking his beer.

Why could the man not leave him alone?

Dan looked regretful. He said, "It took some effort to find you. I had to . . ." He fumbled in a pocket and seemed to think better of it. "I had to get a P.I. He . . . figured out the name thing. You're not Paul anymore."

No, not Paul, and not yet Frank; he'd been going by Gerald then. He felt such a sense of loss. He'd now lost a second name. He was known again; *Gerald Paul* was findable, no longer safe. Dizziness enveloped him. In silence he found power. He would be like Iago and not speak.

"Dad and I wanted to know if you were okay."

He compressed his lips.

Dan spoke slowly. "You don't want any part of us, I can accept that, if that's how you really feel, even though I don't like it. We have a lot in common. Blood. We're all doctors, it turns out. But if you want to be left alone, I'll leave you alone. It's just . . . there were times I felt nobody knew how to *get to* you but me. That even though you hated me, hate me, you also know I care . . . Never mind. So. Are you okay?"

He shrugged, a compromise.

"I wish that for you. The way you left, though, just disappeared, means something. I'm trying to interpret it. I mean, I bought it, that you were going to your mother. When I finally got in touch with her, she said she hadn't seen you or heard from you. I've been trying to make sense of it."

A group of people came into the bar laughing. For a moment, the door hung open again and this time it was a group silhouetted there before the door began to shut.

"Look. Here goes. If you had anything to do with Ted Luckey, it won't go away."

Won't go away. A threat.

They looked at each other. Did his eyes flicker? He tried to keep them steady. He wanted to stay silent, he was afraid of speech. When people argued, things slipped out of them in the anger. If he spoke, he would point out, ridiculously, hating himself, "It's Ted Luckey you care about and not me at all." He would say, "This need to see me is not love, but some sort of vengeance." So he tightened his lips.

"I can't get over the feeling, the worry, that you were involved. I wanted to ask you straight out about it seven years ago. I didn't. And then you left. If that's why you left, if it is, I think you have to come back, turn yourself in, do your time for it, whatever that is. It was probably part accident. I've been over and over the facts of it. The Seconal. Maybe you took some from Dad."

Dan wore a short-sleeve shirt and jeans. He looked large, uncomfortable in the chair across from the padded banquette. He studied his big hands, flexed them, and said, "After you left, this thought kept coming at me that I didn't want to let in, but it wouldn't go away."

Somebody shouted at something on the television. They both looked up. Baseball game. The hulk of a bartender checking everyone's glass with a forefinger out, as if counting.

Once he looked away he didn't want to look back at the big, inquiring eyes.

"I wish you'd speak," Dan said.

He looked back, met the eyes. "I have nothing to say."

Encouraged, Dan leaned forward. "How can I ask the right questions? What am I to do? All right, all right. You look at me as if I'm some sort of idiot. If you did it, you have to deal with it. You can't run. It doesn't work. You'd probably get a very limited sentence, maybe a hospital assignment in prison, and even though prison is unbearable, unbearable, you would find a way to bear it, become a kind of . . . hero."

This was Dan, imagining how he himself would overcome any shame. This was Dan's fantasy, nothing to do with other people and what they were capable of.

"I found you and you won't talk."

He had to say something, he realized, if he was ever to get out of this. The bar was noisy. His own voice didn't startle him. "I'm a year behind you. I don't have a residency until the year after." He took the last sip of flat beer. The bartender came over, and he said, "Two more. On second thought, make that two bourbons, straight."

Dan looked a little taken aback at the turn of conversation, but he rallied and said, "Well, you worked for two years. At that restaurant. Is that how you put yourself through school?"

So the P.I. had found out all sorts of things. "That's my business. How's *your* life?" he asked.

For a moment he thought Dan was getting angry. A fight in a bar in Michigan. Not Dan's style! Then Dan nodded and said, "Good. I'm doing my residency next year. I managed to get placed back home."

"Where back home?"

"At Presby. I wanted Montefiore or Presby."

"Is the old man still working?"

"Yeah. He was drinking too much but now that's pretty much a thing of the past. He realized what he was doing and he stopped."

Drink had been a factor all right, the night he needed the alibi. His father was snoring at eight o'clock and snoring in the same position at eleven-thirty that night.

"He's not exactly lovable, I know," Dan said tightly, "but he's ours."

"Yours maybe. He adores you." The whiskeys arrived. He slid one toward Dan, pulled one toward himself.

"Oh, I don't know. He depends on me, but I don't think adoration is in his repertoire." Dan looked contemplative, took a sip of bourbon. As if reluctantly, he continued speaking. "When I took the residency, Dad said I should live there at the house, but I told him no, it was time I got an apartment. I did find one in Highland Park. It's small but it's cheap, which is good. I'm getting married next year. Elizabeth is her name."

Elizabeth is her name. He could still hear Dan's voice saying that.

"I never thought I could be so lucky. She's amazing. I wasn't connecting with anybody. I was going through a kind of depression, I guess it was. Then I met her and she was so . . . alive. And warm. There are people who make the world work. They have a healing touch. She's one of them."

"You're lucky."

"I am in that. I wish you would tell me about yourself."

Something, he told himself, something. "I'm not too bad. I really could use a vacation, but hey, it doesn't look too likely until August. I'm going with a girl named Mary. Very Irish, curly red hair. She's a bit of a sad sack, though, not the type to lift a guy out of a funk. That's all. I guess the thing I need to say—and that you don't understand—is that I'm okay, that I needed to get away, I never took well to being thrust on you and the doc, I just wanted to make my own way."

"I wish you felt differently."

"I'm sorry you think so badly of me."

That's how he said it. Leave me alone. That's how he said it. The indirect hit, the making an ogre of your tormentor.

Dan backed off. "Your mother . . . ?" he asked.

"I haven't seen her for eleven years. Think of me as an orphan who made good. I had some bad beginnings, but I got over it. I became someone else."

"I don't think people can divorce themselves from their pasts. Successfully."

"They can. They can and do. And Dan?" He leaned forward and made eye contact. "There are some things you don't know about. That's all I can say. When something awful happens to you, you try to fill in with fantasy, make sense of it. Some things don't make sense. Luckey's death. No sense at all. I'm sorry he died. I'm sorry you lost him. But I didn't have anything to do with it. This is a . . ." He waved a hand in a circle at the right side of his brain and he was thrilled that invention was coming to him, the machinery was working. "A crazy obsession. A problem you have. You saved him, you rescued him from *despond*, so you want to believe he couldn't have lost his connecting string with you, done something dumb, talked to a stranger—whatever happened to him. It has nothing to do with me. If it did, I would tell the police. I'm more honest than you understand."

Dan's face went soft, believing.

An old feeling tugged, of almost loving Dan for his naivete. But he scrabbled backwards from falling into the pool of Dan's benevolence. There was no way to explain what happened to him when he allowed himself to believe in Dan's way. Death. He let Dan get hold of him and he felt death.

"I know I don't understand you," Dan said. "I know that. I get caught in wanting to make friends with you and not knowing how. I thought maybe you might want to come home."

He shook his head. "It doesn't appeal to me. I'm the orphan runaway. You're not responsible for me."

Dan looked troubled. "Before I came here, I thought I knew what happened. I wanted to try to help you stop running. Now I don't know what I think. I should have remembered the way you get me turning, spinning."

He was dying. Dan was spinning. That was the dynamic.

A funny thing then, and a lucky one. Mary came in, frowning from both the dark of the bar and her insecurities, looking for him. And even though he was ending things with her, knew now he was going to bolt for sure, he didn't want her meeting Dan and vice versa. So he said, standing up hurriedly, leaving money on the table, "Look, I have to do something for a friend. I'm not your problem. I'm sure you mean well, but let me go."

Dan fumbled to get up.

But he was gone before Dan knew it, an arm around Mary's shoulder, a head close to hers—poor Mary, who thought, as he whisked her out of the bar so fast, making her surprised and happy, that he'd had a change of heart, that he loved her again.

A bad scene, as they say. And he could call it up, beat by beat. That was in Detroit. That was a long time ago. The year the Steelers won the Super Bowl and the Pirates won the World Series while the hapless Lions and Tigers could hardly win a game. If a person cared to remember the minor things. Detroit.

He's in Pittsburgh now, near all the old haunts, but Bridget thinks it's L.A., so he must remember to give her some L.A. tidbits when he calls. Little stories.

"Another bourbon?" the waitress asks. He's had three.

"Yes," he says. "One more." He's done it, two hours in a bar in Squirrel Hill, right on Murray Avenue, near the old house and a fraction of a mile from the Pocusset Safe House in one direction and his new place in the other. Ghosts, yes, but nobody coming in to find him. No Dan. Poor old Mary is God knows where. He can't afford to keep track of people or they might be able to keep track of him. His life is fluid, watercolor thrown haphazardly over paper. Looks like something, doesn't it?

SEVEN BLOCKS FROM WHERE FRANK RAZZI IS HAVING A BOURBON, Darnell Flowers has an appointment at the Safe House. He owes Commander Christie since he screwed up by talking to Jones. It's kind of like a trade.

The place sure is clean. Matching blue chairs. He sits on one in the section where there is a waiting room and small offices. "Darnell Flowers," a woman says in a quiet voice. He jumps up.

He expected her to be white, but she's a caramel-skinned, slightly round woman of forty-something. Her hair looks as if it's supposed to be neat and rounded off, but throughout the day she ran her fingers through it and it went punk. She keeps smiling. When he passes her to go into the office, he can smell garlic.

The small office is militarily neat, everything brand new. The chair she motions him to is leather, so smooth and cushiony he gets a surge of fear this comfort is a trap of some sort.

"Darnell," she says again. She takes up a legal pad, which makes him feel he's in court. If he just leaves . . . what happens then? Does somebody report to somebody? "My name is Ms. Mecon. I'm here to help you talk about whatever you want to work on."

He sits alert for a second, wondering what to do. He has nothing to say and yet he stops looking at the little clock after a while and a word comes out of him and then another word follows. Somehow he puts in an hour just filling Ms. Mecon in on who he is: the father gone when he was two, the bad grades, the not too many friends, the accident of helping out Commander Christie a year and a half ago, the current no-friends status—well, not exactly true, but he still feels he has none—the current good grades, the mother who doesn't ever say anything about the good grades, just talks about how she hates the police and he's a slab of white fish making friends with one of them and wanting to be a detective. He tells about the way his mother doesn't get along with people. Neighbors, salesclerks, delivery men, cousins. Nobody. The sound of her yelling is what he remembers most, a voice rising up in pitch.

When the hour is up, Ms. Mecon says she would be happy to see him again. "Next Thursday, week from tonight?" she asks, smiling.

He wonders what tricks she did on him to get him to talk for so long. Even if he nods that he will take the appointment, he can cancel later.

He stands outside the Safe House, not wanting to go home. Absolutely predictable what will happen when he walks through the door and sees his mother. He'll get yelled at. Still, he starts walking toward the bus stop.

Mecon said, "Sometimes yelling is hard to live with. Does it make you tense?"

"Yeah. I shut it out a lot. Have to."

A little speech came out of Mecon then—he couldn't tell if it was rehearsed or just for him—about how when you shut out one thing, your body hardens against others. "You have to know what you're reacting to so you can be . . ." She used her hands to illustrate flexible. She was okay, he guessed. Just a person.

He wishes he were a detective already, grown up and older and out on a job.

Moments later, Darnell stands on Murray, fully intending to get on a bus and get himself home. "Sometimes parents and children don't match up," Ms. Mecon said.

He has five dollars in his pocket. He crosses the street and orders a gyro, which he eats hungrily, just standing outside the shop, feeling foolish and hopeful. Then he takes a bus home.

THERE WERE TWENTY MARY OR M. CONNELLYS IN THE DETROIT area. Christie called twelve of them before eight o'clock and was running out of steam when Marina said, "Let's try the ex." She pulled her long hair back in a rubber band and went back to the computer, looking determined. There were four doctors named Connelly. Before the night had ended, they contacted three of the four. For this, Marina got on the phone and said she was an old friend of Mary's who needed to get in touch about a personal matter. In each case, she asked if the doctor she spoke to had once been married to Mary Riley. The third man answered tersely that Mary was his ex-wife. However, he refused to give her number.

Christie was tired. There were dishes to do. "Tomorrow," he said. "We have to stop sometime."

Marina nodded, but her eyes were bright. She got like that, tenacious. Acting, teaching, whatever. She went into the high schools, artist-in-the-schools program, taught acting and Shakespeare most days, and she worked hard, worried about the kids. But she was meant to be acting, onstage. That was the work she should be doing. This tracking down Gerald Paul and Mary Connelly was some sort of substitute. She didn't stop until ten-twenty that night when an R. M. Connelly answered the phone in a light reedy voice and said yes, she was the one.

On Friday, Christie got up at six and dressed in a soft wool polo and pants, no tie. At six-thirty, Marina handed him a thermos of coffee and a bag with two sandwiches in it. By six thirty-five he was on the road for Michigan, wishing, as Marina had wished out loud, that she wasn't working that day and could go with him. Eight o'clock he called in to the office from the road to say he was tracking a trip that Dan Ross had made and he'd be away from the office for a day. Chief would ask him, "Recent trip?" It would be easier to just say yes.

Mary Riley Connelly was curious enough, upon hearing

the name Gerald Paul, that she had agreed to take off work and stay home to meet with Christie.

By one o'clock he knocked on the door of a two-story house among a string of ranches. The woman who answered the door had long wavy red hair, faded with gray. She was pale and her face was lined a little more than it should have been for her age. Mary Connelly invited him in.

They sat at her kitchen table, his choice because he thought it's where she would be most comfortable. "I'm curious. Is the R. M. a reversal of Mary Riley?"

"Rita Mary." She blushed. "I never liked the Rita."

"Ah. Interesting."

"What's this all about?" she asked.

He had told her on the phone that Gerald Paul's death might have an impact on something he was doing now and that he wanted to ask her some personal questions. "Thank you for making the time. We're trying to retrace what happened to your friend."

"He died. In Atlantic City. Exactly a week after we broke up. But you know that."

"You ended the relationship?"

"No, he did."

"How did you hear about the death?"

"It was awful. Nobody told me. I didn't hear until maybe ten days after, when the obituary finally got into the paper. One of my friends called me."

"That must have been horrible for you."

"It was. Absolutely the worst day of my life. Hearing like that. I had to call the newspaper to find out where they got their information. Then they tell me about this mother of his—he said he had nothing to do with her, so it was just a grim joke that she would be the one they'd call and not me. I called her then and she said, yes, it was true, he was dead. Shooting heroin, she said. I told her that was crazy, but she said it wasn't too crazy, unfortunately. Mostly she didn't want to talk with me and we weren't on the phone for long."

"Where is he buried?"

"Ashes. In the mother's backyard. Somewhere up where she lived. There's no grave to visit, or I would have."

Interesting, interesting. Christie looked at the sink—newly washed dishes drying on a rack. Dishwasher broken? It looked old. The linoleum had chips in it and so did the counter.

"Tell me about yourself. You have kids?"

"Two boys. Twenty and twenty-one. They're in college."

"Impossibly expensive."

"It is. It's the whole reason I keep this stressful job at the university. I'm in administration, financial aid office. Last thing I thought I'd do with my life, but it gets the boys through college."

"They live here with you?"

"The young one did for a while, but they're both in apartments. I'm on my own now."

"Not married at present?

"Done with marrying. Divorced. I couldn't take it again."

"I'm going to ask you some questions that might help me. Okay?"

She looked nervous. "Okay. Do you want some coffee or something first?"

He saw that none was made and said no, for he imagined it would take her too much time. She was fragile. Something about her was. He took out his notebook.

"Here goes. In the time you went with Gerald—how long was that?"

"Two years and a little more."

"Did he talk about a brother and father?"

She was clearly surprised. "No. Never. I assumed the father just took off. He had a brother?"

"He did."

"What lies must he have been telling me?"

"There were others?"

"Well, he said he had lost track of his mother. He thought of himself as an orphan, but his mother was the one they called when he died."

Christie nodded. "Did you have any notion that his name was altered from his birth name?"

"At the time, no. I got his mother to send me the Seattle paper and— No, I didn't know."

"Okay. See, this isn't so hard. Had you seen any evidence of drug usage?"

"That blew me away when I heard it. He must have been hiding it from me all along. Really, I can't explain it. I knew he messed with speed when he had to study and Valium when he had to stop the speed high, but all the doctors were doing that, I hate to say. Med school is ridiculous."

"How devoted was he to his studies?"

Mary had small, delicate eyes that were pink with worry and strain. She blinked before answering. "He was a hard worker. I always assumed he had a . . . a mission to save lives. But he never *said* that. He said the usual stuff about making decent money and he told the usual jokes about not believing in death."

"What other lies do you think he might have told?"

"I don't know. I really thought I knew him and I didn't at all."

"Did you ever feel frightened of him? Violence of any sort?"

Her eyes widened. "He wasn't . . . He didn't shove me around, if that's what you mean. The funny thing—I really can't imagine what brought up that question."

"It's a standard police question. What was the funny thing?"

"Well, it would occur to me. As a possibility. Even though he never did."

"The impulse was there?"

"Maybe." She collapsed into a slump. "I feel so stupid. These questions make me feel awful."

"I'm sorry. I'll try to be quick with the rest. By the way, did you find any pictures or anything I might take a look at?"

"No. My husband asked me to get rid of them and I did

a pretty good job. I looked last night and this morning, but I didn't find anything."

"Too bad."

"Yeah."

"Did you, did it ever occur to you, I know this sounds wild, that he didn't die, after all?" He watched her blanch. "That some kind of a mistake was made?" The question froze her for a moment.

"Are you saying it happened?"

"No. Nobody knows anything except the official version, that he died in Atlantic City and his mother buried him. It's only an idea."

"He did this, you think, to get away from me?"

"No. It's just an idea, like I said, and if it happened, I don't think it had anything to do with you. I wouldn't bother you with it, except . . . if anyone might have received a phone call from him, saying, 'I'm still alive,' I thought it could have been you."

"No. Nothing like that." She swallowed hard.

"What?"

"Nothing . . . specific. Once, about three years later, I had a series of hang-up calls and I had the feeling it was Jerry. I called him Jerry. I said the name once and the person didn't hang up right away. I stayed on the phone for a long time, maybe twenty minutes, and so did the other person. I thought I was going crazy. It was right after I had my first kid, so I figured I was going through some kind of postpartum depression."

"The person didn't speak at all?"

"No. Not at all."

"Why did he break up with you?"

"Just tired of me. He was always kind of anxious and he said I weighed him down. He wanted to date other women. Just an ordinary breakup except for him dying right after."

Christie left her, feeling he'd hurt her with these memories, and he felt badly about it.

Next he drove to a restaurant that was owned by a man

who had once owned the one where Gerald Paul worked for two years, according to the P.I. but not according to any Social Security records. The owner, Lasorta, was a brusque man of about seventy. He wore a turtleneck and jeans, and must have exercised regularly, because he had no paunch. He looked good for his age.

The man was doing accounts when Christie approached him at about three P.M.

"Pittsburgh Police?" Lasorta whistled. "What's up with which of my employees?"

"From a long time ago."

"Yeah?"

"Gerald Paul LaBeau."

Lasorta laughed. "You're on a very cold trail. I read the guy died a long time ago. Slightly different name, but I knew all about the name monkeying back then."

"What can you tell me about him?"

"Bright. Go-getter. Clever. Charming. Dishonest."

"Tell me the dishonest part."

"Worked for me long hours. I . . . Shit. Here goes. He asked me if I would pay him under the table and I did. So sue me. Tell me this isn't what you came about?"

"No. Go on."

"I got to trust him. I could call him in anytime and get his best. I paid him the usual wage, just didn't record it, and I knew he definitely earned great tips—he sure knew how to work the customers for tips, but he was good, too. This was over at my other place I had, The Duck. We were the fancy place in town, so the customers had it to give. Then I get the word from my bartender that the kid was stealing from me. I'm not a sentimental man, but I didn't want to believe it. I took a good long while watching. He was stealing, all right."

"How much?"

"He made twenty, twenty-five a year that I knew about, mostly tips. He must have taken that much again."

"You prosecute?"

Lasorta paused for a long time. "I found out he was

spending it on college. Putting himself through. Socking it away for med school. It killed me."

"You didn't prosecute."

"My wife has not let me forget that for one day. No, I did not. I felt like I was his substitute father. I couldn't. I wanted him to work it off, at least some of it, but then there was the chance he'd do it again, so I just let him go after he returned ten thou. He got it out of his savings account. Bank check. Strangest employee I ever had."

"In what way strange?"

"Too good to be true, I mean. Likable. Yet I didn't know him. Obviously. And even when I realized that, I still more or less felt responsible for him. He told me he'd been in an orphanage and then foster care. Turned out that wasn't true, I guess. From the obituary."

"Guy seems to be a good liar."

"Yeah."

"Did you ever hear any rumors or otherwise get the feeling he was still alive? Might still be alive?"

Lasorta's jaw dropped. "Fuck. That's a curve, all right. I mourned, even lit a few candles for him. What is this?"

"Just an idea someone had. I'm following it up. He could very well be dead still." Christie smiled at the oddity of the phrasing. "The Social Security number was never used again. Never earned a wage."

"That's it, then. You can't go a whole lifetime without your number. The guy dropped it."

Life. Dropped it.

Christie noted that a four o'clock start from Detroit would get him back at ten. A long day, he had very few facts to add to what he knew, but he did have a growing sense of disquiet about the character study he'd begun.

7

BRIDGET HAD SPENT THURSDAY NIGHT TIPTOEING AROUND THE place or sitting quietly in her room, and being nerdy—*her* room, funny thought—as if he were going to pop back and see her being too free or something. He was the whole way in L.A. for the weekend, so why not cavort or yell or whatever she needed to do to express herself?

He had fetched her between his Thursday class and his flight to take her food shopping. They ran home to eat a quick lunch, and while she put the food away, he began packing a travel bag and put it in the car. He drove her to the office and back home right after she finished work and then he took off. As soon as he left, Bridget felt lonely. Looked out the window at the land. There were no near neighbors. It was a shame she didn't know him well enough to drive him to the airport and then use the car.

Friday morning, the sun was shining brilliantly. What a morning, gorgeous, a gift, an Indian summer Halloween. As she got out of bed, she fretted about clothes; she had nothing good to wear for the interviews she hoped she'd have once she walked into town. Frank had tried to let her off the hook. "Don't bother to job hunt if you don't feel like it," he said. "Relax for a few days. It's okay with me."

As she was making coffee, still wearing her sleeping sweats, her eye caught an old strap-style lawn chair in the back, just outside the kitchen door, and she thought, Why not, why not? It seemed something an adult would do, someone settled. The kitchen door scraped on the linoleum as she opened it, and she heard her stepmother saying, "Have to sand that door down someday." Why, she could do it for him if he had sandpaper. That would be a small enough favor.

Outside, she saw a perfect little crooked table to use with the chair. The ancient table and chair could use a paint job—by Razzi? He didn't seem the type, but you never could tell. There were plenty of crackly autumn leaves on these bits of furniture. Bridget swept them away with her hands. The movement gave her a feeling of elation. Free, she felt free. She walked about the yard stretching. It was cold, but a good kind of cold, brisk, getting ready to warm up. A squirrel watched her, unthreatened. Several birds gathered on a half-broken tree limb just up to her right. *Splat* went the purple shit down to the ground, missing her and making her laugh. Although she'd heard getting hit with it was good luck, still, she'd rather not receive luck in that form. If Jess could see her now, with a whole house to roam in, and grounds around it.

Why not? She went back inside and placed two strips of bacon in a frying pan, cracked two eggs into another, put two pieces of bread into the toaster. She found an old tray under the sink. Okay! When everything was ready, she poured a cup of coffee and took the whole breakfast outdoors. Heaven. She was in heaven. The eggs were delicious. Bacon was something she always craved—meat and fat and salt, what tasted better than that? The toast was nubbly and crisp. No breakfast was better than this, ever.

Thank you, Frank Razzi.

Go look for a job, she told herself when breakfast was done. Then answered herself, I don't want to. I could watch TV all day; he said so. The thought of it made her laugh. She'd never felt this loose, ever. Other people her age slacked off for days at a time, but she was a doer.

It was early yet. The air was still chilly. She took the tray inside. Books, he had lots of books. She could sit outside, read, later watch TV, and still look for work on Monday—and for an apartment, too, a share somewhere—all of that before Razzi got back. Okay. Monday, bus to the university, read the bulletin boards, choose *some*thing. She would not go back to St. Louis, that was for sure.

She selected a book and sat on the couch with a blanket over her knees. All the while she kept thinking she would move herself outdoors, but she drifted to sleep around noon (just like the book's messed-up narrator), and woke at one, feeling just a little worried that languor might overtake her life.

The clock told her to make herself lunch but she wasn't hungry yet, so she decided to earn her keep and clean the kitchen. "If you want to," he said, "if you're not out looking for work or something." Once she got started . . . That's how she was. She put on the radio and began with the stove, then the refrigerator, taking out all the newly bought items and washing shelves and bins with baking soda, then putting the fresh foods back in, just so.

She allowed herself only half a sandwich for lunch, and after she'd eaten, she tackled the cupboards, then wiped down the counters and mopped the floors. By the time she finished at four in the afternoon, the kitchen looked pretty damn good. Her real mother would have approved, yes, absolutely, and she was one very clean woman.

In the bedroom she slept in, Bridget looked in vain for a large mirror, then tiptoed to Razzi's bedroom, where she took off her sweats and looked at herself. She hadn't looked for a year or more, because she didn't care to disappoint herself, and when Jess was around, she was afraid to *think* about herself. She wished she were thinner only because it seemed to breed a certain confidence. It wasn't better in any purely aesthetic way, but still. . . . Five pounds, seven. Wouldn't hurt. If it made her lean and mean.

Finally, she is taking a long hot shower. As she's toweling her hair dry, thinking, How crazy to miss the afternoon outdoors, crazy, she's got to dry her hair and get out there right now, the phone rings. Pick up or not?

From the bathroom, she hears his voice on the machine in the kitchen. "Bridget? Go ahead and answer if you're there."

"Yes?" she says breathlessly.

"Just getting in?"

"No. No, I was just coming from washing my hair."

"Oh, having a good day?"

"I'm having a wonderful day."

"Good. You go in to town?"

"No. I just stayed and cleaned and read. Your kitchen looks gorgeous. I sort of hate to make dinner."

"Order takeout. Have something delivered."

The thought of it, doing whatever she wants, still amazes her. "You'd be just . . . just having lunch now, right?"

There is a little silence and he answers, "Right. In a bit."

"Is everything okay? With your meetings and all?"

"Two hours describing what a Thora Birch type is . . . You're curious about all of this, aren't you? The business."

"You know I am. What is a Thora Birch type?"

"Young and uninhibited, I guess. You can get more story out of inhibition. In my opinion. I can give you my two-bit lectures when I get back."

"Okay." She waits to find out why he called, but another little silence goes by, so she explains, "I'll look for work and a place to live on Monday. I plan to get the house here shipshape, though, before I go. I'm very appreciative. You got me out of a bad situation."

"I was glad to help."

"I'm reading one of the books I found here. I hope it's okay."

"Absolutely okay. Which one?"

"Preston Falls."

"Good one."

"Yeah. It's . . . it's pretty funny. I was thinking, shouldn't I have your cell number? In case I need to get in touch?"

"Not a bad idea." He recited the numbers. "The thing

is . . . use it sparingly. The ceiling fell in on your head, that kind of thing. I'm in meetings most of the time, so it's better if I check in when I can."

"Oh, I agree."

A woman? A woman friend. One in each port. Men do that, even when they're getting over a death, but she feels disappointed in him.

She sits outside as soon as her hair is dry, finishes *Preston Falls* that night, sleeps deeply, and wakes to realize she can eat outdoors again, clean two bedrooms and the bath easily, read something else, walk into the village, where there is a strip mall she noticed when they went shopping, just for the exercise. There's time for everything. She also realizes she is just on the verge of feeling lonely again. By nighttime on Saturday she realizes she *is* lonely. Ecstatic, free, independent, and screamingly lonely.

If she were someone else, someone accomplished in the world, she would walk down to the strip mall where there's a bar that advertises music and dancing. She would order a drink, talk to various strangers, say, "Hey, want to dance?" if nobody asked her. She would feel a little buzz, relaxed, and let herself fall into someone's arms. In her mind, a sinewy working-class man who smells of cigarettes holds her tight. A decent fellow. Maybe not too smart, somewhat undeveloped as a thinker or as a talker, but decent. She'd think, That's okay, why not him?

"Pop your cherry?" he'd ask, surprised. "I'd be delighted. About time, wouldn't you say?"

No, no, he wouldn't say that. He wouldn't be some Brit nerd. He'd be grade-A American beef, her cherry-popper would. He'd say, "Okay, uh, if you're sure." His T-shirt would be a faded navy and it would smell of smoke. His kisses would be wet, eager.

For a moment, she stands outdoors, almost willing herself to walk along the road, where she'd have to watch not to get hit by speeding traffic—down the road to the mall and someone who can like her. But she feels frightened. And there's music and reading and food handy here in

Razzi's house. And even booze. He said to be free with things. He said so.

She reaches back in the cabinet to the right of the sink. Couple of choices. She pulls out a whiskey of some sort. Smelling it just to be sure, then tasting it, just a finger to the bottle and then to her tongue, she thinks, Why not, why not, and pours herself a shot or more in a tumbler and begins to sip.

SURPRISE, ONCE MORE, BY THE WAY THE CONNECTION WAS made finally.

Not looking. Pot not watched. Only going out to buy something for dinner on Friday, plain hunger pushing him, and the pot boiled. There, at a different angle in the other driveway was the son, cleaning his mother's car! They were all there this weekend, he wasn't sure what it was about, but the kids arrived, all right, and there seemed to be life and activity coming out of the place.

As he started for his garage, the boy lifted a wet sponge, nodded. "Hi."

His own hello came out too quiet and then he couldn't think what else to say. Once he got the car started up and backed out of his garage, toward the street, he became aware that the young man had just swerved the hose and shut it off, politely.

Frank rolled down the window to say thanks and looked openly at the young man. He didn't look much like Dan. A little, around the eyes.

"You're the new neighbor?"

"Frank Razzi," he said, extending a hand.

"Welcome. Jeffrey Ross."

"Thank you. Ross did you say?"

"Ross, yeah, not Roth." Jeffrey looked toward the house Frank Razzi had just rented, wondering, no doubt, was there a wife, kids? A girl his age?

Frank said, "Just me most of the time."

"Oh."

"And not even a lot of the time. I have to travel a good bit. Fly, unfortunately. You fly much?"

"Kind of. From school a couple of times a term."

He nodded. "Where's school?"

"Up in Providence."

"Brown!"

"You went there?"

"No, but I had a sister who did. She loved it. What do you study?"

"Film."

Frank froze. He had not expected this kind of luck. He had been about to say he practiced entertainment law or traveled for a company that sold software, but the truth was far more useful. "Film. That's what I do."

"For a living?"

"More or less, yes. I go to L.A. a lot. I lived there until just recently. I don't mean to mislead you, though. I've done more TV than film in the last, say, ten years, but I've done all of it one time or another. The writing end of it."

A whistle. "No fooling. Any chance I could talk to you about it sometime?"

Right in his lap, just like that. "I'm here this weekend. Straight through. Just come to the door. Knock hard enough and I'll hear you." He'd put a phone in, using his ex-wife's name and numbers, so he could hook up his laptop. Who would look for him through Lisa Davis in Pittsburgh? But still, he didn't want to give out phone numbers just yet.

"Thanks."

He drove away, at first thinking he would go to the local supermarket, but once he started moving, he decided to just drive a couple of miles out, to some other neighborhood, do his shopping while the trick-or-treaters came around and thus avoid them.

Jeffrey. Doesn't look like Dan but looks a tad like his old uncle, his old uncle Frank. A bit like young Paul used to look, but better because not quite as ragged and desperate, but . . . Interesting, how that can happen, the old doc's genes leaping around through the generations.

Frank ended up at a market in Edgewood. He added chips and salsa to his cart. That and beer and a little flattery and he'd make friends with the little bugger.

First thing he did upon getting home, something he'd intended anyway, was move the bed from the little room where he watched the house next door to the big bedroom. He'd play music low enough that he would not miss a knock on the door.

No knock Friday night or Saturday day. The family, all dressed up, and not too festive-looking, left the house at five on Saturday. The girl held on to her mother's elbow. The boy walked ahead of them. Took the driver's seat. Something was up.

Patience.

Patience.

Saturday night, Frank sat by the open window and graded papers. When he got hungry, he put on a jacket and put his keys in his pocket, but then stood in the living room, unable to move. Restaurants. He had spent much of his life in them, one way or the other, but now, here . . . Sitting in that bar had buzzed him right up—heart rate, jitters.

He took the jacket off and boiled up some rotini, tossed a little garlic into the olive oil, grated some cheese on it, and ate three helpings. Polished off a bottle of wine. Watched the family next door come home and carry boxes and bags into the house. Would Jeff want to talk career tonight? No. The boy moved the car forward in the driveway and went back inside. Lights burned everywhere in the house. He went upstairs and watched from the little room, standing. For a long time, Elizabeth didn't go to her room. Then the lights went out in other places and she entered the bedroom and opened a book. He could feel the silence. It calmed him until finally he was able to go to the other room, where the bed was now, and sleep.

BRIDGET REALIZES SHE DOES NOT KNOW WHEN FRANK IS COMING back. Today, Sunday? He said he'd be away until when? Was she not listening? He teaches Tuesday, so either Tuesday morning, one of those red-eyes, or maybe Monday night. She realizes she doesn't know which flight he's on or anything like that. Then there's the two-hour drive from Columbus, where the nearest airport is.

It's fifty-five degrees, but sunny, so once more she takes her breakfast outdoors, wishing it were summer.

By Sunday noon, she realizes she's waiting for the phone and this makes her angry with herself. So even though it's early, she walks along the highway, terrified, really, down to the strip mall, where she dawdles in a discount store and then tries the barroom door. Closed. Well, not surprising. Peering though the door's small diamond-shaped window, she thinks about how Frank Razzi's house is now pretty darn clean, but she supposes there is more she can do if she thinks about it. Reorganize the cupboards. Something. Also, she must finally do her own laundry and there *is* a setup of washer and dryer and drying line in the basement.

She would love to be able to mess around on the Net with Frank's computer, but she probably shouldn't. When she gets her own place she will set up an account and maybe, maybe, maybe write to her father. A feeling of oppression hits her to think of Daddy logging on in Egypt or Morocco and saying, Oh, dear, Bridget, wonder what she wants now.

The bar is dark inside, not particularly attractive. Just as she's turning from it, a man approaches with a key aimed at the bar door.

"Desperate for a drink?" he asks. It sounds like a joke, but she isn't sure.

"Just curious."

She hurries away, embarrassed. Desperate. Hardly. She looks about. Do buses run today? She sees none. Sighs. All right. Onward.

Walking back on the highway, she jumps every time a car toots at her, even though *sometimes* it's a friendly warning to keep to the side of the road, not always a blast of irritation. What are you doing endangering yourself at my expense?

one mean driver says by laying on the horn in a long, unvaried monotone.

Back at the house, she makes a sandwich for lunch and reads for an hour. She's started a novel called *The Mourners' Bench*. How interesting. These books he has are so different from one another. She likes this one, too, sad and intriguing. It's got a lot of feeling. The woman in this book pretty much likes the life she's made, all alone, very eccentric, but *hers*, until the man she loves shows up. Would it make a movie? That's how Frank must think about everything he reads. Yes, she thinks it would.

Mid-afternoon, without exactly deciding it, she slips into Frank's room and turns on his computer. She'd hear the car driving up if he came home now, wouldn't she? Take some chances, girl, she tells herself, and she sees with joy that Explorer is available with a click. But her eye goes to a regular folder that says *Friends*. She sees immediately when it opens that it's an episode for the television show by that name. Wild. She reads it, thinking some of the jokes are dumb, but others are okay. How exciting, though. Did he doctor this one or is it original?

Two other files that she opens are the beginnings of something, notes for screenplays? She reads bits of them. He's very prolific, she can see he must have two hundred scripts in there. About eight are for *Cybill*. After two hours she feels mighty guilty and shuts down. He would have to work all the time, wouldn't he, to accumulate that amount? Which means there was limited time for the dying wife and any others, right? She admires productivity, she does.

Tomorrow, look for work. An idle mind is a crazy mind, or something like that.

Thank heavens for *The Mourners' Bench*, which occupies her through the next hours.

THE KNOCK ON THE DOOR COMES AT THREE IN THE AFTERNOON when he has stopped looking, waiting. Jeffrey stands there uncertainly. "You said you'd give me a few minutes," he begins. "I don't know if now is a bad time for you. . . ."

"This is perfect. Give me just a sec." Frank scoops up the papers he's been grading and puts them on a chair, then puts a stack of newspapers over them. He can see Jeffrey standing just inside the doorway, watching him. He's not sure why he's disguising the student work. Habit. To give him options.

"I'm not very moved in yet. Have you had lunch?"

"Yes, thank you," Jeffrey says. "If you haven't, I could come back."

"I had a huge breakfast. Coke, beer, wine?"

"Coke, thanks."

The boy sits in the only chair in the living room. Frank hurries to get out a couple of Cokes and to grab the chips and salsa. When he comes back into the room, Jeff has not moved. "Here. We can just have some chips. All of a sudden, I realized I was hungry. Tell me how I can help."

"Well, I'm a film major, as I told you. There are people who hear that and tell me I'm being impractical."

"Parents?"

"Well . . . no, not them. But I don't want to end up wasting my time. I know it's very competitive everywhere, but especially in anything to do with film. I guess I want to know what your experience was. I wouldn't like living in L.A. I don't think I would. And yet, I think I have to. So I might as well know, what are my chances of actually getting work if I'm somewhere else? And if I really want to do experimental rather than commercial . . ."

Frank nods. He takes his time. He dips a chip in salsa and says, "A lot depends on you. If you're embarrassed to be doing the work, it's going to be hard to get ahead. There was a theatre director, Erwin Piscator—ever read any of his essays?"

"No."

"Said he felt ridiculous working on any kind of fluff after he'd been a soldier in the trenches. World War I. What good was theatre, he asked. Anyway, Piscator started to do political theatre so he could feel better about himself. Serious people in film go through the same thing."

"What kind of film did you do? Do you do." The boy took a chip, dipped, held a hand under it as he brought it to his mouth.

"I worked in a very minor way on *The Killing Fields*. And on *Good Morning, Vietnam*. Actually there were some pretty jerky people invol—"

"I know! Spalding Gray nailed it." Jeffrey is energized by the fact that he knows something about all this.

"You've seen *Swimming to Cambodia*."

"Seen, read it. Love it. What Gray means . . ." He pulls himself up and rephrases. "Sometimes the quality of the product has nothing much to do with the humanity of the people making the product. To me it's like bad presidents doing good things and good ones doing bad." The boy makes a graph of organ pipes with his hands. Up and down. Things happen in columns, he seems to be indicating.

"You're not shocked?" Frank asks.

"No. I figure, in a project like that film, some of what happens is chaos. Some of it is luck. Some is maybe a tiny wave, seed, whatever, at the beginning that was pure and then the people go on to do what they do and get corrupt, but they're still carrying the better intention along with them. I read that Spalding Gray is depressed, even suicidal. That's so sad."

"You bet." The boy was laughable, *young*, but Frank felt almost frightened of him. Yes, he sounded a little like Dan. Talking about purity. Important to be on guard with a person like that.

Jeffrey flushed. "I know I'm talking too much. All that stuff I said about humanity . . ."

"I thought you made sense," Frank said simply.

"Thanks. Well. If I want to be on the editing end of things, at least for a while, I have to be in L.A., right?"

"It would help."

"And what are the steps? After that?"

"Foot in any way you can. Eye out for the chance. Show what you can do. Move up."

"That's your story?"

"It's part of my story." For some reason, he is going to tell the truth. "It's the beginning. I got restless, then bored. I wasn't coming up with what they wanted, which, believe me, is not what you're going to want either. I'm not a success," he said. "Maybe a survivor. I made enough money to live well and to freelance some, as a writer. I did mostly trouble-shooting on other people's projects. It's not what anybody imagines, starting out. I survived way longer than most."

Jeffrey leaned forward, alert. "Where do you teach?"

He had to hold something back, he had to make something up, so he left out the Ohio job and gave one lie, one truth. "L.A. and here. Pitt."

"That doesn't sound like a terrible life to me. Especially the freedom. I could have sworn your car had an Ohio license."

"It does. It's actually my older sister's car, which I am buying from her whenever we get around to the paper-work. She lives in Ohio. Never married. Took care of my father until he died. One of those good souls." There. He felt better, making up a life, and Jeffrey was liking this family portrait.

"The one who went to Brown?"

"Yes."

They talked for a little longer, eating chips. Frank wrote down the names of places that might take summer interns.

"Where do you live out there?" Jeffrey wanted to know.

"I keep a tiny place in Brentwood for when I'm out there, not much more than a hotel room. *Used* to have a tonier place in Malibu." When he felt his ability to invent fading, he unearthed the student papers he'd gone to the trouble of hiding. "These are what I'm doing now," he said. "Got to grade them."

"Thanks for your time," Jeffrey said. "Thank you very much."

Nice enough kid, he thought. Nephew, ha. Nephew. And the kid had liked him. Crazy, though, crazy. What does he do when the kid asks for a letter of rec?

Two hours later there was a tap on the door, and when

Frank answered, he was surprised to see Jeffrey had returned with a large paper bag. "This is food," the boy said, wincing slightly. "I don't know if you want it. There was a . . . a dinner last night and the caterers, who know my mother, insisted on giving her a whole box of food. It was too much for her. She thought maybe you could use some."

"What about you?"

"I'm taking some back to school, and my sister already did when she left. If you don't want it, toss it."

"Thank you," Frank said. "Should it be refrigerated?"

"Probably. There are a couple of steaks, uncooked, and a couple of pieces of chicken that *are* cooked, some bread, some tiny potatoes that would need to be heated up. Do you have a microwave?"

"Not yet."

"Too bad. Things might get dried out. Well, I hope you can enjoy some of it."

"I'll make it up to her."

"Oh, no need."

He watched Jeffrey get packed into the car. His mother was driving him, six P.M. If the Pittsburgh/Providence flight went on time, she'd be back before eight.

SUNDAY NIGHT. DARNELL ARRIVES AT THE POCUSSET SAFE HOUSE without calling first, only four days from his first visit there. His light tapping on the door goes unheard, but after he knocks loudly, a man answers.

"I was wondering if I could stay for a night."

"Come in."

The house is quiet. The man who has let him in is young, black, handsomely dressed. In the background, there is a television going. The man leads him to an office and asks him to sit. "I'm Sherman," he says. "You are?"

"Darnell Flowers."

"How'd you hear about this place?"

"First from a friend. Commander Christie. From the police. Then I came for counseling on Thursday."

"Who brought you on Thursday?"

"I came on my own."

"Today?"

"Same thing."

"Does Commander Christie know you're here?"

"I didn't tell him or anyone."

"What made you come in on a Sunday? You asked about staying?"

"My mother was hitting me with a hanger."

"Why?"

"I don't know. She woke up crazy. I was getting ready to go out and she started on me."

"She wanted you to do something?"

"I don't know. She didn't say. I was getting madder and madder; it's just a hanger, but, man, it stings."

"I'll bet. One of those old wire ones?"

"Yeah. I didn't want to strike back or talk back or any of that. That makes things worse. I held her hand back, that was all. So I just left the house, even though . . . yeah, that's what it was about to begin with. But if I'd've *stayed*, she would've kept after me. I messed around for a long time, just going to the park and stuff. Got hungry. Thought about this place."

"Did you call anyone?"

"Nah. I almost called Commander Christie since he kind of sponsors me, but he has things on his mind. Cases. His family. If I called every time she gets out the hanger, I wouldn't be his friend anymore. I usually just leave the house."

"Who are you seeing here?"

"Ms. Mecon."

"You want me to call her in?"

"No, I don't want to be any trouble. I just wanted to get something to eat and have a place to sleep."

"We'd have to inform your mother. It's a rule. And we ought to give Christie a call, too."

"Jeez." He feels foolish. Man, it was just a hanger. He's had it plenty of times before. What he needs is a job so he has a reason to be out of the house; then, too, with a job, he'd have his own money. That way he could buy whatever food he needed.

"Fill this out. I'll make a few calls. Everything will be okay. I'll make you some dinner."

"Is there anyone else here?"

"No, not tonight. You have to be at school tomorrow? Where is that?"

"North Side. I know how to take a bus."

"We'll see about that. You want to come in the television room? There's some jerky movie on. I was getting into it. You can eat in here if you like."

"Okay."

They go into the adjacent room, where Sherman rattles around in a cabinet, and then a small refrigerator. "You like soda?"

"Yeah."

"Root beer okay?"

"Yeah."

"Here, catch." Sherman does a little feint, then tosses a bag of pretzels over, which Darnell in his surprise almost fails to catch. "Don't think I'd better toss the soda, huh? This isn't dinner. This is just a little something to tide you over." He opens the can and puts it down in front of Darnell. "I'm going to go make my phone calls."

"It's really okay?"

"You picked today. You were making a stand."

Now, sitting there with the pretzels on his lap, the TV going, the heat pumping out, the murmur of Sherman's voice from the other room, he thought, what if he could come here a lot?

He sank into the leather sofa, being careful of crumbs.

Sherman smiled when he came back. "Your mother wasn't too polite, but she accepted it after I said a few things that usually help. Christie is on the phone now, wants to talk to you."

■   ■   ■

WHEN ELIZABETH GETS HOME, SHE FINDS A BOTTLE OF WINE with a note taped to it between her two front doors.

Thanks for the food. It came in handy. Otherwise I would have had to go out, since I've been doing nothing but grading papers. Your son is serious and smart. I hope I helped.

Wine. There's a solution, drink her heartache away. But she does nothing, puts it on the kitchen counter and sinks into the sofa. Twenty days now.

Ten minutes go by. She cannot move. The Pocusset Safe House is open, finally the banquet over with, speeches recorded (Karhakian sycophantic, Christie plainspoken and brief). Christie has had his look at the not-usual suspects. Next week she will deal with the sale of her husband's place in the business and then start on his papers. Things that have to be done will come knocking at her door and it's not in her nature to "put off until tomorrow."

A tap on the door. Literal one. The man who washes windows come to collect on a Sunday night? Kids selling candy? Through the glass panel she sees it's the man from next door.

The tumbling of a lock later, before she can say, "Thank you for the wine," he says, "It's Frank Razzi. I put a bottle of—"

"I got it. Thanks. You didn't have to."

"My pleasure. Wine I've got plenty of. Food I was getting a little low on. Listen, I don't know if you've opened the bottle or not, but I've got a nice bottle open already and some of that bread that you sent me and some cheese I had. I just thought I'd see if you had a couple of minutes to share a glass. Tell me about garbage day and all that."

"Garbage day is Wednesday."

"That works," he says, nodding. "Okay. Well, listen, all I wanted to say is, if you want a little cheese and wine, I've got it sitting on the dining table. I can't grade another paper tonight. I have to take a break. For sanity."

The man has a pleasant smile. He seems eager to get back to his wine and cheese. She sees he is growing a beard, looks like an academic, but also like what Jeff said he was, a media person. What's the clue, the haircut? She puzzles briefly over this. She is ravenous, but bread, cheese, are these things she can get down? Ice cream, she'd thought, or yogurt or cereal. Pudding. Mashed potatoes. "Oh, I don't know."

"Well, it's there. The nine o'clock snack." He begins to move away.

Snack sounds like something do-able, quick, brief. "For a couple of minutes," she says. "I have some things I have to get to tonight."

"You work at home, too?"

"Sometimes."

"Do you want to get a coat, keys?" He moves back to wait for her.

"Just keys. The cold feels good."

She is about to tap the keypad for the security system, when out of pure habit, she pauses. "Go on," she says. "I'll be over in a second."

"I need to get one of those installed," he comments as he leaves. "Another thing on the long list."

She pauses for a minute, then puts on a few lights, looks at the little clock on the table and at her whole place as if from another set of eyes. This furniture, not always her choice, is more traditional than she would have liked. It's made well enough, it's comfortable, but negative on style. If ever she gets her energy back, as everyone keeps telling her she will, she plans to redo the house, make it brighter, but exactly what look she will go for she doesn't know. In a year maybe. She will start getting magazines and study the possibilities. Ten minutes till nine. She doesn't want to stay past nine-fifteen. The man has a slightly needy look. Ha, who is she to cast stones?

She closes the door to her place and for a moment just lets the cold damp air hit her. It moves softly around her legs, curls her hair a quarter inch tighter. To feel something concrete, it's good, elemental, cold air, cold damp ground. She stands there, not wanting to move. She has the idea Daniel is back in the house, the shade of him, admiring the old furniture and protesting her idea to change it. Okay, okay, she relents, it was just an idea. She leaves quietly, as if he's on the verge of falling asleep in the big chair.

HE ARRANGES THE CHEESE, A NOT-VERY-PASSABLE CHÈVRE, A LIT-tle bit of pecorino, medium hard, also not of the best quality. Shaking, he must not shake now.

Her eyes kill him. They are beautiful. What *makes* beautiful? The lashes, the clarity of the whites, the blue that flashes? Maybe. The skin around, the shape. No, more than that. Thought. Grief. The thing about grief that is so beautiful is the way it softens, mutes, confuses, deflects.

He must buy better things from now on. The wine is all right. Should he cut thin slices of the chicken she sent him and reoffer that? No, something tells him no. He puts a few olives on a plate and is slicing a tomato when she taps at the storm door, and he calls, "It's open." She tugs at his storm door and walks in.

She is looking around, surely she is, even though she doesn't seem to be.

He calls to her, "It's nothing to look at, I know. I have a ton of work to do on this place and no time right now. Deadlines."

"You're writing something?"

"Several things." Sounds believable. He wishes it were so, but he hasn't been writing these last weeks, a fact that has to change soon. His laptop is open on the new dining table. Tags cut. "Please, get comfortable, have a seat." He moves swiftly from the kitchen and pulls out a chair. Catching a hint of hesitation, he stands aside and waits for her to sit. He's acting like a waiter, moving the already-poured wine an inch closer. He poured it before she arrived to remove ceremony. Yes, he understands her. She frightens easily. Everything, even the wine, is a betrayal.

Her eyes move quickly, to disguise the fact that she is studying him. She's kind of tricky.

Frank Razzi, safe, safe, he tells himself.

He does not clink her glass, but takes a sip of his own

wine. He's already got a whole bottle of it in him. Red badge of courage. "Ah, what am I thinking of?" He goes to the kitchen and fetches the plate with the tomato and olives and two other dinner plates—too large for the nine o'clock nibble, but all he has in this place.

"My son says you were honest with him. Which he appreciated. He is so afraid of making mistakes."

"That isn't good."

"I know it."

"The best things happen when you're not thinking like that."

"I know."

"This is not a very good cheese. I know the difference, honestly, but the supermarket didn't have anything better."

"You have to go down to the strip."

"Oh, where is that?"

"Penn Avenue, almost downtown. That's where you have to go for cheese."

" 'Strip'?"

"There are a couple of different routes you can take."

"I'll check a map. Thanks." What would happen if she looked into his garbage and saw the wrapper from the Kroger's in Athens? A small problem, but he likes it. The sister in Ohio is ready to be conjured if he needs her.

"It's not bad. I've tasted worse." She breaks the bread into tiny pieces and spreads the cheese on. She takes an olive. Good. Sips the wine. Good. He has to try hard not to stare at her.

"You travel back and forth to L.A.?" she asks.

And he tries to talk comfortably. "I have a teaching job out there and a small job here. Just one seminar at Pitt. Mostly I freelance. But. I got tired of the life out there. This is a good city for housing, so I decided to make my base here. This house would be five times more expensive out there."

"Five times?"

"I'm not exaggerating. I'd rather put in my time and money on the flights, because I'd rather live here than there."

"How many times a week do you have to fly out there?"

"Once. Middle-of-the-week classes, Wednesday and Thursday usually." Aha, he sees the problem now, but he knows how to finesse it.

"I would hate all that traveling," she says quietly.

"Ah. Well, it's hard. I had a trip the beginning of the week, last week when I first moved in. . . ."

"I remember."

"That was to New York."

"The hot spots."

"If you want to call them that. I think the only thing I miss is the food."

"You just have to know where to look here. Food can be managed. Good wine is harder because of our state system. This is excellent." She turns the bottle, studying it. "Margaux. Not a local wine," she almost kids. "Which store did you—?"

"I don't remember." She takes another sip. "I think that bottle I already had. From Ohio. When I stayed with my sister."

"I know people who go to Ohio just to buy wine."

"That seems extreme."

She nods, sighing.

He *should* have asked her what she does for a living. He *knows* what she does and so he forgot to ask. A misstep there.

She eats another piece of bread, looking around the room openly.

"It's awful, I know. I have no time. It's like a camp."

"No, it's not awful. There's something comforting about it. Walls and floor and a place to sit. It kind of echoes, though." She smiles, so something is right. She's relaxing.

"Easy to clean, look at it that way."

"That, too."

"The bread is what you sent me. Tell me where to go for bread, then."

"The deadly baguette," she says, taking another piece. "I love white bread no matter what bad things I hear about it. I like either Breadworks or Bread Company."

"Addictive." He calculates, moves forward, left and straight, knight to queen. "The problem is, they're not all that good in France most places. You have to be just as picky there." Little flicker of something there. Okay. "Well, I guess you know that."

"I keep hearing. I haven't been for a while."

"It's true." He nods. He manages to take brief looks at her, and he already has a strong sense of the way her hair waves, how bright her eyes are. Could he draw her nose, mouth? No, not yet. She wears a black sweater and black pants. Silver earrings that twinkle under her hair. He plain out likes her. He would, even if he didn't know who she was.

France is a good subject, he deduces. And food. He doesn't ask, nor did he ask Jeffrey, the things he most wants to know. What does she think, what does she feel?— although he can guess. How are they all coping, although he has bits and pieces of the family's calm public dignity. And he's seen her private grief and solitude, watches it when he can.

She eats hungrily. She's ravenous.

"Furniture stores. Not that I have time now, but where are the good ones? Not too expensive."

She looks surprised and sympathetic. "There's a strip in Shadyside with a couple of stores. A Pottery Barn, a Weiss, a Baker's, but that's expensive. There's something on the South Side, the name won't come to me, a little bit funky. It's a long time since we've bought furniture. There are the department stores, of course. Then there are those highway strips with big stores. Either go toward Monroeville and read the signs or get onto McKnight and you see the same thing."

"I wish I had an eye, as they say." He goes to pour her more wine.

"No, not any more for me." Her hand rests gently on top of the glass.

He needs to buy wineglasses. He bought only two when he swept through Ikea. As he pours more wine into his own glass, he says, "Hopefully this will get me through the last batch of papers. I probably won't be able to rest unless I do them tonight." He smiles at her.

"Jeff said you only just started teaching."

"Just lately. My life seems to be shifting away from the . . . the extroversion, toward a kind of almost quiet and meditative life."

"Better for writing, I would think."

"There are different theories about that, I guess, but better for me in general. You teach?" She looks surprised by the question. "Your son didn't say, I just wondered."

"No, I'm a therapist."

"What sort?"

"Psycho." She almost laughs.

"You fix people all day."

She purses her lips as if he's too dumb to understand how it really works. "I try to be useful. Whatever that means."

She's going to be flinty, the way she closes off suddenly like that. Not that that deters him. Flashes of haughtiness don't put him off. Like attracts like.

"I have to go," she says, looking at her watch. "I have a lot of work to do tonight." She stands and wavers unsteadily. He gets up to support her but she has righted herself with one hand on the table and the other out to assure him she's fine. "Thanks for talking to my son."

"Anytime. Thanks for your company." He walks her to the door.

"I hope the papers turn out to be interesting," she says.

"They will. They are. I'm not jaded. Not in that. I'm just . . . tired." He sounds like a candidate for a turn-of-the-century tonic. Loss of will? Loss of appetite? Those things are called depression in her line of work. He says, "Okay, and a little down. But some depression is justified, don't you think? As a real, honest reaction to life."

"Yes, I do."

"Well, I'm working my way back. Slowly."

"Good for you. Thanks again. Good night."

■   ■   ■

ELIZABETH SHIVERS ON THE WAY HOME. LAST THING SHE WANTS is to play therapist to someone in her off-hours. Although he wasn't asking. In fact, just the opposite. The new neighbor is right about the fact that some things you just slug through alone.

Food. It tasted good. She could have eaten more, but she didn't want to stay. She ate hardly anything at the banquet last night and she skipped over the food at breakfast and lunch today, until Lauren noticed and gave her a lecture. Supper she missed, taking Jeff to the airport.

In her kitchen, she removes from the refrigerator a rind of cheese and from her freezer an unbaked loaf of bread. It's almost funny that she's given away food again, but at the time, she didn't want it and now she does.

While the oven is heating, she rattles around for something else in the cupboards. Some roasted peppers, all right. A tinned version of good salmon, even better. She puts most of this on a tray, thinking how pretty it looks. The bread will take a while, so she switches on the small kitchen television and watches—what else?—news, the current idea of entertainment. Iraq, and other horrors. Her taste buds request another taste of the wine she had one glass of. Well, there it is, waiting for her. She opens the bottle and pours some into a tumbler, wondering if she'll have a headache tomorrow since a second glass usually produces one. Sipping, she waits for the bread.

Finally, she carries everything upstairs to the room they called the home office, she and Dan. It holds her file cabinet and his. And now it also holds one crate of files Christie returned to her today and that Jeff carried up. At first she sorts through a handful of folders, sitting at the desk, and eating. Then she takes the wine and folders over to the sofa.

"Tax materials, 1999." "Tax materials, 2000." "Tax materials, 2001." She will have to do taxes on her own now. How organized he was. New Products. In that folder are articles he's clipped about everything from tongue depressors to heart-monitor machines for infants. Elizabeth touches the

Post-it, a note in his handwriting that says, *Copy to hospital purchasing.* Then she reads the typed note.

Dear Dr. Holtz, This is another article on the machine we talked about the other day when I was in the hospital. As I said, it's been in use in a few places (I can get you more details) and is superior to the ones we have in the ER of Children's Hospital. The buying contract we now have precludes our getting the better machine. I would like to ask your help in finding funding for this machine or figuring out how to do a special amendment to the ongoing contract that allows purchase of a superior instrument from another maker. Let's talk soon. Anytime. Call my office and I will arrange something. Sincerely, Dan Ross.

He was still fighting the system on this when he died. He's here in this correspondence, polite always, even when at odds. Did Christie find anger here?

In her mind the scene she's constructed plays again. A boy, nervous. Wants something, money or drugs. Words of anger. Dan tries to be reasonable, not frighten the boy.

A wave of nausea hits her. She closes her eyes against the rest of it. But she is not crying. Why? Alcohol, the turn-of-the-century tonic, depressive in itself, but it mutes things, doesn't it, the great buffer. And it tastes good, too. She takes another drink. Her body says, No, can't, no more. She's lucky in that, she supposes.

"Last Will and Testament, Robert Ross." His father's will bequeathing the money that ended up in the Pocusset Safe House. "Let's make my father's money mean something," Dan said. "We don't need it for ourselves."

"We're not *rich.*"

"But we're okay. We'll always work. I want the kids to work for what they have. Every kid I've seen who's been on the dole is spoiled. We need to have something to retire on, yes, I agree. . . ."

"With some luxury, I hope."

"What luxury?"

"Good hotel rooms in Europe."

"That I promise you, if that's what you want."

"If we ever get there."

"Touché. But it's the most amazing thing. The very house Ted Luckey used, the one he called his 'safe house,' is up for sale. For peanuts. It's a sign. We could really do something important."

No way to say no to that. A man with values and a vision.

The rest of the folders she's grabbed are the ones they both used, the common folders in his cabinet. "Brown University, Info." Mostly it holds the form letters they send parents. "Brown University, Statements." This one holds just that, bills. Which she'll be paying. "George Washington University, Info." The information sheets with their bits of proselytizing. "George Washington University, Statements." The bills. "USAirways." Various tickets from last year. Frequent flyer numbers for the family. She begins to put them back into the almost-empty drawers where the remaining manila folders sink with the slack.

Insurance. She needs this folder, for she has an appointment on Tuesday evening with the agency's attorney. Once more she turns over the strange idea that money can somehow make up for a loss by becoming something concrete, desired: new furniture, a vacation.

Someone thought, He's a doctor, he's rich, he'll have tons in his wallet. They didn't know he was the sort who *gave* it away. He was alone, unprotected. Someone wanted three dollars, ten, twenty, whatever they could get for drugs, maybe for food. He stopped and talked, trying to help. He saw something was wrong, but he didn't run the guy down. If she keeps imagining the scene, will it come to her one day, whole?

8

IT'S THE HAIR AND HER GENERALLY DORKY WAY, BRIDGET FIG-
ures, that get in the way of employment. By Monday at five,
she has filled out no less than twenty applications for
everything from secretary to waitress to bartender, and
now she plods up the road, walking against traffic, in the
only shoes she owns that were appropriate for job-hunting.
Sort of flats, small raised heel. With the short black skirt,
plain sweater—really dorky-looking. What else is new?

Not that she wants any of the jobs. And, unfortunately,
she is honest, so she had to leave blank the spaces where
she was asked what past experience qualified her for the
jobs she didn't want. Where's the brokerage firm analog,
the *Working Girl* world, where she can rise up in some organization and either skip school or make enough dough
to pay for it?

Her goal used to be a university job with tuition benefits,
but Platt has made that a virtual impossibility. She's put in
applications to a law firm and a doctor's office, about the
only professional settings outside the university in Athens.

What are your goals?

Enough money to get out of town.

In the six or seven mini-interviews she had, she found
herself trying to hide the ends of her hair, and thinking
she should have just cut off the neon parts before heading
into town.

Try not to be negative, she counsels herself as she trudges back to Frank's place. Maybe someone will call.

At the bank she deposited most of her check but didn't buy herself lunch, except if you count the big pretzel, because she's still mighty nervous about money. Her stomach sets up a large protest she can hear even with traffic whooshing by.

An insistent tapping horn makes her jump and move as far to her left as possible, even though the sound is coming from way over on the opposite side, which makes no sense. The horn-blower pulls over onto the berm on his side and toots again. Frank Razzi, smiling, beckoning, motioning that she should cross the road carefully.

Which she does, aware suddenly of how much her feet hurt. She limps to the passenger door.

"Not a moment too soon, eh?" he says.

"This is lucky. I spent the whole day job-hunting. I'm winded and wounded. I guess I'm not very athletic."

"Neither am I. How did it go?"

A groan is her answer. When she gets some food into her, she can maybe make it all entertaining, but not now. "How did your West Coast stuff go?" she counters.

"Very well." He's wearing jeans today and a nice tan shirt. Leather jacket in the backseat on top of the overnighter. This is airplane wear, she figures, but also the way people dress in L.A. in the media business. If she could earn enough money to stake herself, she would just go out there. Leaving Athens does not have to mean going back to St. Louis.

"What time did your flight get in?"

"Hmmm?" He looks at his watch as if the answer is written there. "Two-thirty. Two-nineteen, something like that."

"Baggage claim takes time," she says cautiously. "But then you don't have any baggage, really. Did you check something?"

In a manner reluctant to come back from some inner world to deal with her, he explains. "No. But we taxied forever on the runway. Even so, I made great time."

"Well, I'll cook something tonight as part of my employment as your housekeeper."

"Housekeeper? Very Victorian," he chuckles.

"Wait till you see how clean the place is. I'm kind of proud of it. I know how to bake a chicken and put in a baked potato. I can make a salad."

"*Roast a chicken,* the phrase is. Even I can do that. We'll order in. Chinese. You can surprise me with a chicken meal Wednesday night."

"How about tomorrow?"

"Tomorrow I have to go somewhere."

"Oh." She thought she might be gone by Wednesday, or rather *ought to* be gone, but then if the place keeps being empty . . . "Do you have to leave on Thursday again?"

"I do."

"What a life. Exciting."

"I want to hear all about your day in town."

"There isn't much to tell. Nobody's offered me a job yet. I had to give your home phone in case somebody *wants* to. I'm sorry about that, but I had no other way to get the message."

"It's okay."

"I sort of covered most places. Tomorrow I'll go into the university and read the bulletin boards for apartments."

"Bridget?" His voice has a minor, little-boy quality for a second. "Remember I said I had some work for you? I can't pay you a lot. Room and board and a couple of dollars will make it a bit above minimum wage. Is that too awful?"

"It's not awful at all, but—"

"I doctored two screenplays last week. I have some on disk, some on the hard copy, wrote a few new scenes. I could use the help. Then I could get to my own work."

"I just hope I'm capable."

"I suspect you are. I'm going to put my trust in you." Just about then he pulled onto the dirt road that led to his house. It narrowed and finally branched off.

Bridget wished once more she had a car. A bike. She

should spring for an old unwanted bike! Where would she find the ads for such a thing?

But Razzi is in good spirits. She helps him cart things into the house. Overnight bag, laptop, jacket. "See how clean everything is?" she asks.

He nods soberly, then walks about inspecting everything. "My room, too?" But of course he can see it's so. "Amazing. You must have worked the whole time." He pats her shoulder and withdraws his hand.

"Well, no, I read three books."

"What books?" he asks.

"I told you. On the phone. Don't you remember?" Middle-aged memory loss? With a twinge of disappointment, she names all three again.

He says, "I haven't read *The Mourners' Bench* yet, but I can take it with me when I'm on the move next weekend."

"Gosh, I'm sorry I read it before you got to it yourself."

"Nonsense. Books should be read. They get lonely sitting on a shelf."

"Will it be L.A. again?"

He needs a moment to understand her question. Then he says, "Yes. On Thursday. It's what I do. Oh. Sally and I are on the outs. I'm here tonight. Don't worry. I'll be way out of your way."

He takes his things to his room, closes the door, and stays in there for a little while. Bridget fetches the car keys from the kitchen counter and checks out the backseat and the trunk to see if there is anything else she can carry in. The box of wine that was in the trunk is gone, all twelve bottles gone. What, he slugs it at the airport? Or Sally took it before dumping him? He's been driving around somewhere, too. The odometer is way up.

Frank orders enough Chinese food to keep her in lunches for a week. Egg-drop soup, moo shoo pork, fried rice, shrimp in lobster sauce, egg rolls. An Asian delivery boy hands over a large brown bag full of cartons.

"You don't think you overdid it?" Bridget asks.

"Take your shoes off and put your feet up."

"What if we get food on the sofa?"

He shrugs. "Buy a new sofa." They eat in the living room with the television on, watching about ten minutes of *The King and I*. "You want to see what inhibition can do for a story," he says, "watch *From Here to Eternity*. Some people only see the cool surface, but oh, no, watch her. Terrific." He nods to the TV. He means Deborah Kerr. Bridget's face gets a little numb on one side from the MSG, but she doesn't mention it because she doesn't want to ruin the mood. Her fortune cookie says, *You will succeed at what you are doing*. His says, *Even if you have tried before, you must try again*. He rolls his eyes and looks suddenly tired at the thought of it. He takes something out of his pocket, two pill containers, from which he shakes a pill each and tosses them back with his beer.

Bridget hopes Frank is not ill in some sort of serious way. This does not seem the right time to ask about the pills, so she takes a sip of her beer and watches. That's who she is, and always has been, the watcher. She sips, tries not to wince at the bitterness, alternates with a glass of water.

"How about a game of Scrabble?" she asks.

He looks a little bit angry, not to mention surprised. "Where'd you find a board?"

"I had one with my things." Has she been too forward, too proprietary?

But then he gets thoughtful. "Wednesday you're on. Are you good at Scrabble?"

"No, not at all. I'm not even sure why I suggested it."

"Unfortunately, I have work to do tonight. Tomorrow morning I'll show you what I want you to do. The script stuff."

"How long will the work take?"

"What I'm going to give you, three days, but I have some of my own work needing the same treatment. Altogether, say, two weeks."

"Wow. That's a lot."

"I have a lot going on. For the rest of tonight, kid, you're on your own. Sorry. TV is okay. It won't bother me. Oh. I

should bring you a couple of videotapes from the office."
He begins to gather himself up. "You said almost nineteen
years old, huh? What happened to that year?"

"I lost two years of school when I was thirteen and fourteen. Schlepping around Turkey with my father and stepmother. The school back home wouldn't let me skip two
years, but I was able to skip one."

"Ah. You lost your friends, your age group, too, probably. Right?"

"Yeah." It surprises her that he can think about such a
thing when he can't remember which books she borrowed.

"Go ahead with the TV if you want. Nothing bothers me."

She watches for a while, then picks up another book.
Being Dead. Intriguing title. When he comes out of his
room, she asks, holding the book up, "You don't mind?"

"Not at all. Good, huh?"

"You looked at it for a movie?"

"I can't help looking at things that way even when
they're not available."

At ten-thirty, she closes the book and listens to him
typing—not fluidly. It's the seven-key, one-key tap of Internet browsing. She tiptoes to her room, locks the door, and
keeps reading.

FOR OVER A WEEK, CHRISTIE AND THE ATLANTIC CITY POLICE
department missed each other. When they finally did connect on Tuesday morning, Christie asked his question.

His counterpart, Ted Rawson, said, "Oh, shit." Christie
waited him out. "I got a dead hooker today and two dead
druggies from a couple days ago. Yesterday a twenty-year-
old girl unconscious, we can't find the boyfriend. This is
real old shit you're asking about."

"I know that. It might be important."

"I'll have somebody look it up and give you a call as
soon as that's possible. If you want my honest opinion,
you shouldn't hold your breath for at least a week."

"Do your best." Before he made a fool of himself he

wanted to see what the death of Paul LaBeau, or Gerald Paul, as it was then, looked like on paper.

"Let me write this down. What is it you're going to want again?"

"The autopsy reports and the investigations report. I know you can fax those. But I'm curious if there's anyone who remembers and also if any specimens were kept—"

"I wouldn't hold my breath. Our specimens lab has been moved three times. Once one of our sweet killers tried to shoot it up to get rid of evidence."

"How did he know where it was?"

"Don't ask." The Atlantic City Police Department wasn't known for its hospitality. "I'll get back to you," Rawson barked.

Christie had a nagging feeling that some piece of paper might be removed from the files and he'd never know. "I could send somebody to help look through things," he offered. Dolan, Coleson, McGranahan, he ticked off. One of them could take the wife and hit the slot machines, have dinner. Who would like that best? McGranahan.

"Let me get it started. Let's talk later this week."

As he hung up, a frowning Dolan was heading toward his office. Dolan came in, saying, "Man, I haven't found a park or bus-stop regular on the whole North Side knows anything about who dropped that wallet. Best I got was *maybe* some kind of black foreign car, *maybe*."

"There'd be a lot of those around. Make, year?"

"Don't kid me," Dolan laughed.

DARNELL ARRANGED TO STAY SUNDAY, MONDAY, AND TUESDAY in the Pocusset Safe House until things cooled down with his mother. She was invited in for counseling but she refused to come. On Monday, the house was busier. Another kid came in that night to stay, and there was counseling going on, people coming and going. But most of the time, it was lonely.

On Sunday night, Sherman had washed his clothes and handed them to him fresh on Monday morning. On Tuesday, Sherman offered a change of clothes. A pair of jeans and a Steelers sweatshirt. Darnell hesitated. People would know these weren't his clothes. They might laugh. He was about to say no when he saw Sherman's expectant smile. He took the clothes and wore them. All day he felt different. Wearing a new identity, it felt like, and after a while, he liked the feeling.

When he got to the Investigative Branch on Tuesday after school, Christie was there, waiting for him. They talked a bit and Christie drove him up to the Pocusset Safe House since Sherman was expecting him for dinner up there. After Christie left, Darnell took a long pee in the bathroom and washed his hands well. He stood at the bathroom window for a moment, thinking the rhythm of the driver of the black BMW that drove by was kind of funny, the sort of thing he'd report if Christie wanted any of his observations. Which he didn't. Christie wanted him to study and keep his nose clean and that was about it.

ELIZABETH MET THE INSURANCE MAN AT HIS OFFICES DOWN-town on Tuesday at six. He was Bennie Smith, short, blunt, with a brush cut and an expensive suit. "A square guy," she heard Dan say teasingly, and she smiled to herself at this reminder of his voice.

The square fellow opened a file folder so carefully, it might have been wired for explosives. "First let me say how sorry I am about your loss."

"Thank you."

"It must be harder with no closure."

"Yes."

"Well. I had all of this ready, but I didn't want to bother you. The police were here, of course, and I gave them the same information about the policies. Our own investigators have cooperated completely with police."

She almost laughed to think she was a suspect. Everything was graceless now. Nodding to Smith to go on, she thought, Just be quick.

"Your husband took care to leave you with enough

money that if you wished you could retire early—now, in fact. Now, you wouldn't be rich, but you could live."

"He knew I wanted to work for a long time."

"That may be the case, but he did provide. And there is enough for college tuition. He talked to me personally about that. He wanted tuition and living expenses, a little start-up capital beyond that, but not a lifetime trust."

"We all talked about that as a family."

"Good. Well, the only thing is, we've been asked not to cut a check until our investigators give us clearance. Does that burden you?"

"I can manage. My bigger question is the lag time in the business. It costs money to run it before the buyer's transaction is complete."

"Oh, we accounted for that in the business policy. Insurance should give you a check for the amount of earnings until the business is sold. However, investigators still have to give the go-ahead," he said formally. She almost laughed, suddenly, because Smith appeared ridiculous to her, money was ridiculous, and people who dealt in it. Vertigo swept over her. The whole thing was comical, unreal, like an old Angela Lansbury episode.

"Here are the figures." He handed over four sheets of paper, which she studied before leaving.

The parking garage was dark, since some of the lights seemed to be out. It, like everything else, reminded her of the night her husband was alone, going to his car. In her fumbling, she hit the car horn accidentally and a woman rushing to her car jumped. "Sorry," she said aloud, but the windows were closed, and the poor woman she'd frightened didn't hear. Elizabeth started her own car up and handed a ticket and a ten-dollar bill to the sentry.

She had no food at home still, so she drove to the Giant Eagle on Murray, but before she went in, she realized she wasn't up to the glaring lights and the crowds of shoppers. Instead she walked across the street to Gullifty's, also glaring and crowded, but it had a darkened front bar, where she ordered a takeout dinner of fried chicken. She waited, in the dim light, drinking a bottle of water while she imagined a cook plunking down her order check, pinning it back up to the wire, and dumping her chicken into a fryer.

Music from somewhere.

Time passes—how much, she isn't sure.

"Elizabeth? Is that you?" A woman she knows from when her children were young comes toward her. She can't remember the woman's name.

"Yes. It's me."

The woman has those tiny inadvertent backing-away muscles at the ready. "I heard on the news. I'm so sorry."

"Thank you."

"He was so wonderful with our kids. I just wanted to tell you that."

"Thank you."

"Take care of yourself, now." The woman's eyes drop to the bottle of water.

"I will. I have fried chicken coming."

The woman whose name she doesn't know looks hopeful. Grease and salt and carbohydrate, her face says, these show you will make it. "Enjoy it." The woman catches herself on the briars of the many things she might say that would be wrong.

"I hope it's good," Elizabeth says simply.

"Take care," the woman says, and backs away.

Seen, living. Grief is so unseemly. Karhakian is wrong. Nobody wants to be around her.

All around her the air is filled with television sounds and the thrum of conversation. The killer is probably somewhere in the city, walking around, having a drink, popping a pill, shooting up. Or sitting in a place like this.

She has time to think about work. A teenager today who is feeling powerful because she's gone down on ten boys, counting trophies, as so many of them do. A thirty-year-old who is having an extramarital affair. Tomorrow, Harry Vittles, who got himself a date last week. There is time to review the roster a couple of times before the chicken is ready.

■   ■   ■

". . . STANDARD PLOTTING," HE IS SAYING, "IN WHICH THE CHAR-
acter is searching, pursuing, whether it's a day off from
high school"—he gets his laugh—"or getting out of prison
and having a tasty morsel and a good bottle of Chianti."
He gets his laugh.

Stand-up comedy might have been an option. Way back
when. But he's losing energy all of a sudden, so, as if there's
an actual transition, he pushes the button and lets
Casablanca play. He knows every frame. He knows it so well,
he almost can't talk. But soon enough the film prompts
him. "Did you notice how she is dressed? Ilsa? Her outfit
matches—what?" Nobody answers, so he does. "Rick. Rick.
They're paired." It was lucky Bergman could wear anything
and look great, give her a tie and a fedora, she comes out
gorgeous. . . . "And notice the stripes here and the slatted
venetian blinds there. You see? Everything fits. Was this a
conscious design choice? Yes. Lucky? Yes, also that."

He twitches. He's very tired. When you think about it,
he's working mighty hard these days. Driving back and
forth like a maniac, like a lover, requited.

"Pursuit. The war effort. Victor Laslo drives the thing.
Is his name an accident, I wonder? His life work once
made Ilsa pursue love. Ilsa's supposed betrayal makes Rick
pursue what?"

He waits. Nobody wants to answer. Talk is an interruption. They are watching the film and wish he would just
shut up.

He hates to wait, so he answers. "A life of pleasure and
forgetting."

"Is that a pursuit?" one boy asks, to show he is listening.

"Is it?" he hands the question back. You bet it is.

"It seems more like revenge," a girl says.

That's true, too.

He talks in and around the moments of the film. "How
many of you have seen this before?" Only a third raise

their hands. Amazing. "Well, after you watch it with me talking, I suggest you watch it again on your own."

When he's finished with class, he drives home through the park and takes the out-of-the-way road—well, only a few blocks—so he can get a look at the Pocusset place again, which he couldn't see very well when he drove by earlier. Can he get Elizabeth to talk about it? This idea of her husband's started the whole thing. Pursuit. Dan was pursuing an obsession while he was pursuing his freedom. Or maybe he wanted a life of pleasure and forgetting.

Subverting himself, he drives by the thing that's now called the Pocusset Safe House once again. Who would know it, all cleaned up and painted. How did they get the mold out? What did they do with the books? And the addition, double the size of the original, what is it for? He can't help but be curious.

When he drives to his own house, there's the luck again—she is just getting out of her car with a bag that appears to be food. Will she want company? He ate only a pretty bad turkey burger at Pitt. He taps the horn.

She nods. Brusque. Busy tonight, her nod says.

THAT SAME TUESDAY EVENING, BRIDGET FLUMPS ONTO THE sofa, in a kind of bad mood because she knows absolutely nothing and can't figure out how she keeps forgetting to ask Razzi the right questions. He went somewhere again after class. Surely not L.A. this time, because there isn't enough time, so maybe Sally is back on after all, unless he has a new woman. And anyway, where did the wine go last time on the weekend? Not to L.A. She's not ready to believe he carried coals to Newcastle. No, it seems more likely he stopped off somewhere, but she knows nothing. What if someone called and asked, "When will he be back?" Again, she doesn't even know that. In town or out? He took a packed bag to class today and that was that, magic disappearance. If it's Sally back in the picture, why not say so? He's planning to be somewhere. Then what? Go straight to school tomorrow and do his office hours and then come home? He teaches Tuesday, Wednesday, Thursday; you'd think she'd know when to expect him. Promising herself to look at the odometer again, she flicks the remote control and settles into an old *Frasier* on cable.

An idea hits her suddenly that maybe Frank is sick. The idea has a certain appeal. He takes pills, after all. In a fantasy that might be spawned by the sitcom, he has an appointment tomorrow at the Cleveland Clinic. He's getting into bed in some motel right now, fasting in order to have tests in the morning. Frank Razzi sits up in bed contemplating his mortality while she heats up and eats leftover Chinese food. Well, tomorrow she will just ask straight out where he went. Why bother to wonder?

She does not miss anyone, except her mother, who is dead, but not her father, stepmother, aunt, Jess and company, high school buddies, nobody. And except Frank Razzi a little bit, but that's another kind of thing, more a need for continuity. When she goes to the kitchen to scrape her plate, she makes sure everything is there for tomorrow's dinner.

The work she did today was all reading and noting discrepancies. And she got distracted looking at her future work, for this morning he hauled up from the basement three cartons filled with pages. Her job will be (when she's finished with his current script-doctor work) to find sequences in each of the drafts of some twenty different projects that seem to be pretty much his. Sometimes a folder will stop at sixty pages, sometimes at a hundred and forty.

There are stray pages everywhere. To do justice to the assignment, she will have to speed-read everything again and again. He said he expected the work to take a pretty long time. And it will. But does he actually *need* these scripts or is he pretending in order to give her charity? Sometimes she suspects the latter.

She's stacked the cartons in her room because they look so bad everywhere else.

She turns the TV off and starts again on the doctored

scripts. It's so weird to *read* a TV script. It's almost like *watching* the tube. She's read a documentary on Andrew Carnegie, one on Roberto Clemente. Another, different, *Friends* episode.

A little of everything. Not that anybody's asking her to judge, but it seems like pretty good, if not brilliant, startling, work. In the biz, they don't want anything too edgy or standout, anyway.

Frank told her he would let her use his computer tomorrow! As if he needs to be there to launch her. Is he afraid she doesn't know how to use one? At one point, she puts everything aside and tiptoes into his room, where she leans forward and presses the ON button. Looks simple enough. Internet comes up automatically again. She clicks on EXPLORER and types in *Orbitz,* idly.

RETURN and she's in Orbitz. Ha. She will not abuse this. Only find his flight.

After studying the screen, she decides he must fly America West. It's the only really logical choice. Even she, living in poverty, would pay an extra fifteen bucks to fly direct. Surely he wouldn't choose USAirways, which would take him inefficiently east to Pittsburgh before west to L.A. There's Northwest, but he'd have to go to Memphis or Detroit or Minneapolis on the way, which can't be fun. Ha. Even America West (for *more* money) is willing to offer him a layover in Phoenix! She checks the recent activity button to see if there are any plane reservations on the computer, but there are not. She goes back to the schedules of America West flights out of Columbus.

Bridget looks around furtively and then presses the buttons she believes will make the printer print out this information, which she plans to put in her room for reference. But once the computer sends the message to the printer, the brain of it goes crazy and it wants to tell her about *all* the flights, all the airlines, all the possibilities. No matter which keys she pushes, nothing will stop it. Paper falls to the floor. The printer spits more out, trying to tell her every damned flight that exists from Columbus!

"Jeez," she says, "enough already," and she looks out the window, terrified, praying he does not, for some reason, drive up now.

When the printer sighs to a stop, Bridget gathers the papers and gets everything shut off. Whew. Lights, too.

In her room, she decides he probably will fly out on the 5:20 on Thursday and get back at 4:03 on Monday. Doesn't quite match when he said he got in last time, but he has a hazy manner and maybe he got it wrong.

Where he is now is another mystery. Chiding herself for wondering, she reminds herself he owes her nothing. It's the other way around. He is giving her money, food, a place to live. If he has to cat around like a jerk, well . . .

Or maybe the Cleveland Clinic, being given the bad news. Lungs. Inoperable.

Or good news. There was a shadow on the X-ray last time but it turns out his lungs are free and clear, perfect little drums. Bellows.

Should she tell him she's worked ten hours today? Will he toss another twenty her way? She throws open the back door and shouts, "Hello. Hello." And because it feels so good to hear her voice, she shouts, "Calling Central," then "Move those cameras in, now." Then, "Places, everyone."

Chortling, she goes back inside and goes blank in front of the TV.

He's home before nine in the morning on Wednesday, futzing in his room with this and that to take to the office. So, Cleveland Clinic is out, probably. In fifteen minutes at his computer, he points out to her five files she will need for her current work.

He gets in again at four in the afternoon, with a bouquet of flowers and a videotape of *Chinatown*. As soon as he's set these things down, he goes back out to the car and brings in a box, which he places temporarily near the bookcase. "Some tapes for you. When you want to watch." He takes a few out and stacks them horizontally on the bookcase.

"Do you want any help?"

"No." He leaves the box and comes to her where she's

standing in the kitchen, looking out. He puts a hand under her chin. "No. You don't have to be a servant. You're . . . you're fine."

Her face flushes with confusion. "What time is good for dinner?"

His smile is a pursed-lip affair. He appears to be figuring something as he continues stacking tapes and nods toward the one on the coffee table. "I have to review that film for class. How about if we watch it together—if you're not busy—having a few glasses of nice wine while we do. Then you start dinner."

"Okay. If I start it then, it won't be ready till eight-thirty." She looks at her watch to be sure. "Yeah, eight-thirty." She's hungry now, but she knows some people eat very late.

"We can have something to snack on while we watch. What's in the house?"

"Crackers. Peanuts."

He moves past her and begins to open cabinets. When he turns, he is holding a tiny can. "Salmon mousse," he says. "You spread on crackers or toast points or whatever."

Crackers, then, if she's the one getting things ready. Good old, plain old crackers. When she brings everything into the living room and sits down, he pats the sofa next to where he's seated.

"No, I'm okay." She has chosen the high-backed armchair.

"Is that a Scrabble game on the table?" he asks just as he points the remote to the TV. He looks genuinely curious.

"You said we'd play tonight."

He winces. "Did I? Would you forgive me if I didn't get to it? I have to watch this, then we eat, then I have some notes to go over. I don't know, maybe I can manage it."

"Never mind. It's okay. I only got it out because when I asked, you said . . ."

"Oh. Hmmm. Have you tasted the wine?"

"No, not yet."

"Go ahead. It's a Barberra."

Whatever the hell that is. She takes a sip. The beer wasn't

to her liking and neither were any of the wines back at Jess's place, but this, this she thinks she could get used to. "Is it expensive?"

"Moderate. You like?"

"I do."

"There's plenty more. Be my guest if I'm not here." He pats the sofa. "This is more comfortable."

"Really, I'm fine."

"You're not afraid of me, are you?"

There's a high-pitched hum in the silence. "I think I'm afraid of everybody and everything, when it comes down to it."

"Fear no more. You're going to be fine. I know success when I see it, and you're going to be fine. Even your fortune cookie said so." This is the Frank she likes—teasing, warm smile. And he remembers the fortune cookie. Just when she thinks he has no short-term memory, he's all there. *Preocupado* most of the time is what he is.

During the first half hour of *Chinatown*, Bridget works to get comfortable with the social arrangement, just two strangers sipping wine and watching a film. During the second half hour, she works on physical comfort, subtly moving her head away from the TV every time she reaches for a peanut or a cracker with the salmon stuff on it, because her neck is stiff from the angle of the chair. Moving the chair itself—she has considered it—would amount to too big a fuss.

After an hour, he says, "You neck must be killing you."

"Not killing me. Just a little . . . stuckish."

He laughs and pats the sofa again. "I won't touch you. I'm an old tired guy. Come on."

Her heart begins beating hard. She moves over to the sofa, feeling nervous enough to cry.

"Bring your wineglass. You need a topper-upper."

She moves to get it and back. It's like practice, going from the chair to the couch, singleness to companionship. He fills her quarter-full glass to the top again. "It's very nice, isn't it?"

The next half hour Bridget spends trying to sink into the sofa cushions. Her body won't do it, but is rigidly on alert. After that, the last forty minutes of the movie engages her and she does relax some even though Frank slides down in his seat and his upper arm touches hers.

In the movie, when Jack Nicholson as Jake Gittes finally figures it all out and gets crazy with anger and horror, Frank wobbles her knee. "You understanding this?"

"Yeah. It's . . ."

"Gross?"

"I was going to say 'sad.' "

"Uh." He nods.

Yes, she feels the weight of the ending—Faye Dunaway gone and the terrible father spiriting the young girl away. "You're going to teach this?"

"Me and everybody who teaches. It's way better than the usual, isn't it?"

Nodding toward the TV, she asks, "Does L.A. look like that?"

"With a lot of color and updating." The credits are still rolling but he doesn't switch the thing off or rewind. He doesn't move.

She starts to get up, saying, "I should—"

He pulls her back by the hand, until she sits again. "Let it settle, for God's sake. Is getting a potato or whatever into the oven so important? Honor the art of it for a minisecond."

She sits, trying to honor the film. He still has hold of her hand. His hand is warm and moves on hers, massaging it. "Nobody has ever been good enough to you," he says.

"I'm okay."

"No, you're not, and you don't know how smart and terrific you are. You don't have any idea."

She feels three years old, or six, awkward, unsexualized—but that's a lie she's fond of telling herself. "I don't want to do this."

"What?"

"Be one of your girls in port."

"I won't let that happen. I won't let anything happen that you don't want. The truth is, I'm a very lonely man since my wife died. You brought a little life into the house. I'm grateful." He still has her hand. Slowly he brings it to his lips. "Did that hurt?"

"No."

"If it did, I won't do it again."

If only her body would quit imploring her to lean over and kiss him. He can hear it. He can.

"You're so alert to everything. Young and open, like a little . . . a little bird."

"Well, maybe young." Clumsy like a little birdie. Artless. She will not say those things, for they're too fancy and they'll require an answer from him and it will go on and on. Everything she says gives him a hook. She must *talk plain.* "Baked potatoes," she says, extricating herself, "don't need to go in yet, but chicken does."

She must leave this place. This will not do. She throws some spices on the chicken and takes out the salad vegetables she washed. The table is already set. Does wine make people weepy? She feels a little raw, but it could be the aftereffect of the movie. Out of the corner of her eye, she can see Frankly Jazzy sitting in the same position she left him in, looking defeated. It's too early to start poking the poor chicken with a fork, so she casts about for something else to do in the kitchen.

"Let's play Scrabble," he calls out. "I was wrong not to stop the movie halfway and let you put all this stuff on so we could be eating soon. You should have insisted."

She peers at him from the kitchen door. "You could do your work now. Then it would be done."

He shakes his head. "Not in the mood. At all. Can't. Let's play Scrabble."

"Okay."

"Set it up. Where do you want to play? In here? Or at the dining table?"

"Table."

He carries the wine bottle and both glasses to the table and begins to fill the glasses.

"No more for me." Too late. He's poured it.

"Get yourself a glass of water or a soda, whatever you want."

"We don't have soda."

"You're kidding. I can go out later and get you some. In fact, tonight or tomorrow, I have to take you shopping, get some supplies in because I'll be gone for a while."

"For four days."

"Yeah, about that."

Bridget gets herself a glass of water and comes to the table. She moves the two dining chairs to positions across from each other at the game end of the table and sits. Briskly, she sets up the board and letter-tile holders.

He watches and laughs his nice hearty open laugh. "You said you weren't any good. I have a feeling I'm going to get slaughtered."

"You know plenty more words than I do."

"Well, that may be, but will they come to me when I need them?" He knocks his head, then goes about the business of choosing tiles and arranging them. He stares at his. "I think I'm having some bad luck here. All vowels. That's a little loose, don't you think, kind of heavy on the yin?"

Bridget has often had the feeling the Scrabble board knows. Decks of cards know, too. They're like Ouija boards. If you're up, they mirror you. Down, they show you so. *Pigs* or *gypsy,* which should she spell? Use up the blank and the *y* so early, or not? Across from her Frank takes two pill bottles from his pants pocket and shakes a pill from each.

Brain tumor acting up again? she wants to ask. Just one of those bleak little jokes she loves. She sneaks a look at the little plastic pharmacy bottles, but can't see the typing.

"Antidepressant, antianxiety," he says, holding her gaze. "I'm an old, tired, bummed-out, *nervous* guy."

"What are you bummed out about in particular?"

"Work. Not Athens, but the L.A. end of things, the part you're helping out with."

"Trying to," she says, putting down *pig*. Save the *s*.

"And death. And loneliness."

Of course, of course, it must be disturbing him even though he pretends to move on. "When did your wife die?"

He winces. "A little over a year ago."

"I noticed you have no pictures around. I wondered what she was like."

"Before she got sick, she was a nice-looking woman with long dark hair. She worked in telecommunications. Sales. Nothing exciting about her job and she minded that. She wanted to do something more artistic but she never got around to it. I suppose it isn't very healthy, putting pictures away, but I never did like living with pictures. She was sick for a long time. In a way, she's been gone for a long time, in another way, not."

"I'm sorry. What was her name?"

"Carol."

Carol, she says to herself, trying to get an image of a woman who is pretty, competent, unsatisfied, and ill. "And no kids?"

"No kids."

A pretty woman, but very thin, wiry, because the illness was there all along, eating at her. Carol. Okay.

He has not put down any tiles. "You don't want to play," she says. "You're distracted."

"I'm sorry. Make me a shopping list and I'll run out now."

She says, "I can go with you." It's great to have a house to crash in, but is she ever going to have a chance to be out and about? He could sit in the car, she could run around the supermarket.

"You be the chef. I'll go provide. I don't have time tomorrow." He starts to get himself up.

"Maybe you could leave the car. Tomorrow."

Her words bring him to a halt. "What?" he asks, sharply.

"If I drove you to the airport."

"No." He frowns, resumes movement. "No. I need the car. Sorry. What . . . what did you need it for?"

"Well, I don't need it. I just thought I'd drive you, pick you up, you wouldn't have to pay parking, and I could go to the store if I needed."

He begins to speak three or four times, but cuts himself off. He paces for a moment. "Well, for now, let's just do the list. Everything you could ever want."

"That'll take a couple of minutes. Are you sure there's time?"

"Sure there is. Ten minutes to Kroger, ten back at most, fifteen minutes to fill the cart."

I can go stay somewhere else. I can take the boxes of manuscripts with me and work anywhere. She almost says these irritable, strident things, but the space, the TV, the books, the videos, the stereo call to her. And he does, too, he does.

FRANK BUYS SODA, PRETZELS, NACHOS, SALSA, PLENTY OF CHEESE, crackers, cereal, milk, yogurt, bread, ice cream, green beans, corn, rice, sliced ham, mustard (he can't remember if he has any), mayo, lamb chops, more chicken, ground beef, more eggs, bacon, lettuce, tomatoes (although they look iffy), green peppers, bath salts, body lotions. Do eighteen-year-olds know how to make lamb chops? He runs back for detergent, bar soap. At the checkout line he tosses in razors, breath mints, a couple of candy bars, and a copy of *Glamour* magazine.

Well, he could make it for four days on this, he hopes she can. He doesn't much like her going out of the house. People will ask questions, call him certain names, point out her age.

She's smart, smart. He likes that, but he's also aware he is going to need to call more often, keep track.

SOMETIMES HE MEASURED WEEKS BY WEDNESDAYS, WHEN THEY had the kids at the house. A week ago Marina had been bringing in groceries and after that she helped him to a Friday trip to Detroit. Now he was thinking about another one, two days from now. Maybe. If Mary Connelly had never surfaced, things might be different, he might be less haunted.

Three weeks since the murder.

He sat on the edge of the bed. Marina came to him, kneeling behind, and began to rub his shoulders. Then she reached over and started unbuttoning his shirt.

"What are you doing?" he said softly.

"Taking charge."

He was glad. He let her do all the start-up and then he snapped to. They were quick and quiet. Fifteen minutes of up and down. Hey, better than nothing. When she got up and came back to bed in a short nightgown, hair streaming, he said, "Right now you look like a little kid."

"You like that? Next time, start with the nightgown?"

He knew he was unsophisticated in that department—no names, no games, just straight shooting. Was she disappointed? He smiled, not answering her. She climbed in beside him and they fitted themselves to each other, tight.

"Are you teaching Friday?"

"Yeah."

"Can't get out of it?"

"No, what's up?"

"I was going to take you on a trip, a mini-vacation."

"Pretty mini. Kids come Friday night."

Right. Good. That great gradual haziness came over him and work seemed blessedly unimportant when he fell asleep.

9

HE HAD CHOSEN ATLANTIC CITY BECAUSE HE HAD A MEMORY OF the doc always promising to take him and Daniel there, even though it never happened. Some great childhood, he used to think even then—mother dumped him for "his good," so she said. Father was definitely no fun. And Dan . . . he had to put up with Dan being everyone's idea of wonderful. Pittsburgh was okay, but his father's household had a darkness about it, an uncared-for quality, a hangover from mourning the death of Dan's mother. Anyway, it was a dull household. The doc didn't take vacations, even though he muttered promises from time to time, had a few shots of whiskey, and then forgot. Twice a year maybe his mother called, in her cups each time, and if he wasn't there, it didn't much matter to her. She was willing to wait another six months for another urge to connect. He didn't call her. It was a vow to himself that he kept. Not to show need.

By the end of his second year in medical school, he hadn't seen his mother in eleven years and he'd barely talked to her. He thought he was done with her. He told Mary he had no idea where she was.

He got into his car, a repainted and banged-up VW Beetle, and headed for the Eastern Shore. He remembers this slice of his life even more clearly than most. He can remember the smell of the salt air, the squawking of the gulls. He took a cheap room in a basement. It smelled musty, but was only ten dollars a night. He paid for three nights in advance but told the man he planned to stay a whole week, so the landlord should not rent the place out from under him. He planned to work for a couple of days—washing dishes or bartending if necessary, probably waiting tables to make some quick money for expenses.

He poked his head into a couple of places, hoping to snag a dinner-hour shift so that he could have some time in the sun. He hadn't anticipated it would be that difficult to find work. But people told him the season was winding down; one man said he'd maybe need someone to wash dishes in a day or two when one of his boys went off to college.

Money was low. He wandered around for a long time, looking at things, cheap red plastic rafts that looked as if they would fall apart on the first use, T-shirts with junk on them. Thirty dollars got him into and out of a bar, pretty tanked by two in the morning, and he still wasn't sleepy. He hadn't eaten and now he was down to a couple of dollars and some change. He got into his car and drove, then parked up against a building on the edge of town where he'd seen a bar flashing its lights at him somewhere back around the corner. He walked, found it—a dark dive of a place—and he ordered a beer. Then another. Then a whiskey. He was sort of philosophically watching the last of his money go. There were about two dozen customers in the place and the music screamed. Doors opened and closed, people came and went. A lot of the traffic was internal—that is, something was going on outside the back door.

The bartender put his whiskey in front of another guy.

"I think that's mine," Gerald Paul said.

The bartender said, "Oh, sorry, I thought he was you. I thought you went out back and came back in."

"I'll buy it for him," the other man's voice piped up, and when the bartender moved out of the way, Gerald Paul saw the person who spoke looked a little like him. He thanked the stranger who had bought him a drink; the stranger came over to sit beside him.

He didn't notice much about the young man right away.

Then slowly he became aware of a silver bracelet on the left wrist. Underneath it he noticed a faint scar. The fellow had once halfheartedly tried to off himself, and was now strung high or low. Then Gerald Paul LaBeau realized the guy was coming on to him. He hadn't been noticing. He'd been thinking about Daniel's visit and that business about going to jail for Ted Luckey. Which was real. What happened to Ted Luckey was real. He sat there fretting, half-crazed, trying to figure out what to do to get Dan off his back. The guy beside him kept asking him questions and he kept telling lies. Said he was born in Lubbock, Texas, had seven sisters. Said he was a grad student in English in Chicago.

The guy—he was just a boy—unrolled a fistful of money. "Whatever you want," he said. The money dropped from the boy's hands to the bar top, to the floor, and he tried to pick it up, but his fingers had lost all dexterity. He was young and thin, and his long hair was a little like Gerald Paul's. He said, "My name is Frank Razzi. And I don't do anything. Just get high."

Gerald Paul, helping to pick up the money, said, "That sounds good, doing nothing," but he didn't mean it, he was only pressing the buttons for automatic speech. He owed speech, no matter how banal. Frank had bought his drink.

Nothing else. He had no other thoughts.

He didn't want to make love with the guy. He wanted to disappear from his own life, that's what he wanted, go off and do something exciting, leave the doctoring to Dan, but he didn't yet know how to make disappearing possible. He wanted a new name, but he hadn't thought in concrete terms how he would go about getting one.

"Gonna tell me your name?"

"Ted.

"Ted what?"

"Luckey."

They talked for a long time, with the TV going and music blasting and people coming and going. People who looked, if they did, thought they saw a pickup in motion.

The drugged-out boy, the real Frank Razzi, finally said he was from outside Boise, Idaho. His parents hated him, disowned him because he liked boys, and he hadn't been back home for years. They couldn't handle his being gay and he couldn't change it. He'd gone to the West Coast for a while, then the East Coast, looking for love.

"Where's the money come from, then?" Gerald Paul asked.

Frank said, "Here and there. I've met some wealthy people. I've sold some stuff."

Stuff. Himself or drugs. Gerald Paul made a professional assessment and said, "You're in bad shape. You know that? You ought to take better care of yourself. Whatever you're on has got you cockeyed."

"Where you staying?" Frank Razzi asked.

"Dinky little place. What about you?"

"Don't have a place yet. Stayed over with somebody else last night, he got religion this morning."

Gerald Paul laughed. He was made uncomfortable by the thought, This is opportunity presenting itself. He wasn't sure how, exactly, this meeting was going to turn out to be opportunity, but he heard the knock and listened for more.

"What are you on?" he asked.

"The good H." The boy, Frank Razzi, made a shot motion toward his arm.

"That can't be good."

"I don't take it for the highs anymore. Just to keep from feeling sick. It used to be great. Once upon a time."

"You can't ratchet it up to great anymore?" That's what he'd said and he wondered later if it sounded like a recommendation. If so, then this one counted against him, too.

The real Frank Razzi looked at him for a moment and said, "I'm going to the john, do some stuff." When he came back, seconds later, he said, "Too many people in there."

"You've probably had enough."

"Where's your place?" the boy asked again.

"Couple of miles away."

"Shit. I don't know if I can walk."

"I have a car. I'll take you someplace. Someplace else."
He didn't want the guy to crash with him but he felt something. Was it responsibility? He wasn't thinking that
clearly. He was very drunk.

"You don't want to get together?"

"Not that way. If you need a ride someplace, want to go
to a hospital . . ."

The real Frank Razzi laughed. "Fuck you, then. You're a
jerk."

Gerald Paul said, "Right. I am."

"You don't have any money," Frank Razzi said, as if
reading his thoughts. "You don't have anything."

"I don't. I'm going to the john now. Then I'm going
back to my place. The offer of a ride is good."

"We could do a little something outside," the boy,
Frank Razzi, said.

"Not my thing."

"You think you're somebody special? Somebody
high up?"

"No."

The boy looked at Gerald Paul with a deep dislike, an
about-face from the earlier come-on. "Fuck you, son of a
bitch," he said angrily, and he left the bar.

Gerald Paul went to the john. He pretty much forgot
about Frank Razzi. His mood was low, and in that low
mood, he had a fantasy of not even going to his car, just
sticking out his thumb and going to whatever city he
ended up in. He could use Ted Luckey's name until he had
some money, and then who knew what? He imagined the
Detroit teachers, like a jury of fathers, hearing he had
skipped out, scratching their old heads. In the bathroom,
he realized he was very drunk. He lurched out of the place
and ended up leaning against the walls of the buildings he
passed on the way to his car, worrying he would pass out.

The walk seemed unbearably long, the couple of blocks
to the corner where his car wedged up against a building.
From a distance he could see someone slumped on the

ground. Blue windbreaker. Frank? Was it Frank? Slowly he realized it was. A feeling of panic hit him. He hesitated, then hurried up to the body. Frank. Needle in the arm. Hadn't had enough after all. He took a pulse. He felt Frank's neck. Nothing. He put the body on the ground and knelt over it to do CPR. Minutes went by. Nothing. The guy was real dead. He looked up and around. People? Where were the people? He looked at his watch. It was four in the morning. A car went by a hundred feet away, that was all.

He didn't think. He acted. He was getting shut of Dan finally, once and for all. He was getting rid of the self-righteous son of a bitch, the tilted head, the sympathetic eyes. The man was like a wasp, a fly, nagging at him.

He took everything out of Frank's pockets and put the things in his. He took everything from his pockets and put them in Frank's, including the key to the room he'd rented. He was about to start out for his car when he snapped to alertness and made two more decisions. He dug his wallet out again from the dead man's pocket and, shaking so that he could hardly write, filled in a blank on the ID card where it said "In case of emergency, contact:" It now read *Michelle LaBeau*. He'd had to put in the old phone number. He didn't even know if it was good anymore.

Who can a man trust if not his mother?

He hurried to his car. Still no one around. This was meant to be, then. He drove the car, without lights, around the corner and right up next to Frank Razzi's body, so that it looked as if Frank had been trying to lean against the driver's door when he shot up and slipped to the ground. He, in his last moments as Gerald Paul, had to get out of the car on the passenger's side because otherwise he would step on the body or bump it with the door on the driver's side. For another moment he hesitated. The car was his only possession. He came around to the narrow space where the body was wedged against the car and he pressed the VW key into Frank's pocket.

He walked. For a long time, he walked. He felt so crazy,

his scalp seemed to be lifting off his head. And drunk, he was very drunk. He walked forever toward the lights. Finally, he leaned against a building and looked at what was in his pockets. He had a driver's license. A hundred and fifty dollars. A Social Security card. A charge card. He wouldn't use that, too risky. An address book. A bottle of some sort of pills. A handful of change. The kid was not yet twenty, five years younger than he.

He thought, I won't do it. I'll go to the police and tell them I was drunk and crazy.

He thought, she, his mother, would not be able to pull it off. She'd screw it up and he'd be accused of murdering Frank Razzi. He thought again, I'd better come clean, explain all this.

And then what? Jail time, med school contacted, the seedy story told. Shame.

Instead, he called his mother from a pay phone. At first he dialed the old number, and when it turned out it wasn't hers anymore, he called information and got her new one. She answered the phone, still awake. He could hear a television going. It was only a little after one o'clock in Bellingham. He told her everything he needed for her to do. "They're going to call you," he said. "Just say your son wore a silver bracelet. If they ask you if there was a scar on the left wrist, say yes, a little one, say a not-very-serious suicide attempt. Just say it. They'll ask you to come in to identify the body, do it, say it's me, and I'll send you money to cover whatever it costs."

"You don't call me, and then you call me with this? I can't. How could I do all that?"

"Sure you can. Just say yes. Remember the bracelet and the scar, then they'll probably ask you to come in. Say six foot tall, long brown hair."

"You killed him?" she asked.

"I swear to you, I didn't. But it could look like I did. And I have other reasons. . . . Give me this. You owe me."

She made a sound, a moan, a sigh.

"You can do it. It's better all around. I'll call you tomorrow to see what's happening. Ask . . . ask to have the body cremated."

He watched the sun come up. He waited for a coffee shop to open, got himself two cups to go, and looked at the ocean some more. Around nine o'clock, he got himself onto a bus.

It turned out the police bought it easily. He had written it just right. They called his mother and she mentioned the bracelet and the scar. That was enough for them. They were busy. Fifty deadbeats in a week; one positive ID put them way ahead.

When she explained she had no money, it only made the ID seem stronger. The police accepted her request for cremation because it made their lives easy. It was the cheapest of the possibilities, less bulky than a coffin. When he talked to her, he understood that she had pulled it off. He had dreamed the plot-turn in his life, dreamed it and not believed it could happen. But it had. He had found a busy police department with too many cases. And his new life began.

His mother seemed almost to believe he *had* died and that she was talking by phone to someone else who gave her various instructions. She entered into the fiction, he could tell she did, and saw to it that appropriate obits were written and published in Bellingham and in Detroit, just as he requested.

The morning after the first Frank Razzi's death in Atlantic City, the new Frank Razzi, hardly used to the name, or his new age, was on his way to Philly, and the next evening he was waiting tables at a pricey place. He bought some clothes with his first tips. September came. The school term started just about everywhere, including at Wayne State. He imagined people packing up his room, his books, in Detroit. He kept working. The restaurant owner clapped him on the back and said he hoped he'd have him around for a long, long time.

A month later he was on another bus going west.

A memorial service had been held in Detroit at the med school early that September. Gerald Paul read his own obituary a year later by going to a library in L.A. and getting the *Detroit Free Press* on borrowed microfiche. That was when the old name finally died for him.

WHAT CHRISTIE SAW ON FRIDAY AT THREE IN ATLANTIC CITY WAS what looked like a simple case. The ID of the dead man matched the registration of the car. An autopsy, though they hardly needed one with the needle still stuck in the arm of the dead man, showed a drug and alcohol overdose. There were no foreign prints on the syringe. The room key in the pocket of the deceased was finally identified in a door-to-door search. The landlord said the name of the person who had rented the room was Gerald Paul. He confirmed there were Michigan plates on the car of the young man, a VW bug. Fairly overwhelming evidence.

The boy's mother was called and given the news, asked the usual questions about identifying marks. She said he wore some kind of bracelet in the last couple of years but that she thought he chose it because he was embarrassed by an old scar. And bingo, there was a scar on the dead man's wrist. They asked her about her son's friends, sexual activity. The mother said she hadn't been in touch with her son for a while, didn't know what all he was up to lately. All of this was recorded in one particular detective's handwriting. Christie could almost see the invisible exclamation marks. Luck! A quick case! Christie expected to find something about Michelle LaBeau coming into Atlantic City, but note after note showed only phone interviews; and then he found a phrase: *ashes to be sent to her.* He read on. The fact was, she *hadn't* come in. And this was the thing, in spite of the overwhelming evidence that Gerald Paul was dead, that fascinated him. She had committed the body to ashes without *looking.* Cremations weren't so popular twenty-five years ago as today, and besides, most people wanted to *see.* . . . There was another scribble about a charitable organization that coughed up enough for the costs of the cremation and shipping the remains.

Cremation meant no dental records, no DNA even after the fact.

Find the mother. If possible. Christie copied down the old phone numbers and the address in Bellingham, Washington. Looked the same as what he had up at the office, way out-of-date, but he copied them anyway.

What happened to the car? Some cop copped it for a daughter? He kept turning pages of official reports for the next week until he found an answer. *Sold to a junk dealer for minimal contribution toward funeral expenses, the rest covered by charity.* The car would be waste by now, nothing left.

Had anyone gone to Detroit? No. Had anyone flashed a photo around Detroit? Fingerprinted the items in the wallet? No. Sloppy, sloppy. Busy, yeah, they were busy that August.

Another reason for the sloppiness was sadly clear. *Possibly homosexual,* the detective had written. *Wears shiny underwear and silver bracelet.* That was the reason, all right, a homophobic cop, to whose mind a puff drifter was better off dead.

Fingerprints of the dead man at the end of the report. Good, but what does Christie match them to? Gerald Paul's are not on file.

He got on the phone and bothered Mary Riley Connelly once more. "Tell me, think back, did your friend Gerald have a faint scar on his left wrist?"

"No," she said slowly. "Nothing I ever noticed."

"Did he talk about an attempted suicide?"

"No."

"Did he wear a silver bracelet?"

"Definitely not. No jewelry."

"Satiny underwear?"

"Never. Tell me what's happening."

"I'll call you again as soon as I know. Can you not talk about this to anyone?" He thanked her, hung up.

Around three-thirty, Christie is in the old specimens lab, where it's clear they need a few more employees. He examines jar after jar of specimens with yellowing labels, but does not find one for Gerald Paul.

He dials up Ted Rawson. "I'm here in town," he says. "Got antsy. How about missing-persons reports for the couple of days I'm interested in? Where could I find those?"

Rawson, sounding both less friendly and less harried, tells him which building to go to.

The clerk in the Records Department is a young, large woman whose breath comes hard when she moves around and whose natural expression is murderous. "Let me look."

Soon Christie is presented with stacks of papers, but the clerk is not in a chatty mood. When he tries to say something to her, she heads him off. "We're supposed to hand over, keep track, not discuss."

"Oh." In the background he sees another clerk, much older, also grim-faced, who looks briefly at him, then away. "Friendly place," he grumbles to himself.

He looks through the reports for the week before, during, and after the death he's studying, sorting for young men in their twenties. *After* is more likely, he thinks, so he takes the names of the people who could possibly match up with the deceased. Jotting them down quickly, he makes it through several months. He catches the old clerk's eye when he can, but she seems very busy. When he returns the files, it's only to the counter, no one in sight. It's closing time.

Out in the hall, leaning against a wall, tired and hungry, he dials Marina from his cell. He can see that inside, the large woman has come to snatch the files back. "Anything?" Marina asks.

"Nothing conclusive, but my gut tells me yes. If Gerald Paul, or Paul *LaBeau* is how I think of him, went off and pretended to be someone else, who did he pretend to be and where did he go?"

She mused, "Family or old friends? Eventually?"

"People do. But the Social Security number never surfaced again. What kind of guy would pretend to be someone else? Forever?"

Marina says, "Someone with enormous will. And an actor's personality, able to . . . to adopt a fantasy." Christie stretches his back against the wall, wondering where to go next. Marina asks, "Didn't anybody at Forensics remember anything?"

"No, they just provided paperwork. Same as with the missing-persons reports. For all I know, Rawson took something out of the files so they wouldn't look so bad. Get this: They never even brought in the mother to identify the body."

"How can that be?"

"It happens in places where a lot of people pass through. Because a lot of people . . . come to die, in a way. I don't know. I feel like I'm nowhere in particular on this. Wasted time. I hate it."

"So you're staying?"

"Oh, no. Absolutely not. Get home to you, have an actual weekend."

On the way to his car, the old female clerk who was way in the back at the Records Department appears and walks along with him. His breath catches. Is this purposeful? Does she know something? Her face is creased and hard, but her eyes, he sees now, aren't particularly mean.

"Long day," he says.

She nods. "Glad to see the weekend."

"I have to go the whole way back to Pittsburgh. Don't know if I'll be back next week. Old missing-persons reports are not a thing I get a lot of time to pursue."

"Who were you looking for?"

He lets a little pause go by while he lets her tone filter in. Kind. She's being kind.

"Don't know who exactly and don't know what. Looking *into* the death of one Gerald Paul LaBeau. Thinking it might have been a misidentification. A mix-up. It was a long time ago." He looks straight at her.

"There was a guy here a couple of months ago looking into that case. Same case. Does that help you at all?"

His heart jumps but he realizes what the answer is going to be before he asks. "Who?"

"A doctor. He was here on a convention, he said. But he spent a couple of hours in with us looking through records. Real worried-looking. They let him see what was legal to show."

"Did he find anything he liked?"

"I don't know. He never said. He was quiet and kept to himself. That's all I know. Honest."

"Thank you. You have a good weekend."

"You be safe home."

ON SATURDAY, WHICH IS REAL BAD WITH LONELINESS, BRIDGET, while working at Frank's computer, starts to study his filing system. Almost everything is neatly tucked away in a file, in a file, in a file. Under "corres," she finds "consum," "med," "ag," "ms. sub." She is aware that if things are buried, she shouldn't unbury them, but she takes small peeks. Right. Agent. Consumer. Medical providers. Submissions letters for manuscripts. Just a peek. It's just a break from the work. But after she's worked a while longer, she becomes aware of what she'd most like to dig up, and she looks again—in vain—for notes on airline tickets and flights, but there is nothing on the computer. That puzzles her and it sends her to the desk drawers. In one drawer, which seems to be filled with receipts of various sorts, she finds old boarding-pass stubs, from L.A. to Paris to L.A. Another L.A. to Tampa, Florida. One set of stubs is for a return flight to San Francisco. And another set is for New York. Guy gets around. However, looking more closely at the dates, she sees they are not current. Also, paper-clipped together are a series of road receipts from all kinds of places. California, Nevada, Iowa. This would be his drive east to take the job.

It sure would be great to talk to someone every once in a while, she thinks. "Going nuts," she says to herself aloud.

Playing spy, detective, is making her nuts, too. She paces the house, back and forth, opens the back door, trots around the backyard, which butts up against the scraggly woods, then the nice woods. "One, two, three," she counts, working to get her voice moving. She's noticed it's hidden away in her throat from lack of talk. "Seven, eight, nine, ten!" So what if someone hears her. Ants in pants. She knows what that means. She can hardly sit still. "Okay, investigate. Do it."

She trots back into the house.

Desk drawers. In a paper file marked "MasterCard" she finds bills which include the flights she has just found evidence of. No flights on the most recent bill, though. Still, it arrived on October 7, so okay, maybe the recent travel just isn't on it yet.

She sits at his desk, thinking. The Tuesday–Wednesday trips don't seem like flights. Definitely not L.A. on that quick a turnaround. And besides, he puts some miles on the car when he heads off. Because she looked at the odometer before he left and when he came back, thinking he'd been to Columbus, but the odometer showed he'd racked up too many miles to account for a simple trip to Columbus. A road trip? A woman in Akron? A secret vice? Zipping around town with Sally? He's a mystery, that's for sure.

She's rolling around on Razzi's desk chair, reading another paper file marked "Correspondence," when she finds a letter that shocks her. He's requesting termination of the lease as of the end of November. Three weeks from now, the end of term. Her first thought is, What will happen to me? It's only been ten days there, only five working for him, but she's gotten lazy about dealing with her own life. Here she is trying to figure out his. Never thought to tell her he was leaving. Okay, apartment hunt tomorrow, next day. Find something and move.

But the free lodging is seductive. She's become accustomed to doing her own thing, getting what she wants from the refrigerator, watching TV until two in the morning.

Doing her laundry. Adult feelings come with this much freedom. She feels a certain weight of adult responsibility when she reads Razzi's letters; it reminds her of how much time in life is spent just explaining what you just paid, what you need to terminate, what you wish to order.

She has retyped parts of six manuscripts, three that he's doctored and three of his. And, of course, read all six several times start to finish. The man *works*. He's not a slouch. In this, she identifies with him.

After looking out the window and seeing there is no activity on the little road whatsoever, she opens the center desk drawer. Ah, a letter that has been opened and is as yet unfiled. *From* the realtor. She slips out the piece of paper. The agent has written to inform Mr. Razzi that, by the constraints of the lease, he may terminate at the end of November, but will have to pay rent for December as well, even if he is not in the place. Someone will be coming by to do an assessment of any damages. If he fails to pay December's rent, his security deposit will not be returned. If there is any damage to the place, he will be called to court.

Adult life leaves little to be desired. You can get a finger-wagging that makes you feel seventeen at any point, she supposes. Well, she keeps the place super clean, so it will pass any tests the realtor wishes to levy.

But where is Razzi *going* at the end of November? If he has to pay anyway, might he let her stay on, in the empty house? Take her with him to New York or L.A? Now, there's a thought. She didn't invite the thought, it came to her as a joke, but by evening, it has not gone away. She takes a shower, puts on his robe, which she likes because it's a soft, dark blue plaid that just seems like something with a certain *quality*, and she paces the place once more.

When the phone rings, she runs to it.

"Everything okay?" Razzi asks.

"Sure. Except all I do is work. Where are you?"

"Just in the lobby of a hotel."

"Oh, a nice one?"

"It's just a plain old Holiday Inn, but I'm not staying here. Just meeting someone for a coffee."

"Oh."

"You have my cell for emergencies."

"Right." She can't imagine calling.

"I'll have to get you to a movie or out to hear some music or something next week."

"Yes!"

"You're working on the stuff I gave you to do?"

"Yeah. Making progress."

"Good work, Sawyer. Keep up the good work."

"Sawyer?"

"From *42nd Street*. The heroine-hoofer. Musical. I don't have the video."

God, he knows everything. All evening she paces even when she eats a bowl of pasta at seven. The call from Razzi, just speaking and being spoken to, has excited her. She puts on her best jeans and a light blue sweater that has a low neckline. She forces herself to sit and watch TV. Finally, at nine o'clock, stir-crazy, Bridget starts on foot toward the bar at the strip mall, dodging traffic and terrifying herself twenty times on the way there.

The bar has the sharp, yeasty smell of spilled beer. A jukebox is playing, two televisions are going, men bellow, women shriek, and it takes time to separate out the sounds and lights, one from the other. Bridget spies an empty stool across from the bar and heads for it. As soon as she sits down, she watches a woman holding a beer in one hand and a basket of fries and something else in the other. She holds both up high so as not to jostle them, comes straight toward Bridget, who is about to say, "That's not my food order," when the woman says, "That's my stool."

"Oh, sorry."

The woman, who, closer up, looks tired, tosses permed blond hair as she's seen it tossed on TV, then promptly begins to hog down fries and calamari, washing everything down with beer. Now, *she* does not seem self-conscious about being alone. Bridget moves several feet away and wedges herself between groups of people who lean up against a narrow counter.

A hawkeyed waitress sees her not spending, squeezes through the crowd, and asks, "What'll it be?"

Alone and *young* and *not a good drinker* is stenciled on her forehead, that's for sure. "A beer."

"What kind?"

"Draft. American."

"Light?"

"Sure."

Slowly, Bridget becomes aware of the beckoning of fatty and salty foods the bar specializes in: fried clams, onion rings, cheese sticks, fried zucchini, fried wings. According to Frank Razzi's scale, she has lost three pounds in her ten days there. In spite of the fact that she would like to keep them off, she orders wings when the waitress returns. A frown of irritation greets her order. What has she done wrong, taken up two minutes of the woman's time?

At least she wasn't carded. She must pass.

For a long time, nobody talks to her. Bridget sips the beer as slowly as she is able to while she watches the way the band sets up—inefficiently, moving amplifiers, bumping beer bellies against microphone stands, staring at things, plugging things, muttering to one another. New screeching sounds join the rest of the cacophony. The dance floor, Bridget can now see, is a tiny thing, and will only be big enough for a couple of show-offy pairs doing that stroll thing to the two-timin'-man song that surely this group will sing. The singers are a sad lot, swollen and greasy, but they have that look of confidence that they can be the two-timing type, plenty of women will still want them. Man, does she feel out of it. She just doesn't get it, why some people are so damned *sure* of themselves.

"Can I have one of those?"

She looks up to see a man whom she would describe right off as leering. His hair is slicked down, not too long, and he looks as if he just took a shower, but can't wash the dirty expression off his face.

"One of them wings," he says, revealing some bad holes in his smile. He eats candy bars, she thinks. Always has, said he didn't care about his teeth, now wishes he had the money for implants. What do I know? she chides herself. I can't make him up from a few paltry impressions. But she doesn't like him, so she says, "No. Sorry. Order your own." Then feeling badly, she says, "Sorry. I'm hungry."

He moves off and she thinks she is rid of him, but he returns with a basket of fries and wings, saying, "Here. Have some on me."

She is not sure how to handle him, so she says nothing, just keeps eating from her own basket of food.

"What's your name?" he asks.

"Mindy."

"What's Mindy short for?"

She doesn't know. Melinda? She doesn't know. "My parents just named me Mindy. It's not short for anything."

"I see." He nods knowingly.

She does not like him. One wing left. Let him have it. She slings her purse over her shoulder and heads for the ladies' room. On the way, she tries to find her waitress, but can't see her. So. She has to learn some tricks, that's for sure. Jess would know exactly how to get rid of a guy, how to zero in on the one she wants. She takes a nice long pee, washes her hands, does not plump up her hair as seems to be the required gesture before the mirror, and goes back out. People have begun dancing to whatever it is the band's playing—she can't recognize it. Because she cannot easily cross the dance floor, she stays put and manages to hail her waitress from there.

"What?"

"I need to pay."

"The wings, right? The guy paid."

"Are you sure?"

"You want me to charge you again?"

"No, but here." Bridget hands over four ones. "Your tip."

The woman hesitates then folds the money over and pockets it. She pauses again, then says, "You watch out for that guy. I've seen him around before. You watch out."

Her heart pumps faster. She tries to concentrate on a different man, one she would like to dance with. He's young, light-haired, laughing, a good spirit. She concentrates so hard that he turns to look at her. He seems puzzled, frowns as if he might know her but can't place her. Soon a woman comes up to his side and slips an arm around him. Taken, of course he's taken. Bridget feels a tap on her shoulder and turns to a man who says, "Dance?" and twitches his head toward the floor. He's fifty, fifty-five, wears a Western shirt and slim-fit jeans. She lets him lead her out to the floor, feeling relief that he does not seem mean. He's only a guy dancing to his own 1960s Texas drummer. In some way that she can't identify, he reminds her of her father. She dances with him, a slow fox-trot that has nothing to do with his costume. Something happens. She feels a little heartbreak for him and is about to ask him questions about himself, when she sees the man who bought her wings come up behind him and tap him on the shoulder.

"Oh," her cowboy says, then tips his head once to her and walks away.

Bridget, having missed the moment when she might walk off the dance floor, too, or plead fatigue, is in the tight grip of the slimy man she has been trying to avoid. Her purse slips down her arm, but he keeps holding her tight, too close. His breath on her neck makes her shiver and he doesn't seem to notice she keeps trying to adjust her purse, because, the way he holds her, she can't move.

When the dance is over he walks her back to the spot where she stood when coming out of the ladies' room. He isn't going anywhere. "Bought your wings," he said.

"The waitress told me. Thank you."

"You want to dance again?"

"Not just yet." She looks longingly to the old cowboy,

but he glances aside politely, used to rejection. She looks even more longingly to the young man who caught her eye, but he's not going to be any help to her. When she sees her waitress head to the ladies' room, she says, "Got to go again, wait here," and she moves as fast as she can.

The waitress is in one of the stalls. She emerges, paying no attention to Bridget.

Bridget holds out a five-dollar bill and says, "You know that guy who was bothering me? I can't get rid of him. If there's a back door, I was thinking I could go and you could tell him I bought him a beer. . . ."

"Where's your car?"

"I walked into town."

"Jeez. You're walking?"

"Let me get a head start."

"Forget the money. I'll try to keep him here. Did he do anything we should call the police about?"

Bridget feels miserable, stupid, naïve. "Nothing. He just held me too tight and I don't like him. I want to go. Where's the back door?"

The waitress leads her through two doors and pushes a third door with an emergency bar on it. Three men standing outside watch Bridget begin her fast walk. "Thank you," she says back to the waitress, who looks worried, the same look Bridget misread as a scowl of disapproval at first. She can only hope the waitress will succeed in keeping the man with the slicked-down hair waiting at the edge of the dance floor.

It's a twenty-minute walk home. At least she is going against the traffic, so that if the man pulled up across from her, she could attempt to hail a stranger. Cars going fast usually slow as they come toward her. A few don't. Bridget walks so fast, she makes it home in eighteen minutes, drenched in sweat. She listens carefully as she creeps down the dark dirt road to the house. I gotta get outta here, she says to herself over and over again, opening the door, tumbling inside. She listens again. Quiet. Quiet everywhere. She begins to turn on lights.

The phone rings, jolting her.

When she answers, it's Frank Razzi.

"You went out?" he asks. "I've been calling."

"I only went out for an hour."

"Oh. Who with?"

"By myself."

"In the dark."

"I got lonely. I went to a kind of a pub."

"Oh, Bridget. This is . . . I should have thought about this. I'm so sorry. Are you okay?"

"Yeah. I'm okay."

"Something happened."

"No, I'm okay."

"I'll try to come back early, take you to a movie or something. If I can. I don't know if I can get away."

"Which flight are you on?"

"I don't remember. But I have so many miles, I just switch around if I need to."

"Oh." She hadn't thought of that.

"You need a little company. I'll do better. We'll have a good talk when I get back."

"Okay. I should probably move anyway. Going nuts talking to myself."

He sighs and lets a long silence go by. "How's the work?"

"I love doing it. You're a very good writer. I just get lonely."

"Of course you do. We'll talk when I get back."

"Thanks."

She leaves the lights on, lots of them. She reads until four in the morning, when she reaches that stage of wanting to sleep so much, she doesn't care what happens to her.

SUNDAY NIGHT ELIZABETH IS FEELING THE EFFECTS OF A GLASS of wine she's drinking over at Frank's place.

"Go nuts talking to myself," he said, as if quoting, when he made the invitation.

Maybe he's not the needy one. Maybe it's she. The idea

of spending time with someone who doesn't know her at all appeals to her. So here she is, one week after the first glass of wine with him, on the sofa in a room otherwise sparely furnished, feeling as she used to on vacation, as if she's stripping away inessentials.

"Tell me about your work," she says. "You seem very busy." She nods to the table piled high with papers.

"Too busy to put this place together, you mean?" He smiles. "My work, hmmm? What about it?"

"Anything."

"Mostly, after the first couple of years of working in film, I worked in TV. I let your son know all about that. I'm not some famous film-writer. I still float the occasional film script out there. My chances of getting something made for HBO are slightly better. And the independents, well, maybe. The money's not as good, but I don't care. Shows you how little I belong, I guess. Most people would say I'm fooling myself, but I don't think so. I just fired one agent and now I have another one trying to get to know my work."

"What is your object, then?"

"Just getting the stuff made. Off my desk. In a way, if you think about it, my desk is metaphorically piled too high. A script is never finished until it's sold or made. I can't keep up with all I've started."

"You're prolific?"

"Yep."

"You have to be resilient."

"For sure."

"I don't know if Jeff is. He's never handled rejection well."

"He has to get over it, grow some thick skin."

"I know."

"You have two kids?"

"Yes. Did Jeff tell you he had a sister?"

"No. I thought I saw a girl coming and going."

"Two kids," she answers.

And a husband? He doesn't ask. So she says, "My husband died recently. Did you know?"

"No, I didn't. I'm sorry."

"Jeff didn't say?"

"No. Not a thing. Had it—? It hadn't just happened?" Frank looks uncomfortable.

"Three weeks before."

"Oh. God, I'm sorry. I didn't know. Your son only talked about work and about a dinner event. I thought he was here for something good, some kind of celebration." Frank Razzi seems distressed.

Of course, she had to bring it up sooner or later, and there is no good way to do that. She explains, "The dinner *was* a celebration, of sorts. It was one of my husband's projects, which we're seeing through."

"I didn't have any idea. I hope I didn't say anything inappropriate to him or to you."

"I'm sure you didn't."

"I, uh, I'm widowed, too." She feels the first flash of surprise. "I can tell you . . . the first month is like a dream. It's . . . nothing is real at the beginning. My wife died two years ago and I'm not myself yet. It takes a long, long time."

She had assumed divorced. Separated. Because of his age, which she guesses to be early forties. "She died young, too, then."

"I'm forty-three," he says. "Carol would have been forty-seven now. She was four years older than me."

Carol. Died at forty-five. She must try to remember. Carol . . . as if she's his therapist. She wouldn't want to be caught looking at her notes for a wife's name. Carol. The wine makes Elizabeth feel comfortably foggy-headed.

She watches him lean forward to pour her more wine and sink back in his chair. "For me, if I'm honest," he's saying, "some of what I'm going through is selfishness. I watched her go through a lot of suffering. What I mean is, I catch myself being plain worried about my own . . .

mortality. I'm not proud of that fact at all, that my emotions are selfish ones. I don't know why I'm confessing it to you."

She is not sure what to say. Her own strongest emotion is of wanting to undo what is already done. "Maybe I seem priestlike." She smiles.

"You do, sort of."

". . . that thing about therapists being lay priests."

"I'm sorry to be making you work on a Sunday night."

"It didn't feel awful. Really."

"Well, to make it short, Carol was sick for a long time. I got used to that. That was my marriage. I was a pretty decent caretaker. We found ways to . . . to talk about what was going on. And here's the funny thing. I thought I was prepared. Stupid, stupid, but I did. I thought so. Then she died and I realized a person is never prepared." He leans back in the chair, lets his head fall back, and she does suddenly feel she's at work, something about the expression that crosses his face. "I had a lot of trouble working. I wasn't happy at Paramount and they . . . weren't too happy with me in the last year. I told your son that part, too. As a kind of preparation for him. So he would know that people can falter at all ages. I was always able to be productive, and I was saner than the other writers, so I never thought I'd be the one to lose it. But then I did, because what I needed was change. My mind was trying to tell me that."

There's music playing upstairs. It seems as if somebody else is in the house.

"What?" he asks.

"I can hear jazz." She points upward.

"Sorry about that. I leave radios on for company. It's a bad habit I have. I'll get it."

Before she can say it's not a problem, he's gone to turn it off. He tiptoes around her grief, not asking anything. It makes her feel badly, as if she's lied. She told him her husband died, and if she adds nothing, it sounds like an ordinary death, from illness.

The wine has had a strong effect on her. She sinks into

the couch, feeling passive, even though she's thinking she really should go soon.

"I like the jazz station," he says when he returns.

"I didn't mind it. It seemed friendly. I almost told you that but you—"

"I acted too fast. Sorry. Here, I've got it tuned in down here, too." He switches on an ordinary boom box that sits on the floor near the dining room windows. Stooping there, he lowers the volume gradually until the music is just a sketch in the background.

"One of your changes was moving here?"

He nods. "It's got a good rep in the film business. Very livable. I'd been here on business twice. I find it interesting. There's an energy. Maybe it's the mix of the gritty working class, the old mill workers, with all the high-tech stuff. Universities, good hospitals, sports. Anyway, it's a city that appeals to me. Even though I couldn't find the good cheeses right away." He's moving around, almost pacing.

"Did you know my husband was a doctor?"

He stops. "No. No, I don't think I know anything about him." His look is a question: Did he not take care of himself? "And he died young."

"He was shot."

"My God. I'm sorry. How awful."

Yes, awful. Terrible. Tragic. All of those things. "Someone shot him coming out of his office in Shadyside. Took his wallet."

He shook his head. "They know who?"

"No."

For a moment, she thinks to ask him if he has any connection to those television shows that help to track a killer. But most of those shows must be made after the fact, once the thing is solved.

"I wish I could do something for you," he says quietly. "Do you have any faith in the police? Are they on to anything?"

Christie asked her not to talk about the case, at all, to

anyone. Standard procedure. It's so easy to talk here. Her heart starts to beat hard with the feeling she has already said too much.

"I can tell they haven't, by your expression."

"My task is philosophical," she says. "Inner. I have to come to terms with it, however long it takes. People think I'm good at that. Being rational."

"Rational might be a little overrated."

"Might be." She was surprised to see it was almost ten o'clock. "I said one glass of wine, I've had two, and I'm still here." She stood up to go.

"Don't rush on my account. Talk is good. I can do the rest of my work tomorrow morning."

"It's okay. It's past time."

He opens the front door for her and walks her the twenty-five feet home, not touching her elbow, but hovering behind her as if he might. "Try to take care of yourself," he says. "You deserved a better deal."

"I'm not sure anybody *deserves* anything," she quips. "The machine is very arbitrary."

"I'll maybe debate that with you someday."

CHRISTIE, HAVING DROPPED THE KIDS OFF, HAVING STUDIED HIS list of names, taken out the garbage, yawned, and climbed into bed, wondered what detective he would torture with this new work of running down old missing persons. He could hear the groans. It was drudgery, checking Social Security numbers, trying to locate families—important drudgery, but nonetheless . . .

Marina said, "You want me to do something for you?" reading his thoughts.

"No, I can't let you. It's not your worry."

"Okay. Use me, though. Another mind, anyway."

"Well, people tend to go back to their right names. Eventually. Use their Social Security numbers for something somewhere along the line. Wouldn't you think? We ought to be able to catch him that way if he's alive."

"I would think so. Usually."

"I keep not telling the widow about this part of the investigation because there's got to be some reason her husband didn't clue her in."

"Maybe he was embarrassed to be obsessed."

Christie nodded, slid down into the bed. "I should take you on a nice trip. Where would you like to go?"

"Cayman Islands. France. Italy. Greece. Sometime."

He felt his eyebrows raise, but he said a quiet, "Okay." Elizabeth Shepherd had wanted to go places, and they never got to do it. He didn't want that to happen to them, truly he didn't, but the idea of trotting off to Europe didn't appeal to him, either. Well, it *did*, but only if he could have a personality transplant in between. He would need to shed some of his Americanness and become a discerning, walking *appetite*; he would have to get contemplative about cathedrals and ruins and paintings. He could do it; he just couldn't do it easily.

The house made its settling night noises and he thought, I really should get some sleep.

She said, "I'm a good detective, you know I am. Uncredentialed, but, hey, what does that matter? Sometimes, I seriously think to get some P.I. to take me on. I could be useful. It might be as close to acting as I get."

"You're almost serious." She needed to get herself cast in something pronto. Why was nobody doing *Phaedra* or those things she said she was good at? She was amazing and meant to be *looked at* while she spoke and did things. Her job in the public schools wasn't going to satisfy those emotional needs to go down deep into a role. Acting needs.

"Almost."

"You were great with the kids this weekend."

Her eyebrows went up, down. He has never seen eyebrows like hers in his whole life, so perfect—completely natural, arching, graceful—a person just wanted to reach out and make sure they were real.

"Catherine must say things about me still. To the kids. That I'm the person who interrupted your family life. Whatever."

"She probably does say things. Out of her own unhappiness. But what made you think of it now?"

"Only that no matter how great I am with them, I'll never be Mom, and they'll never be really free with me."

"But they are free with you."

"No, no, they're not. You just don't see. They're performing a little. They know how they're supposed to be."

"I think maybe you see performance a little too easily wherever you look." He was surprised at how irritable his voice was.

"Maybe I do. But every time they come here, I start all over again. The good feelings don't accumulate and stay still. Like stocks or something. They're there, but devalued, depleted. And I'm waiting for them to plump up again."

"I'm going to talk to them."

"It won't do any good. It just is. A fact of life. I'd give anything not to have brought it up at bedtime."

"You have to say what you think."

They tossed for a while, both of them, before falling asleep.

ELIZABETH HELD A PILLOW CLOSE TO HER AS SHE USED TO WHEN she was pregnant. The memory came back and was sweet. The pillow shifting under her hip, between her legs. Dan spooning behind her, asking if his arm bothered her, trying to find the spot between breast and belly that would not add pressure. Nice, nice. She can almost feel him. She drifts, numb with too much wine, drifts into her past when things were growing, not dying. *Toward* versus away from; *life* versus death; *growth* versus decay. The needle makes jagged mountains and valleys, a design that says diastole, systole; the needle flatlines. Just like that.

Sleep arrives.

An hour later, she is wide awake, the pillow tossed off the bed, her nightgown twisted. She's sweating, lying without covers over her. What was the dream? She can't catch it. Her heart is pounding. Her body feels thin, wiry, her stomach concave, not pregnant, but the other way, hungry, waiting to be filled.

She gathers the pillow up and curls over it again, waiting for Daniel. He's not behind her, holding her, but in front of her at a distance. He's the film she's watching, the dream she's having. He's sitting in his car, about to start up. A boy comes up to him. Says something. He's surprised, but he talks quietly, trying to calm the boy. He doesn't move fast. He doesn't want to alarm the boy, who is desperate, scared. Anger, anger would have been better. Doesn't he know that, after all these years? It's the gentleness that maddens the boy. The gun. He doesn't quite believe it. He thinks, No, please. The shot. Pain? No, she decides, no, something more important in the last seconds, coming to terms with. That would be Daniel, working to understand.

Why did he not hand over the wallet?

Trying to save a soul. It wouldn't have been the money. Or pride. It was soul against soul.

She cannot sleep.

She sleeps.

IT WAS SIMPLE. HE WAS SHAKING WHEN HE WALKED UP TO THE car. He said, "It's me."

Dan was older, had not aged well, the man who was now Frank Razzi thought. Dan had become middle aged, with tired circles around his eyes. "I knew" was all he said when he looked up and recognized his half brother. "You must have had a hard time all these years."

Now, why did he assume that? The anger Frank always tried to tamp down blossomed and filled him. "I've done all right."

"Where are you staying?"

"I live here. In town," he lied. His lie surprised him as much as it apparently surprised Dan, but he liked it, he savored it, because it said, *You've missed something.* "I've lived here all along."

"That I didn't guess. Doing what?"

"Never mind."

"I think maybe . . ." Dan had been confused, undecided about what to do next. "Do you want to get in? We could go to my place. I'll just call Elizabeth. She was after me to get home and get something to eat. I'm sure there's plenty and we could . . ." He began to reach for his cell phone.

"No. Put it down."

"All right. All right. I hope to talk to you, though, if not at my house, somewhere. How can I do that?"

"And what, put somebody on my tail? Try to get me locked up?"

"I'd do whatever was necessary to help you. I don't know how to convince you of that."

"You can't."

"If you're not going to let me help you, look, I'm going to go home. If you can't stop running and making things worse for yourself, I don't know what to do." Dan reached toward his key in the ignition.

Frank almost laughed. "You said I never had a chance anyway." Dan looked up, surprised. "Didn't you?"

"The newspaper, you mean? I think I said, 'not much of a chance.' To me, that meant you had odds against you, but it didn't mean you couldn't make it with, with . . ."

"Effort? Moral backbone?"

"My phrasing bothered you, I see that, but look where it was coming from. I didn't know what to think. I thought you were dead. I mean, I believed it, but then I got the idea maybe you weren't. As if I could sense it. Come with me. We'll sit calmly and talk this out."

"No. Say what you have to say here. Ask what you have to ask."

Dan looked distressed. "Did you kill someone in Atlantic City?"

"Now that, too!"

"I don't know what to think."

"But you've told people to look for me. Who?"

"No one."

"I don't believe that."

"No one. I looked for you. I never even told Elizabeth because I didn't want to upset her."

"I don't believe you."

"It's true."

"What do you want with me?"

"I want . . ."

That's when he showed the gun, right there in his hand as he gestured. "You want me to go to jail to please you? Self-righteous son of a bitch. Why is it up to you to condemn me?"

Finally, Dan was scared. He reached for the phone.

"Drop the phone."

He didn't drop it. He tried to tilt the keypad toward the light.

Frank shot. He didn't plan to shoot, nor did he expect it to be so perfect a shot. But there it was, a done thing. "Please no, please no," Dan was saying, even after it was too late and the blood was pumping out of him. The phone dropped.

"Help me," Dan said simply.

But he hadn't meant what Frank thought at first, not something about help for the body. It was a done thing; the two men of medicine knew it. "Elizabeth . . ." he whispered quietly. He tried to reach for the phone. That was it. Speech ended abruptly and the head went back. The heart was a swift, speedy death.

Once more he could say he hadn't intended it. But he must have. He had taken the gun with him, after all. He had shot once and got the heart. He had to decide what to do. He leaned against the car door, casually, as if chatting. He listened for sounds of people coming toward him. Nothing. Sirens? Nothing. Automatically another part of his mind took over.

He felt for a pulse. He reached for a wallet. He walked away. Again. Again.

10

CHRISTIE CALLED DEREK JOHNSON AGAIN AND GOT HIM ON THE first ring. Who was the woman who had disturbed Ross with a story that her cousin had seen a man she thought was Gerald Paul LaBeau at an airport in Florida?

The retired P.I. said Dan Ross never told him the name of the woman. Just that it was someone who had a relative, a cousin, who lived in Phoenix and saw a man she thought was LaBeau when she happened to be traveling in Florida. Johnson said, "I'm not even sure what airport it was, but it runs in my mind it was not Miami, because he didn't say the name of a city. I didn't take notes. I tried to tell him I was retired and didn't want the case. Of course, by the time I said all that in a polite manner, Ross had already treated me to a few details."

"Ross seemed like a guy who would keep going once he got an idea."

"Yeah. I gave him the name of another P.I., John Lipinski, he's a guy I trust. But Ross said he would handle it on his own. He must have, because last time I talked to Lipinski, he said he never got the case."

Christie called Lipinski anyway. The P.I. muttered that he could have used the work, business was slow, but no, Ross had not come to him.

Thin trails, for sure.

That afternoon, he sent a detective to Taylor Allderdice

for a yearbook for Ross's class and the one before it and after it.

When it arrived, he couldn't help being fixed again on the pages that included Dan Ross and Gerald Paul LaBeau. They didn't look much alike. They were boys. Young. The youth of both of them touched him. Dan looked hopeful, worried, kind—that tentative smile. But looking at Gerald Paul, he wasn't sure. Cagey? Clever? Alert? Or maybe just trying to fit in, not quite natural or comfortable. He flipped the pages for Ted Luckey. Engaging. Hopeful *and* clever.

Christie combed the books himself for same-name classmates, although cousins would not necessarily have the same last name. He found seven, but only three were sets of women. The problem was to keep gossip about the investigation from getting around, but he was going to have to take a few chances. He called the school again and got the name of the person in charge of the last reunion— last June, it would have been—and she turned out to be the class president as well. She was Amy Berkholtz.

"We're tracking down some random details," he said. He made up another story, a simple reversal: Ross might have told a patient something that bothered the patient. "We have to check everything, even if it's flimsy. Do you know anyone in your class who had a cousin in the class?"

"Cousins. There must have been at least a couple of sets of cousins."

"Two women," Christie said.

"Nothing comes to mind," Berkholtz said. "And I thought I knew it all. I could ask around."

"How discreetly can you do that?"

"Very discreetly. You have no reason to believe me, but I can. I'm not a gossiper. And . . . and I want the person who did this to be found."

A day later, Berkholtz called him back. "We had a woman in our class who had a cousin in our class that she was pretty close to. Dana Straub, our classmate, doesn't live here anymore. She lives in Phoenix. The cousin *was*

Maureen Hamilton, but now it's Maureen Peterson. I don't know if she was a patient or a friend of Ross's. I couldn't ask that kind of thing without arousing interest."

"Thanks."

"Commander? Oh, never mind."

"What?"

"I wondered if I could ever find out if I helped."

Christie made a note. "I'll call you."

Okay, reason enough to call Straub in Phoenix. It took him two days to get the actual person answering her phone. He didn't want to leave any information on the machine.

The woman who finally answered the phone had a businesslike voice.

After he introduced himself, he made his inquiry, trying to sound casual. "You had an idea you saw the brother of Doc Ross. It's always so tricky when someone has died and a story like that gets started. I mean, it can be crazy, turn into a rumor, all that, but I need to track it down," he explained, "just because we track down everything that's part of a case. What made you think it was the brother, adopted brother, wasn't it?" He could hear the woman moving something and then putting dishes in the dishwasher—an unmistakable sound, water running and then the clink of cup against glass.

"Something in the manner," she said. "I got it like a flash."

"He wasn't a dead lookalike?"

"No, he was older and darker and handsomer. Well put together. The kid was kind of geeky."

"Then your guy at the airport was pretty different-looking?"

"Yes."

"Was a lawyer, is that right?"

"Practicing in Detroit. So he said. I could have sworn there was some sort of recognition when I asked him *how* I knew him. Then I told him I was *sure* I knew him from somewhere, maybe high school, and the man kind of twitched."

"Maybe just a surprise reaction of some sort."

"It looked like shock. But then right after the sort of *snap* to attention, he was very smooth and formal. He made a point of sitting far away from me. I thought that was odd and it made me think all the more I was right. Then the connection and the name came to me, high school, Paul LaBeau. I figured he'd become a hot-shot lawyer and didn't want to be bothered with anyone from his past. And it kind of pissed me off."

"I see. Which airport was this?"

"Tampa."

"Who did you tell about this meeting?"

"A couple of people out here. The only person I'm in touch with back home is my cousin. I don't go to reunions or anything like that. I told her and she said, no way, LaBeau was listed on all the reunion rosters as deceased. Last thing in the world I thought was that she would go straight to the doctor with it. She can be really dense. Apparently she got the same snap reaction I got. She upset him. I never would have wanted to hurt the guy—Ross, I mean. But even now I can see that other guy's face. I heard Doc Ross got killed. A street thug, my cousin said."

"Yes," he answered slowly.

"So, is everybody sure Paul LaBeau died?"

"It sure looks that way. Very dead. Would you know of any reason he would be dangerous if he hadn't?" Which was a very weird question, but it didn't stop her.

"Well, families, you know. Money and all that."

"Yes, I suppose."

"Are you looking into that?"

There was something about her directness he didn't know how to avoid. "Yes. I have to look into everything no matter how far-fetched. Describe the man as well as you can."

"Six feet, possibly an inch or two more. Trim enough. Expensive clothes. Brown hair, a little bit of gray. Brown eyes. Fairly regular features." She paused. "He sounds like a lot of people."

"Kind of. You could be describing me if you found my features regular, which you probably wouldn't."

She laughed. It was kind of a relief to him, maybe to her, too, her being less defensive now.

"There was something that caught me, I don't know what. Aura or some shit. Well, I guess there are doubles. If I'm dead wrong, that could explain it. People have doubles."

"Absolutely. I hear that all the time."

"Okay, so it wasn't Paul, then."

"We all get excited by wild ideas like that. They're almost never true. But I'm checking it out. I'd appreciate it if you didn't talk. Especially not to your cousin. Until I call you back." That last phrase would hopefully fix her cooperation.

"Okaaaay."

He thanked her for her time. The manner of the man, she had said. Not the nose or the ears or the eyes. Was manner more lasting?

ELIZABETH PUTS MUSIC ON HER CAR RADIO TO TRY TO GET HER spirits up while she packs the car. Lauren can only come for one night to their cottage, only Friday. Elizabeth tried to let her daughter off the hook totally, but Lauren insisted she would come for Friday night and most of Saturday if her mom could pick her up at the Breezewood interchange. Anything, anything, Elizabeth thought. Breezewood was nothing. She would happily drive the whole way to D.C. to get Lauren. She carries a couple of boxes of her husband's papers to the trunk of her car and tucks them in along with a little bit of this and that—some food, an extra set of sweats, a copy of *Interpreter of Maladies* (which sounds a little like a textbook for therapists)—she's taking to the cottage. She will stay the whole weekend even though Lauren can't stay long.

Alone out in the woods when solitude hurt . . . Kind of strange to cure her heartache with more of the same, like a drinker having a few hairs of the dog the next morning. Why hadn't she called Margot to see if she could come along? Even now she could call to invite her; or Margot could come up on Saturday. But no, Margot would feel like a caretaker. And Elizabeth would hobble around, trying not to drop forty pounds of grief at Margot's feet. No, she would try to enjoy her daughter's company on Friday, then grind through Saturday and Sunday alone.

So she was packing the car after work on Friday, when she saw the BMW turn the corner and drive up the driveway next to hers.

"Perfect timing," Frank Razzi said. Then his face fell. "Oh, you're going away somewhere?"

"For the weekend."

"Oh. I was just going to ask you if you could—I was going to offer to cook you dinner tomorrow night."

"Oh, sorry, I won't be here."

"If you'll be back on Sunday, if you feel like it, that is, I could make it then?"

"I don't know. . . ."

"It's okay. I've been where you are. You just want to hole up. I don't mean to intrude, only to let you know I'm here. I'm going to write down my cell number. You just call me if you think you're up for it."

He pulled out a small notebook that looked almost new, but Elizabeth could see there were tidy notes in much of it as he flipped through to look for an empty page. He wrote neatly, then tore the page out. "I hope you're going someplace nice." His eyes caught the boxes in the trunk and then the grocery bag with a bottle of wine sticking out. He seemed pleased by something.

"Our cottage," she answered.

"Good. Good. You have a long drive?"

"No, it's not far."

"Well, you have my phone number in case you need it. Is there anything I can do, watch the house, anything?" He was dressed a little formally today, in roughly woven wool pants and a jacket, a shirt but no tie. Elizabeth had the impression he would be driven crazy by a tie. She could picture him claustrophobically clawing at anything around his neck. But then, she was just playing the shrink's guessing game. And the one thing you knew if you were any good was that people were surprising. Strange and marvelous snowflakes.

Elizabeth cataloged her passing feelings and came up with a truth. She had wanted to go to the cottage this weekend partly to *avoid* Frank Razzi. She had been afraid she would be weakened by loneliness and would end up sitting next door in his funny, nearly empty house, drinking wine, letting him tell her stories about *Cybill*, *Grace Under Fire*, things she's never even watched. Now she faces the accuracy of her prediction; she has an invitation to do just that.

"Let me know, anytime," he is saying. "I'm not going anywhere, too much work. So if you're up for it, it's nothing fancy, just a little pasta. Maybe toss some shrimp into it. Do you need to have anything carried in or out before you go?"

"No, I'm set."

"I'll leave you alone to get started."

A TALK WITH MICHELLE LABEAU, WHO WAS NOWHERE TO BE FOUND in Bellingham or anywhere else, would be mighty interesting. Hadn't she *wanted* to see the body? Straight to ashes. Had she believed it herself? Christie put one of his best people, John Potocki, who turned out to be good on the Net, to study the real estate history of the house in Bellingham.

Potocki came back with the following information: The house had been sold twice. The present owners had bought it from a man who bought from a group of co-owners in the late seventies. Christie looked at the list of names, the co-owners, conjuring the aging hippies who had once lived there. Where were they now? Probably in sales and insurance, not playing guitars. People flipped one-eighties.

LaBeau's name was not among the owners, but she had lived there, according to the old phone numbers. Now, if anyone was still in touch with her . . .

He patted his young detective, Potocki, on the back and asked him to search out current addresses and phone numbers for the people who had once owned the house. There, no need to bother Marina.

"Call them, too?" Potocki asked.

"No, just bring me the names. And go back to looking for Michelle LaBeau again, using other cities."

"Okay."

When he had all that organized, he called Bellingham and found a detective with a little time on his hands. "Cold case," he said, as if offering a candy.

"How old?" The voice was skeptical.

"Thirty years at its oldest." That was no doubt the age of the detective he was talking to. Outside in the main office, he could see his own detectives answering phones, reading, carrying pieces of paper from one desk to another. Blood on the pavement. Drug overdoses. Stoolies in prison. Things that were a year old, two at most, could start to feel ancient.

But the young Bellingham man, Dave Bittle, said, "Why not?"

Christie asked him to go out to look at LaBeau's old address, nose around.

"What's the case?" Bittle asked curiously.

"Murder of a doctor here. Could go way back to who said what to whom a long time ago. Could. No guarantees."

Bittle called him from a cell phone two hours later. "It's a real nice house now," he reported, "completely renovated. Young couple who bought it do all the work themselves. The wife was actually working on the exterior paint this morning. She had just gone in for a coffee and answered the door and showed me around, no paranoia. Unfortunately for you, there's no junk left over anywhere. She was pretty proud that anything left in the basement she'd carted out a couple of years ago. And she didn't know a thing about a woman named Michelle LaBeau. Mostly I had to listen to how she and her husband had sanded and stained the floors, even though they had kids under ten, two boys—that kind of thing."

"Kids'll challenge a floor."

"That's what she said."

"Did you tell her there used to be marijuana plants in the backyard?"

"I didn't mention it. All that's there now is an apple tree right in the center. Kids use the yard," Bittle said, "basketball hoop, that kind of thing. It was real nice. I'll tell you, it's exactly the kind of place me and my wife are looking for."

"Do you have any more time to give me?"

"Yeah, so long as my lieutenant gives me the okay."

"Can you ask around the neighborhood about LaBeau? Where'd-she-go, where-is-she-now kind of thing. And at the old apartment where she'd raised her son? Mind you, in both cases there will be renters and owners in between, but sometimes a person knows something. Anything might help us."

"That won't take long. Anything else?"

Jeez, Christie thought, don't say no to this kind of offer. "Here's a thought, then. Go by the schools the kid would have gone to. See if by any chance there is anybody there who worked there thirty-five, forty years ago. That's not likely, so ask about records on LaBeau's son. This would be a student named Gerald Paul LaBeau. Got it? They'll try not to show you anything."

"Okay, I know that. But what am I asking?"

"Whatever you can pick up."

"Okay." The detective sounded uncertain.

Christie *felt* vague. He didn't *know* what he was looking for. The Bellingham detective probably wondered what aging, dithery people were on the force in Pittsburgh. He summoned an idea. "There might be alternate addresses for the mother in the files. A relative, an aunt. See if you can sweet-talk somebody into coughing something up."

"I'll do what I can. Sir? What's Pittsburgh like as a place to work?"

"I like it. Why?"

"I think of getting me to a city sometime. In my future. That's all."

"If you come for a visit, look me up. I owe you a big dinner and a tour at least."

"Thanks."

Coming to move in where the old fart who lost his edge couldn't cut it anymore, Christie laughed to himself.

LAUREN IS ALREADY STANDING AT THE TURNPIKE INTERCHANGE when Elizabeth gets there. She has a backpack at her feet and an overnight case propped up on a metal railing. Her brown hair has the rag-doll layers that are considered fashionable. She is in blues—a polo shirt, jeans, a light down jacket. She looks thin and sad, her large brown eyes focused on something way up ahead, so she doesn't see her mother drive up. Elizabeth taps the horn as lightly as she can, just a few little bleats, but it makes her daughter jump.

Lauren lifts her two cases and hurries to the car before Elizabeth can get out to help her. "I've got it," she says. "Stay put." She tosses everything into the backseat. The backpack heavy with books thuds to the floor. Lauren climbs in, kisses her mother, and starts to buckle up.

"Let me look at you."

Lauren's hair swings over her face as she messes with the buckle. "I look bad lately."

It's true. She looks tired. But her being able to come for only one day, this a good thing—doesn't it mean she has friends, plans? Another football game? Or is she just taking care of her mother? Yes. She's managed three weekends already.

"Is anything happening?" Lauren asks.

"No," Elizabeth says.

"They don't have any idea who did it?"

"No. They're looking for someone from his high school class. Did Dad say anything like that to you?"

Lauren shook her head. "What's that all about?"

"I don't know. I think they're heading up one blind alley after another."

"I liked Christie." Lauren clicked her seat belt and they

started out. "You did, too. But maybe he doesn't want to tangle with the tough guys."

"He swears they're doing the usual stuff with addicts and informants, all that. They ask around in the jails to find out who heard what. He says he's personally following up the eccentric ideas. If you think how many guns there are, how many guys on dope, how many people in need of money in any city the size of—"

Lauren says thoughtfully, "He prefers some other story to the deadbeat story."

Prefers. And she, Elizabeth, prefers the deadbeat story.

Suddenly Lauren says, "Jeff is seeing someone. Did you know?"

Elizabeth, starting out, pulls over to the side of the road and pauses to take in what her daughter is telling her. "No. He didn't say."

"You know how he is. But when I called him, his roommate thought I was someone named Jenna. So then when I got him on the phone, I said, 'Who's Jenna?' He said she was this very nice person, and gorgeous, and he kept being surprised she was still interested in him. Anyway. They're together all the time, apparently. That's why it's so hard to get hold of him."

"He didn't say."

They're stopped just short of the ramp that will put them back onto the turnpike, going west to the Donegal exit. A truck brakes, then curves around them.

"This isn't a great place to stop," Lauren says. "People might think this is a lane and bash—"

Elizabeth starts forward again.

"He's afraid to tell you, I think. Because, why of all times is his life looking up now?"

Elizabeth knows why. Just that measure of vulnerability in him.

"I think I'm one of those people who's going to be alone forever," Lauren says simply.

"Not true. These things take you by surprise, you know that." Lauren, her Lauren; Elizabeth would die for her, no question. It hurts her that Lauren doesn't know she's fine-looking and way above the average in every way. "Are you hungry?" Elizabeth asks. "Want to stop for a milk shake on the way?"

"Milk shake. Good idea."

They pull off at the next service plaza and order their shakes from TCBY, leaving the car running while they're inside so they will be able to drink the shakes in a heated bubble. As they hurry back to the car, her arm around Lauren, the sun bursts through the clouds. Here it is, again, perfect weather. Elizabeth doesn't want to let go, doesn't want this time with her daughter to be over. She asks, "What time do I have to get you back to Breezewood tomorrow?"

"Two-thirty is my ride."

"Same person?"

"Yeah. Remember Billy Krauss, went to high school with me? He dropped me off, he'll come and pick me up again."

"Billy. I remember. Cute guy."

"He's just a friend, Mom."

Elizabeth nods. "Well, I'm grateful to him for helping you out."

"He's a good guy." Then, as if reading her mother's thoughts, Lauren adds, "I have to get back, not for anything fun, but because I have three hundred pages of reading on reserve."

"Three hundred is a lot."

"Tell me."

A few minutes later, Elizabeth turns to see Lauren has tears in her eyes.

"What is it, honey?"

"I think there were whole years I didn't talk to Dad, really, you know what I mean. And now I miss him and I never can again."

"Think of something you did talk about when you did. Hold on to it."

Lauren nods. Then she starts to laugh and cry at the same time.

Elizabeth waits, drives and waits, hoping for this little piece of memory to be shared.

"It was before junior prom. I didn't have a date and then I finally got one at the last minute. It seemed so important at the time. He hugged me and told me I was great, that I was all these wonderful things—I won't even try to list them." Lauren is still laughing, kind of, crying, too. "I have character, he told me. And a sense of humor. Health. Endurance. Political perspective. I mean, a kid of sixteen just wants to be attractive, acceptable, *hot*, but he tried to tell me all this other stuff."

Why is Lauren laughing? Once more, Elizabeth feels adrift.

"I wore that red dress. Remember? My date said, 'You're kind of flat-chested.' He was horrible. I never told you. I said, 'Yeah, but I have character.' He just looked at me cross-eyed, trying to figure out what that meant."

"You're wonderful."

"Thanks." Lauren's eyes fill up again. And maybe she hasn't quite rejected the compliment.

The cottage is a four-room log cabin fifteen miles off the Donegal exit, near Seven Springs. There are four acres of land on the property, which is all they have to keep people from building encroaching weekend houses. The place has a large living and dining room, a kitchen, and two bedrooms. When the whole family used to come, Jeff would sleep on the pullout sofa in the living room. Elizabeth's idea was to add a new large master bedroom with lots of windows on the woods, so they'd feel they were practically sleeping outdoors, but they hadn't gotten around to it.

"Will the kids want to come here after they're off at college?" Dan wondered.

Elizabeth said, "If they don't right away, by the time they have children, they'll want it again."

Oh, she had asked him from time to time what was going on with him. Inside. Nothing new, he'd say, gently touching her hair. Hard work.

She and Lauren move automatically through the cot-

tage, opening windows to air the place briefly, starting a
fire, checking the back door to be sure nobody has broken
in these last months.

"Everything is dusty," Lauren says.

"Sure."

The wood floors need only a dust mop. The leather furniture could use a damp cloth, the carpets a vacuuming.
When the fire is roaring, Elizabeth pours a couple of buck-
ets of water into the toilet to get it moving. She opens the
kitchen cupboards and sees the hot chocolate Dan sometimes drank here. She opens the closet that is both laundry and pantry, to find a couple of six-packs of Heineken
that he put there maybe a year ago, and a set of his underwear on top of the washer. She folds his things carefully
and puts them aside. In the bedroom, the bed is neatly
made. She flicks on the electric heater.

"Whew. It's colder in here than outside." Lauren shivers.

"Always the way. It takes a day to warm it up."

"I know."

Of course she knows. They've been coming here since
Lauren was seven. They've had birthdays and Thanksgiv-
ings here. She's lugged the turkey and all the fixings. Lauren
has brought friends for a weekend. Jeff has, too. All these
memories—sleeping bags, videotapes, music that made Dan
go out for a walk, pancakes for breakfast, sweet chaos—surface and sink downward again. Mother and daughter wan-
der through the cottage, back and forth, hearing each other
think, feeling each other feel, not intruding.

SHIT. HE'S BEEN ON THE NET, FOUND THE COTTAGE LISTED IN
county property records, but lost his patience with the
map of rural routes. The phone is unlisted. With a phone
number he could get an exact map. What is he going to do
anyway? Go there?

No. Go back to Athens for a day. Make little Bridget
calmer. But what excuse can he give her for a turnaround
trip to L.A. that would have him there for an early Friday

breakfast and nothing else? He could spin it, but his mind is moving too fast to pin down the story.

He stands at the window, wishing he could get in next door. See how they lived, as if his fertile imagination can't provide most of it. Well, he's not going to try any doors of a place with an alarm system. Shit. Shit.

And he's got bigger problems. He reaches into his pocket and pulls out the container of Valium. The doctor with the braid wouldn't give him a refill. Only two left; went to a second doctor in Athens, a kindly man, who said a kindly no; he had tried to tell himself he could do without them, but that was wrong, wrong; he has to get more. Monday in Athens? And if Elizabeth comes to dinner this weekend, what kind of shape will he be in?

More Valium. A quest. He's been too lax, should have gone eight places, trying, but too busy for that shit. He kicks at the kitchen cabinet as if he's starting up a machine that's cranky, then his body is moving to the driveway, the car, even before he has decided *how* he will do it.

Four-thirty. He drives fast, too fast, to the office in Shadyside, parks on the street as he did the first time, and walks toward the building. Cars are pulling out, people—if they are looking—see only a guy walking calmly toward the building. A prescription pad left unattended is what he wants.

He enters the building, feeling courageous. Dan walked here, and here *he* is, too, not afraid. Not afraid. Two floors, the second rented out to plastic surgeons. Get my otoplasty checked, he laughs. Go in for the bletharoplasty I've always wanted! Do my Botox!

Another man comes alongside him at the elevator. Not safe. He goes to the stairs and climbs up the single floor.

The receptionist in the Center for Plastic and Reconstructive Surgery says, with a snap, "We're closed."

"I just need to make an appointment."

She sighs. "You'll have to call on Monday."

"But I'm here, so we should probably make one right

now. I'm actually hoping for a cancellation on Monday that would get me in right away."

"We're booked for four months."

"I know that, see, I'm a friend of the . . ." He can't remember any of the doctors' names he's seen on the door. "Never mind. You wouldn't care who you're rude to."

"I'll need to get the books out again, but there isn't going to *be* anything."

She is so uptight, so vain and stiff. He feels an instant dislike of her that is so undistilled, he is afraid to talk much longer. What if she decides he's too much to handle and calls the police?

"Are any of the doctors still here today?"

"Are you kidding? It's Friday." She is fuming. She slaps the appointment book down and looks. "There isn't anything."

"Please." While he forces his voice down to slow and reasonable, his eyes are canvassing the place, looking for where the prescription pads are kept. Shit, this isn't going to work. Shit. Only two pills left, he waited too long and if this doesn't pan out, he's going to have to go to the emergency room. "Honestly, I'm sorry about the time of day. The Film Office wanted me to do this right away and I'm supposed to ask for the doctor Phil Moravian had."

She looks at him with contempt laced with just the slightest interest. Film Office, well, she twitches a little at that, not much, but a little.

"The Film Office should have given me more detail," he offers.

She hesitates.

Standing there, waiting, he looks at his shaking hands like some fifth-act Lady Macbeth. No blood on him. He never got blood on him. His name is completely different. There is no proof of anything. All he has to do is deny it. "Please. I'm sorry."

"The files are in the back." He almost laughs with relief as she swings her little butt around the desk and out of the reception area to what is presumably a maze of a hallway.

He listens to her footsteps recede, then leans way over the counter and begins opening drawers. Shit. Nothing. It's not going to work.

Her desk is pristine. But the other one behind hers, against the wall, is not. He listens again and, hearing nothing, leans way over the counter and cracks open the door she left by. He can see her at the end of the hall, fuming, looking through folders.

Not very athletic, no, but with one push he could make it over the counter, he could, but what would he say if she . . . Before he knows it, he's over, looking at a much messier desk. He lifts legal pads, coffee cups, stray pencils, a book of some sort. Ha. Ha. There's one stray prescription sheet. It's still in his hand as he hauls himself back over the counter. He's just putting it in his pocket when she comes through the door.

She looks at him. His hand comes out of his pocket, holding car keys.

"I can't find any Phil Moravian in our files."

"Damn." He pinches two fingers to his eyes.

"Do you want an appointment anyway?"

"Yes."

"I can squeeze you in next Friday morning. Early. Like seven-thirty."

"Okay. Good."

"Your name?"

"Ted Luckey."

"Spelled l-u-c-k-y?"

"Right," he says. As if she'll ever see him again.

Close, she's so close, she creates airwaves, moving to the door just behind him to lock up for the weekend.

In order not to have to go to the elevator when she does, or let her see him walking to his car, Frank stops at the second-floor men's room. In there, he goes into a stall, where he stands for a good long time before he pulls out the prescription paper. Stray pencil mark on it. Precious, though, all the more because it's for Type II restricted drugs. Hooray. He'll need some story about why he gets

Valium from a plastic surgeon. Muscle spasms from what sort of surgery? Maybe he can get himself a little bottle of OxyContin, too, while he's at it. A clammy sweat breaks out along his neck and back. He feels the beginning of a throbbing headache. Soon it'll be muscle cramps in his legs and back. That's the trouble with starting on the stuff again and not having enough of it because the bitch in Athens was so, so . . . fucking responsible. It's twenty-three days, he's been breaking the damn things in half, trying to go easy, and saving his last two little pills in the hope he wouldn't feel this much withdrawal. . . .

It's funny when he thinks about all those guys in L.A. juicing themselves up with cocaine, and him with the opposite problem all along—so much natural "brain cocaine" that he needed downers to take various edges off.

Leaning against the door of the stall, he writes a prescription for OxyContin, and he's about to go for Valium, when he changes his mind and writes it for 2 mg alprazolam, Xanax, because he likes Xanax better, always has, even though it's much more dangerous than Valium, so he'll have to watch the booze. In a moment of inspiration, brilliance, really, he makes the scrip out for Daniel Ross. That way, if it doesn't work, nobody will be looking for Frank Razzi. After he tucks everything back into his pocket, he leaves the building by the stairs, and the door he came in. He passes an old couple standing around waiting for a taxi or something, but that's about it, they're talking to each other. He drives toward East Liberty, then Lawrenceville, trying two Rite Aids and one Eckert, chosen for their placement in these low-income areas, but the number of questions he's asked by sleepy-looking pharmacists who are on the *lookout* for bad scrips alarms him. In each case, he says, "It's okay. I'll just go to my local pharmacy. I was just on this end of town. It's fine."

It's six-thirty and he's not sure what to do. Rush-hour traffic is not over yet and certainly not what he's in the mood for, but it occurs to him to try the opposite kind of pharmacy, something upscale. It all comes down to the individual pharmacist anyway. So, he heads south, thinking he will try the Mt. Lebanon area.

Calm down, calm down first, he tells himself. The nerves are churning stomach juices and he's hungry. He stops the car at a strip on Banksville Road, goes into the Union Grill, and orders a meat-loaf dinner with mashed potatoes. Sitting there, he shakes out one of his remaining two pills and takes it, washing it with a sip of water, and concentrating on the scratch of the pill going down his throat with the promise of calm, calm. After scooping some ice cubes out of his glass, he downs the rest of the water in one long drink. Good. Water. Healthy. Cleans out the system, right?

Alcohol, too, washes out the system. Kills germs, purifies, provides communion. The waitress delivers a glass of the best wine he could find in this place, a passable Shiraz, and Frank takes a nice big slug of the good, purifying stuff.

Now. Calmly. Very calmly, think. He saw the sign for Medfast Pharmacy on his way into this little strip of stores. Medfast. Never *heard* of it. And he didn't see a *storefront*, so it must be *inside* the Kuhn's supermarket two doors away from the restaurant. He stuffs down a piece of roll, thinking, Follow the dots, huh, why not try it? Nobody will know him here. Dan's name. Powered, as always, by something not exactly logical but inspired by thrill, sensation, he beckons the waitress and says, "I'm just going to run this prescription to the drugstore. I'll be coming right back."

"No problem. Your food will be here in about five minutes." She smiles at him as if she likes him. Great smile. Things are looking up.

There's nothing to associate him, Frank Razzi, with the car out there with its Ohio plates, and so he continues into the Kuhn's and over to the Medfast counter where it seems to be kind of busy. The pharmacist looks at his piece of paper, so skillfully and professionally written, it's almost unreadable. He sure does know how to write a prescription. "ID?" she asks.

He fishes it out, Dan's driver's license flipped over quickly, then his hospital ID card.

He watches her. She smiles and writes down Dan's name. She reads the prescription where he's added, *as needed for spasms in groin,* and *as needed for pain.*

"Hmmm," she says.

"Don't ask," he laughs. "It's not the best thing that ever happened to me." To himself he laughs, too, to think of what kind of plastic surgery a man would have to his nether parts.

"I need your address and your insurance card, then."

He gives Dan's address, while quickly showing the insurance card and saying, "I'm switching insurance. I'll pay cash."

"We're running about a half hour behind. Can you pick it up then?"

Perfect, perfect, have his food in the meantime.

The hot meat loaf and mashed potatoes are a good, old-fashioned delight. He orders a second Shiraz and pays his bill out of the left pocket, as Frank Razzi.

He scans the parking lot for police, the store for police. Nothing. All is calm.

The prescription—he gets a smile and a sympathetic shake of the head—he pays in cash as he promised. He searches the pharmacist's face, sees nothing except pleasantness, and walks calmly to his car. The Valium has hit, done its magic. He feels good, real good. He knows without a doubt that little Bridget is pining for him and that Elizabeth will cave in soon.

Once he's back in his house, he calls Bridget. "Hi, lovey, worried about you," he says. "You terrified me last week. Are you hanging on okay?"

"I'm good."

"Why is that?"

"I dunno. Maybe I got used to being alone. I sing to the records. I'm really, really enjoying your work. Do you know what I counted just in the boxes? One hundred manuscripts. Altogether. Some are really old."

"I'm really old. Many of them are no good and lots of them aren't mine, either, about half are ones I doctored, as the expression goes. You're seeing twenty years of work."

"The ones you gave me to work on are pretty new, though."

"True."

"And yet I never see you writing. Do you write when you go away for the weekend?" Her question is sly, playful.

He laughs. "I wonder what you really want to know."

After a long silence, she says, "More about you, I guess."

"I wish I could tell you. I wish I could be there right now, relaxing." He's sitting at the kitchen table in Pittsburgh, with a new glass of wine in front of him, and a delicious lethargy coming over him, too delicious to wave away. No way could he get his butt the whole way to Athens tonight.

BRIDGET HAD PANICKED WHEN SHE FIRST REALIZED EVERY MOVE she made on the Net was recorded in the history. She called the university's hot-help-tips line and described herself as Razzi's secretary. Now she knew how to delete a day's spying: TOOLS, OPTIONS, CONTROL, click, pass OPEN, pass OPEN NEW, and choose DELETE. A day wiped out so that he could not see that she followed him, traveled his paths. Now, having heard affection in his voice, she feels a confusion about her shoddy behavior that makes her blush. He likes her. But then, where does he go? L.A. or not? She votes not.

It *feels* as if he's calling her from an apartment across town.

And. There's the odometer, which she's checked twice now. Four hundred miles one time, four hundred twenty miles the other. He either goes to some airport other than Columbus or goes somewhere in addition to Columbus or goes somewhere instead of Columbus. Those are the choices.

Which is it? On his desk is a stack of mail, unopened. No. No, it's criminal to steam open an envelope. And he's been kind to her. Gave her a hundred dollars to go to the supermarket on Thursday, and let her drive, too—which is how she had a chance to check the odometer the second time.

Brainstorm.

Among his receipts are slips of things he's charged. With his number, she can call the card company to check on his bill. This is something Jess used to do all the time because she could never remember what she had spent. Friday-night blues, tomorrow the Saturday-night variety. She needs an activity to keep her from going back to the Go-Bar. As if she had a decent time there to begin with, which she did not.

She makes herself a bowl of pasta and dresses it with a bought pesto sauce. Not bad, not bad. Slowly, not rushing or panicking, she gets the 800 numbers for Frank's AMEX card and his MasterCard. She tries AMEX first and stumbles when the voice-mail system asks her for a Social Security number. Of course, of course, and they're going to want a date of birth, too. All that stuff. Saddened at what she is doing—spying, lying—she takes a deep breath. From the desk she removes a small file-cabinet key, and moments later she begins to go through hard-copy files that have been locked away.

Manuscripts. More manuscripts. Medical plan. Hospitalization plan. Investments. Everything has the L.A. address. Insurance. Well, the insurance folder gives her the Social Security number and birth date anyway.

She dials again and punches in these newly acquired numbers to AMEX, but gets a message that the information is no longer available. The intelligent and watchful computer seems to remember she hesitated too long the first time.

Her ride of the MasterCard train is smoother. Of the last five transactions, however, they give her only amounts, not types of purchases. She pushes a zero for an operator.

"May I have your name and account number?"

"I just keyed all that in."

"That's all right. We need it again."

In a less-than-steady voice, she speaks these numbers.

"And who am I speaking to?"

"Mrs. Razzi."

"And may I have your Social Security number?"

"Mine?" She gives her own. "But the card is in my husband's name." She gives his number.

"I cannot give information if your name is not on our records."

"Oh. Oh, it was just something simple," she says, feeling so sick she thinks she might toss the pasta.

"And what is your question?" The actual operator has taken on some of the mechanical qualities of the computerized voices.

"Well," Bridget begins, "we try to keep really good records and we forgot to get our gas receipts the last two times we filled up. I wanted to get the amounts."

There is a silence. In it, Bridget can hear the woman saying to herself, "You've got to be kidding, right?" But after a while, she says, "I see a BP charge for $19.82."

"Empty tank," Bridget laughs. She sounds like an idiot. "And where was that?"

"Rodi Road."

"Oh, shoot, of course. 'Road-Eye'?"

"Yes."

"Oh, right. And there was another one. Yesterday."

"Exxon, West Virginia."

"Right. Thanks."

She really thinks she might throw up. The operator must have thought she was a wife checking on an errant husband. West Virginia. West *Virginia*.

What was that movie she saw where the woman went through her husband's things when he left the house? No, the husband went through his wife's things, wasn't it? No, both. Both. They spied on each other. Is that what she's been reduced to? She's nuts, that's what it comes to. Nuts and— No. That's the old thinking.

She is not bad-looking. She has a little wit. And he wants her. She knows it, feels it. Maybe it's only the kind of wanting that counts for very little. She can't help but feel touched by it. When they talk, she can see she lifts his spirits, and it feels good, being the bright entertainment. He's depressed. He takes those pills. Whoever he visits can't be making him very happy.

His date of birth is January 15, 1960. He's twenty-five years older than she is. Twenty-five. That's too much.

He has such sad eyes when you catch him unawares.

The phone rings.

"I . . . I felt worried about you," he says. "Don't go out to those lousy places, okay? I'll do better by you."

"I'm not going out."

"What are you doing?" His voice is slow, mellow, lazy.

"Absolutely nothing. Staring at the wall." In front of her is his open file cabinet, just yawning out his secrets. She is turning out to be a rotten person, a liar. "I'll be okay," she says. "I'll sit tight."

But he left the key there in the desk, didn't he? And he kept her there, "sitting tight" in his place. People's ways are circuitous.

They are both creative. They both have a kind of mettle.

HE CAN HARDLY STAY AWAKE, EVEN THOUGH IT'S ONLY EARLY evening. Finished off the Valium! and drank the better part of another bottle of wine and can't stay awake. The girl is coming around. He hears it in her voice, she has turned some corner, is ready now. Tomorrow, Saturday, start on Xanax, drive back then.

For the first time in a long time, he lets himself think of Dan. He reaches deep into his left pocket and pulls out the new wallet with the library card and the driver's license, the medical card, the insurance cards, the family pictures. The kids, twelve or thirteen years old, toothy and awkward. Dan and Elizabeth, their arms around each other, a small section of a snapshot.

Elizabeth is in bad shape now, that's for sure. The sorrow is all over her, in her walk, her skin, the fall of her arms. He can't stop looking at her, that's the truth.

Frank studies the picture of Dan with Elizabeth. Five

years ago? Her hair was longer. He was possibly trimmer. He wears the classic Dan expression, slightly shy, slightly . . . Fury creeps in past the Valium and the wine. Frank puts the picture down and tries to get his breath under control. Everything feels soft around him, fuzzy. He must hide the wallet. It's unsafe to keep it in his pocket. Even driving back from the pharmacy, he should have put it somewhere, deep in the trunk, deep under the carpeted flap.

He looks at the driver's license. The pharmacist didn't even so much as blink. Why, he and Dan look nothing alike. Well, she didn't look, then, did she? He has gotten away with it and has enough Xanax now for a couple of weeks, if he takes it wisely. Always there are those good intentions: to cut down, taper off gradually, do without chemicals. He hobbles to the small powder room on the first floor, studies himself in the mirror, studies the picture, lets out a large sob, which he stifles. Doesn't want to know what the sob means, doesn't want to know.

Everything back in the wallet. He makes his way out to the garage, opens it up, powers the door down so there will be no passing witnesses. He opens the trunk, tucks the wallet under the spare, which is under the flap. He would get rid of it altogether, but he might need it again at another pharmacy. No, no, the truth: It feels good to have it.

After that, he sits in front of the TV like a zombie, tamping down rage and memory, getting rid of days, weeks, like most of America, now that he thinks of it, so how is he any different? People prance and get serious and kill each other in front of him. How is he any different, in the big picture?

ON SATURDAY MORNING, HE HAS A BIG EVERYTHING—DICK, HANG-over, headache. It hurts to move, but he moves. By the third cup of coffee, which is around eleven o'clock, he realizes the coffee is not going to do it, so he pours the rest of the wine, about half a glass, and downs it. Slowly, things begin to get more right. His work, his own work. He approaches his laptop warily, sighing. He can't do it. Not today.

He hasn't written anything in a month. Write what stirs you, he tells his students. Ha, if he dared, if he bloody dared.

A little ride. A little getting to know "da 'burgh." A little brush with it, coming close to it, the big *it*, the way he did in going into that medical office last night. Armor-building, he supposes a shrink would call it, skin-toughening. Eye-of-the-stormishness. Damn, no, he laughs, aphrodisiac, more like. The car hums. He passes the Pocusset Safe House, which he's now pretty toughened against, and he drives into Oakland, where Ted Luckey used to work. All gone, no restaurant there anymore. Drugstores. Everywhere. Which shows to go you just how many *chemicals* we Americans take. He loops around and drives up over Beacon to Dallas, over to the Homewood Cemetery, which has, as he remembers it from a long time ago, some kind of stone building and an entry for cars. Right. He parks the BMW and goes into the office, where he watches an attendant mark a map for an old couple in front of him.

". . . wanted to bring flowers," the old woman is saying.

"You can order them here," the young ponytailed attendant tells them. She points. "At the greenhouse. The Thanksgiving and Christmas orders are coming in now."

"I don't understand," the old woman says.

"Holiday orders and standing orders. Some people have orders for flowers. At the greenhouse. Then we put them on the grave." She works to explain herself to the old woman. "People who can't get here. We put the flowers on for them."

It makes him laugh, it really does, how some people actually like their families.

"I wanted to be the one to put them on the grave."

"There are flower shops on Murray," the attendant says kindly. "Do you know Murray Avenue? It's close."

The man nods. "It's okay, Hannah. We got all day. What does it matter we backtrack?" The attendant watches them shuffle out as if they might trip and fall without her concentrated attention.

In turn, Frank watches *her*, wondering what her life is

and what it will become and why she seems happy working here in a graveyard.

"May I help you?" she asks.

"Grave of Daniel Ross, recent death, about a month ago." Armor-building, skin-toughening.

"I know who you mean. His wife comes every couple of days. Very sad. Lots of people knew him."

His face flushes. "I'll need a map."

After she taps something into her computer, reads it, taps another couple of keys, she marks a map for him.

"It's walkable," she says. "It's just a left, a right, a left. A short distance."

He walks it. Stone upon stone. Why, he played here as a boy, sort of, scaring himself, and once came on a scavenger hunt when he was supposed to get a bouquet off a fresh grave. The temperature has gone down to thirty-eight. His light jacket is not enough to keep the shivers away.

There it is. There they are, both of them, father and brother. The real wife, the woman he knows only from pictures, Dan's mother. And a place for Elizabeth. No stones for his mother or him, of course. He looks around to see if anyone is looking. No. He spits on his father's grave, kicks it once, but hesitates before Dan's, saying, "If only you had left me *alone.*"

He walks back to his car and is soon on the Parkway, where he makes his way in a few short minutes over to the North Side and a few short minutes later to West Park. He parks on Resaca, crosses the street, walks through the park. Nothing bad happens to him: he is not struck down, he does not go into an apoplectic fit. Armor holds. He says, "Yes, I did it," aloud, and a moment later, "I had to." The park is not empty. There are old men on benches and young men jogging here and there. His path leads him to the spot under the bushes where he spotted the rags that made up a bed for someone. Same path, same bushes, no rags. He figures by now the guy must have used the charge card and got himself arrested. Surely. Surely. But not indicted for murder or it would have been in the paper. But he is walking on, toward the Aviary, for it wouldn't do to hesitate anywhere—no, he needs to look purposeful.

The Aviary has a schedule of fees and a list of hours posted on the glass. He goes in and automatically plunks down a ten, takes up his change, walks into the atrium. Birds squawk at one another or at the people come to look at them. Even with the high ceiling, the food, the space, it's a prison. They can't get out. This is not living. You can't have a zoo or an aviary without hurting the creatures you put in there, so far as he's concerned. Better to die a natural death out in the wild than this pretend sort of caring. Preservation. Species conservation. What for?

Again, he feels himself close to tears.

No, he's not afraid. In a way, he's as brave as they come.

Back to his car.

AT TWO SHE DROPS LAUREN OFF AT BREEZEWOOD. THEY STAND hugging each other for a long time. Billy Krauss sits in the car right in front of them, waiting patiently and politely looking aside. Elizabeth kisses her daughter, who is like Dan in so many ways. "You need to make time for fun and friendship."

"I feel so stupid jumping around like a maniac at a ball game. I tried. I did try."

Elizabeth says, "Look, I've been thinking . . . you want to go to Europe at Christmas break?"

Lauren looks surprised. "Maybe. You want to?"

Elizabeth says, "I think I do. I'm going to look into it. France, I think. I'll see what's possible." She looks toward the car. "We can't keep him waiting much longer."

Lauren kisses her good-bye. "Will you be okay at the cabin?"

"Yeah. If I'm not, I can go home, right?"

An hour later, she's pretty sure she's *not* going to be okay. There are signs. She has to notice that she did not build up the fire again, but let the embers burn out. That she has cleaned the coffeepot and has the dishes draining. She has to notice that she's partly packed and that she's taken off the big sweater of Dan's she had on and put on her own tidy sweater. That she's not the person she thought she was, not at all. She can entertain thoughts that shock her, not that she means to act on them, but there they are. There are gates, she tells herself. You can go through one without going through all of them. Fumbling in her purse, beneath the tangled receipt from the supermarket, the receipt from gas, the card from Christie, is that other piece of paper. Friendship offered.

He's in his car. She can hear tires on pavement, car noises when he answers, the radio, which he turns down.

"No problem," he says. "Whenever you get there, the pasta goes on. Time doesn't matter."

I AM BONKERS, BRIDGET TYPES. THE LITTLE LETTERS LOOK drowned and silly on his screen. He was coming home for a day, then *not*, just like that. His life is out of control. He was *in a car*, talking to her. Five minutes later he called back and said he couldn't come after all. You don't hop planes, just like that. "Work," he said, as if she believed that.

He hasn't told her what he's writing these days, but she's ready to bet what it is because of the research he's doing on the doctor in Pittsburgh who got killed. He's bookmarked three articles from the newspapers on his computer and gone back to them repeatedly. It makes sense, since he's written about other murders in other works. Violent stuff, too. Lots of it violent and mean. People putting shit in other people's drinks, car accidents, all kinds of drama. But definitely more interesting than sitcoms so far as she's concerned.

The bar down the road beckons, but he asked her not to go. As if he cared. Which he does, he does, she can feel it.

Thinking very hard, she realizes her biggest problem is solvable. Mobility. She could have rented a car and taken herself to Nelsonville, got a haircut, gone out to dinner, to a movie. An expensive solution, with the extra forty bucks for the car, and maybe not the funnest excursion, but sanity has its price, right?

She leaves the computer on, frantically looks up car

rental companies in the phone book, even though it's Saturday evening, too late for anyone to be open. She decides, though, she will do it tomorrow, or next week. With that small decision, a feeling of comfort comes over her. Then she thinks, maybe four wheels aren't necessary. Try two. A bike rental might do the trick. Could she bicycle to Nelsonville? Surely if she's careful and takes breaks— A wild feeling of freedom, independence comes over her, at the mere thought of mobility.

This is how prisoners entertain themselves, this is how old-time housewives survived. Fantasy of deliverance. Meanwhile, you get yourself all bent out of shape about getting the sheets clean and fresh, you maximize the little things, you talk to yourself, find joy in small things, read and read—and truly, is there a better world?

In order not to go down the road to the Go-Bar, she opens the back door, runs around the yard fifty times, wondering if fifty laps is a mile or not, comes in winded, drinks a shot of whiskey from the bottle under the sink, and plops in front of the TV, which she watches for three hours.

ELIZABETH REALIZES SHE'S FRACTURED INTO A LOT OF PEOPLE, not yet able to put them together. One of the people she is checks her hair and earrings before she goes next door, while another person who is a part of her shakes her head in condemnation. Why do you care how you look? the condemning figure asks. The vain and rebellious one tosses her hair so that it looks less tidy and leaves the house without an answer. An uncertain child crosses the lawn, bearing a pint of ice cream. A steady, easy, mature neighbor says a simple hello when Frank answers the door with a cheerful "Ice cream!"

"It's Häagen-Dazs coffee. It keeps me awake, but I like it anyway. You don't need to serve it. It's just for you."

"I wasn't doing too well with dessert. I bought two slabs of cake up the street."

"Nothing wrong with that."

"We can have either/or or both."

The table, which he has set plainly with a couple of straw place mats and plain white dishes, is a comfort to Elizabeth. The unfanciness suggests no pretensions, no pressure, even before he speaks.

"This is just pasta," he says, "and salad and bread. The only things I have to do are make sure the bread doesn't burn and the pasta doesn't get overcooked. I buy good ingredients, but that's the only thing I can say for my cooking."

"It's not important. I used to think about what I ate. Now it's anything, fuel, that's about it. Cooking . . . I just can't get interested. I buy prepared things lately. I never thought I would, but . . ."

He bites his lip a little, listening, nodding. "It's shock. You'll be okay. One day you'll be cooking again."

She wanders around, stopping and starting, not that there are many stopping places on the tour. Couch, table, wall.

"If you want to look around, it's okay. There's nothing to see, but it's okay."

"Bathroom?"

He hesitates. "There's a little one down here. The one upstairs is nicer. This place needs a lot of work."

It might be delicacy that has him sending her upstairs. What woman wants to pee in earshot of a stranger who is cooking her dinner? A date, she almost said to herself. A date. She shivers and climbs the stairs, trying not to look left or right, not to snoop. But her eye catches a bedroom, bare, neat, to her right. The room that looks out onto her house is empty, completely empty. He has more room than he needs, but of course everyone can find ways to spread out, a whole room as a dressing room, for instance, leaving the bedroom calm and neat.

Plain shower curtain. Blue. Blue and beige tiles. A couple of rose-colored towels that don't match anything. No carpet on the floor. A bachelor. A widower. There is an echo in here. She pees noisily, washes her hands, dries them on the rose towel that seems fresh, clean, and descends the stairs,

curious about what they will find to talk about. Houses?
Decorating? No doubt about it, she feels better when she
talks, as if, like a teenage girl, she becomes identityless
without the use and sound of her own voice.

He is in the kitchen, staring at a large pot that has, as
yet, no fire under it. "I don't want to rush, if you don't
mind," he says. "Let's have some olives and that sort of
thing first. And wine." He has already started on a glass of
wine, a deep burgundy. "Which?" he asks. She reads the labels of two unopened wines, a Graves and a Pinot Noir,
and the one he is apparently drinking. It's partly thrift,
partly not caring; she points to the open bottle, three-
quarters full. "That."

"You like reds. I do, too."

He seems a little absent, not that she can detail it, for he
pours the wine efficiently, moves the bowl of olives toward
her on the counter.

Leaning against the refrigerator, she's thinking it's better not to sit formally in the living room as she did last
time. It makes her feel so captured. Stiff. Staid. Now she
can move. A sip of the wine goes down tangy and strong,
warming her whole body, weakening her elbows and
knees. She shakes her head at her small capacity, but
there's nothing she can do about it. Small-boned people
are easily knocked off their pins.

The first thing he says is "Talk to me."

She tells him about Breezewood and Lauren, how good
it was to see her, just for a day.

"The cottage is near?"

"An hour from Breezewood, hour and a half back this
way."

"That resort area."

"Yes." She remembers this kitchen now from a party
she came to three owners back. The countertop is an un-
usual combination of muted coral and aqua tiles, good
tiles—small, imported rectangles, much more artful than
anything else in the house. "I like this," she says, tracing a
finger along the grout.

"I do, too. Look at this, though." He shakes his head at the inexpensive linoleum flooring. "I'll tear it up, someday. Ceramic or wood, which do you think?"

"I like both."

He nods. "It's awful to have not enough time and not enough heart to do what has to be done. Which is a pretty normal state of affairs." His voice is rougher, raspier in that way voices are when a person is slightly naked emotionally. He takes a sip of wine and closes his eyes. Elizabeth is aware of studying his face, or rather of his letting her look at him.

"How's your son?" is the second thing he asks.

"He's okay. I think he's doing way better than Lauren is. He's . . . doing okay, I think. I'll see him at Thanksgiving." How can it be Thanksgiving so soon? In under two weeks. Absently, she traces the tile again, watches herself, stops herself.

"Will you cook?"

"It's not that big a bother."

"If you're not up for it, go out. Go to Europe. Surprise yourself."

"Funny you should say that." Her heart goes a little faster, wondering if he can read her mind.

"What?"

"Well, Christmas, I was thinking to travel. I can squeeze two weeks out and so can the kids. So, maybe then."

He nods hesitatingly. "There you go."

"You think it's a bad idea?"

"I think it's a great idea. I know some places there, in Paris and in the south. I used to spend a lot of time in France. Let me know if you need suggestions. I travel a lot. I know I told you that."

"I might ask you about places to stay." The south? She hadn't thought to go south on such a short trip, but that might be exciting. Reaching forward, she chooses an olive, a slice of cheese, and something of the familiar pre-dinner ritual grabs at her heart. Dan. Gone. For a moment it was as if she talked to him about a family vacation.

The third thing Frank asks is "How are you managing? How are you now?"

When she looks up, she doesn't hate his face, but she doesn't like it, either, as she had moments before. His eyes widen too much with curiosity.

"I've never felt less steady," she answers honestly. "I have friends, and they call me, but I don't want to see them. I have too much anger in me."

"I don't see that in you. At whom?"

She swallows. The kitchen clock chimes lightly, a shy seven strokes. Good. It's early still. She will be home at nine. His face is still asking, Who do you hate? And she answers, "Whoever did this to him. To me and my kids."

He moves awkwardly across the kitchen, pours more wine, sighs a large gasp of a sigh. "I'm listening. You loved him?"

"Yes." She almost said, "Of course." He had loved Carol. It seemed so from the way he talked.

"You miss him."

"Desperately. I want to talk to him a hundred times a day. I go to the cemetery—before work, after work—even though in my heart I don't think that increases the . . . closeness. It's more that I'm trying to get used to the idea."

"I wish I could help." He puts down his glass and comes to her quickly. Before she knows it, he has enfolded her in a tight embrace. The first thing she thinks is how ridiculous it is, her arm with the wineglass outstretched, her head turned too far to the side. But he adjusts the embrace and it's deeper, more comfortable, as if she knows him, has known him for a long time. He smells clean, nothing perfumy, just soap or shampoo. He releases her, takes the glass out of her hand, and holds her once more, much more comfortably. The second thing she thinks is that she hardly knows him, so it makes no sense to feel this calmed by touch.

She's used to comforting others, but she can't bring herself to put her arms around him, although he's in mourning, too. Recipient only, an unequal moment, her with her eyes closed, standing there, being enveloped, held.

The third thing she thinks is that she was not wrong.

Something in the pattern of his breath on her hair—the embrace shifts, a sixteenth-inch of a crack opens between them, and sex walks in. Not that it wasn't there in the house, hovering around stairways, making its way down the stairs from the second floor and up from the basement. But now it's right there, held between them.

She doesn't want to let go. It's almost funny. Life is so ridiculous. People are. She is. Where is sense? Where is reason? It comes when she calls for it, and she releases herself.

Dash of cold water, reason is. There she is, in a kitchen next door, no window dressings on any of the windows, an echo when she walks, nice colored tiles on the counter next to the sink. A big old refrigerator that does its job, poor-quality flooring that will have to be replaced in time. Her lips are dry. She licks them. Suddenly she's parched. "Water," she says.

He hurries to get her a glass, takes a jug from the refrigerator and pours. He watches her drink. "Okay?" he asks.

"Um. Olives and wine, I guess."

"All the good things." He smiles. "Then good old water."

She thinks that thing about being made up of water and thinks that thing about *drinking* water being a way of becoming more of yourself. It's one of those thoughts that comes to her for no good reason because the mind, dreaming or not, has its own pathways, its own linkages and patterns. He is looking at her. "What?" she asks.

"Were you ever a dancer?"

"No."

"Something made me think it. You're extremely . . . graceful."

"Thank you." She feels herself flushing. "Is there anything you'd like me to do with the salad?"

"Are you good at dressing it?"

"I'm excellent at dressing it."

Silently, they begin to move, he to light a fire under the big pot, she to open the refrigerator and find a little mustard to add to the dressing. Even at that point, she thinks she has escaped, that she will eat, drink, even carry a dish or two to the kitchen, go home. She thinks, Dan, how could you not run, drive, get away from the thief? How could you not? And she wonders, as she mixes the oil, the vinegar, the mustard in a small bowl, what surprise or fatigue or sorrow kept him from moving.

"SATURDAY NIGHT," BRIDGET SINGS TO HERSELF. WHEN SHE CANnot stand TV anymore, she has another shot of whiskey and fumbles for the small key that opens the files she is not supposed to open. Well, he didn't say never open them. A key is a key.

Every time she thinks she hears a car, she jumps. But now, in her state, even little scratching noises seem as if they might be cars creeping up the road.

She thumbs through the file cabinet, looking for something telling, something that will give her a sense of him. Looking for anything that might say "Photographs" or "Pictures." Or something that says "Condo" or "House," so that she could see how he *lived* once upon a time, at any rate, in L.A.

He must hide things. Certain things. Pictures. Real life. Frank Razzi, worker bee. "Paramount," she says aloud.

She reads what's within. *Contracts.* Wow, did he ever make the bucks! Wow. Although an L.A. buck is not an Ohio buck. Worth a quarter, she's told. *Letter of termination.* Now, why is that in the back of the file when everything else goes the other direction, newest in the front? She answers herself. He didn't like to look at it.

Her hand stops on a folder unmarked—no, it's actually marked in light pencil. "Notes. Ideas."

It's thick. Filled with notebook pages, old envelopes, every funny kind and shape of paper. Now, this is something. This is rough, quick, closer to the unseen Razzi, right? Tiny handwriting some of the time. Just ideas. *If it were a girl. Vivian. Circumstances could be the same. Poor family, no reason to break records, but she does. The brother loves her.*

Handwriting is . . . naked. Something about it breaks her heart. But the fact that she has come close to the real

Frank makes her nervous. She puts the folder back, locks the drawer. She listens for traffic sounds. No. He's not there. She's alone. Completely.

Picks another novel off the shelf. *The Reader*.

In her bed, door not locked, she reads, "When I was fifteen, I got hepatitis. It started in the fall and lasted until spring." So sure. Facts. A finished book. So unsubjunctive. Not like "If it were a girl." Nor like "Circumstances could be the same." She reads one thing, thinks of another, wondering what Frank was writing, wondering why there is a *feeling*, even in the notes. No matter what, Jess was right about one thing, sex is everywhere, in and under and around things, just everywhere you look, everywhere.

THE DIRECT ATTACK. HE KNEELS BEFORE HER. HE RUNS A HAND along her inner thigh and closes his eyes. Can he smell her heat? She thinks he must. He stretches forward and kisses her. It isn't a difficult kiss or a foreign one, just an ordinary kiss that is not too pushy and is easy to return.

The lights aren't bright but still she's aware there's nothing at the windows. He sees her looking. "It doesn't matter," he says. "I'll turn the lights out in a minute."

Afraid she will say something stupid about how it can't mean anything except need, need, need, she doesn't say anything. Why insult him with "You can never be Dan, never."

As if she's said it *anyway*, his eyes cloud over. In spite of herself, she touches him, cheek, ear. "I think I'm not a very good bet. I'm full of sadness."

"You talk as if there's something to decide." Is he laughing at her? Almost. But his eyes are nice again. Sometimes the brain is no good at all. His hands move up her thigh, belly, over her breasts, and she is almost sick with wanting it so much. The lights are too bright. People will see, someone will talk. She's going to want to do this in the dark. She leans forward to let him kiss her. It's grief, one of the dances of grief, can't be helped, the body is already moving.

"You have to come with me," he says. "I'm not going to let you go for a second."

He lifts her up, keeps his arms around her, walks her to the wall switch in the kitchen. "Off," he says. They walk to the living room, to one lamp. "Off." Another. "Off." Only a candle left burning. She feels safer. They kiss for a long time, not moving away from the table, where the candle burns. Then he lifts the candle and carries it with them. "I'm going to hate myself," she almost says, but why burden him with that, it's hers, all her problem. Slowly they climb the stairs to the middle bedroom, where she knows, from looking before, there is nothing but a neatly made bed in the room. The little dream she walks in to, why, it's like being a student, it's like being young again, except everything is neater and of a better quality.

He doesn't let her go; he knows she might come to her senses and leave if he gives her a moment.

He's a quiet lover, serious and attentive. He undresses her slowly, methodically, saying, "You're beautiful. So beautiful." These are those moments of negotiating half-truths, putting some things away, fanning others into credibility. He needs her, that's the part she doesn't want to know about, for what will she do with him after, when she has time to think how he isn't Dan, never could be?

He is brown-haired, brown-eyed, his body is average, trim, not heavy, evenly sprinkled with hair. He was starting to grow a beard, but he's shaved it off. Earlier today, he says, just felt like it. He smells clean. She knows hardly anything about him, might be annihilating herself, who knows where he's plowed before. But he works her body, turning it over like soil, working out the knots, finding his way in. This is something he knows his way around, all right, and he's granite hard with wanting it.

11

WHILE LYING IN BED ON SUNDAY MORNING, BRIDGET IS THINKING she really ought to get up, walk down the road, find a church, find a bicycle shop—or call a nonexistent cab, go to Kmart, buy a bike, cut the tags, ride it home. Excellent ideas, the brain is cooking away, she tells herself, yawning, lying abed still, reading a bit more. She is working out equations that go something like "If he does not come home today, I will pack up my things and just leave. See if he notices."

Ridiculous. She came here not wanting him, and has turned without much warning into a woman spurned, scorned. It's amazing how easily a thing like that can happen, the mind subverting itself. She needs classes in Women's Studies, she's sure, but for now, she enjoys the prickle of woman-wronged thoughts like If he could consider flying home on Saturday (or driving!), why couldn't he fly (or drive) home on Sunday, then, why not? Does he have a meeting (ahem) on Saturday night and Sunday and also at dawn on Monday? Someone has him by the balls.

She reads for a while, not concentrating, thinking how she has acted as a super-secretary-assistant, typing and splicing and merging pages. She's even written a few lines for him when she couldn't figure out where the right pages were and needed to get on with it. He will probably never notice. Or care. Or thank her. Maybe he'll fire her! Freedom!

In thought sketches, he does energetic things with a

nameless, faceless person in a bedroom in California. She blinks, reads, in order not to spy. Can her own imagination be rude?

All the work he gave her is done. Boredom makes anyone nuts.

Fantasy edges in. It begins with where she is: She is still in bed, reading, there are soft footfalls, she does not have time to dress, he is standing at her door, he approaches her, book aside, covers aside, T-shirt and sweatpants off, bedding pulled back up to cover her nakedness. Various words: She is wonderful. She has lifted him up. The ages are wrong, according to the world, and he has resisted for that reason, he explains, but he can't any longer. She is his Lolita, but he won't force anything, he won't kill her mother, he won't put her in musty hotel rooms, he will just love her. And take her to L.A. with him, where all they need is the magic of time.

They will make love everywhere, in the car, on the airplane, in L.A. at parties, as she becomes older, riper, wiser.

Time passes, working its magic. She learns to fight with him. Wears little red dresses with spaghetti straps. Angel-hair straps. No straps.

Her notes. Just notes. Foolishness. But the fantasy makes her feel so alive; it beats feeling nothing by a long shot.

She gets dressed and moves, out of the house, down the road. Walking for an hour, she doesn't find a bike or a church, but it's okay, the brisk walk does her good, anyway. Airs out the mind. She buys a bottle of water, pressing her rolled-up change from a twenty into her pocket.

Returning, trudging up the path, she feels almost lean. It's because she's skipped breakfast and *moved.* The feeling interests her. Lean and hungry makes a person more purposeful, more . . . sexual, awakens the killer instinct, probably some primitive thing going on in the head, like *What will I kill for lunch?* No wonder people say their brains change when they become vegetarians. Suddenly she remembers her parents patting her on the head and calling her precocious when she was a child. They murmured that she *thought* too much. The memory makes her want to cry.

A man walking his dog passes her. He smiles and that makes her want to cry, too, because his smile is so kind, as if he knows she's alone.

East of Eden is the television noon movie and it unhinges the "want to" and allows her to cry in earnest. Rapt, Bridget watches the vegetables wash away, the rain come down; she watches Aaron hurting himself on the train window, Julie Harris bursting with love, and she lets the tears flow. The crying brings contradictory thoughts, that she will hide out for a long time until her father notices he doesn't know where she is; that she will call his answering service on Razzi's phone this afternoon and tell him exactly where she is, shocking him. Simpler to start a Net mail account and write to him. Two o'clock and she hasn't eaten anything, which has her feeling a little faint. She hobbles to the kitchen, looks around, teary-eyed. One slice of toast, nothing on it, will be her allowance. She eats it, standing at the window, letting the crumbs drop into her left hand, opens the door and brushes them off for the birds or the ants, whichever get there first.

Then she takes off her clothes and walks to Frank's room. In his mirror, her white nakedness shocks her. It takes her a while to get used to seeing it; she has to keep looking, thinking, Is that me? Okay, yes, she is thinner.

For a few minutes, she walks around naked, considering a second piece of toast, considering going out to the yard and running around in her skin in order to shock someone, have an effect on someone, but it would take a passing hiker, looking through just the right crack in the trees, to see. Fear is a sensible emotion, she tells herself. Really, her life is so strange, she's practically a runaway and nobody knows it, nobody cares. Her stepmother doesn't know where she is, her father doesn't, Jess, her supposed caretaker, doesn't. In a way, she's gone to a teen safe house like the one Razzi keeps bookmarking on his computer. The Pocusset Safe House. Well, she'll call this one the Razzi Safe House. A bed, food, drink—same great deal, except without the talk and the love.

Bridget hops from one foot to the other, puts her clothes back on, and commences what she calls "stair-master exercises" by running up and down the basement steps for a good thirty or forty minutes. When the phone rings, she is panting, exhausted.

"How's the fort?"

"Watched."

"Good. I . . . I don't know when I'll get back. I'll have to keep you posted."

"I think I might go crazy."

"Why? What's the matter?"

"Loneliness," she says simply. Had he not thought of it? His very good wheels grind slowly in the silence.

"I have to figure a couple of things out," he says quietly. "Maybe I'd better find you another place. Can you hang on for a day or two?"

"I guess so. I finished the three scripts you gave me." Her voice has a childish sound she hates. No wonder he doesn't take her seriously.

"There's more you can do, but I can't explain it now. Let me think. I'm actually going to need to pack up some things, but it's too hard to explain which."

"I ended up working twelve hours a day, thinking you'd be giving me more work." Still the voice is the one she hates in herself.

"Relax, then. Do you have enough money?"

"Yes. To do what with?"

"Are you crying?"

"I was, earlier."

"Over being alone?"

"Well, I was watching *East of Eden*."

"You, too," he says. "It holds up, that's for sure. Puts tears in your soup."

When she hangs up, she's thinking of the "soup" and wondering if she ought to have some. Then she thinks of the "You, too," and what it means. Either he watched the movie over breakfast on the West Coast or he watched it over soup somewhere nearer by, on Eastern time. That he feels a need to lie makes her bristle.

She gives five other films on TV a try, but can't concentrate. Razzi is the most interesting story around. Why not give in? She goes to the locked file cabinet, where she chooses the folder of notes she held last night and another folder marked "Beginnings." A part of her is already purifying the act, thinking, Maybe I'll find some work I can do, make myself useful instead of just sitting around.

Back in her room, sitting on her bed, she begins with the notes, putting aside the page she has read and looking at the next.

A girl is killed. Spring day. Wet earth. Feelings of longing. Make it a girl. Good in school, poor family, all that. Okay, same story as before . . . A list of characters' names follows. Robert. David. Michael. He seems to have chosen Robert, because on the next page, there are a few lines and it's Robert who is walking through the park. Schenley Park, it's called. Is that a real park or a made-up one? She scans the page, with its tiny writing, thinking briefly of *East of Eden,* how sad it was, but how absolutely, incredibly cool James Dean was. Her first real look at him and she is smitten, like an idiot. Like Julie Harris, she likes the ones who need to be lifted up.

Walks through the park all the time because he's seen her there with Robert.

Why, she has to be like a detective, to find out who the *he* is. If not Robert, who is the he who walks through the park? Making her way through the page, she decides it's somebody named Michael. Two brothers vying for a girl. Why, it's *East of Eden* all over again! Or the Skakel story. Is he writing about Skakel? She's seen newspaper clippings among his work from time to time, but there are none here. Not Skakel. The bits of paper feel old, aren't yellow but feel old, so this is an old project that maybe made it to completion, maybe not.

Guilt at her plunder makes her heart thump but she doesn't take the things back to his room. Getting to know him is the best part, forcing this private, intimate look. On the next page the handwriting is larger, less careful. *Uncompromising, cold, but no one knows. He has respect. Keeps his distance from people. Robert is damaged. Robert thinks he has escaped, but—*

She reads, trying to piece together what he intended.

Wants to take her away from her mother, who is a hopeless drunk and has a stream of men in and out of the house, and take himself away from his father, who is just as bad in other ways as her hopeless, defeated mother is, and his half brother, who is someone he doesn't know what to do with.

Who is the *he*? This last set of notes is on the back of an envelope addressed to someone named Gerald Paul. Jeez. A long time ago. A 1977 postmark. Long before she was born. Gerald Paul was some guy in Detroit. An envelope dropped at a train station, she decides, and Frank picks it up and writes his ideas on that.

FRANK, UNABLE TO WORK, WATCHED *EAST OF EDEN* FROM TWELVE to two. He dialed Elizabeth's number twice during that time, but she didn't answer. Her house was quiet, no activity. Was she going to pretend it hadn't happened?

She had cried a little in the night and talked about Dan—missing him, she said, and feeling she was betraying him. He knew he would hear those words, and that they would make him angry, he knew it, so he worked to listen sympathetically. He must have done okay, because she talked freely. "I had a wonderful life," she said. "I'm trying to be grateful for that." She was lovely, with pale skin, a long, thin back, and soft, thick hair. As she talked, he stroked her shoulder, her arm. He told her he was grateful for his time with her—some numskull phrase like that. He told her anything was okay, he just liked being with her. She had looked at him, straight at him, searchingly, and they had made love again. Then slept. Then held each other and talked again. When she asked him about his work, he focused on his early days in Hollywood, funny stories to distract her and keep her from getting fidgety.

He told the truth. How he'd worn a tie to his first inter-view, almost didn't get the job for looking too wrong, too stiff. How he corrected the clothes right away, but then had to stand at copy machines for months, feeling he'd made a mistake, there'd never be a place for him. Finally, got an as-signment to read through unsolicited scripts. Which is pretty much how everybody who breaks in breaks in. Did it so well, so thoroughly, with copious typed notes and all, they gave him a few more. Pretty soon they gave him stacks and stacks. Let him doctor one, and again he did a good enough job on it that they gave him two more.

She seemed interested in his grit and survival story.

"I'm a script doctor, mostly," he said. "I say, 'This char-acter needs to be excised, this line needs to be stitched to that, we need an artificial pacemaker to drive it.' " He gets his laugh. "Then of course there's the 'Physician, heal thy-self' aspect to my life."

"Your work?"

"My own stories, yes."

How did he meet Carol, she asked. He had to begin in-venting then, since there was no Carol and therefore no long illness and no dead wife. Invent, create, it was so much what he did that the words came easily. He made up a courtship, said he and Carol had met at work and even though they were both dating other people, they had eyed each other for two years, then one day he asked her out.

Elizabeth nodded, probably the way she did when pa-tients talked. "What was her job there—where was it, was this at Paramount?"

"Research. This was at NBC Burbank."

"How old were you then?"

"Both in our thirties. Both of us had made our way out to L.A. in our twenties, so we were natives by then."

"Where did you live?"

"Glendale. More than one apartment there, but I stuck to modest Glendale." The truth. What had he said to her son? Brentwood, Malibu?

"I don't know my areas."

"It's a faraway place."

"Did Carol have a large family?"

He thought that was an odd question, but he made up an answer. "God, yes, sisters everywhere, four sisters and one brother."

"And they were all involved when she got sick?"

A careless invention. He suddenly saw the need to be rid of these relatives he'd brought into being. "Two of the sisters were okay through the illness. The rest of the family is all off in far-flung places, Hawaii, and the Far East. Well, North Dakota, which seems far-flung to me. And to be fair, all of them had work and families, so even the two who did come always had to get back. Mostly it was just the two of us, facing it down."

She nodded again and watched him. He was propped on an elbow, talking. "What about *your* family? Large, small?"

"Only child."

"Oh. I thought you had a sister. In Ohio."

He snapped to attention. What he had told Jeff? He tried to remember. He said, "A stepsister. Came much later in my life. My father remarried late, but no, none of them were around when Carol died, because we weren't, aren't, that close."

He shifted his position and touched Elizabeth's hair, partly to distract her from the imaginary Carol and her family, a subject he needed pen and paper for. "Nothing so bad as what you went through," he said.

She shook her head. He was not sure what it meant and he didn't know how to get the conversation back on her, so he waited. Between the wine and his calming medications, he had a detached feeling, as if *she* were just a story, a supposition, and she might blow away with the piece of paper she was written on.

When she spoke, her voice was low and real, sending his heart into an erratic rhythm. She said, "I'm a kind of dull true-blue type. I had two boyfriends in college. Then Dan.

I never had an affair with anyone after I met him and so it means I was *with* him for almost thirty years. You're only the fourth person I ever slept with."

"You did well," he teased. When she didn't laugh, he made his face more sober and said, "I'm honored," and then she smiled after the fact at his joke.

It was something like four in the morning when she went home. "I'm sorry," she said as she left. He watched her cut across the two driveways and go in her back door.

Sorry? What the hell did that mean?

Let her go, he thought, she'll be back. He didn't know all the math and the magic, but his charm was with him, his luck. He imagined lights on briefly at her place, lights off, then a tap at his door minutes later. But her place had stayed in darkness. She hadn't come back last night or this morning, and now he was less sure that she would be back. He felt this uncertainty in his knees and elbows as a kind of weakness and fear. He walked to the small bedroom he'd once slept in and looked out the window at her house, but he couldn't see anything.

Finally at two-thirty on Sunday afternoon, he dialed her number again. Her machine picked up. He was about to hang up as he had the several times in the morning, when he went still, listening to the sequence of beeps telling him she had other messages piled up. Suddenly her voice on the answering tape asked him to leave a message, too.

"My door is open," he said. His voice was raspy, needy. He wished he could undo the message, but there he was, finger on the hang-up button, too late, too late.

So now it is three o'clock and he still can't work, he's too nervous to work. He has watched *East of Eden*. And waited for Elizabeth. And called poor little Bridget, whom he never meant to keep for so long without figuring out when to have her and what to do with her. Little bird in a cage, singing uncertainly.

Everyone is uncertain. Underneath the layers.

Now an unease fills him. Has he tripped himself up,

said something that contradicted something else? Is Elizabeth on the phone checking up on him? His heart is trying to pick up speed, fighting the drug that's telling it to relax, forget it, nothing he can do. He feels in his pockets for the two pill bottles he carries around with him, his hand tightens around them, but he stops himself from doing more. He's taken exactly what he, playing doctor and patient both, prescribed for himself, no more. Another Xanax might knock him out.

He hauls a stack of papers off the floor and up onto the dining table, gritting his teeth. An hour later, after he has read the same twenty pages over and over again without comprehension, he notices he's shivering and gets up to raise the thermostat two degrees. Just as he sits down again to his papers, the door opens and she comes in.

Her face is sad. She has been weeping. "I don't want to hurt you," she says. "This can't be anything. I'm obviously not in good shape. This can't *be* anything and maybe you don't want anything, but I feel completely . . . I must be going nuts. This isn't really me. . . ."

Dismissed at the start. His face goes to stone with anger. He feels his jaw clenching, his lips tightening. "Don't say it can't be anything," he snaps. "That reduces both of us. Don't say it. Don't believe it."

"All right, then."

All right? Just like that? She's a hot one. When she wants it, she'll say anything. He takes her hand and pulls, leads her up the stairs, motions with a nod to her clothes, which she is already taking off. "This counts," he says. "As some fucking thing."

"All right." She's not crying. Almost laughing.

CHRISTIE WAS STANDING IN THE KITCHEN JUST BEFORE SUPPER on Sunday, talking to Marina, when the phone rang. The caller was his man in Bellingham, Dave Bittle. "I didn't expect to hear from you today," Christie said, surprised.

"I put in some weekend hours," Bittle said. "I owed about four hours, and there was nothing going on except for the usual tips about drug sales, so I did some looking around."

Christie nodded slightly to Marina to let her know it was a good phone call, no need for her to call him to some pretend emergency.

Bittle was saying, "I found a woman who was once married to a guy who used to be in the house you asked me to look into. Don't ask. It was one of those A to B to C to D things. They divorced seven years ago. The guy died like four years ago. She'd met the LaBeau woman somewhere along the line during the marriage years and didn't like her too much, that was clear. Could be because the husband had. Seemed to love the idea the police were interested in the woman. Said LaBeau was in Florida the last ten years or so."

Christie thought, Okay, okay, now we're getting somewhere.

"Apparently she went off with some guy something like twenty years younger than she was, the relationship didn't make it, and she stayed."

"Did your contact know where in Florida?"

"No. Not Miami. Somewhere on the Gulf side, she thought, not inland. That was about it. She didn't know anyone else who would know more, I asked that."

It fit. It fit. "Name of the guy she ran off with?"

"My contact didn't know."

"Anything else about LaBeau?"

"Drank. Had a superior attitude. Ran through men."

"Anything about a son?"

"Not a thing. This woman didn't know a thing about any family at all."

"Good work," Christie said. He pinched his fingers over his eyes, wondering the best way to trace her. She hadn't come up on regular computer searches for name and address. But there had to be some way to find her. And when he found her, he'd have to ask the awkward question: Did she know if her son was really, honest-to-goodness, dead?

"I'm going over to the grade school and middle school tomorrow," Bittle said. "See what I can find."

Christie thanked him.

Marina dumped a handful of onions into hot olive oil, sending a wonderful smell all through the house. "Are we going to Florida?" she asked, teasing. "It isn't Rome, but I could handle that."

"I'll use local police," he told her, ploddingly serious. "I have to stay here because the potential yield down there is. . . ." She looked disappointed. "I can't take another travel day on a maybe. I do need to look at a map, though."

"I know where the maps are. Keep an eye on the onions."

When she returned with a U.S. map, he was stirring absently, wondering, What would make a woman like LaBeau talk now if she hadn't talked before? A scare? How could he scare her?

Marina took over the stirring while he spread the map on the kitchen table. "There are plenty of places for her to be on the Gulf side," he said.

She nodded soberly. Then she turned everything off, so that they could look at the map together.

"The mother liked the water, it seems," Marina said. "Did she have a profession, was she pursuing any art?"

"Drinking, apparently."

"Well, you can do that there, too."

After dinner, Marina went off to her computer and came back saying, "There's an e-saver on this weekend. Don't laugh. If there's one next weekend . . . Think about it. Not you. I could pay my plane fare and the rest might not be too bad. Four days in the sun."

"That's not your ideal vacation."

She bit her lip. "But it might help you crack the mother's story. Only, if I'm going to do that, we need an address for her. And we're up a creek on that, I know. If you get an address . . . Don't worry about me. I like to do things."

Her eyes were bright.

She was good, too, Marina was. If anyone could talk to

the old lady, she could. The idea, once spoken, kept coming back to him that night, about as often as the tomato sauce did.

WHAT BRIDGET FOUND IN THE FILE OF NOTES WAS A PLOT SYNopsis for a story about a killing done by one brother, suspected by another brother, who haunted him and tried to get him to confess. It seemed kind of good, making her wonder if he had ever written the whole thing. She turned to the folder marked "Beginnings" and found various starts on the story. One was about the weather, one was about the innocent brother's feelings of love toward the girl, another was about the guilty brother's hatred of his brother. She read through them, pretty much deciding these were all old notes, and she was about to put them away, when slowly, the idea filtered in that all the versions took place in Pittsburgh. The idea scratched at a memory, but she lost the memory for an hour or so, napping with the folder on her chest, and then getting herself into the kitchen, where she heated a bowl of canned soup in the microwave for a very late lunch.

Bridget burned her mouth on the soup. It seemed only lukewarm at first, then the heat snuck up on her. Damn. Every time she used the damned microwave, it tricked her. She hopped around, getting herself a glass of water, swirling it around in her mouth, keeping the soup bowl at arm's length until it cooled.

The bookmarks on Frank's computer. The doctor Frank kept reading about was in Pittsburgh, the Safe House was in Pittsburgh.

Forgetting the soup, she went to Frank's computer and logged on to MapQuest, where she asked for driving distances, Athens to Pittsburgh. The answer came back: 193. Dead-on. That's got to be it. He does four hundred miles plus each time he leaves, double the distance to Columbus, so Columbus makes no sense. She can't find Road-Eye Road, but she can see where West Virginia links up to

Pittsburgh. Schenley Park! There it is. And then, after a long search, *Rodi*, not *Road-Eye*. Okay. He goes there, but is it for research or a woman or both?

Curious, she rechecks his bookmarks about the doctor in Pittsburgh. There are the old ones, the obituary and the articles about the home the man founded, and one new one, a thing about a dinner, picture of the doctor's widow and children at the Pocusset Safe House from something called the SEEN column. Frank's next project? A documentary on a do-gooder?

After deleting her work, she shuts off his computer and goes back to her now-cold soup. Agitation prompts her to down it fast, drinking most of it from the bowl. *Put those folders back*, she thinks, *you've gone too far*, but she can't quite explain her feeling. She hurries them back into the drawer, lingers, closes the drawer partway, sees folders tucked in the middle with no labels at all. She feels them, half lifting them. There's something inside. No, no more. She puts them back. Just read one of his many books tonight, tomorrow. Take walks. Ask him straight-out what she can read and what she can't. Ask him straight-out about the research in Pittsburgh.

While it's still light out, she trots down the road, going nowhere. The man who walks his dogs passes her, preoccupied. No smile. Her spirits drop because he doesn't notice her. She's completely desperate for someone to talk to. All right. Jess or one of them at the house. She hurries back home.

Home.

The old number rings three times before anyone answers. The voice of the man who answers is mature, dark, an unfamiliar voice, so it must be the new guy. Is he a lot older, then? "Is Jess there?" she asks.

"Just a minute." In the distance she hears him calling, "Jess. Jess, it's for you." He sounds like somebody's father.

"It's me," Bridget says when Jess answers.

"How's it going?"

"Okay."

"You're home?"

"No. That's why I called."

"Where are you?"

"Well, I'm staying with someone. If my stepmom calls, pretend like I'm still there. Okay?"

"I can be vague if that's what you want. Is that what you want?"

"Yeah. Just say I'm coming and going until I figure out what's next."

"Where are you crashing?"

"A house. It's rural. With a prof."

"You're shitting me."

"No." Bridget weakens. She can't pretend there's more to it than there is, she can't, she's not a good enough liar. "I just stay here. It's not a love thing."

Jess laughs. "You got yourself a sugar daddy who's timid."

"No, it's just a place to stay and food and some cash."

"Sounds good," Jess says vaguely.

"Who answered the phone?"

"We call him Guy, but it's not his name. His name is some ugly, complicated thing I can't pronounce right."

"He sounded older."

"He's getting up there. Almost daddy material."

She can't handle Jess, never could, can't now. All she wants is to hang up. "Just play it cool if anybody calls. And jot down this phone number, but don't give it out. Okay? It's just for you to call me if anybody calls for me."

"Hey, I got it."

Bridget gives the phone number and hangs up. Having talked to Jess, she feels, if anything, more lonely than before. The person who is nicest to her is Frank.

Men are so puzzling. She keeps dreaming wild, embarrassing dreams, where she's with various men. She does bold things, reaching under their coats or into their pants. Then one dream last night, she was with someone, who was it, with a giant erection and a smattering of interest in her, but he kept having to deal with people knocking at the front door and the phone ringing and other people wanting things of him, and somehow the whole dream went by and it didn't happen. This will be her whole life, no love, no touch.

The dream was Frank, wanting her. He does want her.

She finishes *The Reader,* such an odd book about an odd relationship. Prison, death. Next she selects and starts on an old paperback, *The Assistant,* which she likes very much and reads slowly so it will get her through Monday.

"I HAVE SOME STUFF ON THE KID," DAVE BITTLE SAYS ON MONday, what is late afternoon in Pittsburgh. "One woman let me see school records. I took notes. Should I go ahead?"

"Shoot."

"The boy was a puzzle, according to the school records. Decently behaved a lot of the time, top grades, but flashes of violence. Note that he was a bed wetter. Wouldn't you know? And he set a fire once, and the counselors seemed to get pretty scared by that. There was one note—the fire was supposed to scare off some guy his mother was involved with. Anyway, they put the boy on the usual drugs and the notes indicate the drugs seemed to calm him down. The thing is, though, all through it, teachers went to bat for him, and so did counselors. Everyone wanted to help the kid. They liked him. Mostly they liked him. One of the teachers wrote he was 'bright and engaging.' That's about it. Nothing I read gave any alternate addresses for the mother, no relatives, nothing like that. Not until the records show he moved to Pittsburgh to live with his father."

"Sounds like he was destined to be trouble and managed *not* to be a lot of the time."

"Right. That sounds right. Like one of our volcanoes. Like, you know it's there, you're waiting. Also, I'd say destined to be successful. Well, maybe this was a lesser school system, but he was at the top of it."

Christie was about to hang up when he got an idea. He had been banging around all day looking for a contact with the IRS and nobody was getting back to him. He began slowly. "You've been invaluable. There's one more thing. I'm sure you thought of it, but do you have contacts of your own with the IRS? Ours are fizzling."

"Sorry. If I had them, I would have used them by now. LaBeau has to file. Legally."

"Yeah. She sure does. No guarantee she has, though."

"Right. Just a— I just had a thought. The woman who hates LaBeau. She's an employee of H&R Block. I suppose it's a long shot that she'd know someone on the government end, but she'd be motivated to try maybe. Especially if I hinted it would lead to trouble for LaBeau."

"Do what you gotta do."

"I'll do that."

Sitting at his desk, Christie drew a circle with about ten spokes going rim to center. He put *Gerald?* in the center and he wrote on the spokes, *bed wetter; new family; Ted Luckey—drugs and alcohol; medical school; A.C. corpse—drugs and alcohol; name and soc. sec. for Gerald Paul/Paul LaBeau disappear; mother moves; Dr. Ross killed with gun after publicity about P.S.H. hits papers.* Could be a mishmash of several cases. If not, if there was one answer to it all, if the answer was the LaBeau boy, what were the other connections, the other spokes? You could know a ton and know nothing.

Potocki at the Pittsburgh office was the lucky guy who drew the assignment of making roughly twenty phone calls a day in and around his other work—to people who once reported missing persons in the Atlantic City area. Sometimes it took all twenty calls just to locate the person who'd put in the report, so the whole process was going slowly. Generally, the missing person had shown up or been found a long time ago. "Keep going?" Potocki asked lightly. Christie told him yes. The danger was in losing faith, losing interest. The next phone call could always be the one.

ELIZABETH LISTENED TO CLIENTS FROM NINE IN THE MORNING until one in the afternoon without taking a break. By one, she was famished and exhausted. She lay on the couch in her office and tried to think. Margot, she would talk to Margot about this need of hers for Frank Razzi. Need. People act on it all the time. Her body feels alive, yes, there's that, but it has something to do with talk, too. Is that the aphrodisiac? Why, he talked to her for four hours yesterday, about sadness and his recurring bouts with depression, about being an only child. He diverted her. He fed her dinner again, asked her what music she wanted to hear, asked her about *her* childhood.

He's nice. She likes him.

He makes her nervous, scares her, too, but she doesn't know why.

He's a nervous man. She can see him steadying himself at times, taking deep breaths, or it looks as if that's what he's doing. So there's anger or pain or deep emotion, probably more than she wants to know about.

Where can it go? Nowhere, and that's why she tried not to go back.

She will end it eventually, he'll get too close, want too much, but she doesn't want to insult him.

Margot. She must talk to Margot.

When she gets up from the sofa, she's hit by a dizziness that makes her grip the edge of her desk. Low blood sugar. There were no lunch makings in the house; she knew she'd have to go out for something. Today is cold and rainy, wouldn't you know. The pants and soft wrapped jacket she's wearing aren't quite warm enough. She slips on her raincoat and leaves the office, hoping a fast walk down the street will throw off the chill. It's a laughably short walk, only two minutes at most, going at a clip, to the fancy grocery, not enough to count as exercise. After impatiently waiting in line for help, she orders herself a chicken salad sandwich and a Coke. On the way out, she buys a package of peanut butter crackers and one of cookies, in case she gets another attack of hunger later.

Sometime, the next time, she must cook something or at least buy takeout to offer Frank. Next time? Her children would be shocked and angry to know what she is up to. Is she falling in love? It sometimes seems so, the way she longs for his company, yet the idea of having him come into her house, to sit at the table where Dan has sat, horrifies her. She wants him, but only in certain circumstances. *Marginalizing* is the in word for what she's doing, relegating to the borders.

Climbing the stairs to her office, opening the door, sitting down with her sandwich and drink, she wishes she could talk to Dan. Funny. She almost says his name aloud. Where is he? Why can't she conjure him anymore? She closes her eyes and tries to hear his voice. Can't. Frank's low warm voice is in the way.

It's a quarter to two. She eats hurriedly, washes the whole thing down with the Coke, and hurries to the bathroom in the hallway she shares with other shrinks who rent in this building.

Thanksgiving. Jeff called last night and left a series of questions. Where are you? Thanksgiving? The cabin, as usual? Then he said he was thinking of bringing a girl with him, a friend, but not to worry, the friend could stay at a local B&B. However, Elizabeth should call him so they could talk about it.

Ho. It's a fever, a flu, they all have it. The mourning disease. Like Spanish fly in the soup. Will Lauren fall, too? Elizabeth *hopes so*.

She brushes her hair at the mirror. Faces change. A stranger has her hair, her lips. She studies the stranger, trying to figure her out.

She must talk to someone. Margot.

A message on the machine is the best she can do. "Margot? Are you by any chance free for dinner tonight? Could use a talk." She imagines the conversation in advance, Margot saying, *There's a reason for everything*.

Two minutes to two, she composes herself to wait for the two o'clock, who will be exactly one minute late.

WEEKS AGO, FRANK, THUMBING HIS WAY THROUGH THE YELLOW Pages, called several movers and rejected the big companies. They did too much record keeping. He also rejected companies based in Athens. He told Heinz Ersicher that he was moving straight back to L.A. because he doesn't want Heinz or anybody to know about the Pittsburgh house. The quarter ends just before Thanksgiving, only nine more days.

He has chosen a "personal mover" from Pittsburgh's Dormont area, and without any illusions. The ad means a couple of guys with a truck, no insurance or bonding, but also no ties to any big company. He doesn't own anything highly valuable, so it's the best way. In nine days, he won't be driving back and forth all the time.

Then?

There's some waste. The Athens house he has to pay for until the end of December.

That thought brings him to another. He will have to do something with Bridget. A couple of nights with her, a gift of a plane ticket to St. Louis. She is exactly as he'd guessed, eager and smart and unsure of herself, his type. Elizabeth is also eager and smart and unsure of herself. The whole fucking league of females is, what's the secret?

"Dormont Personal Movers," says the man with the high voice who answers the phone. The man sounds winded. A baby screams in the background.

"Frank Razzi. I want to go ahead with you guys. We should talk timing—when you'd get to Athens next Tuesday morning. If you come early, I can be there while you pack up, but I can't start out right away with you because I have to teach a class that day."

"That's okay."

"What'll you do, kill a few hours until I can get back here?"

"Better for us to keep it tight," the man says. "Give us a key. Tell us where you want everything. We'll do it." The man's breath is coming over the line in short jabs.

Frank decides if he puts a few small boxes and a very important suitcase in his car, everything else, the file cabinets, the desk, they just have to be careful with. "Let's finalize plans," he says.

"We'll start out six, be there by nine-thirty, say ten if we run into any problems." The baby continues to scream in the background.

"That works. My daughter might hang around to supervise."

"No problem," the man wheezed. "We done things like this. We need a deposit, though. We don't do credit cards."

Perfect. His kind of place. "What about a contract?"

"We don't do all that paperwork."

"Fine," he said. "I'll trust you."

"We're trustworthy."

Frank laughed. "When do you want your deposit?"

"ASAP. So we don't take on another job for that date."

Frank checked the cash in his pocket. "Three hundred okay?"

"That's real good. I said eighteen hundred for the whole thing, right?"

"Right." He got directions, and realized that on the way to Dormont he'd pass the Kuhn's where he got his prescription, precious Xanax, which was doing him up just beautifully. Unfortunately, it wasn't time yet for a refill. He had, what, twenty-something pills left. Twenty-six.

Before he left the house, keys in hand, he called Bridget, announcing, "All kinds of things are happening. I'm going to be clearing out of the house in a week."

"In a week?"

"End of the term."

"But doesn't the lease go longer?"

The way she asked it, with the slight slide at the end— she's read something. What? Letter in his desk. Okay, okay, he can play this. "I have to move to L.A.," he says simply. "I'm getting some bites suddenly. I probably should have stayed there."

"Can you get me work out there?"

"Maybe. Eventually."

"Shit."

"Bridget. Did I do badly by you?"

"No."

"Didn't I give you a place to stay? Food?"

"Yeah."

"I'll buy you a plane ticket to St. Louis—"

"No. No, I'll just go to L.A. on my own, then." Her voice was husky, on the verge of tears.

He could picture her turning her toes inward, like a young child. She had a way of making him feel tenderness. "Look. I'm due in tomorrow morning. We'll talk about this. Okay?"

"I thought you were coming in today."

"I can't."

"Sure you can," she said. "Pittsburgh isn't that far."

They both went silent. She knew. How did she know? He laughed uncomfortably. "You're a funny kid."

"Whoops," she said. "I meant L.A. Slip of the tongue."

He thought, Put her on a plane to St. Louis or even L.A. She won't be able to find me, but she'll make it. Get her out of there before she brings it down on herself.

He stood at the back door looking toward the garage. "I've got to give you some time," he said. "Play a little Scrabble."

"I put the board away."

"You don't like me anymore."

"I don't think liking has anything to do with it. I just want the respect of you telling me the good old plain old truth."

"I'm not sure you do. I think you might be enchanted by falsehood." That took her off guard. It was what he did, his job description: surprise, invent, win. Never lost yet. Not in the big things.

He turned away from the back door, looked out the window to next door, a familiar sight. "What else did you read?"

"Nothing."

"Tell the truth."

"Nothing."

"You're a bad liar."

"Why do you care? Why do you care what happens to me one way or the other?"

"I just do. Don't make me explain it. Are you in love with me?"

He heard her gasp. "No. Why would I be? I know you have a woman in Pittsburgh."

It was a question masquerading as a statement. He said, just standing there, almost still, "I have a job in Pittsburgh. It's a job."

"Research?"

"Yes," he said slowly, wondering exactly what she meant. Unless she'd read everything. He hoped not. He hoped she had not become that much of a danger to herself.

He turned back to the door and opened it quietly.

"Something keeps you away," she said. "It's dumb to rent a place you never come to."

"People do it all the time. You're lonely."

"Tell me about it."

"And you like me a little?"

"I don't know that I do."

"That's love, then. We're going to have to talk." He stood looking toward the garage. And the next thing came easily. "I've been worried about taking advantage of you. It's why I stay away. You needed a place, the thing with Sally broke up, I had work to do, and I didn't want to land on you."

He could almost see her swallow hard, search for words.

"Now I might like you a little," she said.

"I'm going to come in tonight."

He tightened his fist over the car key and thought of what he needed to pack into the car—nothing much, laptop, papers—to leave right after he paid his deposit to the movers.

Let Elizabeth pine. Good for her. Keep her from thinking she was doing him a favor.

OUT ON BANKSVILLE ROAD AT THE MEDFAST, MEGAN SMITHY, going over her records, lets the thing that's been nagging her come to the surface. That guy. She didn't run it by insurance even though he had an old card that he said was expired because things got so busy. Both Xanax and Oxy-Contin at the same time, payment by cash, she should have run it by. She knew it that night, driving home, and here the worry is, still coming at her, three days later. Can't remember the guy's name, but she does remember he lives in Squirrel Hill.

Because there's an inexplicable lull in things, she has the leisure to check the records, and after a few minutes, she finds the scrip. Daniel Ross. UPMC Insurance, but he didn't use it. She keys in the information with today's date, as if he's standing there, getting the prescription today. The system is slow getting back to her, so she strolls the store aisles on her break, reminding herself of the things she needs to buy before going home. Would she know the guy if he came back? Maybe something would jingle her bells. He was pleasant enough, nice-looking, but she can't come up with a picture of him, only the memory of letting something go that she didn't have time to do right.

Bananas, cereal, milk, frozen burritos, frozen pizzas, that would about do it. She isn't too up for cooking and she's pretty tired of feeding her hopeless boyfriend the junk he likes so much. Why can't he bring some food over once in a while, huh?

Back behind the counter, she checks the computer. "Daniel Ross, terminated." She taps the RETURN button for more detail and the screen tells her "Deceased." Shit. It was a bad scrip. Shit. But the guy showed ID. She stopped. Maybe there was some plain and simple explanation for it. The guy had the same name as his father, the father died, the guy— No, it doesn't come out good, no matter how she plays it.

Call headquarters and she gets in trouble.

Simple. Let it go. Don't tell anyone. Don't do it again.

A couple of hours later her boyfriend comes to pick her up. "Take me for something to eat," she says.

"Don't you want to take the bags home first?" He tilts

his head toward the things she has put in the backseat of the rattletrap he insists on driving around.

"No. They'll keep." She pulls down the visor and checks herself. Blond waves, dimples, clear skin. Still there. People smile at her automatically. So if sweet Tony doesn't get it together soon . . .

"Where do you want to go?"

"Atria's is fine," she says.

"We'll have an hour wait."

"It won't be that long."

The restaurant is only a few yards across the road and even though it's a downscale, homey place, it features valet parking. Three valets in red sweatshirts zoom around and the one assigned to the not-restored antique Falcon smirks when he hands the ticket to Tony. She knows Tony is thinking, Two bucks to park and we could have left the damned thing in the supermarket lot. All it would take is dodging across the highway. True, he has no money; his face gets that desperate look.

They will have a twenty-minute wait for a table. The hostess invites them to spend that time at the bar, where loud men are watching football news. They smile at her, one after the other, notice Tony hovering, drift back to the televisions.

Tony moves in close behind her and puts his arms around her. "It's noisy in here," he murmurs.

"It'll be better when we have a table." They both order beers, draft.

"What's the matter?" he asks.

"What do you mean?"

"You seem funny."

Between sips, in dribs and drabs, Megan tells him about the computer system, how she usually keys things in, but didn't the one time she had a fraud pulled on her.

Tony looks alarmed.

"Nobody will ever know," she says.

"What did the guy want? You think he's selling them?"

"It wasn't enough to sell. Not big-time. Modest quantities."

"What does it mean he wasn't in the computer?" Tony asks this with such naivete, it seems he pictures tiny little people living in the electronic city, raising a hand from time to time when called. Here. Me. My prescription.

"He was in there as dead."

Tony says, "Oh, maybe some relative still wanted the stuff."

"Probably, but it's still fraud."

"What about the picture ID?"

"I don't remember."

He stays close behind her. For a while they watch the television just like everyone else.

When they are finally seated at a table, Tony declares, "You should report it."

"They'll only ask me why I didn't in the first place."

"You'll tell them how you just realized."

"Give me a break. That isn't going to sound too good."

She watches Tony's scrunched-up face as he tears off a piece of bread and swallows it pretty much whole, saying, "Starved." He keeps surprising her. She thought for sure he'd tell her to forget it, cover her ass, and here he is being the goody-goody.

"No mistake about the name?"

She shakes her head.

"A weird name?"

"No, a common name. Daniel Ross."

Tony considers the name, chewing his cheek, like a P.I. deciding whether to take a case. She has to laugh. What a character. And all hers. He orders a burger, the cheapest thing on the menu, and a good value. She considers everything else, but ends up ordering a burger, too. Tony looks at the high-up television in the back room where they've been seated. He is easily mesmerized, news, commercials, anything. His eyes blink a couple of times and he comes back to her. "What was the first name of that doctor that was killed in Shadyside?"

"I don't know."

"Daniel. I think it was Daniel."

"It's a common name. Could be a son or something using the card. I'm not even sure the name is right."

Tony is really taking to his P.I. role. He leans forward and says in a low voice, "You could call the news station and ask them. A wallet was taken, remember?"

"Who'd hang around and use the dead guy's card? No. This guy was pulled together. He had money. He needed the scrip for a groin injury. I remember now. Or some kind of surgery in that area."

"He told you this?"

"Yeah. Okay. I'll look into it tomorrow."

Ripping into another piece of bread, Tony says, "You could be sitting on something. We should go back tonight."

"I can't. That would arouse all kinds of suspicion. And I'm not sure of anything."

"You should flag it, though, in case the guy comes back. You could be the one to cook him."

"Tomorrow, then."

They dive into their burgers. Tony eats the second half of hers as well as his own. She takes pity on him and begins to pull out her wallet, but he gets to his first and pays, looking both proud and sorry at the same time. She insists on handing over the two dollars to the valet.

THERE, IT'S DONE.

He is asleep, not very asleep, just a little bit asleep, with an arm across her. Bridget has pulled the covers up for decency, and now without moving too much, she's trying to see his face. It's innocent-looking, boyish. The beard was nice, too, on him, but it's gone. He's not . . . not ugly or old. His hair has a tiny bit of gray and his skin isn't as young as hers—so what?

It's done, she told herself as soon as it was over. I'm an adult now. Her delicate parts burned and throbbed. She wasn't sure she liked it all that much, too many sensations, not all of them pleasant. But then, lying there, maybe two seconds went by and suddenly she wanted to do it again, what sense did that make? She's *heard* you get hooked. Do it once, Jess said, and you can't get enough.

Is he asleep? God, a dick is an amazing thing, hard, soft, medium. And hard it's a wonder, it really is. Just this big thing sticking up. Not that she hasn't seen one in movies of the blue sort back at the other house, but close up it's kind of more impressive. All that emotion and blood and force going from everywhere to the tip like that, a big testosterone capsule. Bridget likes the idea she might be earthy. Frank's word. She's almost used to the icky-sticky feelings. Womanly, she feels. Rooted and able. The type who can clean up a baby's diarrhea, kiss her husband's butt, no problem.

A kind of elation occupies her that she can feel these things.

He stirs. She goes still. Quiet again, although his eye opened for a moment, she saw it.

Yes, he told her, yes, he goes to Pittsburgh to do research.

Something good? she asked.

It's a passable idea.

For a documentary?

No. He looked puzzled. No, for a possible feature-length film. Maybe.

Oh, she said, raising her eyebrows a little, and he laughed, as he almost always did when she expressed herself. How good it feels to make him laugh. She wants to touch his face, to wake him up, but that doesn't seem fair play, sleep is precious.

"I never did this before," she'd said.

"So, you see why I stayed away? You're delicious-looking, delicious in every way, but I don't want to be a bad guy here. I'm forty-three. You're a baby. A delicious baby, however."

Forty-three is pretty old, but Bridget isn't like those other people her age who think nobody does it after the age of twenty. She reads all the time and so she knows better. She knows people in their forties used to marry people her age all the time, all the time, because first wives died in childbirth. Now it still does happen in Hollywood, with the young wives impregnated by the old actors, who still look pretty good. Frank is Hollywood, has that Hollywood need for young flesh. Delicious flesh, whatever that is.

"Are you going to take your clothes off?" he said when he came home and held her for a long time and kissed her. "I'll only do what you ask, no more. Let me look at you. I'll only do what you say is okay to do."

How strange it felt to take off her clothes. She felt so . . . so . . .

He said, "Tell me if it's okay to touch you."

She told him to go ahead. It occurred to her that hands took the place of clothes. If he looked, she felt naked, but when he touched, especially when he ran the whole flat of his hand over her, she felt clothed. "You like this," he said, "your breathing is excited. Let me, let me touch you. Ah," he said. "You are so hot. It's as if you have a fever! You must be a hundred and five degrees. You're burning up."

She was. She felt it through his words. A hot number, a hot item, *her, Bridget?* A fine old slut, Jess always called herself. In those moments it suddenly seemed a good thing to be, the only thing to be.

I knew we would do this, she thought. I knew it would happen eventually.

Now she is lying here thinking, Wherever he goes, whatever he does all weekend, it's nothing that makes him nearly so happy as this. She saw it in his face, joy, she saw it.

His wineglass sits by the bed, empty. Hers is on the floor beside the bed, still full.

He stirs. An eye opens. "I'm sorry. You've learned the worst thing about men, they fall asleep after, just when you want to be held."

"I watched you sleep."

That thing he does—freezing, going still—then he moves again. She is reminded of a film getting stuck in the projector. At the little theatre in St. Louis her father used to take her to—he'd curse the cheapo theatre that never got its equipment fixed—the movie on the screen would shiver, stop, then continue.

Frank's arms go around her. He holds her very tight, breathing into her neck. "Are you okay?"

"Yeah."

"What do you do here all day when I'm gone?"

"Sometimes I go out to the grounds in back and run around. Just in a circle, like running laps. Sometimes I take a walk down to the strip mall."

"Where you went to that bar. God, that scared me."

"Well, I didn't go back. I did my work that you gave me. Ate. TV. Mostly reading."

"And what did you read?"

He sounds . . . different. Suspicious. She feels nauseating guilt, which she covers by naming the novels she has read, one after the other.

"Books?"

"Yes."

His body smells musky, woodsy. He's over her again, turning, kissing her, looking hard at her.

She feels the baton hard against her leg. She moves more fluidly this time. His hands feel good. "In you," he's saying. "In you." A game of prepositions.

That's what sex is, a game, she tells herself the next morning when she watches him pack up the overnighter again. He's about to leave for class and then, he says, work he has to do out of town, after class. He doesn't say where; she doesn't ask. Tuesday again, and he will leave. For a day. Why can't he talk about it?

He seems scattered and at odds, going to the shower, gathering his things, slurping coffee. Going to his other woman, no doubt. Guilt? Confusion?

She waits for him to call. She has, if nothing else, the ability to endure. He likes her. She makes him laugh. She can hold on to that. He's . . . something about him is beautiful.

About above across after against along among around at before behind below beneath beside besides between beyond but by down during except for from in into like near of off on out over through till to toward under until up upon with within without.

MARGOT WAS NOT AVAILABLE FOR DINNER ON MONDAY NIGHT, but she and Elizabeth met at nine for a drink on Murray Avenue. It felt so strange being out at a bar, just sitting and talking. Only a month after the murder. Five weeks.

"I'm sleeping with someone," she told Margot.

Margot looked surprised. "Someone I know?"

"A stranger."

"Clint Eastwood?"

"Funny you should say that. No. He just seems ordinary and lonely and we started to meet."

"Anything you do is okay with me so long as it's okay with you."

You could hardly ever stop a person from getting hurt. Both of them had seen people get into relationships six months after a death, get married three months later. Of course it didn't work. Elizabeth knew that. "I'm not the type. To be doing this."

"I know."

"It feels strange when I'm not thinking about Dan every moment. At the beginning, after he died, he was everywhere. If I turned a corner, if I went to my car. He was with me all day, in my thoughts. I don't want to forget him."

Margot frowned. "I'm sure you're not forge—"

"It feels like it. This new guy, Frank, has a certain power. He occupies my thoughts."

"Where did you meet him?"

"He's my next-door neighbor. Convenient, huh? I didn't look far."

"Did he know Dan?"

"No, no, he never did. He's a new neighbor."

"You like him?"

"I'm drawn to him. It's pretty confusing." Elizabeth

looked at her glass of wine. "He poured me wine one day and we talked. One thing led to another. I know what he is. He's wine. He's a . . . a buffer. I know it must be that."

Margot's only wisdom was to take it slowly, not be hard on herself, talk when she needed to talk. They broke up at ten. Elizabeth was surprised to see how dark Frank's house was when she returned home. Sleeping or gone? She looked out again at eleven and the place was still dark. She missed him.

HEINZ ERSICHER CAME UP TO FRANK IN THE HALLWAY ON TUESDAY, saying "It's been great having you here. What's next, huh?"

"Back to L.A.," he said, turning aside, so his eyes would not show the lie.

He stood in his classroom, looking at faces. Interested, bored, distracted, ordinary faces, and he thought, Who am I, what am I doing here? A student smiled, raised his hand, waited to be recognized. A pain seized Frank's heart. The boy looked like Ted Luckey, sweet and upbeat, a ghost looking at him, saying, "I'm not dead, I just waited thirty years, and here I am, here I am to talk to you."

But this kid was only ordinary. He wasn't *smart* like Ted Luckey. He didn't look through you like Ted Luckey did. Ted Luckey had eyes that held the sadness of the ages. "What's the matter with you?" Ted Luckey had said. It was a soft, modulated challenge. "Jealous is the only thing it could be. Mr. Wonderful for a brother."

Dan was *not* wonderful, *not*. Dan looked *downward upon*, not *up toward*, not *equally to*. And that was ego, that was self-satisfaction. Dan didn't have a self, only the selves he lifted up, like Ted Luckey.

"Are you okay, Mr. Razzi?"

Clawing his way out of the claustrophobia, he looked at the class. "It's hot in here," he said.

And wouldn't it be, wouldn't it have to be the same kid with the sweet face, who was saying, "Mr. Razzi, are you all right?"

For Ted, even at the end, drank the bottle of beer with the ten Seconals in it because he was asked to by a boy so wrought up, so fevered with anger and grief, that he didn't want to disappoint him. Before the pills hit him, Ted said, "Paul, you got to get hold of yourself. What the hell is the matter with you? So, okay, I drank with you, you wanted to be friends, I'll be . . ." Ted tried to laugh but he got scared then, his body was going numb on him, he climbed out of the house toward the air, hit himself in the stomach, tried to throw up, tried to throw a punch at the person who followed him outside and had made him drink. He went still for a moment, understanding, then he tried to move but he was slowed down, and he slid in the mud. "Oh, my God," he said. His voice was slurred. "What did you, what did you do?"

He slid. He wanted to put his head down on the wet ground. He wanted to rest. Paul saw that and it seemed to him rest was a good thing, a wonderful thing. Cool mud on the forehead.

No exams tomorrow. No coming in second tomorrow.

It wasn't a simple thing. He panicked. He was willing for it to be over, reversed. "Get up," Paul said. "Get up and fight me."

He lifted Ted Luckey up, but Luckey's feet wouldn't take hold. "Call Dan" is what Ted said. Then Ted started to cry. "Where's Dan? Did he know about this . . . ?"

The very idea. Paul was caught off guard, almost elated to hear Dan blamed.

Ted staggered and fell backwards, then down the hill, rolling, his body stopped by a tree. He didn't move. Time passed and he didn't move. Paul squatted on the ground in front of the house, watching for movement. Thunder rumbled, rain began, large splashes of it, and lightning zigzagged its way down to the earth, missing the tree Luckey rested against.

He got scared and ran. It was done, too late.

■   ■   ■

WHEN CHRISTIE GOT BACK TO THE OFFICE, HE RETURNED A CALL to Bittle out in Bellingham. It turned out the guy had done it. He had an address for Michelle LaBeau. She was in Fort Myers. She'd married a guy named Walt Walker, now deceased. Phone was in Walker's name. He called Marina on her cell and said, "You're going to Florida if you want."

"Hooray."

"When is the only question."

"I might go Thursday night if they have a seat. Otherwise Friday. I can get a sub for Friday and the Thanksgiving week is completely free. I could stay on if I have to."

He felt an immediate pang of separation before the fact. She was glad to be leaving. He would bump around missing her.

12

ONLY CRUSHES, DUMB LITTLE THINGS, BRIDGET HAS HAD BEFORE.
Now, lying in her bed, she feels an ache so deep, she can't
stand it. And also a lover's suspense. To see if he is the same
as he was. To ferret out what he is thinking. To see if he
smiles at her. If that angry look that puzzles her comes over
him again. What does he *look* like? She thought she knew
but now she can't picture him.

Decisions come to her in tiny leaps that must be faith:
She will go with him, where he goes, in the BMW to Pittsburgh, on a plane to New York, on a long drive out to L.A.,
and allow whatever happens to happen. Could be that before this, nobody stuck close to him, nobody hung in
there with him. There's an aura of isolation all around
him. Jess would say it's just how men are. Adults. Who
have seen a lot of up and down in their lives. Edgy and self-
protective.

He was gentle with her.

She feels languorous, remembering. But she can't sense
him in her own bed so she goes into his room. She feels a
kind of ownership now and lies down freely on the larger
bed, where the covers are sloppily pulled up. She gets up
briefly, cleans up the wineglasses, straightens the covers,
lies down again.

Tomorrow. It seems forever until tomorrow. She will
have a dinner ready for him, and she will be showered and

dressed nicely. At least she can do that. She moves herself again to the kitchen, where she takes a chicken out of the freezer and puts it on the counter to thaw. As she does this and wipes up the counter, making everything orderly, it runs in her mind she saw a clothing store down on the strip where the Go-Bar is. The window display of the store was anything but enticing, but there might be better things inside. Give it a try, might as well. She's due for an outfit, all right, that's clear when she puts on for the thousandth time her tan cords and sweater. Clothing needed. Frank gave her two hundred dollars cash toward the hours she put in, getting his manuscripts in order. More to come by check.

She hesitates. What if he comes home and she misses him? What if he reconsiders rushing to Pittsburgh and comes home to see her, to say something. She waits, sitting at the kitchen table, drinking coffee. So it's a good two o'clock and he's long gone when she takes herself out of the house and down the road to the clothing store.

The pickings are as bad as she thought they would be. There are the kind of sweats middle-aged women favor, with spangles on the sweatshirt part. The clerk mutters, "You should go to University Mall. Even New to You, near the campus, there'd be something for someone your age."

"How do I get to the mall from here?"

"Oh, a bus comes every once in a blue moon. It stops right out there." The girl points.

What else does she have to do with her time? She has not been anyplace where students go in almost three weeks. Amazing how life proceeds.

Bridget waits for the bus for forty minutes, gets off twenty minutes later, and finds herself among people her age. When she first came to this town, she felt happy, thinking she was in the world, making it on her own. Now, among students, Bridget feels more like an outsider, and they seem like *kids*. Will she run into any of the people from the old house, Jess's house? Could happen. Warily, so as not to be surprised, she starts to look for them in the doorways of Penny's, Elder-Beerman's, Goody's.

She slips into a small shop, where, from the rack, she chooses things to try on—three clingy little dresses in case Frank takes her out to dinner sometime, a pair of cropped jeans, and a new shirt with shoelaces tying up a V-neckline. Sexy clothes. She considers briefly a pair of sandals she likes, but puts them back on the shelf, away from temptation, because she should save some of her money, just to have some. In case the thing with Frank doesn't work out.

Her hands clutch tensely when she allows herself to think about a parting.

He's not old-looking. They match in a funny kind of way, in spite of the age difference. Both of them are hard-working brainiacs with lots going on underneath. Underground river meets underground river.

"Try those on?"

"Yes."

The clerk shows her to a fitting room.

The jeans fit. The shirt fits. She looks good.

She has made love. Like other people. Only to her it was important. Jess doesn't take it seriously, lots of people don't, but for Bridget it was serious as church.

Didn't he try to say something of a warning this morning? "Don't rely on me."

"What do you mean?" she asked.

"I'm not always able to . . . do things for people."

"I think you got it backwards," she teased. "I'm the one who does things for you."

That's when he got angry. Only for a moment, but he got angry. Men are like that, from the little she's witnessed. With no personal experience to speak of, she senses they're prickly when it comes to questions of who does what to whom. She will have to learn the poetry, the things said, the things not said.

All the dresses fit. She chooses a black one that's form-fitting with a Chinesey top.

"That works," the clerk says, opening the curtain.

Haircut? At a shop?

No, trim her own, save the money. Also, with bad hair, it won't look like she's trying too hard. A slick new 'do might freak him out. After all, he liked her natural, with fucked-up hair.

ELIZABETH MADE HERSELF GO TO THE SUPERMARKET ON THE way home from work. She bought a plump roaster and a few vegetables. More ice cream.

As she parked in the driveway, took out the groceries, she wondered if she was watched, seen, and she got a little flicker of stage fright, an odd feeling. Assembling things on the counter, she kept an eye on the house next door—no activity that she could see. It was okay. She would make the chicken anyway. She went about the routine, so familiar, of moistening the skin with olive oil, spraying oil inside the bird, filling it with onion and garlic and one large sprig of rosemary, chopping rosemary for the outside. She put it into the oven, scrubbed a couple of potatoes and cut them into wedges, sprinkled them with oil and garlic. Next, she cleaned asparagus and lined it up in a roasting pan. More olive oil. Salt . . . fatten me up, she thought, elasticize my skin, turn me into a plump bird.

If he didn't want anything to eat, well, she'd have food for days. Plenty for herself.

Her inner voice had changed its rhythm. She listened to its flip, defiant chatter and didn't disapprove.

THE BUILDING HE TAUGHT IN WAS THE CATHEDRAL OF LEARN-ing, a big, thirty-six-floor gothic tower that he liked. In a Hollywood sense, it transformed ordinary grousing and cheating into something medieval and sacred. In his small, second-floor classroom, people with cell phones and headsets got to tap into something remote and monk-ish. He went in on the ground floor, from which most of the gothicism was absent in favor of institutional tile walls. As soon as he entered the building, the sharp smell of coffee hit him, for right in the center of the floor was a Starbucks, which ground and poured and spilled America's favorite drug all day long. The smell was so seductive, he stood in line every time to order himself a cup of something, even though he hated to feel jumpy.

The line was long and slow-moving. He tried to squelch his impatience with people, ordinary people who crept along and couldn't decide and couldn't find their money, or had to get rid of nickels and pennies, but what he felt was a deep contempt, something strong as black coffee juicing him up. Move, move, move was the feeling he had. Dull people! When he had the coffee in hand, he saw that he had twenty minutes to kill before class.

The old lady.

She's been on his mind lately. Lots of years have gone by with only phone calls between them. She has not seen him, would not know him, probably. He has seen her but she doesn't know it. When he traveled there last summer, he thought to sit down with her, talk to her, and yes, settle old scores. But he went to Fort Myers, sought out her address, and then stood frozen before it. He must have walked up and down the street fifty times, when he saw an almost-stranger come out and move down the road and into town, walking slowly to a restaurant. Alone. Where was the new guy she was supposedly with?

An old woman now. He followed her. He watched her go, as if by habit, to one of the cheaper restaurants. She seemed tiny—drawn and withdrawn. He might not have known her except for the address. He might not have. He followed and took a table in the next restaurant, where he could just manage from where he was sitting to watch her.

Her hair was cut into a short, pixie style and it was carefully dyed a light brown. She wore a bracelet and earrings with plain pants and a sweater. Like somebody's mother.

He sat and ordered the marlin special, all the while thinking he would go over to her, approach her table, or follow her home and announce himself. But he had a need to watch her first. The phrase that came to him amused him. *In her natural habitat.* She ordered some kind of chop. The way she worked over her food, got everything off the bones, made him think of an animal, practical, storing up until the next kill.

He was only a boy like others. But she hadn't wanted him.

She drank a couple of glasses of house wine with her dinner. He watched her pour from a flask and drink. Anger filled him.

He imagined pretending to be a stranger, seeing if she knew him, then walking with her, back to where he was staying, at a simple hotel on the water. Let's sit on the rocks, he would say. Let's watch the water and have a few drinks. Let's. He would help her down. One rock. Two. Them sitting in the crags. He would pull out a bottle and let her drink.

Say, "Who do you think I am?" And let it come to her. And when she knew, what?

He imagined killing her, a hand over her mouth, pressing. It made him sick to think it. He abandoned the thought or leapt past it to himself, later in the film, sitting in his hotel room. Hearing sirens on the beach. Having a tired detective at his door. "We're questioning everybody along this beach. What time did you come in? Did you see anything? Ever see this woman?"

And him, lying perfectly, beautifully. Shrugging his shoulders, saying, "I was here reading. I heard nothing."

"Your name?"

"Frank Razzi."

The police would leave him. Nobody would have seen.

Film image: a woman flung back on the rocks, awkward, released. Gulls squawking, water rolling in.

He did not kill her. Or even go to her and introduce himself. Instead, he called his waiter and gave him eighty bucks, and told him to go next door to the other waiter and pay for the woman's dinner, to take their tips out and give her anything that was left over. He watched the waiters talk, move, look back at him. He had the feeling they were going to be scrupulously honest.

Before they approached the old lady, he put another fifty on the table for his dinner and walked away. He didn't kill her. He loved her.

It was the only time he saw her in all those years.

She didn't know his name, she didn't know he was called Frank Razzi.

He sent money from time to time, when he had it, wasn't that filial duty?

She didn't know where he lived, not anything about him. That pleased him.

He never called her from the same place twice. Always from a pay phone, with coins (before cards), now using pre-paid cards.

He went to the phone bank in the Cathedral, thinking: Catch her before she goes out for the night. His cup of strong coffee sat on the ledge in the booth while he dialed all the numbers on his phone card and then hers. When the ringing began, he lifted the cup.

"It's me," he said.

She told him she had a cold. "Where are you?" she asked, carefully. "Are you here?"

"Where?"

"Here."

"I'm nowhere."

SHE HEARS HIS CAR. SUDDENLY SHE CAN'T BREATHE. WHAT IS this thing happening to her?

Is she falling in love, ridiculously, immediately upon widowhood, like that old bad joke. "My husband just died, my husband just died." "Don't cry, lady, you're pretty, you'll get a new husband tomorrow." "I *know*. But what am I going to do tonight?"

Her phone rings. "You're home," he says.

"I've made you something to eat."

"I should come there?"

"No. No, I'll bring it." This is the problem. She can't imagine letting Frank into her house, and that means, doesn't it, that she's taking advantage. Doesn't it? But the mind, the body, have their own programs, secret programs you have to follow. She needs him, can't stay away, misses him when he isn't home next door. Something about this plain man, this semi-failed, semi-successful screenwriter who has offered her small kindnesses, pulls her in. Is it simply that he's a world apart from her world?

Time with him is like entering a dream. Like going to a movie. Reading a good book. He's the whole of it, all the rules. For a time.

It takes her only a few moments to put the roast chicken and vegetables on a platter and that platter on a tray, then to walk over there. She can't open the door with her hands full. He sees that and comes running.

"You weren't kidding," he says. He takes the offering from her and puts it on the table. He stands with bent elbows, looking at it. She has the impression he's hurt or angry.

"I haven't had anything to eat yet," she said.

"Then we'll eat now."

"You already ate?"

"I don't remember. No, no I didn't. I bought a coffee before class, I had to make a phone call, that's right, then I bought a muffin at the break from class and that was it."

How funny not to remember. He looks overburdened with worry, distractions. "I can get some plates," she says. In the kitchen, she finds the almost-empty cupboards, just a few plates. There's something so appealing about having nothing. Even at the cabin, they have too much of everything. Potting soil, Tupperware, paper clips. She finds the forks and knives. Again, there is very little to choose from. Curled on the counter are the rolled-up place mats and napkins they used the last time she was here. And salt and pepper, always a good bet. She gathers these things up and takes them to the table.

"Was your class good?"

"Not very. It's not completely their fault. I'm thinking about other things."

"I can see. Should I go?"

"No. No. Let's eat."

She's done a good job, olive oil on everything, the potatoes and asparagus and chicken tender, not overcooked. They sit quietly and eat, as if acting out some exercise in self-restraint.

"I keep thinking about you," she says. The admission tumbles out, shocking her. He doesn't flinch.

"It can't be helped."

What an odd thing to say. There's something else he almost says and doesn't. What could it be? She's afraid of it, whatever it is.

They eat very little, complicit. There is no need to load up. They can eat again after. He comes to where she's sitting, kneels, kisses her breasts, her whole body. The lights are on, the windows open, so they are the current erotic flick, a little treat for the neighbors. And soon again, she is in the bedroom, feeling the sense of ritual, how she gives up trying to figure things out up here, but all the while knows this has something to do with wanting to die, wanting to live, something to do with grief.

There are no lights on up here, but she stretches back as if every window in the house is a camera lens and she's free, free. He kisses her all over, her whole body, making her wait. He's hard, but he doesn't give it to her right away. He's using her and there's hatred of some sort mixed in with it, her shrink's mind knows that much, but so what, so what if he needs to show her his power, her powerlessness. These are games teenagers play.

His body is trim except for the smallest, slightest rounding at the belly. He's not weak, but not muscular either. His shoulders—and this is slight—turn in a little, just that smallest amount of apology.

Her body is a fine thing. She feels pride in how well it works, how liquid she is, how good it feels to be filled up, the final puzzle piece in.

Silence.

"You need this."

"Yes."

"You've been neglected."

"I'm middle-aged. It comes with the territory."

"What is it you want from me?" She goes still to listen. "When you think of me."

"I don't know. An answer of some sort. Only I don't know the question."

Studying him, she sees his right knee is knobby, because of the position it's in, but his left, flatter, shows the little lines of age around it. The gray in his hair seems like a glow of some sort. His eyes seem familiar already. He turns to reach for the lamp. There is a small scar behind his left elbow.

IT'S EASY TO SEE SHE'S BEEN HURT, ABANDONED. IT MAKES HER sexy, all that want. And on Wednesday morning, after he gives a lingering touch to Elizabeth's body, an arousing touch to keep her alert all day, he watches her drive to work. She's uptight and not. She packs up her troubles in an old kit bag and smiles like a soldier. Leading lady, definitely, definitely.

On the drive to Athens, Frank jolts himself into remembering he has various responsibilities at the university and then he will have to deal with Bridget, whom he can hardly imagine, hardly remember. A child, right, a sexy little child in his rented house there, reading his books, waiting for him in Lolitaville, his budding soubrette.

He meets the students, four of them, and goes over their work, without remembering to take a break, without remembering to get so much as a drink of water. Mail has piled up at the office. Grading instructions, grade forms. A note from Alice asking him to stop by to sign several pieces of paper.

Heinz Ersicher bounding down the hallway, giving something between a wink and a blink.

Alice, who is expressionless, tucks her hair and hands him forms to sign. He wants to say, "I killed my brother." Without any trouble, he can imagine her puzzled, dead expression. Then he would add, "I didn't want to and I wanted to very much. The second feeling won. I shot him. In the heart. And nobody knows. There was something about him that infuriated me. Reduced me. Made nothing of me." And her expression would be only a little less puzzled. She would think what he was saying was some kind of joke she just didn't understand, something with flow and intention, but just out of her league. "Because he wanted to embarrass me," he would tell her. And that little eyebrow of a phrase she would understand.

He says nothing. He signs the forms for old Alice with the geometric hair. He gets out of the building and into his car and home. Home.

Bridget is a sore thumb in her new outfit. Don't you know, Bridge, he wants to say, a new outfit should not look stiff. The L.A. way is expensive grunge, don't you know. Bridget is sitting and reading, pretending not to be eager to see him, pretending. She puts a bookmark in her book and looks up. She looks different in the face, still a dumpling, but an older one.

"Your hair isn't so red anymore," he says.

"I cut it. Kind of. Tried to make that shaggy look by taking off the reddest edges."

Not bad. It looks pretty much purposeful. He lifts a trendily errant strand and kisses her on the forehead.

"I made you dinner," she says.

He looks at the roast chicken and tries not to laugh. The roast chicken circuit.

"Why are you smiling?"

"It was sweet of you to cook. What about the duds? New?"

"Yeah."

"Very nice."

The table is set. How funny. My God, another chicken dinner.

"What do you want from me?" he asks when he is seated across from her. "Now that I've done a certain job for you."

"I want to . . . go to L.A. with you, see if we can make it."

"I'm an old man."

"You're very handsome."

"Nobody would say that. I'm just okay."

"To me, you are. I love how you look." She is trying to cut into the chicken breast and it's giving her a little what-for and she looks as if she might cry.

"This is not the usual thing, you and me," he says quietly.

"Nothing in my life has ever been or will ever be usual." She cuts firmly and a tear rolls down. "At least you're smart. And interesting."

He smiles. "It's my brains you like?" Without much jubilation, he takes a bite of slightly dry chicken.

"No. It's something else. If I say it, you'll laugh at me."

"What is it?"

"That you seem broken. That you seem hurt and you let me help you. There. Now you'll hate me."

Oh, no, another Daniel, a little Daniel. In the soul business.

And so, when the inevitable happens, after he's removed her stiff little cropped jeans and her starched little blouse with the laces at the chest—"What do you call this?" he asks. "I call it a pirate's shirt," she says—they lie in his bed, her curled toward him and clinging, and he says, "Tell me which of my things you've been reading."

"The things you gave me to work on."

"Come, now, Bridget, tell me the truth."

"What do you mean?"

"It's because of who you are, curious, strong, intellectual, eager, all those things. Hungry for information. I know, because I know these things, that you would have to read something more. You like me, you think you love me, you want to know about me. Right?"

"I do want to know about you."

"And so you looked around, right?"

Now he turns to search her face so that she can't lie without his seeing. "So tell me what you read."

"Well, I looked in your desk."

"And what did you find?"

"That your lease only goes to the end of December. I got all worried wondering what would happen next. To me, too. Then you said—"

"I'm leaving a lot earlier than December."

"In a week, you said."

"Next Tuesday, probably." She is frozen, still. Ready to cry. "I'll take care of you."

"I don't want charity. I want to go with you."

"We'll talk about this. It depends, if you still like me. What else did you read?"

"The locked files." She can't look at him. Head downward, looking at her knee, then his thigh, she swallows hard.

"And what did you find?"

"You're being mean."

"What did you find?"

"More plays, files, notes for stories you were going to write."

"What stories?"

"Something about a teenager who kills a girl by putting a bunch of sleeping pills . . . in her booze. At first, I figured that's what you were researching in Pittsburgh."

"What made you think that?"

"Nothing." Scared. He's scared her off. She knows something.

He says softly, "Tell me. You're very good. I knew you would be. Clever as sin. And maybe my soul mate after all. What made you think that?"

"Because I figured out it was set in Pittsburgh and then you seemed so interested in the city anyway."

"I don't get how you figured out I was interested in the city. I love how smart you are, Bridget. Go on."

She looks uncertain.

"You know you're amazing, huh? You could probably do about anything you set your mind to do. Tell me how you did it. The history on my computer?"

"Yes."

"And what did you find?"

"Some guy who died. You read about him a couple of times."

"And you thought . . ."

"I thought maybe a documentary on him, or maybe an *Unsolved Mysteries* kind of thing."

"Did you find him compelling enough for that?"

She nods. "He sounded as if he wanted to do something good. That place in the park for teenagers, that was his idea. The newspaper said he was an amazing man."

"*Unsolved Mysteries,* huh. I never thought of that."

"Did you ever finish writing that other idea, the boy who murdered the girl?"

"A million times."

"What do you mean?"

"Maybe not a million, but a lot."

"Could I read a finished version?"

"Maybe." He could see her eyes flicker as she wondered where it was. "I tried to tell you I'm not a good-hearted guy. You see me as generous because of this arrangement we have, but I'm not. You're going to be disappointed when you realize that."

"Are you thinking about your wife?"

"Who?"

"Carol."

"There is no Carol."

He could feel her adjusting, thinking about the strange world he inhabited, where things changed, truths were hard to find. She said she didn't appreciate lying, she could handle anything if it was the truth.

He had to laugh at that.

In the middle of the night, her arm went around him in her sleep. In the morning, he told her he'd be gone for the weekend.

ELIZABETH IS ABOUT TO CALL MARGOT ON THURSDAY NIGHT IN the hopes Margot will be tougher with her, less delicate, when next door, the black BMW pulls in, and Frank walks to his door without looking her way. An hour goes by. Lights on. No phone call.

Is he giving her a night off? She wants to ask him things, she wants to talk about Dan and herself, ask him more about his childhood, where he went on his trip this time, what happened. Facts. She wants facts. Maybe it only seems like love, wanting to know.

THAT THURSDAY NIGHT, BRIDGET OPENS THE FILES AGAIN AND begins. Skip nothing, she tells herself.

She's trying to get used to the idea that she will not see him until Monday. Reality. A reality she never thought she could get her mind around, and yet here she is, being one with this unacceptable idea, sharing him with someone, compromise, waiting. Pretending, game playing. Not her thing and yet of course there is a whole world of adults who do just that.

Some of what she reads is incredibly boring. Some of it is stuff like life insurance, an adult preoccupation she can't begin to relate to. But yes, there was a woman who got listed as a beneficiary between 1991 and 1997. Her name was not Carol, but Lisa. Lisa. There were furniture bills, electric bills. Funny how he saves everything. Not everybody saves furniture bills. And taxes. Lisa is listed on taxes, too, as a spouse. Is *she* in Pittsburgh now, putting the screws to him in some way? His heart is split, that she knows, between her and someone, something large. Taxes paid every year. All very orderly. Letters. A million letters of the business sort. She begins on them.

Dear Mr. Razzi, I met you at a pitch meeting in April of 1983. Since then I have rethought my goals with the piece. Would you be willing to read ten pages of the new version?

Frank had answered. That was nice. He wrote a lot of letters back to people he didn't have to write back to. He provided amazingly detailed reports of everything he read. *I have a few ideas of my own I might develop when I get time,* he

wrote in the last paragraph of several letters from the early •
eighties. He was not the most aggressive wannabe. Too polite, that's what she'd say.

A folder, marked "Unfinished." Another beginning, but
this one goes on for forty pages. A woman who drinks lives
right at the sea somewhere. West Coast. She is drinking
and pays no attention to her son. She has boyfriends, one,
then another, vying for her attentions. The boy is more
and more neglected.

Bridget starts at the beginning and reads again. This one
is kind of *good.* It has a physical effect on her breathing and
heartbeat—that she takes seriously. The woman wants to
get rid of her son. Frank has tucked into the folder a newspaper clipping about a woman who drowns her son, but he
doesn't write that. In his, the mother takes the son to another family, tells them to raise him. They are a pathetic
couple, not a thought in their heads. The boy is bored.

Oh, another forty pages, as if beginning all over again.
A mother takes a boy to a family and asks them to raise
him. But it's a different family this time. A father and his
son. The father is a doctor and the son is a stellar student
in the high school. The boy is very shy, awkward, and
doesn't know how to fit in. He is jealous of the other boy.
At school he's taunted about being adopted.

The boy is called Michael and the brother is Robert.
Aha. Recycled characters. Aha. She has seen these characters before. Robert is extraordinary. When he speaks, he
sounds wise. Very kind. Understanding. Michael sulks for
a few pages but then he looks at Robert with admiration
and gratitude.

Bridget is involved. This one is *very* good. Even though
it's old, and somewhat old-fashioned, it *stands up,* as Frank
would say.

Why did Frank never finish this script? Why? This one
lingers with her.

Between Thursday and Friday, Bridget reads or scans
everything in the whole file cabinet, four drawers of lateral
files. And still, she can't catch him, doesn't know him. On

Friday night, she goes back to his computer and begins slowly to go through the places bookmarked. He knew she would do this. He expected it. So why not? The part about the dead doctor, he wasn't surprised she knew he was working on that. No script for that one yet, nothing on the computer anyway.

Where is he and why does he not call her? If he can't break away for a minute to call her, then it's hopeless between them, the other woman has won.

She can't quite make herself believe that, but on Friday night, unable to stand it, she walks down the road and to the Go-Bar. Let him reprimand. Let him. She's human. She orders calamari and fries and beer. A different waitress waits on her this time and the man she wants to avoid is not there, although she keeps checking, fearful he will appear when she drops her guard. Two older women are sitting beside her on the stools against the wall. Both, she would guess, are in their forties. Both are hefty, permed, perfumed, and wearing large earrings. Going for life, Bridget thinks, wondering who she will be at that age. Married, happy, or still alone?

"Cute outfit," one says to her. "Where'd you get that?"

"University Mall, a little shop."

"My daughter would like that, all right."

"Thank you," Bridget says, after the fact.

"We always think we're going to meet Mr. Wonderful in here," the other one says. She laughs, looking over the pickings. "We are really hopeless. You don't think you're going to meet Mr. Wonderful, do you?"

"No."

"That means you think you already met him." The woman to the right gives her a wise, head-down, eyes-up look. "And he's being a jerk and you want to get even."

Bridget smiles, an admission that that's definitely one way to look at a fairly complex situation. "So where do you two come from?" she asks.

"We live in the boonies. We work at the university," the one on the left says. They look a little alike, sisters, friends.

Same hairdresser probably, same makeup, same clothing shops.

"Where at the university?"

"Food service. Good benefits. Bad food."

Bridget laughs agreeably. She had wanted to ask about Frank. Did they know him, process his paycheck?

"You a student?"

"No."

"Good for you. College is for the birds. The smartest kids are the dumbest, you know what I mean?"

"Yep." Talking to them helps to pass the time. But after a while, they drift off. Nobody asks Bridget to dance. She talks to a man for a while but she can't seem to help him get beyond "Sure you don't want another drink?" She could never in a million years imagine kissing him.

The two women from food service move close to the dance floor and ask men to dance. Bridget watches them, doing their best to have a good time, and she admires them for it. A lot of people are unhappy. Frank is. He's stirred-up water. Muddy and obscure. Gets to her in a James Dean–Julie Harris kind of way.

CHRISTIE CALLED MARY CONNELLY ON FRIDAY AFTERNOON WITH a fresh question. He'd been sitting at his desk, doodling, looking at his picture of the wheel with the missing spokes. "I never asked you, what kind of work did Gerald Paul *want to do,* if not medicine. Did he talk about other work?"

"He didn't," she said.

"He seemed devoted to medicine?"

"Devoted doesn't seem quite it. Determined, maybe. He waited on tables for years before he went to med school, then that was it."

Pencil to paper, more doodles. It was pure luck that he didn't ask another question, for it gave Mary time to think. "You know, I think you have it wrong. Ever since I talked to you, I've been thinking about him nonstop. He got angry, he had a lot of anger in him, but he tended to suppress it. He also had sentiment, compassion. Some-times a lot of it."

"I could have it wrong. I've been wrong before. What kind of compassion?"

"Well, he watched a lot of movies. He never said it, but I think they allowed him to cry."

"Hmmm. Interesting."

"He even tried to write screenplays. Went to some guy in the English Department and showed something he was working on."

Hair up on the back of his neck. "And what was the upshot?"

"Nothing much. Some statistics about the minuscule chance of writing anything that anybody wanted."

"You think he ever continued?"

"He did, a little, just messing around."

Christie called Potocki in and said, "Film business. How about checking for names like LaBeau and Paul and Gerald in funny combinations?" Thank heavens Potocki didn't ask "How do I do that?" because Christie didn't have a clue.

Meanwhile, if, if, if. Ridiculous. The guy was probably some cameraman named Bob Jones or something.

And meanwhile Marina had landed. When he answered her call, she had already rented a car and made the drive into Fort Myers.

"How is it? The town?"

"Everything is low and square and unfancy. My place is pretty . . . basic. Richard? The address we have for LaBeau? I've already been by once. There's no name on the apart-ment mailbox and nobody answered my knock. I'm going to keep trying."

He already missed her.

THEY ARE IN BED, LYING ON THEIR SIDES, TURNED TO EACH other. Elizabeth is trying to pinpoint something—what?— a funny way he has of talking about himself. "Did you go to a lot of movies as a little kid?" she asks. "Did you know you wanted to be in film then?"

"No. Made up stories, though. Had imaginary companions. The usual nutty kid stuff."

He sounds too breezy, she thinks. "Who were your imaginary companions, then?"

He stops to think.

If a person remembers any friends, it's the imaginary ones, in her experience. The ones that are made up are right there, still with you, the nondangerous form of schizophrenia. Why does he need to think?

Frank says, "A boy. He was a little bit Tom Sawyer but I was a lot Huck Finn."

"Huck was the more interesting," she says gently.

"Do you think so?"

"I think Twain did. Most people do."

"I don't know. I was one or the other."

But why did he need to think? "And only the stepsister, you said? No siblings?"

"Very clever," he said. "Your shrinking skills. Very clever. I had a brother once. He died young."

Something sinks in her. There will be a tragedy here, something that explains him. "How?"

"Drowned."

"It changed your life, then." A statement.

"I don't remember."

Carefully, she asks, "How can you not remember?"

"I was very young and my parents didn't tell me until years later. When I asked for details, they always just said he had an accident at a pond."

"Were you there, too?"

"Apparently, I was."

"Apparently?"

"I was nine months old at the time."

Nine months. So it couldn't have been his fault. Nine months. And maybe not a memory. But he's clever enough to know the imaginary friend would have been conjured to make up for it. Why doesn't he say those things, then?

He closes his eyes, lies flat like a dead man.

If any of it is true. She can't tell yet, she's getting bull-shitting vibes, and he is a man with invention at his finger-tips. If it turns out he's a liar, well, it's no good, she can't have anything to do with him.

Everything in her is alert. Love? Or work? Is she work-ing? Questioning, listening, trying to help—only, in a bed-room, naked, with kisses in between, letting him travel her body, explore her as a safe vessel for where he can put the secrets?

SHE GOES HOME AT TWO IN THE MORNING AND TRIES TO SLEEP, but can't. It's almost four. In all her life she has not felt this unmoored. It's like jet lag cubed. Her mind races. When she is on the verge of sleep, the kaleidoscope begins and people become puppets that become dogs that be-come vases that become plants. Everything is one. Truly. String theory. Just rearrange the strings. Everything is one. The kaleidoscope is frightening, so she stops it and puts on the lamp. She opens a book and tries to read, aware now that if he should go to the small empty room in his house and look out the window, he would see her light, see her reading, unable to sleep.

Trying to read. Forcing herself to concentrate, she begins to make progress, stepping through a sentence, a paragraph, and then that thing happens, she reads whole thoughts that aren't there, wakes to witness their absence, reads again, makes things up again. The mind invents, invents.

A thought slips in, so horrible she wakes shaking, but can't find it on the page and moments later can't remem-ber what the words were. Finally, she is asleep.

When she wakes at eleven in the morning, she lies there thinking she has not slept to this hour in her adult life ever except on a trip to Europe when time was turned up-side down. Not even, in her memory, with a cold or flu. She had kids, a life. She always got up.

Now, lying here alone in the bright light of morning, she feels an arousal so deep, she wonders at herself. Lust, it always means something. What? A. That she did not love Dan in a passionate way, but only as a good friend. B. That God is a joker and the body, the spirit, have to be renewed with a stranger. C. That she is being trapped, mesmerized by something false and delicious that will disappear when she finds the trick of it. D. That she is falling in love again; an interesting man happened into her path, timing be damned. E. That she is crazy and this is nothing but the flip side of grief. On the SATs, GREs, other intelligence tests, what would she answer? F. All of the above. The answer keeps changing.

Her phone rings and she knows it will be Frank, wants it to be.

"Okay? Only checking in."

"I just woke."

"Good. It means you needed it."

"My day is gone. I feel foggy."

"Take it slow. Take it easy."

"After I have some coffee and a shower, I'm going to take a walk in the park. Do you want to?"

His hesitation is palpable. "I'd better keep plugging. Dinner, though. You're coming for dinner."

"Am I?"

"No question."

Seven-thirty dinner, then. It helps. It gives her the impetus to do laundry, decide which clothes to take to the dry cleaner.

HER SKIN IS SO PALE IN THE CANDLELIGHT. SHE SEEMS FRAIL, delicate, ready to blush at everything. He wants to shock her.

"Did you write today?" she asks.

"I started again yesterday."

Interestingly, she does not ask what he is writing, but looks sideways toward the pile of things on the dining room chair. "Good. Good. Do you write very autobiographically?"

"I have seventy-five manuscripts that aren't at all auto-biographical. I can't say *not at all*, but they don't sting. The images come from me but they aren't personal. I have twenty-five somethings, scripts, screenplays, *starts,* a lot of them, that are in various ways autobiographical."

"I would love to see those."

"Maybe. One day." His muscles tighten at the thought of it. "The thing about a film," he says, because she's listening, "it goes out everywhere. Film, you're talking to people in China, Japan, Australia, England. Up in little huts in Appalachia. It still astounds me. Still, after all the years and the crap in the business, it astounds me."

"You want to talk to a lot of people?" She asks this gently, but her face is searching him intently with the question, What do you want to say? He wants to say, Good people hurt you more than bad ones do. Moral rectitude is a form of punishment. No one knows what anyone else goes through. Prison is impossible, impossible. Freedom, prison, are in the heart. There is no such thing as a lie. Every invention is true, if only you can figure out how.

"Images," he says. "The words tell the story, the action tells the story, but there are also those images you never forget. Visuals. The story in a moment."

She makes a face, unsure what he means.

"Mrs. Robinson shrinking."

"Oh. Yes."

Woman in a bedroom, crying. Man holding cell phone in open hand, like a surrender.

Bird on a branch, branch bobbing, uncertain footing, bird flies away. Even then, as early as that, he sees it, an image he will use.

"ARE YOU GIVING ME THE BRUSH?" BRIDGET ASKS, WHEN HE calls her on Saturday to say he has been thinking about her and they have to talk seriously soon. "Because why wait? I could just pack up and leave now." Amazing how anger just pops out that way—she decided not to challenge him, not to act on anger and pique, not to ask for anything, but to put in time, being kind to him, letting the good parts flourish. So much for resolutions.

"We are going to be packing up, *both* of us. Giving up the place. Remember I told you I was leaving Tuesday."

"I remember."

"I need to pack Monday, when I get back."

"In two days?" The words are three high notes in minor key. But he keeps surprising her with shrinking time.

"That's right."

She looks around with regret at the place she got used to, the kitchen counter she's worked at and that she stands at now, the scratches on the peach-colored countertop she knows well by now—one set of knife-lines looks almost like a game of tic-tac-toe. The place is familiar. Maybe *she* could just stay. "Is it your ex?"

"Who?"

"Lisa," she tried.

After a brief pause, he said, "No."

"What about us?"

"How about a little trip, just a few days, the two of us, to see where we are?"

Breathlessly, she asks, "Where?"

"I don't know," he says impatiently. "Off by ourselves. A cottage somewhere."

When she hangs up, she looks around at what is essentially cottagelike and off by itself and wonders, Why not here?

And she thinks he can pretend a million things, but she knows one truth. He's happy around her, no matter who or what he's running off to see.

She forces herself to read something, picks up *Why Did I Ever*, and falls in love with the hard-drinking, drug-taking wit of the book. While she's reading, it seems the only way to be, tough, funny. When she puts the book down, she knows full well she's flunking out of the school for hard-assed people.

On Sunday, Bridget makes a thorough search of his desk, the files again, his clothes closet, looking for something, not sure what. She begins to pack things up, without being told to do so. In the basement she finds some boxes, which she puts the few dishes and pots in. There aren't a lot of boxes, so she puts food like crackers and cereal carefully arranged, so they won't spill, into large garbage bags tied tightly.

If only she could get into his e-mail! Back at the computer, she goes into his history and sees that the last time he was home—it must have been when she took a shower, since they were together all the time otherwise—he went into the Net history and looked again at the picture of the woman and her two kids.

A terrible thought hits her. Not Lisa on the road to reconciliation, not some new hot number, but this sad woman who was married to the man who got killed? If he's looking at her picture all the time . . . She rereads the article but it doesn't say anything that answers her questions. A funny feeling grips her as she tries to stitch together the bits and pieces of his life.

She has worked so efficiently that the house is no longer pleasant. With everything in boxes, there is nowhere to sit without being reminded she is in transit, in a temporary mode. He does not call.

On Sunday night she goes to bed early, *his* bed, reading *Why Did I Ever* until she's finished it. Tomorrow morning, she will wash and pack up the bedclothes and she might as well see if anything of his needs to be washed. Then if there's time, she will organize his clothes, pack them. Everything will be ready. They can go out to dinner, talk, go to their cottage, talk.

Bridget sleeps fitfully, an hour at a time, until, at five in the morning, she konks out hard. At ten-thirty, she stares at the alarm clock in surprise.

Coffee. She drags herself through breakfast, using up the eggs since those don't pack well. She dunks bread into the egg yellows, wondering why the whole world seems to have given up on eggs for breakfast. Then, even though she's still in the sweats she sleeps in, she puts on her coat. Once more, for routine, she goes outside and walks around the grounds, toward the edges where the woods begin. It's colder now, cold enough that her breath makes clouds as she walks the periphery. Last time, she thinks. Good-bye to this place. Jogs, slows down, walks. She entertains the thought of splashing water on her face, putting her things into the duffel bag, and just leaving, like a five-year-old hobo runaway. Make him find me. Walk into town, go to Jess's place. Test him. Make him find me. If he cares enough, he will find me.

Back inside, she showers and puts on her old jeans and a sweater. Stripping both beds, she thinks, Work is the only thing that makes sense. Without it, she's not sure who she is. One washer load of sheets, another of towels, and maybe another if he has any odd socks that need to be done. But she doesn't know what time they are leaving. Is she washing the sheets only to put them back on the beds for tonight? Never mind. It's all right.

He has an awful lot of polo shirts of a nice quality. She uses her duffel bag for those since her clothes aren't that good. All through her body is the beginning of a crying jag, mini-convulsions, a feeling of stinging fullness in her eyes and cheeks. She's so close to crying, she is sure she will be weeping into the washing machine when he arrives, quite a picture, bound to make him love her.

The basement is full of stuff, but most of it, she is pretty certain, belongs to the house and not to him. A broken chair. Motor oil, can't tell whose that is. Furnace filters. A rack for hanging clothes. The three suitcases would be his. She decides she will pack the rest of his clothes.

The first suitcase is a large tweed thing, fairly heavy. She hoists it off the pile, picks up a hanging bag, which is next, and gets those things up the basement stairs. She opens them on the bare mattress, but then stops herself. It's an intrusion, packing his clothes. She's not sure what order he would like things in, and she probably never should have used her duffel for his things.

For a moment, she sits on the edge of the bed, defeated. It's a gray day. She would like to curl up and sleep. How wild her imagination is, to think of tramping down the road with her possessions slung over her shoulder. Pretty pathetic. Not too cute, not too Norman Rockwell.

Bridget starts to the basement for the remaining suitcase, and partway there realizes what she needs is *sound, cheer*. So back upstairs she goes and she puts on Santana's *Abraxas* nice and loud. Let it pound. Make the house vibrate. Give the old house a good jolt before leaving it.

The third suitcase is odd at the first tug. First of all, it's heavy, and second, something slides inside it. Better be careful, she thinks. The suitcase itself is a run-of-the-mill taupe thing, from what little she knows, not at all the quality of the tweed one upstairs. It's pretty darn heavy.

Bridget lifts it more carefully, puts it on the floor, and zips it open. Her heart drops even before she looks into the two boxes within it. Each box is three or four times the size of a shoe box. Fifteen by eighteen, twelve by fifteen. Inside are the secrets.

At first, Bridget isn't sure what she's seeing, but she knows it's important. For one thing, there are photos in one of the boxes. There are pictures of a boy and a woman at the oceanside. They are wearing heavy jackets. A group picture of schoolchildren. Who are these children? She reads their names on a strip on the back and does not recognize any of the names. She studies the pictures and does not recognize any of the faces. It sometimes takes a trick to see the adult in the child. Some people are good at it. She's seen those celebrity games—like which boy is Tom Hanks, which boy is Tommy Lee Jones?

There are other photographs that puzzle her. Teenage pictures of two boys. A couple of pictures of a woman with a sweater over her shoulders and a book in her hand. The woman looks uncomfortable, standing on the back steps of a house. Who is she? Nothing written on the back. The hairstyles suggest these are pretty old pictures.

Grade reports for a child who got a lot of A's. Gerald LaBeau. That was one of the names on the group picture. She locates the boy. Her insides turn upside down.

Couldn't be. Couldn't be. Wrong name. What was that name on the scrap of paper upstairs in the files, the one with the notes for a screenplay on it? Gerald something. She is about to go upstairs and check, but there are treasures here she cannot stop searching. More grade reports. Paul LaBeau. Pittsburgh. She is sick, sick. A school newspaper photo of two boys, Paul LaBeau and Daniel Ross, Pittsburgh. She has to put things down, to breathe, just to breathe. Her whole body is shaking. She can't stop looking. Who would hide these things? Bridget looks up at the basement ceiling. Yes, there's another bulb, and maybe with that on, she can see better. She's been sitting right on the cement floor and her body is stiff when she gets up to reach for the light. She pulls the string and sinks down again to her work. Upstairs the CD goes back to the beginning and begins again, the whole house cat-crying with guitar.

Slowly, matching name to face and face to name, she is able to trace Gerald LaBeau to Paul LaBeau to Gerald Paul. It's Frank. It's Frank, all right, she can see his face in these faces. But the ears are different, so maybe not, maybe it's a relative, a brother. In an envelope she finds a driver's license for Frank Razzi. The first relief she feels is washed away when no matter how she tries, she can't get the face on the license to sit still and be Frank's face.

All of these things in a box. Hidden. Bridget has a certainty now that nothing is simple or ever will be simple again. Never will she believe a person is what he or she seems. Never again.

Leave it. Go. "Fast as you can," she whispers to herself.

But she wants to know what it is she's running from. It's here, what she's wanted all along.

In an envelope are newspaper clippings, some of real newsprint, and others in an old shiny copy paper, sections, pasted together. Obituaries for Gerald Paul. Obituaries. Her mind won't work, can't take it in, yet she keeps going through the papers, puzzling over the collection. Gerald Paul, and another obituary—real newspaper again, all yellow—for another boy. Theodore Luckey. Pittsburgh paper.

It's nothing, nothing. A researcher's, a writer's, files for ideas. The man is interested in the deaths of young people, something he wrote about, plenty of evidence of that upstairs. It's nothing, only her crazy mind.

But why down here, why not in the files?

"Black Magic Woman" is playing. She wants to be happy again, and suddenly it seems that two weeks ago, three weeks ago, she was. Even back in St. Louis, she was sometimes happy. Simple disappointments, she can handle them. Frank doesn't love her enough and she's gone bonkers, okay. She's a baby with a crush. Love doesn't work out. Easy. Easy.

The music plays. She starts to put items, one after another, back into the boxes.

"Hello," he says.

She looks up. Frank is standing at the top of the stairs. His face is not quite in the light. Her face is collapsing inward, trying not to exist anywhere it can be looked at, read.

"What are you doing?" he asks.

Today is Monday, she thinks. I almost left.

DOLAN CAME INTO CHRISTIE'S OFFICE ON MONDAY AFTERNOON. "We had a funny call from a pharmacist in Dormont."

"Yeah," Christie said, abstractedly.

"Seems our Dr. Ross filled a prescription there."

"Get out."

"Right."

It was too much to hope for. It meant LaBeau or somebody they were going to be interested in was around, making mistakes.

"Get this," Dolan said. "I looked up the name of the doctor who wrote the prescription. It's the next floor up from Ross's office. A plastic surgeon. Does that seem a little bit close for comfort?"

"Let's go."

Dolan made a face. "You're not going to like this part. It happened over a week ago. The pharmacist just got around to checking it out. Our man could be halfway around the world and over jet lag at this point."

They had to go to the Medfast first to take a look at the written prescription. Megan Smithy let them have it without a warrant. She was pretty nervous.

"The date is only ten days ago. The person didn't try to make it look like an older prescription, I mean, didn't date it before Ross died," Dolan said.

"We might have hesitated over an old prescription for a pain medication," Smithy interrupted. "Look," she said quietly. "I'm probably in big trouble here at work. We were busy and he seemed nice, ordinary."

"That's the part we want to know."

"What?"

"Tell us anything you can about him," Christie said.

The pharmacist said, "I can't tell you what he looked like. I don't remember. Honestly, I just can't remember. I have the impression of a nice-looking man, nicely kept up, but I can't get a picture. My boyfriend asked me this already. He made me deep breathe and try to picture the guy and I couldn't come up with anything big."

"You'd know him if you saw him again?"

"Yeah, I think so, that's different."

NEITHER RECEPTIONIST AT THE PLASTIC SURGEON'S OFFICE RECognized the handwriting on the prescription, nor, of course, did they have a Daniel Ross in their books, although they were determined to look through them. It was lunchtime. One receptionist was neat and uptight, the other couldn't have been more chaotic. They let Christie and Dolan know they were giving up their break time, but they stayed.

Only one patient was there, a woman who was sitting and reading magazines and being, well, *patient* as a person has to be who comes an hour early for an appointment.

After about fifteen minutes of answering questions, the receptionist clapped a hand to her head and said, "That guy. The one who kept me here after five for some emergency appointment. Then after all that, he canceled the appointment. Said something about having to see whichever doctor this other guy had seen. I had to go into the back to the old files. That's when he could have . . ." She looked accusingly at the woman who had a messy desk. "Did you leave a scrip pad out?"

The other one said, "*I* don't know."

"Do you think that's what he came in here for?" The receptionist turned from Dolan to Christie. "All that other stuff about how he was told he had to get an appointment right away—"

"Told by whom?"

"The film company. No, Film Office."

Christie and Dolan exchanged a look. Film. This was it.

"So he pressured and I finally made him an appointment. I squeezed him in for last Friday. Then after all that, he called and canceled."

"What name did he give?" Christie asked. This was it. He could feel it.

"That would have been the twenty-first." She looked. "We erased it. We erased it and squeezed someone else in."

"You don't remember his name."

"Tip of my tongue," she said. "Damn."

"Can you tear the sheet out and hold it to the light?"

"I never tore anything out of the book." She looked nervously toward where the doctors kept their offices. "Let me just try to hold it up."

The messy receptionist said, "I remember it was one of those names like Money or Darling. Like it's a word. That kind of name."

The neat receptionist went cross-eyed studying the book that she held up to the light.

The patient in the waiting room no longer read her magazine. She found this far more interesting. She came right over and joined in.

"I think that's an *L*. An L name," said the receptionist, as the patient said, "Sorry, I couldn't help overhearing. I'm good at this kind of thing," and then began to volunteer words: "Land. Lender. Lamb."

The neat receptionist looked horrified at the interruption. The messy one laughed right out loud, which further horrified the neat one.

Then out of the blue, the messy one said, "Lucky. It was Lucky. That was the word, *name*."

Christie felt a shiver go the whole way through him. "First name?" he asked.

"I can't read it."

"Theodore?"

"Something short."

"Ted?"

"I was going to say Tom, but Ted, Ted is right."

"Amen," Dolan said. "Our first real break."

"*Lucky* break," the messy one said, thrilled.

13

ELIZABETH DIALS FRANK, BUT HE'S NOT IN.

A glass of wine in front of her on the table. That, too, all right. A Frank substitute. She has always known from the outside what it must feel like to be an addict. And she supposes every therapist must flirt with it, sometime, come to the edges of addiction to understand how the person who wants heroin or alcohol is fascinated, enjoys it, then slips into plain needing.

She talks to Dan, tries to, even though she is having trouble imagining his replies. "About Thanksgiving . . ." she begins. "Jeff has a girlfriend. He wants to bring her. Apparently . . . I hear they're together all the time. I told him he could. Lauren wants to leave early. Jeff wants to stay the weekend. So there I am. . . ."

The person who supplies an answer is not Dan, but Frank. In her mind, he whispers, "Come back here. Come back as soon as you can."

She takes a drink of wine and looks toward the place next door. Quiet.

Next, she dials her daughter to confirm Wednesday at five at Breezewood. The usual arrangement.

Now she sits to open the mail she has not bothered with. Glossy travel brochures slip out of the envelope into her lap. The blue of the Caribbean is slightly different from the blue of Maui, and surely none of it is real.

Dan. Dan. The house is empty, silent. She imagines the thing differently. The shot rings out, glances off his shoulder, he guns the motor, swerves out of there, hurt, but free. Why not that?

Dutifully, she looks through the travel brochures. The woman who gathered them for her is someone she knows and so she gives a little time to balconies over the water, dinners with the ocean at the elbow, happy scuba divers. Gathering up the brochures, she is aware of the expense and weight of the paper. Will she want to look at these again? Indecisive, she walks them to the kitchen trash, then stops short and puts the envelope on the counter.

Too tired to eat.

Evening news. On. Watched. Off.

Stomach growls. So the body insists. Pasta. Something soft. Pasta. Another glass of wine. Another news program, because you can't ever get enough news.

An idea is edging in again, just under the voices on the television, and it's only the shadow of an idea, put aside with another taste of the wine, a slow walk to the kitchen, where she goes still as she waits for water to fill the pot.

"COME," HE SAID TO BRIDGET. "COME UPSTAIRS. LET'S HAVE SOMEthing to eat."

Foolishly, she tried to put the boxes back into the suitcase.

"Leave that. Come on up."

She thought, There is a basement door, where is it? Then she remembered the hatch over in the left corner. Even if he left the top of the stairs, it would take time to figure out the door fastenings, there would be the rattle of metal and the thump—But he was not leaving, only standing there, waiting for her.

"Don't jump to conclusions," he said. "Let's talk. We said we would."

She could hardly get up, her legs were stiff from sitting cross-legged and they were weak with fear. She stumbled like a baby animal. No way to outrun the old predator if the legs would not obey. Bridget made her way up the steps, holding on to the banister, thinking, This is the end, isn't it, I won't be able to fight him.

He didn't grab her. He looked as if he would, but he stayed six inches away, shadowing her.

"Let's sit at the table," he said. "Have a little something."

"It's not suppertime."

He smiled. "Late lunch or teatime, then. No scones in the house, though. I'll have to serve you plain old cheese."

"I'm not hungry." Her challenging tone surprised her.

"Well, I am. Late lunch for me, communion for you." He turned from her toward the refrigerator and looked through the drawer that held the cheese.

Communion. She turned that over, the couple of things it could mean. Communion.

"Maybe it's the weather. Makes it feel later than it is," he said, nodding toward the windows. It was a dark afternoon, clouded over.

"I should just go," she said.

He turned back to her with the refrigerator door open behind him. His face was unfathomable. "Not yet. When I told you how much I cared for you, you didn't believe me? I meant it."

Lies, they didn't fool her this time. She knew he was bad. What she didn't know about herself was that she was religious. She started to pray, Don't let this be it, please, don't let this be the end of me.

"Bridget. I like it better when you talk. Why won't you tell me what you were doing down there? Talk to me."

"Tell me about your trip" is the first thing she squeezed out of her mouth, "who you went to see."

"My trip?" He looked intrigued, a little surprised, as if to say, Still the jealous little Lolita, huh? Maybe he was thinking, Jealousy is good, jealousy is advanced, it's hot, it's *something*. She could hear his voice even though he wasn't speaking. The expressions on his face became words and the words had sound and rhythm in her mind, that's how close she'd come to him.

Oh, help me, she thought, help me to know what to say. Her body and voice were still frozen. The horrible fact she kept coming back to was that nobody knew she was here, nobody knew anything about her. Jess, all right, Jess, but only a phone number. He'd killed before. Surely that's what the stuff in the basement meant, all the pieces put together. This was it. She couldn't think beyond that, couldn't talk.

He moved. She jumped and almost cried out. He put cheese on the small kitchen table, crackers from the cabinet. Everything was just every which way on the table, at angles, not his style. "You want a drink?" he asked.

"No."

"I do. Wine, whiskey, beer, you sure?"

"Nothing."

She watched his hands. Nothing to drink. Three scenes in three scripts with powders or pills pushed into a drink. In the one, a boy dropping pellets into a drink, the victim unable to fight back after a few sips. She would not eat or drink.

He sat across from her. His eyes were wild, but he didn't sit forward on the edge of the seat as she expected. Instead, he pretended to lean back, relaxed, with the plate on his thigh. He was a man who pretended all kinds of things.

"My trip? I cut it short. I wanted to get back here. I wanted to see you, figure out where we were going next." An accusation. You have ruined it all.

Bridget said, "I think . . . I don't know what I was thinking."

"You wanted to go to L.A."

"Yes . . . I did. But I'm not the person for you. You have someone in Pittsburgh, I know that."

"Is that what you were looking for in the basement?"

"Yes."

"Where I was, who I was with?"

She nodded.

"And what did you conclude?"

"Nothing. There were just some old pictures in there."

He leaned forward suddenly and grabbed her wrist hard. She tried to pull away, but his grip was strong. "Bridget, don't lie to me. I don't want lies now, of all times, I want to straighten things out. What did you conclude?"

"About what?"

"The person I go to see."

"I don't know."

"I think you are clever. Smart. And you wanted to know. So you know. Say her name."

Bridget shook her head. "It was just an idea I had."

His hand tightened. "Go on. I know how smart you are. Nothing gets past you. Say it and that's that. It's done. We have it between us."

She looked at her hand, curled, the way he held it. He's strong, she thought. "Elizabeth," she said.

"Yes." He let go of her hand.

She had never seen his eyes like this, positively black. Inky. Outside the window, the sky darkened. She was not breathing right. Her body was all collapsed, like a sack of clothes, like a puppet. She had to breathe. Slowly, determinedly, she began to fill herself out. "I didn't know what to think."

"Not true. You had lots of thoughts. Right now you're having lots of thoughts. Try me. Elizabeth because . . ."

Scrambling for a thought, anything, she said, "She's nice."

"Yes. You saw her on the computer?"

Bridget nods.

"And thought she was nice."

"She had a kind face . . . in the photo. She has kids." My age, Bridget thought, kids my age or so.

"She knows a lot about people. And she likes me very much." He shrugged. "What does that mean? Help me work it out. You're smart. One of the most capable people I ever met."

"It must mean you're . . . complicated. That you have many sides to you." He leaned forward almost imperceptibly. Defiance rose in her again. She said, "The person who would grab my arm the way you just did—that's not the whole of you, there are better parts."

He sat back. "Clever," he laughed. "Giving positive reinforcement to the child." He patted himself on the head.

She didn't know how to talk to him. He was a liar, but he hated evasion and lies in her. And caught them, every time.

"What did you think of the pictures?"

"I didn't know what to think."

"Why didn't you have any thoughts? A quick-witted girl like you."

She gave a bare answer, like a child in school. "People you were doing research on." A partial truth, an early thought she had, before the other ones came rushing at her.

"That was your only thought?"

"What do you mean?"

"A fixed thought? *Idée fixe?*" He laughed. "I was doing research? Your thought didn't change?"

"No."

"We're going to have to really talk. We said we would. You're extremely capable, Bridget. Sometimes I wish you weren't so bright, but on the other hand, it made me care about you, and I have to deal with that. It's my problem. I hate it that you have parents who have no idea how worth it you are."

"Maybe they know. Maybe they're just . . . busy."

"They don't know. You can't go back to them."

Bridget thought, One hour, one hour at most, before it all explodes. I must think of something. She got up and put on the overhead light. The even glare was hardly better than the dark. Everything about the afternoon in the little kitchen was unreal, apart. He ate, and after a while, because he kept offering, she took a bite of cheese, too.

Four o'clock passed. He said, "You know about Elizabeth. Good. You know I've had a couple of different . . . names. Lives. Okay, good. I'm going to give you some time to calm down. Let's go see what still has to be packed for the movers." She has already done a lot, most of the packing, unfortunately, but doesn't say so since movement, activity, might give her a chance at something. "Your room first."

In the few seconds it took to get from the kitchen to her room, Bridget imagined many things. Turning on him, flailing her fists. Running out the front door. Finding his car keys and fumbling, getting into his car before he could catch her. Driving away. Columbus, a bus station. Leave the car, keys and all, motor running. Leave everything behind. Bus to St. Louis. No, he could *find* her in St. Louis. Pick a city, any city. Get on the next bus no matter where it was going. But she needed money. Had almost none because she had deposited seventy-five dollars. She had twenty-two dollars cash in the pocket of her other jeans. If she could find a reason to change pants . . .

As she entered the bedroom, she slowed down in the hopes of making things calm, and he bumped into her. His body felt rigid, frightening. He was a dozen times stronger than she.

"We can work together. We can talk when you're ready."

"When do the movers get here?"

"About nine-thirty tomorrow morning."

"Where are they taking all this stuff?"

"Pittsburgh."

Oh. She was hit by a jolt of anger, as if she loved him and minded the relationship with Elizabeth in Pittsburgh. Crazy, crazy, she couldn't catch her thoughts. He'd snaked into her heart and she wasn't free of him, even now. How could that be?

"I'm just consolidating, putting my things in one place."

They stood in her room, looking at the bags and boxes all around. There was nothing, nothing, she could use as a weapon. He backed up toward the doorway, watching her. She stood at the window, wondering how she could get her money from the other pants.

"I have a house there and it needs furniture."

She nodded and began shifting boxes toward him.

"This single bed could go in a small room that would be a study. There are four bedrooms altogether. My bed and dresser could go in one of the bedrooms. Desk and files in the room with the single bed. This sofa in one corner of the living room. The living room is large. It can handle two sofas. I've been arranging the furniture in my head."

She sensed the thing about the house was true, something he was working out. For some reason, she felt a small leap of hope, as if they were mere acquaintances talking over possibilities. "So you're planning to live there?"

"I'm very torn," he said. He came over and lifted the black garbage bag on her bed. "Is this trash?"

"That's my clothes and things."

He looked inside. She was grateful she'd told the truth, not hidden any of his files in there among her few spare pieces of old clothing. "Where's your duffel?"

"I used it for your shirts."

"Did you?"

"It's only a small cheap duffel."

"Oh, I remember it," he said. He looked sad. "You had most of your things in boxes when you left that other place. I should have bought you luggage. I wasn't thinking."

"Well, I thought you needed boxes for things that had to be packed tight. So I saved them for your records and books and CDs. I started to put my clothes and shoes into the small duffel, but then I just sort of decided your things were neater, so I used the garbage bag for mine."

He shook his head. "How spoiled some people your age are. There's nothing fair about it. The mush-brains that I teach get all kinds of attention paid to them by their parents, and here you are, doing all the work, a plastic bag for luggage."

She didn't know what to say. He was acting, wasn't he? Or maybe not. He lifted the set of single-bed sheets neatly folded on top of the bare mattress. "Where do these go?" he asked.

"They're yours. I laundered them."

"Oh." He stood there holding them, looking thoughtful. "I thought you wanted to pack up completely. I thought maybe you intended to go to a motel."

"Or a cottage. I remember now what I said. 'If we had time apart from things and could talk . . .' Maybe we should."

She took a chance, speaking slowly and quietly so as not to disrupt his reflective mood. "I think I should just go home to St. Louis. For a while."

"It's not home to you. This is home. You said so." He stood between her and the door.

She wanted to run, but there was no way she could. He could trip her, block her. Move, somewhere, anywhere, she told herself. She grabbed at an idea. "We have to clean this place before we leave. I meant to do it, but I didn't get to it. I'll go get the vacuum cleaner."

"I'll get it. You pack your things."

He kept looking back to her as he left the room. No way to run. It took him only a few seconds to fetch the vacuum, but Bridget managed to get the cash out of her other jeans and into the pocket of the ones she wore by the time he returned. Reluctantly, she placed her clothes, shoes, the last of her things in the trash bag she'd started to fill earlier and she checked the windowsills and each corner of the floor. She moved the bed and checked under it, knowing he watched everything. He switched the vacuum on and ran it quickly over the floor. She dwelt over her books and papers for as long as she could, thinking of writing a note that she could hide somewhere in the room as soon as he turned away. *My name is Bridget Stevens. I lived here from October 29 to November 24. I am in danger. The person who finds this note should call my stepmother in St. Louis to see if she has heard from me. She is Elaine Muhler. My father is John Brigden Stevens. If they have not heard from me, notify the police about my disappearance. The man I lived with here at the house was Frank Razzi. Also perhaps . . .*

Oh, she could compose the note, efficiently, too. and if he caught her writing it?

He finally turned away and began to do the hall outside her room. The vacuum cleaner thumped regularly against the wall. Stifling a sob, she slipped out a piece of paper and began. *My name is Bridget Stevens.* She imagined some teenager a year from now finding the note and starting a chain of events that would make her story known after her death. The first line was all she wrote. The vacuum cleaner switched off.

"Finished?" Frank asked. "Let's do my room."

She got up.

"What were you writing?"

"Nothing." She handed over the piece of paper.

He looked at it for a long time. "Note in a bottle," he said. He folded the paper and put it in his breast pocket.

When he'd appeared at the top of the basement steps, if someone had told Bridget then that she would pack and clean and eat dinner, she would have said that was impossible, that she would die of fear first. But she was learning the impossible, the unthinkable, could be gotten around with words. Words and time.

CHRISTIE AND DOLAN WENT BACK TO THE STRIP MALL WHERE the Medfast was, to see if the person who took Daniel Ross's identity used it anywhere else. They went to the supermarket office, the other stores on the strip, the restaurant, the Rite Aid pharmacy across the road, asking if there was any record of any charges to Daniel Ross. They hadn't *expected* it, because the guy didn't use a charge for the prescriptions, but they had to ask.

Nothing had showed.

They were standing in the Union Grill, about to head home, when Artie, always in the mood for food, said, "Hey, you want to get something to eat here?"

"Doesn't your wife want you home for dinner?"

"She does. And she'll have me. Only she's dieting and so all we ever eat is skinny food, and tell you the truth, it's getting to me. I'm in the mood for something with bread around it or breading on it. Something."

It was all the same to Christie. With Marina gone, he'd

keep forgetting about food until it was nine o'clock and he didn't feel like cooking. End up having cereal or toast. Meanwhile, her trip was coming to nothing, as if the old lady got word someone was looking for her and she just wasn't going to show up at home.

The Union Grill wasn't busy yet. They took a table.

"You sure Ross's wife is clear?"

"What made you ask that?"

"Nothing, really. I only met her the one time, right after it happened. She was in bad shape."

"Yeah," Christie said. "Shock. They had the fairy-tale relationship, both of them successful and good. Try to tell her someone who knew her husband could get angry with him and she gets spooked. Anyway. I'd better call her soon. I keep waiting till I have something meaty to tell her."

The waitress who approached to take Christie's and Dolan's drink order was not the person they spoke to at first—the hostess—when they asked about charge cards in the name of Daniel Ross.

"Heineken."

"Guinness."

Christie drew his little wheel on the cocktail napkin.

Dolan laughed. "Wheels these days, huh?"

"Something. Some detail is missing."

"Name wouldn't hurt. Name, address, Social Security number, profession. Any of the above. We'll take anything."

"Mother," Christie chortled. "Anything." Again, not featherlight humor, but it was all they had. Dolan knew the whole scoop about Marina being down in Fort Myers looking for LaBeau.

When the waitress brought their beers, Dolan said, "Just one thing. If you have a sec."

"Sure." She looked at him brightly.

"Think back. Were you working here ten days ago, a Friday?"

She computed quickly and said, "Yes. What did I do, screw up your bill?"

Dolan smiled his most charming smile and slipped out

his badge. "We're trying to trace a man who got a prescription at the Medfast last Friday. The pharmacist didn't catch him fast enough. The pills are heavy-duty and we have reason to believe he wasn't on the up-and-up about getting them."

"Oh," she said, "oh, I bet I know who you mean. Guy came in, ordered, went over to get a prescription, came back. Right. I remember, because he popped something right here before he ordered his food."

"Popped?"

"Took a pill."

Dolan looked at Christie as if to say "Timing, huh, I got it."

"He didn't pay for dinner with a card, though, right?" Christie asked, frowning. "We already talked to the hostess."

The waitress said, "Yeah, I think he did."

"You remember what he looked like?"

"Kind of."

"I sure would like to see that charge slip. We asked the hostess about a charge for a Dan Ross. You remember if that was the name?"

"You don't know his name?"

"It's complicated."

She looked sideways at the hostess and said, "I bet I could find it for you. *She* won't like it, so I'd rather not tell her, but I might be able to look it up. The guy was kind of nice. I mean, I thought so, and so did my pal." She pointed to another waitress, who was oblivious, rushing with plates to another table.

"Nice means what?"

"Pleasant and friendly. Although now you tell me, I can see how maybe he was up to something, you know, a little nervous. You guys don't know what he looks like?"

"The pharmacist told us he was a regular-looking guy, nice-looking, but she couldn't give us any details," Christie offered. "Ugly might have been more memorable."

She thought, then spoke. "Okay. Good haircut. Medium-brown hair. About fifty at the outside, but well put together, that's true. Wearing a shirt and, what was it, maybe a leather jacket. Damn." She almost stamped her foot. "I'd know him if I saw him again. Shoot. I thought I had a good memory."

"Well, let yourself think about it," Dolan said.

"Okay. I'm going to find that charge slip." She lifted her order pad. "What do you guys want?"

Christie ordered pasta primavera. Dolan ordered meat loaf with garlic mashed potatoes.

"I think that's what he got," she said, pointing toward Dolan's place, as if the meal that was going to fill him up had already been delivered. She went off and chatted for a long time with the other waitress, who laughed, listened, nodded, said something. After that, their waitress disappeared for a few minutes, then came back into the dining room and filled some drink orders for other people. When she brought the detectives two gigantic plates of food, she slipped a piece of paper toward them.

Frank Razzi, it said. The name was followed by a Master-Card number.

"Frank Razzi," Christie muttered. A brand-new name.

"You're sure?" Dolan asked the waitress.

"Oh, yeah. My pal over there took a shine to him, as I said. She was tracking him. She went out for a cig break when he left. He drives a black BMW. Something not too new and it has a plate from somewhere else, but she's not sure where. You'll want to hear this from her, huh?"

"We will," Christie said dryly, "if we can pick ourselves up off the floor. You're not making any of this up, are you?"

"Not a bit of it."

"I'm going to have to ask you not to talk about it. And we're going to give you our cards, because if you should ever see him again . . ."

"So it's more than you said? More than a bum prescription?"

"Maybe. Yes."

"Wow."

Christie called the office and gave the MasterCard number to one of the men on four-to-twelve. He told them to set off all the bells and to run the name Frank Razzi for

prints, prior convictions, hell, for anything and everything, phone number, e-mail address, anything they could
get. And to check it on the missing-persons list from
Atlantic City.

BRIDGET WATCHED HIM THROUGH EVERYTHING, WHILE THEY
gathered up the last of the records and tapes and added
them to the boxes that held such things. She would run,
didn't know how or when, but she simply had to. She
spotted his car keys on the kitchen counter and hoped
they would stay there until she found a way. The only
thing left to pack were his files. Since they were completely
out of boxes, she suggested going out to get more, but he
said no and started using plastic bags, as she had, for all
kinds of things. She had come up with a scheme for tying
them off once, tight, and doubling them back for
strength. This was important with the files, keeping them
in order. She took a long time doing each move; the longer
a bag took, the longer she had to figure out an escape. All
the while, it seemed, he would ask, "Did you read this?
This?" The silence was worse.

"Are we going out to dinner?" she asked as casually as
she could.

He answered with equal blandness. "I'd rather stay here.
Get showered after. What do we have? Anything quick?"

"We have some frozen Mexican. Burritos, I think." That
would be too quick. "Oh, I know. There are some sausages,
some pork chops. . . ."

"Why don't you go ahead and thaw the Mexican. I'm going to mix up a pitcher of margaritas. I have tequila, don't I?"

"I think so."

"I'll do the mixing."

"I don't really want a margarita."

"Sure you do."

"I do?"

"Relaxing. Tart. Sweet. Salty."

She watched him opening some sort of mix and the
tequila. He poured things into a pitcher and stirred. She

watched him pour the drinks, by positioning herself at the microwave door and tilting the door until she could see him. She watched his hands. Another person might not have seen, but she saw, she knew what he was up to, she *saw* because she knew what to look for. She'd *been* watching. She'd been listening for the rattle of pills in the plastic container, figuring the sound would warn her. There was no sound. But in the black of the microwave door, she saw him reach into his coat pocket, and she saw distinctly his hand raised above one of the glasses. His fingers flexed three, four times, then he slipped a swizzle stick in and stirred while he took a sip from the other glass.

"We haven't talked," she said.

"I know. Now's the time."

He went into the living room.

She calculated everything. How long it would take to get the back door open and to get out. Too long; he would be behind her in seconds. There was no place to lock herself in the basement. If she tried to lock herself into the bathroom or even the bedroom she used, she couldn't climb out a window without his catching her. And he could break either door down. His car keys were no longer on the counter. Then she noticed the kitchen phone was unplugged.

She turned the temperature to the lowest defrost setting so the frozen burritos would take a long time, then stood in front of the microwave door, waiting, and thinking. He could have hit her or strangled her. Why did he do it with pills? To put her to sleep first, like in the scripts she read. That had to be it. She couldn't drink it no matter what.

"Hey. Can't you wait for those in here? Bridget?" He started to get up off the couch.

"I'm coming." She tried to make her mind work. She had to do something. "I was just getting some salsa out of the fridge. And the last couple of chips. To go with the drinks." A small idea, trick, came to her. She grabbed a ginger ale from the refrigerator and spilled a little of it on the tray with the chips and salsa on it, then poured a little of it under her shirt, front and back, crying out, "Oh, damn."

"What?"

"I spilled some ginger ale. I don't think it got the chips, though."

"I made you a margarita."

"I know, but I'm parched. I'm all sweaty and hot from lifting. If the margarita is melting, you drink it."

She walked into the living room and saw his eyes were black, no light. She put the tray down and tried to sound strong. "Look, I made up my mind. I want to go home. There are buses all the time and I'd like to get myself on a bus to St. Louis. I've been e-mailing my dad and I called Jess and talked to her about it, then I even broke down and called my stepmom. She thinks I need to come home, get a job, make some money, then think about school."

His expression was sardonic and he held it for a long time, staring at her with a pinched face. She tried to withstand the examination, but couldn't, and so she reached for the ginger ale, feeling flushed, terrified.

"You can't go back there just because you've seen something that scares you. Are you going to be grown-up or not?"

"It might not be all it's cracked up to be."

He smiles. But his eyes are still black.

"Cracked up. I'm thinking about the expression," she says. "Cracked up."

"I wish you would come over here. Sit with me." He pats the couch beside him. Bridget tries to erase fear from her face. She shivers once; the ginger ale against her skin feels sticky. Her body feels like lead, but she lifts herself up and sits beside him, holding on to the ideas that she must not anger him and must not drink the margarita.

"I forgot, when does the mover get here?" she asks, sliding into place.

"Tomorrow morning." His arm goes around her shoulders.

"Fifteen hours."

"What does that mean?"

"I could stay here with you until they come. Then you could take me to the bus station."

He looks confused.

"If you don't want to be alone," she adds. The microwave dings and she leaps up, grabbing her margarita on the way. "I'll get them." Six little burritos. Three for him, three for her. She makes a show of taking a drink from the glass as she walks to the kitchen. In her peripheral vision, she can see him getting up to watch her. She pretends to take another sip and he's right there behind her. Holding the glass so he can't see how full it is still, she wonders how much of it she can drink before whatever is in there has its effect. Awkwardly, with the glass still in hand, she takes out two plates for the burritos. "This doesn't seem like something you'd eat," she says.

"It isn't."

"You don't have to. I can eat them. Make you something else."

"We can order in later."

"So you want to stay here tonight?"

"I thought so." His eye goes to the glass in her hand and she drinks some because he's watching. She prays again, Don't let it be enough to kill me. Almost immediately, a dead weight pulls at her limbs—but she can't tell if it's the drug or if defeat has got her.

"Take these in?" she says, handing him the plates. In one quick move, she manages to get a half inch of the margarita down her shirt. A large speck of white clings to the side of the glass and when she sticks a finger in, it does not separate like salt. There it is, evidence. She slides it out, flinging it toward her pants.

He's back in the kitchen, asking, "What is it?"

"Big chunk of salt or something."

She lets him shepherd her into the living room, while she takes another fake drink, swallowing elaborately. When she sits, she allows her head to tip forward heavily and notices he's watching.

"Good?"

"Yeah, but it's very strong."

He puts the plates next to each other. He's listening, watching everything. If she is to live, she must act, act in every sense of the word.

"I'd better go pee," she says next. She picks up the glass to take it with her.

"Why are you taking the glass?"

"Not thinking."

"Leave it."

This is it, then. He will fill it with poison. While she sits on the toilet she dries the ginger ale under her shirt, front and back, best she can. She stands there shaking as she washes her hands. She lurches out of the bathroom, forty-five seconds later, wiping her wet hands elaborately on her pants. Her margarita glass is full again.

Her stomach wants to reject the food, but she forces herself to eat. Whenever she looks up, Frank is studying her. The pitcher is between them.

"I wonder if the burritos are okay. I don't know. I . . . I don't feel well."

He pauses, considering her. "They taste okay to me. I'm getting salt." Somehow even when he moves away to the kitchen, she feels watched.

But she does it anyway, pours more of the drink on the tray, more on herself—this time, her pants, where she wiped her hands.

When he sits down beside her, he looks scattered and sad.

She leans back against the sofa, and a real feeling of dizziness comes over her. He puts an arm around her and soon he is holding her close.

"I don't feel right," she says, and her voice has hardly any strength. She feels far away from everything. She tries to look at the kitchen counter and it looks as if the keys are back. Her only chance. She stretches up slightly and is light-headed again. His voice seems far away.

"Bridget, what are you thinking?"

"I don't know what it is. I'm so tired, all of a sudden."

She can't tell whether she's acting it or feeling it, she can't tell the difference. She doesn't want to give up, but her body is giving up, her speech slightly slurred. She thought she was doing it on purpose, but now she can't tell, it's hard to form speech, her eyelids are closing. . . . "Better make some coffee," she says.

"No, not coffee. That would keep us up and it's already late."

"What time is it?"

"Nine forty-five."

He holds her and he feels nice, kind. "You're right, Bridget," he says. "I have had more than one name, more than one life. I'm responsible for two deaths. If you were wondering, that's the count. Two."

Two, she's thinking. Which two? Stay awake, think. Her heart wants to race, but it can't. Her brain is turning, turning in slow motion, she doesn't want to be giving up. He sounds nice again and kisses her on the forehead, gently. Two, which two?

"I didn't know what I was reading," she slurs, "and I didn't want to make you angry." Could she form words clearly if she wanted to? "People you knew, *cared about*, is what I thought." Is that true?

"You didn't wonder who I killed?"

"No," she murmurs, moving close, nestling her head between his arm and his shoulder.

"Ted Luckey," he says. "And my brother. The other was just a name I used."

He holds her so gently, kisses her, and the smell is the familiar smell of him, Frank, but he's not Frank really, he's someone else. " 'Cared about,' you said, and that's right. Nobody will ever know that. Other people won't figure that out, ever. That's all you, Bridget. Fantastic. Smart. Plucky. I think you know I never wanted to hurt you?"

She closes her eyes, goes limp. Please God, please, don't let him . . . "I have to sleep," she says.

They sit there for a long time. She tries not to move.

"I'm going to get a shower. We'll go to a motel. That was a good idea you had. This place is grim, with boxes packed."

Good, good, a chance to run. The thought brings energy. Behind her lids her eyes are jumping. Relax them. Do not react. Stay limp. Do not react. Stay limp. Eyes must not move.

Bridget keeps her eyes closed, even as he jostles her getting up and then tilting her body to lie across the sofa arm.

Footsteps.

Then the sounds in the bathroom. He could fake it, run the shower and then come out to check on her. She's afraid to move, listening for the change of sound the water makes when a person climbs into the shower. But the thing is, she doesn't hear it. Has the moment passed, has she waited too long? The door opens, but the sound of water continues. Her breath quickens. She opens her eyes a sixteenth of an inch and sees the bottom of his robe, his bare ankles. A part of her mind instructs her, Limp, go limp.

The bare ankles move. Away? Then finally the sound of water *interrupted* that means he has gotten into the shower. Her eyes open. The bathroom door is ajar this time. He's trying to keep an eye on her while he's in there. Nothing to do but run. No hope, no hope, but she has to do it.

She makes for the kitchen, but the keys are gone from the counter, nowhere to be seen.

She dashes for the front door, unlocks it, opens it, closes it quietly. As soon as the door closes, she hears his bellow. *"Bridget. Bridget. Damn. Fuck. Bridget."*

There is nowhere to go. The yard she has run around so many times won't hide her. The woods, thin enough that he will see her before she can get to the thick part, are no good to her. No hope. He will check the car, first thing, no good getting inside it. It's locked.

She ducks behind his car, which is facing the house, ridiculous, putting off the inevitable. Stooping there, she feels around for a tree branch. Nothing. Her hand is inches from the lock of the trunk, she is crouched three feet from where he will first look. Her eye falls on the seam between the trunk and the bumper. Is the trunk un-locked? She pushes it gently and, yes, it moves up an eighth of an inch.

She hears the front door unlatch.

"Bridget," he calls. He sounds . . . mournful.

His voice recedes. Clothes. He has to put on his clothes. She takes a chance, the only one she has, and opens the trunk as little as possible, climbs in, pulling the lid toward her. She uses her shoe to keep the trunk lid from closing completely. He will figure it out, find her, and she has no weapon.

"Bridget!" she hears. She can imagine him running the periphery of the yard, buttoning up his pants, pulling his shirt over his head, looking into the woods. "Bridget," he calls.

Footsteps, receding. He is running toward the house. For the car keys, surely. She has ten seconds, not enough to run down the long path to the road, not even enough to get out to find a stone or a bit of branch. There is no hope.

She can hear him running toward the car. Then the click of the locks popping up. The driver door opens, closes, jolt-ing her. Then the motor explodes into life. The car begins to move in a crazy pattern, making her more dizzy than she was. Back and forth it moves. She grabs the trunk lid by the metal lock, for fear it will pop up, exposing her.

Her heart grinds and slows to one large thump and then another. Her brain is trying to race, keep her awake with terror, and all the while, the car jerks back and forth. Somehow she understands he's trying to aim the high beams to search the woods. Now he's moving differently. The car moves up and over something—the grass and soft earth. But where is there to go except to the edge of the woods, come to an abrupt stop, haul her out, hit her, dig her grave right here. Nobody will ever know.

In another minute, the car moves quickly, the lid bounces once, and she can feel they've come down off the crabgrass and onto the driveway. She holds the lid down while the car moves evenly. They are going out to the road.

Frank stops at what must be the dirt-road exit to the paved road, then pulls out into traffic. At first he goes fast, then slowly. A horn sounds at him, but he continues to creep along.

He is looking for her. He thinks she sprinted down the road and he lost precious time. She begins to count seconds, wondering. The drive is even, smooth, and lulls her. A terrible sleepiness overtakes her, and she has to fight it, squeezing her fingers together, letting her nails cut into her palms. Frank knows everything, so he must know by now where she is. He would think ahead, what he will do, where he will take her, how he will do it. Her clothes are damp and sticky, making her shiver.

When the car stops, she goes still to listen. Motor off. He's parked somewhere. She slips her fingers from under the lid in case he comes around the back. She tries not to breathe or move. Nothing. Then she hears the car door open, close, but after that she can't tell what's happening. Strouds Run State Park? The lake? No, the sound of gravel and traffic, both.

The twenty seconds she's lying there, waiting to face him, feels like twenty minutes.

When nothing happens, she opens the lid a little, peers around, taking in the lights and sound. The strip. The Go-Bar.

He's looking for her inside. She pushes the lid higher and climbs out.

FRANK MOVES THROUGH THE GO-BAR, LOOKING QUICKLY FROM side to side. He's shivering because he threw his clothes on over a wet body; his hair is still wet. Misjudged her. Clever little bitch was acting. He knew she observed everything, but he didn't think she could pretend that well. Two sips of the drink and she should have been out. He put enough in there to fell a much larger person.

He doesn't see her in the bar and she was not on the road, so where? Could he have missed her back there somewhere, hidden behind a tree? No. No, she must have run to the road and hitched a ride. If she did, by now she was talking to the police.

"Where's your pay phone?" he asks the waitress.

She jerks a thumb toward the bathrooms.

No one is at the phone. The Go-Bar is relatively empty, so he takes a chance and opens the door to the ladies' room. Two stalls, no feet. Back to the waitress. "Looking for my daughter. She sometimes comes here. Wears a little pirate shirt and those short jeans. She was wearing just plain jeans today. Hair is dyed red, but only at the ends. Bright red."

"Nope," says the waitress. "Haven't seen her."

"Ever?"

"That's a different matter. If I have the same person in mind, a couple of times, but not tonight. Are you her father, or is that just an expression?"

"We had an argument."

"Why don't you leave her alone, then. She's just a kid." The waitress starts to move off, but he blocks her way.

"She was here, then, tonight."

The waitress meets his look, long and steady. "Not tonight, she wasn't. That's the truth."

He sees himself through the waitress's eyes. Angry, soaked hair, clothes that are damp. Turning from her, he thinks, Bus depot at the Oasis, hurry. Then he thinks, If she hitched a ride, she could be anywhere, anywhere. Then, the right idea just comes to him. Of course. The trunk of his car. Of course. The only hiding place there was.

Frank hurries out of the bar in time to see a truck pull to a stop down the road and to see a girl climbing awkwardly into the cab. Jesus, he thinks, stupid, stupid, and has the strange thought overlapping the first, that she will not be safe. His thoughts tumble over each other while he tries to breathe. Fucking little bitch, he thinks. And when the truck pulls out, although he knows he's got to do something and he doesn't know what that is, he thinks, Bridget got away, good, good.

14

MARINA SLEEPS BADLY. SHE HAS ONLY TWO MORE DAYS IN FORT Myers and although she has made about twenty visits to the house with the phone registered to Walt Walker, she has not seen the woman who was once married to Walker. The woman apparently does live there *sometimes,* according to one of the neighbors, but she has a lover and spends most of her time at his place. Marina comes awake, thinking of the story she plans to spin if she ever sees LaBeau; she turns, feels the pinch of sun on her skin, slips off again.

ELIZABETH GETS UP, LOOKS TO THE HOUSE NEXT DOOR. MONDAYS, sometimes he's here, sometimes not.

There are things to like in him. He speaks well. Intelligently. He's interesting. The last few weeks she's been hanging on his sentences as if he's begun with a subordinate clause and paused with the comma, smiled, and refused to go on, teasing her. What is the main clause? When will he speak it?

Misses him. Misses Dan. The two feelings merge, bewilderingly.

She opens *The Amazing Adventures of Kavalier and Clay* to drop herself into a rich world stranger than her own. Disguises. War. Long absences.

The thought that popped up in her sleep nights ago, and which she buried, slips from its hiding place, crosses the room, and looks at her. She shakes herself. Was she asleep, dreaming? Disguises, war, long absences. No, not possible. She must get control of her unruly mind. But the idea doesn't leave her room, just sits there, watching her until she falls asleep.

FRANK HAS NOT SLEPT. HAS NOT TAKEN HIS PILLS BECAUSE, FOR one thing, he is afraid of muting his responses. For the other, he wants to hoard the pills. Six good pills wasted on Bridget. She tricked him for sure. If she'd taken the four with alcohol, she would have slept deeply or slept forever. Either way. Two fingers to the nose, a hand over the mouth would have finished the job.

Look what she's done to him. He keeps seeing her the way he caught her, in the basement, making her way through his secrets.

Now he will be awake forever, wondering when the police will arrive and what he will say and how he will persuade them of his innocence. He'll say something to buy time, then get away.

Air. To Europe. Use Dan's name.

He's been up and down the roads, no sight of the truck, which was headed west. He's been to the house where she used to live. Seen Jess in the flesh. Sizzling little number, Jess—the way she looked at him, *through* him, amused at the idea of an "old guy" running after Bridget. Another time, he thought, he'd like to get hold of Jess, show her what an old guy could do. He asked her where Bridget was. She smirked, told him to try Lakeside Trailways, out of the Oasis Restaurant; otherwise, her little cuz might have gotten herself on one of the end-of-term charters.

Jess and her pals were staying put for the holiday, she explained, going to turkey-it-up right here.

He didn't even bother to tell her he'd already been to the Oasis and found it closed down for the night. There was no way to know if Bridget had boarded a bus.

He can only hope she stuck with the truck driver and that the truck kept going west. Frank works on an image of Bridget cutting her losses and going home to St. Louis, never to speak his name again. Shy Bridget, embarrassed to go to the police. In his thoughts, he fashions her that way, as if the thought can control the action.

He pours himself a drink, another, and paces from the kitchen to the front door, wondering.

Four in the morning and no police. The suitcase put away, everything tidied, ready for the movers.

He tries to persuade himself to start out right now for Pittsburgh, but he is shaking badly, exhausted, and he needs to be here for the movers. Waiting, he's done it before, all right. If he makes it until one in the afternoon, his last class, he will be gone from here, all traces of him gone. Smart, the way he hired his movers out of Pittsburgh, paid cash.

But Bridget knows about Elizabeth. She said her name.

It feels like a heart attack, the way his chest is tightening. He curses, knowing he should have made an end of Bridget, should have been tougher, less sentimental.

Four-thirty. He hurtles from the darkened living room of the rented house in Athens, out the door to his car. Starts the motor and runs it for three minutes, switches it off. Exhausted, exhausted. If he drives like crazy, he will get there at eight, miss Elizabeth by forty-five minutes, not be able to get back in time for the movers or to give his final at the university. No. Skip out of things and he sets off an alarm, looks guilty.

Better to wait. He's been in limbo before. This is not new.

He doesn't sleep, not at all.

BRIDGET IS ASLEEP. LIKE A BABY. NOTHING COULD STOP IT ONCE she felt the hum of the engine of the eighteen-wheeler.

The truck driver, Jim, was a lucky find. After a while, he stopped asking why she was alone and if she was going to be okay. Her eyes were crossing, she was trying to concentrate on what he said, trying to think what to answer, and then she mumbled that she'd just had a breakup with her boyfriend and she'd be all right if he just dropped her at a major bus station.

"I'm headed to Dayton. They have a bus station."

"It's perfect. I can catch a bus to—" She almost said "St. Louis," but at the last minute, she said "home." Her voice was slurry, she could hear she sounded drunk. He looked at her skeptically. She used all of her will to turn her body around in the cab of the truck to see if a black BMW was following behind. It was not there.

"I got a cell phone here. You need to call anybody?"

"No. No thanks." She wanted to sleep, had never wanted it so much in all her life. Her jaw went slack.

"Police?"

Yes, of course, police, but she murmurs no, because she doesn't know how to stay awake long enough to talk.

Hours later, before the break of dawn, Jim rouses her. "You got to get up now. I got to keep going," he says. "Here's the bus station. I already lost a little time, getting you here. I have a schedule to keep. Here you go." He holds out a twenty. "Don't use it on drink."

Jim. She forces herself to wake up. Jim. He didn't hurt her. He wonders if he is a fool, doing favors for people. He has an uncertain look.

She does not take the money. Opening the door of the cab, she says, "Thanks for the ride. It was important."

He presses the twenty into her hand, and she thinks, Okay, it will help with something to eat, somewhere to go.

She carries nothing, not even a sweater, and almost stumbles toward the building, feeling badly for Jim, who is worried about her. Inside, she finds a bench and curls up. Dayton. Frank won't find her in Dayton. Doesn't matter when she catches a bus. And as she falls asleep, she thinks vaguely it will be a bus to St. Louis and that she will be able to forget what she saw in the basement, what she knows.

CHRISTIE SLEEPS FITFULLY FOR THE SIMPLE REASON THAT MARINA is not there. It can't be helped, he told her last night, Michelle LaBeau did a disappearing act, not your fault, and besides, there are police to do inquisitions, it can't be helped. He told her about the new leads, a name to go on, not one on the missing-persons reports, but a name, Frank Razzi, and she pronounced it on the phone, as if trying it out. Christie wishes he could call her now but it's five in the morning. He puts a pillow over his head, thinking the spokes of the wheel are starting to fill in, but he doesn't even guess at how much more he will know in twenty-four hours.

AT TEN IN THE MORNING, FRANK IS LETTING IN THE MOVERS.

They are big beefy hard workers who grunt and hoist without wasting time on words. By half past ten, the large items are already in the truck and they have started on the boxes and plastic bags with books in them. Frank goes to the windows often, looks out. He starts to take the suitcase, the one Bridget was so interested in, from the basement to his car, but realizes that might be a bad idea if he's stopped by police. "Here," he says. "Toss this into the truck, too, when you have a chance."

"We'll put it real careful on top of something."

"Fine."

"And there are a couple of lighter trash bags you should be careful with. They have personal things in them." Clothes. And Bridget's purse. Better in the truck than buried in the woods here. He'll drive them out to some other countryside.

Frank can't swallow. His throat doesn't seem to work right. He gulps coffee, burning himself. He's more jumpy than usual and considers taking a pill, but he's holding off, hoarding.

By noon, there will not be a trace of him at the house.

Somehow he drives to the university, where he makes copies of an essay exam and then hands it out to thirty people. "It's a short exam," he says. One of the students holds up a shopping bag and says, "Nobody leave when you're done. I brought cookies. We have to give Razzi a send-off." She gives everyone a peek at what look like homemade cookies.

Thirty people look up from their writing. Nobody says no.

"Are you okay?" the girl with the cookies asks. She's the first done.

"Why?"

"You seem upset."

"Just have a lot to do."

The students are still hanging around him when Heinz Ersicher passes by, waving. If the police came by now, all they'd see is sweetness and light, people hugging, dewy eyes. He bids the students good-bye. He gathers up the papers and falls into the black BMW. Sleepy. Wired up. The drive, which is an eyes-closed affair by now, suddenly seems impossibly long. Frank looks forward, backward, left, right. No police. Thank you, Bridget, he thinks.

"YOU CAN'T SLEEP HERE," SAID THE ANGRY POLICEMAN IN Bridget's blurred vision. He sounded as if he were repeating himself.

Her mind still felt foggy and her body didn't want to unhinge itself from the bench. "Sorry," she said, trying to sit up.

"Been drinking?"

"No."

"Why don't I believe that?"

Bridget tried to force herself to alertness. Here was her chance to make her report. But when she looked into his face, she knew he would never understand. He'd write up a report, the subtext of which was, Girl was dumb, put demands on the guy, he got pissed, she has a wild imagination. And so Bridget said, "I'm sorry. I'm so tired," and worked to get awake, look around her. The policeman's fists balled up and he breathed heavily. How could she tell him that she almost loved Frank, maybe does still, and that something so complicated she can hardly grab hold of it herself went on between them? There is no way this man will ever understand.

"You going somewhere?" he asked bluntly.

"Yes. I'll go buy my ticket," she said.

When she stood in line—there it was, on the schedule

board in front of her, so she chose it, or it chose her—the very next bus leaving Dayton was going to Pittsburgh. Yes, of course, she had things to do when she got there. But first, a nice long ride. Sleep.

"THERE WAS A FRANK RAZZI IN L.A., ALL RIGHT, UNLISTED NUMber, some jumping around with addresses, but we traced him." Potocki looked proud of himself. "With the help of the bank his MasterCard came from. Then we sent someone to the condo complex to ask questions. It was eight in the morning there and some people had gone to work already and the other people weren't too happy to be quizzed. However. The guy lived there until last summer. Was a writer of some sort for television. Paramount, one of the neighbors said. That was all my guy could get, though. He called Paramount and got a runaround. Didn't find anybody who knew Razzi."

"Damn," Christie said. "Razzi must have had some friends there. Or enemies. Call Paramount yourself. Spend some time sweet-talking them. Where Razzi is now is what we need to know."

MARINA HAS LOOKED AT THE CLOUDS AND WRAPPED HER BATIK cover-up around her like a dress and started toward Michelle LaBeau's address once again. This time is different. The door opens.

Marina can see right away it isn't much of a place inside. Just a room with a kitchen counter, not something a person would get terribly attached to.

"You're Michelle LaBeau?"

"Yes."

The woman who blocks the doorway has a face that was once handsome, but is now dried out, crosshatched, thanks to cigarettes, booze, sun. "Who are you? Do I know you?"

"I represent the law offices of Huntley and Frederick in Pittsburgh." Marina has watched Richard lie when he needs to get around people, they all do, they lie, they beat up, they take justice into their own hands. Is it fair and reasonable to *trick* a person? "It's complicated, but we have a bequest of considerable size to you and to Gerald Paul LaBeau. There is a hitch, though. May I come in?"

Michelle LaBeau's face twitches, as if to say, A hitch, sure, of course, but the light of expectation has come into her face in spite of her doubt. The door opens.

It's not that Marina hasn't lied before. Why does it feel wrong now?

Inside the efficiency apartment is an unmade bed. The cloth of the bedspread is surprisingly beautiful, a tapestry in blues and purples. Also, although there are a few unwashed dishes, on the shelf above, Marina can see pretty, handcrafted pieces. Interesting woman. Not the usual bum. On top of the small table are newspapers. *New York Times, Washington Post.* And on the floor, a row of liquor bottles. A faint scent of garbage.

A smart woman, ruined, slowly killing herself.

"Can we sit down?"

LaBeau brings in the single chair from the kitchen area for Marina and puts it across from the bed, where she then sits.

"This is about the will in the death of Daniel Ross of Pittsburgh, Pennsylvania. He . . . was looking for his brother, Paul. He provided for him. Quite a lot of money. But he never found him. There's a small sum and then an ongoing allowance for you if you can give us an address. Daniel Ross's widow made that stipulation."

The old woman struggles for some time before saying slowly, "My son died. Dan Ross knew that."

Marina says pointedly, "We know he didn't."

"Are you the police?"

"No."

The old woman considers her, takes in her sandals, her batik wrap.

"I went to the beach," Marina says apologetically.

"Why couldn't Dan Ross find Paul himself?"

"He tried."

"What if I tell you I don't know anything?"

"We know it's tricky," Marina says, working to smile, smiling to disarm. "Names and all. What name and address do you use for him when you contact him?"

"I don't have an address. I call him Paul."

Marina can't tell if she's hearing the truth. Why should she be? The room is thick with evasions.

"Are you the police?"

"No." Marina would like to stop lying. Something about Michelle LaBeau, sitting up straight, trying to figure it all out, gets to her.

"I could use some money, but this isn't about money, is it?"

"I hope there will be money for you if . . . if you do the right thing. A name and address and phone number would help a lot." Marina hopes, as if willing it, that LaBeau will say the name Frank Razzi and give an address. She waits, hoping.

"I don't know his name." The words have the sound of truth. "He never told me what name he was using. He calls me a couple of times a year. That's why I keep my phone."

"You want to hear from him."

"Yes."

The smell of sunlight comes through the open window. The woman's leathered arm rests against the salmon-colored blouse she wears. In the building, somewhere, a television goes on.

"It's very strange."

"I know that."

"You must miss him."

"I think I saw him once. Last summer. I felt someone looking at me. Waiter told me the person bought me a meal. By the time I realized who it was, he was gone. I walked, looking for him, but I . . . never found him."

Marina thinks, This is something extraordinary. She thinks, Please, I don't want to cry. But her body, as usual, betrays her.

■   ■   ■

"HOW'S THIS?" POTOCKI SAYS. "HE WAS THERE UNTIL LAST SUM-
mer. He got downsized or something, even though he had
been there for years. So he hit up some old contacts and,
get this, he goes to teach at some university in Ohio—
Athens, Ohio. Far from L.A., but not too far from here."

Christie takes over, calling directory services for Ohio
University and then asking their operator for Frank Razzi.
It's torture, torture, sitting at his desk, scratching out de-
signs while the operator takes forever to come back on the
line. "You said he's new? I don't have him on the books
yet," she says. "Departments don't always remember to
update us." Next he asks for somebody who teaches film,
and after a long time, she comes up with a woman's name,
Lilly Vanda. There is no answer at the woman's office
number and so Christie has to go back to the operator
again to ask her for someone else in that department. She
gives him a man named Israel Olds, who *does* answer his
phone, in a harried voice, and puts him onto "the head,"
Heinz Ersicher, who says, yes, Frank *worked* there up until
an hour ago, and yes, lived there, too, but the quarter is
just about ended and Frank is headed back to L.A. real
soon, if not today. "Alice can give you the address. I'll
transfer you. I didn't hear you at first. Did you say you're
an agent?"

Agent. Agent? Oh, that kind. "Yes," Christie says, "it's
important I talk to him today."

"Well, then, you could try him at the Pittsburgh job,"
Ersicher says.

"What's the Pittsburgh job?"

"University of Pittsburgh. Film Studies. I don't have a
number handy. What's today? Tuesday. He'd be there today."

"Give me Alice, too."

There it is, lots of stuff to write down, a whole orgy of
facts. A rural address, a P.O. box, a phone number. Christie
then calls Pitt and goes through the same routine before

he finds out where exactly the guy is teaching his course that evening.

Then, covering all possibilities, he dials the Athens police force. After a little folderol, he's on the line with a detective. He gives the address he's gotten from Alice Platt. Christie tells the detective, "This guy is probably on the road, but call me either way. If he's there, take him in for questioning and take the longest route you can find while I get myself there. Get lost, buy donuts, I don't care what you do. If he's not there, well, you'll let me know."

THE BUS PULLS INTO A ROAD STOP WITH A DENNY'S. A MAN TAPS Bridget on the shoulder. "You going to want to sleep through this?" he asks. "Pit stop?"

She opens her eyes to the thin man of about thirty who sat across from her and tried to talk to her about germ warfare while her eyes kept closing. He's a little bit nuts—poor, slightly criminal, bus-rider nuts—not that she's much different. "Where are we?" she asks.

"Denny's. You want something?"

"I'd better go in." Eight dollars left, since the ticket cost thirty-four.

The lights are bright, the waitresses trained to be cheerful. Bridget is embarrassed because she has no suitcase or bag, not even a backpack, and that makes her look trampy. She could buy one, out at the gas station–travel shop, a prop, nothing to put in it. First she goes to the bathroom, where she hardly recognizes herself in the mirror. Her hair is matted. There's a spot of dirt on her chin.

The only thing she can do is wash her face. She has no comb. All she wants to do is sleep.

Fifteen minutes, the man said.

"Bacon burger and fries, large coffee," she orders. Better to eat in the bus, make sure she gets back on. Carrying her large bag of food, she stops at the map on the wall. She's in Ohio still. Outside Columbus. Fear sends a shot of adrenaline through her. What if she heads for the bus and sees him? What if the bus starts out and she sees the black car on the road?

The travel shop is overpriced and Bridget doesn't have enough money for anything substantial. She buys a comb, a cheapo fanny pack, and a newspaper with the last of her money. There. She feels less conspicuous.

In the bus, Bridget opens the newspaper to keep the man across from her silent and she eats everything, every last fry, every crumb. No matter that she drinks sixteen ounces of caffeine, moments after she's finished eating, the words of one particular paragraph dance crazily and she's asleep again.

NOW ELIZABETH HURRIES TO HER CAR AND STARTS IT UP, THINKing, ten minutes to get home, five minutes to grab what she wants, and she's on her way. Away from him. Time to think. Time to look at the idea that won't let her alone.

She wishes she hadn't left him a note this morning when she left for work, not intending to come back again today. The idea that pressed at her even while she listened to her clients blinds her as she tries to drive. What if, what if . . . She doesn't want to see him right now.

Finally she's home. She parks quickly in her driveway and steps over the ground row to the house next door. In moments, she is at his front door, stooping down, but unable to get her note back; too good a job of pushing it under the door. Never mind. Hurry.

Her heart pounds uncontrollably with the thought that he might see her and be able to read fear in her face. When she stands, her knees buckle. She has to grab at his door to steady herself. Carefully, she moves across the yard, over to her house, and in the door. After quickly tapping the keypad for the alarm system, she goes upstairs, finds the latest box of files Christie returned, finds the ones she wants, then scans the bookshelves in the home office until she sees the other thing she's looking for. Dan's high school yearbook. She stuffs these things into a plastic supermarket bag and starts for the door.

The black car pulls up just as she's heading for her car.

"Wait," he calls. "Need help?"

"It's okay." The bag slips down her arm as she fits the key into the trunk lid. Inside is a cooler, which holds the still-frozen turkey.

He's there, holding the trunk lid, taking the bag from her.

Don't let him look inside, she thinks.

He looks. He opens the bag and looks into it, just like that. But there is no way to tell what he's thinking, if anything. "You're off?"

She has nothing to add to the cooler. She pokes at the turkey, as if that's what she intended to do all along, closes the cooler. "Going to be with the kids."

"I'm just on my way to teach my class."

"Good."

"I'll miss you."

He can see something is wrong with her. Her face hides nothing, she knows, it's always been that way. "Sorry," she says. "I have to be with family."

He touches a finger to his lips, then hers. Are his eyes different? Angry? Have his eyes always been that dark?

She tries to breathe. Gets in. Starts up. Waves good-bye.

Time to think. Time to entertain the idea, blast it to pieces, get rid of it.

FRANK LETS HER SEE HIM ENTER THE HOUSE. EVEN IN HIS HURRY, part of him takes in the fact that the movers did a good job. Dropped the keys inside as they promised. "Things are in place, sort of," he imagines himself telling someone, Elizabeth or Bridget. "I mean, you wouldn't want to *live* with the angles they chose, but then . . ."

Where is Bridget now? He can't sense an answer.

She feels very near as he scrambles up to the bedroom and finds the bag with her things in it, the suitcase with his secrets in it, but now that he's found what he came here for, what does he do with the stuff? Bury it all far away. He moves with the things in hand, hurrying toward the kitchen door.

Elizabeth knows something. He passes her note on the kitchen counter, grabs it up on the way out. The movers must have put it there. *Packed and gone early for the weekend. Will call when I get a chance,* she wrote.

Didn't mention the note just now. Everything was in the car. . . . She came *back* for something. Shit. Shit. He knows how to read *signs.* If he knows anything— He's got to catch her, then. He's moving fast. It's now four-forty. If he can overtake her on the road . . .

His class. It doesn't matter. He throws bags, suitcase, himself into the car, and starts up, gunning the motor and going too fast on the city streets, down to Forward and to the Parkway, tangling with rush-hour traffic, being the rude driver who's in a hurry.

But if she sees him, that's no good. She won't see him. He'll make sure he's invisible.

He gets the whole way to the Turnpike before he spots her moving along steadily. She is going to the cottage and not to the police. Good. He stays ten cars behind until there is a nice thick bevy of trucks, then he snakes ahead in the left lane. Beat her to the Donegal exit . . . He'll do it in good time. Park in the back of Sarnelli's, motor running, get his bearings.

He's the man in the black car, going fast in the left lane, blocked from her view by trucks, other cars; she won't see him because he doesn't want her to, doesn't want her to.

Everything's changed. He's running again. This is the end of something.

15

MARINA CALLED IN THE LATE AFTERNOON ON HER WAY TO THE airport in Ft. Myers, saying, "I talked to her. She's his mother, all right. And . . . and he's not dead."

"Wow."

"I didn't hate her, either." As Marina gave him the few facts she had of the strange relationship between LaBeau and her son, Christie nodded and made scratches on his tablet with a pencil. "I couldn't get her to talk about Atlantic City. I did find out something about the earlier years. The father told her he'd take care of the boy if she *never* called or got in touch. She hated him for that, but she caved in. Hears from her son now a couple of times a year by phone. Richard? She told me she doesn't know her son's name."

"So she never said 'Frank Razzi'?"

"No. For what it's worth, I kind of tested her. At one point, I said, 'Well, there's a Frank Razzi wants to be in touch with you, if you think of anything,' and I gave her a pretty good looking-over and she didn't flinch at all. No, I don't think she was pretending. Either she really doesn't know or it's not the same guy. At another point, I said to her, 'Did you know the name of the person whose body you claimed?' She clammed up then and said she didn't know what I was talking about. But it was only form. She let me know with her eyes that we both knew what she did."

After they hung up, he sat there, doodling and thinking, was it time to call Elizabeth, jolt her with: long-dead
relative come to life again?

He called Dolan in. "I need you to work late tonight.
We're going over to Pitt. Hang around."

Dolan smiled. "I'll call my wife. We got him, huh?"

Christie said, "It looks good. We don't look too much
like students, though, do we?"

Dolan said, "Probably not. Night students are all ages,
though." He sighed. "My daughter announced the other
day she wants Harvard, Princeton, or Yale. They're just
names to her right now, but, man, is she smart. I have to
hope for scholarships."

"Doesn't she have a few years to go?"

"Seven to go. They think ahead."

Christie and Dolan got to Pitt a little after five and
found the classroom. They stood down the hall, trying to
keep their distance. At five-fifteen a bunch of classes let
out, and the room they were interested in emptied out,
too. It remained empty for half an hour. Then slowly, very
slowly, the room began to fill again.

It was a long wait for Christie and Dolan, and Christie
hated waiting. Nobody who looked like a teacher, whatever
that looked like, went into the room. At six, when the class
was supposed to start, the detectives walked down the hall
for a closer look. The room was full of students, who talked
comfortably among themselves. No prof.

Restlessness, evidenced by a certain amount of looking at watches, began around six-ten. Christie got on the
phone to the Investigative Branch. He never could stand
just waiting. "Anything going on?" he asked.

"Nothing. We sent McGranahan down to Greyhound
to talk to a runaway who asked for somebody from Homicide. That's about it."

A boy came out of the room and headed toward the
men's room. He looked as if he hadn't washed or changed
his clothes for weeks.

"Hold up a second," Christie said. The messy-haired

fellow turned in a shuffle. "You know anything about how late Razzi is going to be?"

"Why?"

"We hoped to see him."

The student laughed and slouched even farther into the house he'd made of his clothes. "You guys are cops, right? No wonder he took a powder."

A flush of irritation came over Christie, but he buttoned himself up. "You know something about it?"

"I know nothing about it, but if I had to guess, I'd guess cocaine. I hope he's having some fun."

The shifty-eyed boy knew nothing about fun, except for the sort of kick rudeness gave him. Christie said simply, "I don't think he is."

Dolan swore under his breath. Both men were used to being hated, but they didn't have to like it.

The student went and had his pee and cut a curved path away from them on his way back to the classroom. They could hear him telling the others in tones loud enough to carry out to the hallway that the two "uptights" out there were cops after Razzi. At six-thirty the class broke up, but many of the students went on talking as they left.

Christie said simply, "They like him. Razzi. You can tell."

They were on their way back to the parking lot at the Investigative Branch when the phone rang. Detective in Athens saying, "That place you asked me to check on is dead empty, swept clean, not a trace of the guy."

SHE FELT SCARED STILL AND COULDN'T GET A DEEP BREATH. Before she hauled heavy groceries in, she wanted to sit for a moment, pull it together. She went into the cottage with only the bag of files and the high school yearbook. The familiar smell of the cottage fireplace enveloped her—ashes, wood, smoke.

Dan, she thought, Dan, are you here? It helped to think of him here somewhere, just out back, gathering kindling.

Elizabeth put on the lights and sat at the kitchen table.

On an ordinary day, she might have done this, looking over some list, waiting for the kids. She opened the yearbook first and studied the pictures. No. No way. She'd been going crazy, is all. Paul was a blond kid with jug ears. The idea that had been bothering her was preposterous and must have been coming out of guilt. It was six weeks to the day since she lost Dan, exactly six weeks. She didn't return her friends' phone calls, she was in an affair, she couldn't *find* Dan—and couldn't explain to anyone what that meant. She was as troubled, as rocky as anyone who had ever come to her for help.

Look at the files, too, she told herself, finish what you started. Go on.

She leafed through one about the Pocusset Safe House. Nothing new. Then, of course, the one she meant to read, the one marked, "Gerald Paul LaBeau." She opened the worn folder and shook her head at the idea that had driven her crazy. As if Frank, who touched a finger to her lips, could be that boy, that name, that trouble. LaBeau. School report cards, greeting cards, all the things people kept.

Dan's handwriting. A groan escaped her, just seeing it.

Name of the detective Dan had used. Paul's obituary. The photo. Something stopped her. No. She looked at the photo again and couldn't find what it was that alarmed her. Only that the hair seemed different, darker? Her heart began to thump and she turned a few more pages. Then she saw what Christie had been talking about. The detective's phone number, the 724 area code. All right. Dan had worn the wings of justice, couldn't stop, couldn't let it go.

There were noises out on the road and in her head and even in her heart—the little washing-machine-like chugging sound of diastole, systole—and she thought she had better get the rest of the things from the car.

But when she went to the door and opened it, there he was as if he had sprung from her imagination. He stood there, with a crumpled map in his hand. He just stood there and looked at her.

For a long moment, she didn't breathe or swallow. Then he moved forward, and she moved backward, and somehow, without meaning to, she let him in. "You're Paul."

He nodded once. His eyes scanned the table behind her.

"Please don't hurt me."

"That's all you have to say?"

"Please don't. I have kids. Please, Fra— I don't know what to call you. I don't know what you want."

"Frank. Call me Frank. Who told you to look at that stuff?"

"Nobody."

"You're going to put all those things back in the bag again, put the little bag in a big trash bag, we're going to take a ride."

"No, just take—"

"Do it." Suddenly he was there at her side, twisting her arm back until a pain seared through her shoulder. "Do it."

"Coward," she spit out. "Coward. You killed him, didn't you? Say it, say it. You shot a defenseless, innocent man."

The sound that emanated from him was somewhere between a curse and a growl, but he let her go. "Innocent! If that's the way you want to paint it . . ."

She held on to her shoulder where it hurt still, looked around, thinking, What can I use, knives, skewers, a hammer, but suddenly hate filled her up, got her body moving, and she was at him, hitting him in the face over and over with the heel of her hand. "You . . . You . . . Killer. Murderer. You took everything from me."

He grabbed at her hands to stop her hitting. His face looked pink, vulnerable, stunned, and she backed off, panting. "Did you hate him that much?"

"I guess I did."

"Why?"

He waved her question aside and took a few steps, looking around the place. "He built this? Little hideaway? He wasn't big in the imagination department, was he?"

Jealousy, it was all jealousy, then. There was a steady hum in her ears, like a machine saw going at high power. She didn't know what to grab. A chair? The lion was faster than the tamer.

"And. He was a bleeding heart, wouldn't you say? A moral prig. Don't deny it." He paced around, hunched over, watching her, watching what she would grab.

When she went still, he did. It was as if the moment in the courtroom, facing the murderer, was here, had crept up on her. "You killed him," she said simply. "You shot him. You took everything away from me."

He ignored her accusation. He wanted the other conversation. "You must have thought so, too? Sometimes? That his so-called beneficence was something else. Arrogance."

"No. He gave everyone time. Value. He loved people."

"Not me."

Was that it? Another person wanting more of Dan? "He cared about you, grieved for you, and you—"

"No. Not true. You whitewash things. He wasn't everything to you either. Because. You and me." He waggled a finger back and forth, ridiculous. "What was that? Huh? Plain old lust? What was it?"

Outside it was dark. She heard a car on the road, way above. Talking to him—would it buy her time? She said quietly, "I don't know what it was. Do you?"

He made a face she couldn't read and paced the room once more. She saw that he was carrying a gun in his jacket pocket. The tip of the butt stuck out, and she thought, This is real, this is real. She thought, I'm going to die, and yet she also felt she had never been more herself than she was now. She said, "He loved you," without being sure of all that meant. Was she telling him she had loved him? "He wanted to help." She could see how tense his muscles were, how jagged his breathing. He was sweating profusely, and shaking. Oh. Of course. She saw now. He was on something, a drug of some sort, but she didn't know if more of it or less of it was in order.

Hitting him, that had been easy. Running out the door, letting him catch her, hurt her, that would be easy, too. Kill him or let him kill her, easy, easy actions. Instead, she did the hard one. She sat down at the kitchen table.

He looked at her, surprised.

"I take it you want to confess," she said. "You went to a lot of trouble to get to know me."

After a while, he said, "I'd tell you. Nobody else."

"From the beginning? About Ted Luckey?"

He nodded.

Her cell phone was in her purse. Christie's card was in there, too. If only she could— She kept talking. "And the boy in Atlantic City?"

"Frank Razzi was his name. Poor kid."

"Why do you say, 'poor kid'?"

"He was a mess."

"You killed him?"

"No, he did quite a job of it on his own."

"How?"

"Heroin. I saw him after it was too late."

"That's the truth?"

"Most of it. Only that I thought of his death before it happened. I thought, Wouldn't his cards be handy? Got what I wished for."

Her purse was on a chair and she couldn't reach for it. He watched everything she did. She opened her hands to show she had nothing, was writing nothing. I am buying five minutes, an hour, she thought. I might find a way out, I might not. An ant crossed the tabletop and she watched it, latched on to its steady progress. An ant, out of season, all alone, alive. Busy, looking for something.

Frank sat down across from her.

FRANK HAD TO LAUGH. IT WAS LIKE THERAPY AT GUNPOINT. SHE sat there listening to him because she had to, no fee, no time limit, her only way to live.

Her hands were on the table to say, No funny business. She looked calm, couldn't be, but she looked it, a good trick. She had hit him, but the fury that had driven her across the room didn't show now.

"How did you get the house next door?" she asked.

He told her about luck, how he'd always had it, thinking of a thing and then getting it. He wanted to be back where he'd been as a boy, he wanted memory, like other people, but more than that, he wanted her, to show her a little something. And it had happened. Accomplished. Luck or fate. He told her that.

Repressed, she is. Starved. The way the blood rushes to her face. She needed a dose of Frank and they both know it.

"The part about Ted Luckey. I don't understand. Dan never understood."

No tape recorder. No paper. She wants to know things just to know them, before she dies? Just to stay alive. That's how some people are.

He begins slowly. "Ted laughed at me sometimes. He thought he was teasing but it had an edge. He said I was jealous about his grades and Dan's. So what? I thought. What's wrong with jealousy? It burned, because all along, I knew things about Ted and I didn't throw them in his face."

She is very still. Her eyes are full of questions.

"The thing is, I worked for my father in the office. I read his files on patients. I knew all kinds of things about all kinds of people, not just Ted. Ted Luckey's father was a drunk, liver trouble, mother was a mess, on everything sedating there was at the time, Seconal was one of them.

"Ted told me how he and Dan were both planning to be doctors. Dan had been reading all kinds of articles in the medical journals and psychiatric journals and, see, he had discovered the theory that if a mother was loving, a kid could get through anything, anything at all, even her addiction. Whereas. If the mother was abusive or didn't love her kid, it was hopeless. Fathers were expendable, that's what Dan said. The whole future rested in the mother."

"Some people believe that," Elizabeth says evenly.

Her voice surprises him. He wants her to shut up and listen. He wants to shock her.

"Well, Ted blathered on and on about this idea—Dan's idea about mothers. Dan told Ted his mother loved him and that made it all possible. The idea came to me one day and it was like . . . creativity. I wondered if the idea would *work*. It was like a math problem. Work it out to see if you have the answer right. . . ."

She shakes her head quickly, doesn't understand.

"Steal a little Seconal from my father's drug cache. When the idea first hit me, I thought of it as a joke—put Ted Luckey out of commission for finals with some of mother's milk. But then I thought, maybe out of commission for good, I did have that thought, and when I thought it, I didn't freak out. It was just an idea. That it would hurt Dan, that, that was an advantage. I stole the Seconal, that was easy, but I didn't do anything. Then I went up to the Pocusset house where Ted hung out and I talked a lot, chatted him up. Ted was restless, wanted to be on his own, wanted to cram all night, even though he pretended it all came easily. I handed over a six-pack of beer and said, 'Open 'em up. We're going to get social.' He didn't want to, so I called him chicken and he opened them up.

"And after one beer, Ted said he felt bad for me on account of my mother. I said, 'What do you know about it?' He said Dan saw my mother when she came to drop me off, and Dan said one look at her and he knew I didn't have a chance. I said, 'Why?' and Ted said, well, because of her anger and the fact that she didn't care two sticks about me, and didn't want me."

"If he said those things, he was young . . . trying to understand."

"What I'm saying is, Ted looked at me with pity. Condescension. And a terrible thing happened. I started to cry because of how he was looking at me. I cried uncontrollably. I guess in your business, that doesn't surprise you, you know what will make a boy angry. I told Ted, 'That's not true, that shit about my mother.' I tried to defend my mother, but I couldn't believe in it, so he was looking at me like I was a hopeless, sniveling five-year-old. I . . . I couldn't stop crying."

Elizabeth looks as if she will say something, shifts, doesn't speak.

"Ted said he was going to talk to Dan, tell him how upset I was, and that I still loved my mother. I told Ted I didn't want him to talk *about* me to Dan, I didn't want to be the subject of their conversation. Have the two of them pitying me? I had pills in my pocket. I was very careful not to touch anything. Just dropped a bunch of pills in one of the bottles on Ted's side of the six-pack when Ted went outside to pee. So you see, I wanted it. I wanted to wipe him out."

Elizabeth's hand goes to her mouth. She winces.

"I hated him."

"For seeing you."

Are all therapists this green? Of course, of course, he's light-years ahead of her. "Ted came back and drank it all up. He thought he was keeping me company."

"You weren't sorry?"

"I almost stopped him twenty times. But I didn't."

Elizabeth shudders and closes her eyes for a few seconds, as if praying, and who knows, maybe she is.

"Once I'd started the thing, I couldn't stop it. Do you have an explanation for that?"

"No. Poor Ted," she says quietly. "Poor Ted." Tears gather on her lashes, she opens her eyes and they fill again.

"It was like work, like a job I had to do. Same thing with Dan. This is the part you want to know. The other was just delay, right? Your Dan was kind of thickheaded. He never stopped pursuing me over the Ted Luckey thing. He wouldn't let me be dead. I had a life of sorts, I'd made some successes, and he was after me, after me."

She knows to be scared now. Folds her arms in over herself.

"Wanted me to confess and go to jail. Couldn't let

me be. Do you remember what he said in the newspaper interview?"

"No."

" 'Never had a chance.' Still at it. Self-righteous son of a bitch you hooked yourself up with."

"He didn't mean it that way. I'm sure he didn't."

"And what would you say? About my chances? In life and love."

"I think everyone is different. I never knew your mother— It doesn't matter what I think."

Frank laughs. She thinks she'll squirm out of it, live to tell all this. "But it does."

"It does?"

"Yes. I appoint you."

She seems uncertain. "I think you have a chance even now."

"Clever." He smiles.

"What else do you want to tell me?"

"Nothing."

"Frank Razzi. How did he die?"

"Heroin. You already asked me. Surely he's not the one you want to know about? I took his cards. Just like I took Dan's cards. And now the session is almost over."

She snaps to attention. All right! Thought she was the one in charge, didn't she?

He makes an amused expression and pats his pocket. "Going to Europe," he says. "Dan Ross is going to retire in Europe. Wine and women and cafés."

"You won't get away with it."

"Who's going to tell? You?"

Her whole body collapses inward. "Someone will know," she says, rousing herself to fight. "Airport security . . . they look at photos now."

"I have a trick. If I want them to think I'm Dan, they will. It's in the way I engage the agent's eyes. I never got questioned before."

"You don't have the slightest idea how much Dan cared about you."

"And you?"

"Yes. Yes."

"And my mother? She never called me."

She hesitates, then says, "Maybe your father told her not to. Maybe he told her she was a bad influence."

"That would stop her?"

"It happens a million times a day."

They sit there in the quiet, with the bright kitchen light on, and the longer they sit there, the truer this idea seems. Simple and true.

"Maybe you should ask her?" Elizabeth says.

He looks at the phone in her hand. He didn't see her get it, and that frightens him more than anything. Where was he looking? Had *he* closed his eyes?

"Tell me the number," she's saying. But she's already punching something in.

He grabs the phone from her. These honest-looking women, full of tricks. He thinks about how he first saw her, alone in her house, quiet and full of grief. How beautiful she was that way, just drinking it in, the idea of loss. This grappling for life—he understands it, it's his story, all right—is not so pretty. *I'm just a poor fellow that would live.* Line from something. "Stupid of you," he says, "to think I am so stupid."

Phone is in his hand. She watches him punch at the STOP button. He throws the phone. It hits the couch arm, skitters off to the table, the floor. As if it's some kind of joke, the phone begins to ring. Again he laughs. "Don't even think about it."

One of her kids, but she doesn't want to say those words, doesn't want to remind him. To keep them safe, she would do anything. That anger of his, how far does it reach? Not to her kids, let Dan and her be enough for him.

If he would leave now, try to get on a plane, he might make it. Probably would make it. Why did she stop him, why did she say it wouldn't work?

"What did you think of my confession?"

A tricky answer is beyond her. She plods toward the

truth. "The part about Ted Luckey made me sad. The part about Dan made me . . . furious. It made me want to hurt you. Did he know what was happening? Who you were?"

Frank appears to give it some thought. "He knew me as if he'd been waiting for me. At first he offered to take me home for dinner. And to meet you."

"Was he afraid?"

"Yes. When he saw the gun, he got quiet."

Oh. Oh. Dan. In that moment, she rises above her small self, as if, for a second, she can understand all of it, has understood: a boy threatening him, he doesn't want to hurt the boy, and then it's too late.

"He wanted to call you. I made him drop the phone."

"Oh."

"He said, 'Please, no.' Not terribly original. Then he said your name. 'Elizabeth.' "

The tears well up, burn at her eyes, then fall.

"It was as if he guessed what I would do. He gave me the idea. To know you."

It's coming to her, slowly, slowly. He wants to be Dan, wants Dan's heart. "I think you loved him," she says.

"No."

"I think you did."

He shakes his head. "The way he looked at me, it was pity, condescension, arrogance."

"He worried about everything. Including you. You must have known it."

CHRISTIE LEFT A PHONE MESSAGE FOR ELIZABETH AT THE SQUIR-rel Hill address. "Call me. It's urgent. I have to talk to you."

He was just about to let Dolan off at the Investigations Branch when his phone rang again. This time it was McGranahan, who was over at the Pocusset Safe House. "There's a girl here telling a story about the Ross killing. Says we ought to be looking for a guy drives a BMW. She says his name is Frank Razzi."

He hit the gas and they got themselves over there in six minutes, doorway to doorway.

Bridget Stevens was a good witness. Smart, too. Said she thought Frank Razzi was divided, that his actions were divided. That she was half of some equation and Elizabeth Shepherd was the other half. That's what she said, as she sat there, while Sherman put a bowl of soup in front of her. She said, "I think the doctor's wife is in danger."

Christie and Dolan looked at each other. Christie took out his phone and tried Elizabeth's number again. The girl, Bridget, showed how she'd saved some of the drink as evidence, even the chip of a pill she'd slipped into her pocket.

Alarm washed through Christie's body. It was his fault if Elizabeth got hurt. He had not included her. He had a sinking, terrible feeling that he'd botched it.

"We're going over there now," he said. "Check on the house."

When they got to the Beechwood house, it was empty, car not there.

Christie and Dolan drove to East Liberty with the lights flashing, no siren. Up in his office, Christie found Elizabeth's cell-phone number and made the phone call that trilled in the cottage out near Seven Springs after the phone was thrown across the room.

"WE'RE GOING TO TAKE A RIDE," FRANK SAID. "GET RID OF SOME things."

"No, just take the things, then go."

"You have nothing to say about it. You're part of it."

"Better to talk to someone else like you talked to me."

He was incredulous. The whole family was cracked. As if a day could be passed in prison without madness. An hour. He couldn't do it. As if he could tell the things he told her to someone else, and then a new person, and another one after that. His secret. His own small, hard gem, people trying to pry it from him. Pitying him.

She'd lulled him, sitting across the kitchen table like that, playing confidant, tracing the tabletop, like a wife. A husband and wife having one of those big, serious conversations.

He got up suddenly. "Let's go." He pulled at her elbow.

"No." She pulled away and backed up a couple of steps. They stood, five feet from each other, frozen. "You like something about me. Or did. Let me go."

"You can stop shrinking me anytime." He grabbed her and she wrenched away once more. He saw her eye go to the phone. Same thing, same as Dan, she pitied him, blah, blah, blah, she was looking to save her ass.

He went after her, pushing at first, then pulling once he got her off balance. Do it now, he told himself. Now.

He dragged her to the bedroom.

"Please, no."

Just like Dan. Same words, just like him. He threw her on the bed and pinned her wrists down. In one quick move, he let go with his right hand and grabbed for a pillow. She was clawing at him, pulling at his shirt. He began to press the pillow into her face and it was awful the way she fought, struggled. He saw himself as if from a distance. Long scratches on his face and neck. Blood bubbling to the surface. If he hadn't needed both hands, he would have pulled the gun, but even as he had that thought, he shunned it. The gun was messy. By the time he got it, she could run. He'd have to gouge ten holes in her body, just to stop her. She fought and thrashed, then there was stillness. He felt exhausted and wanted to cry. He took the pillow away. Too early. Crouched over her, he watched her eyelids flutter, her eyes open. Nothing worked, her body was failing her. She couldn't get control of the muscles, wanted to breathe, but couldn't. She looked as if she might kiss him, as if she might cry. He wondered what she would do. He couldn't stop watching her. Lips formed a word. *Fuck,* maybe it was, but he thought, *Frank,* something said softly.

It wasn't possible to feel love now, it wasn't possible to be so ridiculous. Her arm flew up, brushed his face, fell. She was trying to hit him, surely, he knew that, but it was soft, soft, the way her hand brushed his face. He hurt everywhere—throat, eyeballs, head. He waited for her to say his name again. Her eyes said it.

He cried out, climbed away from her.

Put it on my gravestone, he thought, I couldn't do it. He backed out of the room and went to his car and drove away.

WHAT HE WAS, WHAT HE KNEW, CAME TOGETHER AT ONCE. THE night was beautiful—cold, crisp, clear. There were stars. He opened the windows and breathed in the stars. Why, he could go anywhere, be anything. Couldn't he? Drive to Kalamazoo or Seattle or go down to Florida and see Mum one last time. Have a drink with the old girl, watch her face soften, watch old Mum feel love.

He sucked in the air.

Dictionary of Synonyms and Antonyms, one of his mother's possessions. He'd loved it, pored over it. Discovered he belonged on the right-hand page. Across from *candid, frank, sincere, honest, veracious, truthful,* which was on the left.

He'd found his page a long time ago, marveled at it. *Knavish, roguish, scampish, rascally, scoundrelly, blackguardly, villainous.* Then the nouns that he was: *a reprobate, a recreant.* It seemed, when he was twelve, thirteen, and discovered his page, a *good thing* to be so full of bastardly life. But it wasn't all comedy, not really, not just the grit and ingenious adaptation to adversity. There were other truths: base, vile, degraded. Deceitful, false-hearted, unfrank, disingenuous. Unfrank. Put it on his gravestone. Treacherous, perfidious, double-dealing, unfrank.

Even now, as he drove fast past Sarnelli's, where he'd hidden out until her car went past, where he'd parked and hidden like a spy, then followed her, even now, he wanted to lie to someone. He'd told nothing but truth tonight, a whole night of truth, and it left a hole in him, got him an ache behind his eyes.

Liquor. He needed a bottle of something. He wound back to Sarnelli's, parked, ran in, and asked where there

was a liquor store open. The man behind the counter drew
him a little map. Ten miles out of his way. What did it matter? Ten miles.

He still felt he had luck. He'd taken it from Ted Luckey
a long time ago and had it ever since. He would find the
shop. All would be well.

A FULL HOUR LATER HE IS ON THE ROAD AGAIN, SUCKING IN AIR
and looking at the beauty of the night as if he hasn't seen
it before, ever. And maybe he hasn't. He knows exactly
what he's doing and exactly when, exactly how.

ELIZABETH LISTENED, LISTENED. SHE WAS AFRAID. EVEN THOUGH
she'd heard a car start up and leave, she thought she would
emerge from the bedroom and find Frank there looking at
her. Or that she would fumble for the phone, turn, and find
herself staring at him holding the handgun. The house was
quiet, but she thought his voice would rise up out of the silence. She attended in a new way to the hum of the furnace
giving way to the roar of the furnace fan, then cars on the
road above, leaves rustling. He might drive back any
minute, overpower her again. She moved in slow motion,
as if to listen better. When she touched a button on her
phone, just to test it, the phone sang back to her. Sitting on
the couch, listening to this familiar sound, she realized she
was still far away, in a dream of the last six weeks, a night-
mare of unsettlement. She got up and locked the front
door, then the side door—as if that would help if he
changed his mind. Then she sifted through her purse until
she found what she wanted, Christie's card. It meant she
had to explain herself. She had no choice.

"Christie," he answered.

"It's . . . Elizabeth Shep—"

"My God, where are you? Are you all right?"

She didn't know how to answer that. No, no, and yes. "I
know now who did it. I'd been seeing him. He moved in
next door and I didn't know. . . ."

"Next door!"

"His name is Frank Razzi. He's . . . he's in despair. He's in terrible shape. He might try to use Dan's ID to get on a plane. He tried to kill me, but . . . he stopped himself."

"Where are you?"

"At our cottage. I don't know how he found it. I never—"

"Give me your address. I'll get someone to you right away."

She gave Christie the address. The shock began to wear off. It was the idea of help coming to her, someone to be with her, that unhinged her, made her feel like a child of five, hopelessly small.

EVERYBODY AT THE INVESTIGATIVE BRANCH DID SOMETHING. APB for the black BMW. Cops on the lookout on any road within an hour of the Donegal exit. Ohio vehicle registration contacted, a plate number added to the orders. Cops at the airport checking outgoing flights, under the names Razzi or Ross, either one.

FRANK DROVE WITH THE WINDOWS OPEN EVEN THOUGH THE cold air bit into him and his body shook. Gun, yes, but that was messy, messy. He had to make sure, that was the thing. Fucking bad aim was what he had.

If he had leapt into the fire he built when he was a boy, he'd have saved a lot of people a lot of trouble, all right. The man had called his mother a cock-sucking whore. Which, if you were being literal, she was. He never told anyone that part of it.

Mum. Looking for salvation in men. Smart, and thinking she was nothing. Looking for her heart in some idiot's cock. Couldn't lift herself up. How he hated her for that. But tonight, the hate begins to float out the car windows, like smoke, vapor.

He flicks on the radio. Thelonious Monk. Oh, glory. This is religion. This is Mozart. Oh, baby.

His name. No way to salvage that.

Jail. No way. He's done jail all his life.

He pulls off at the Pittsburgh exit and smiles as he

hands a five to the man at the tollbooth. "Keep the change," he says. "Beautify the highways!" Ha. In his rearview mirror, the man is waving a receipt in the air, looking mystified.

Air. Monk. Oh, glory.

He takes a long pull from the bottle. Preparatory. A little blood of the lamb before the body.

Monroeville exit. Gun out of pocket and on the seat. Swissvale exit, he reaches deeper into his pocket and wraps his fingers around the bottle of Xanax. The body. It's all he has, it will have to do. Confession made, God take me. Without suffering. Please. Timing, timing is everything.

Two pills in his mouth. A slug of alcohol. Good. Like a little curtain coming over him right away.

Two more. Two more. Another slug. Careful, careful. Follow the painted line. It's working. He has to fight against the softness for a few minutes until he gets past Oakland. It could be any spot, he doesn't need to be particular, but ideas take hold with him, and he's thought of this before, the guardrail, the particular spot, he's had the spot picked for thirty years—go at it hard enough, then the steep drop toward the river. Steep drop, *hade,* a Scrabble word. Off the parkway in Pittsburgh, a mile from home, not even.

He will suffer, but not for long. Everything will be relaxed. Even his brain. Even his dick. Three more pills and another slug.

Then he hears the sirens. He looks behind him and sees there are two cars after him. He accelerates, looking for the right spot on the guardrail over the river. He would like to fall like a parachuter caught on the wind. He's doing seventy, he makes it eighty, ninety, and he's off.

This isn't it, this isn't it—

Sound of metal, sounds, sounds. Feeling of stretching backward. Screaming, all kinds of screaming.

His car is hanging off the guardrail, hanging in the air. Something holds it up. It's laughable. He's just hanging there. He can feel a gash on his forehead, but it doesn't hurt, or maybe it does but there are so many pills in him to soften it. The car is teetering. He tries to shake it forward by jerking in his seat, but it does not fall. Panic overtakes him. There are more cars coming up behind, sirens everywhere. He tries to get the door open and at first he can't, but then he can. The door is open and he's tipping out like an old drunk, hand on the door.

"No, don't move. Hang on, buddy."

His jaw drops. Four cops are motioning for him to hang back, hold on, don't tip the balance. One fat cop moves forward with an arm outstretched toward him and another arm being held by those behind him. "Hold on, buddy." The cop stretches forward. "I got you, if only you—"

Another car screeches to a halt. Something important is happening. He can sense it, by the way they all react. Both car doors open, two men get out. The fat cop keeps trying to hold his eyes.

"Commander . . ." says one of the other cops.

The man who must be the commander comes up behind the group that wants to pull him in. "It's okay," the commander says calmly. "Reach out, Paul. They've got you."

He can't bear it. Can't bear it. He closes his eyes so he doesn't have to look at the poor shits who want to save him. He can't bear it. When he opens his eyes, there's Ted Luckey, standing beside the commander, looking serious, looking sober. Ted Luckey. How did he get here?

Bird on a limb. He saw that image, loved it, wanted to use it. It was beautiful. Bird on a limb, footing, footing, footing, the act of moving on the feet, dancing. Bird feels the limb dip low. Flies away.

"He's drunk," someone says.

He supposes so. Cold air. Dan next to Ted Luckey, both of them saying, "Reach forward, it's okay." Coltrane now slips past the sirens to find him and he keeps his eyes closed and tries to make his way to the great sound.

16

ALL IS IN ORDER NOW. THE BMW HAULED OUT OF THE RAVINE. The body hauled out, buried.

In the family plot, in the cemetery—Elizabeth's decision, one of the harder ones she ever had to make. And the mother brought up for it, too. It was only right, she thought.

The contents of the car, the house next door have been examined and filed. The man dissected, this way and that. Evil or full of something else, not everyone can agree. What sifted out with some certainty is: He needed danger, needed to come close to it, had never killed a woman, after all, and what drove him seemed to go back to a moment when he was a boy, an Ishmael grieving for his mother, who'd been cast out, and him still trying to figure out how to defend the both of them.

Dan *sent* him to her, that's what Frank said. She has turned over all the ways in which this is true. . . .

She had to tell Christie everything: The man moved in next door, she wanted his company, nobody else's. It was a sexual relationship, yes, and hot. That's not a word she used with Christie, but he understood anyway. She could tell by the way he blinked and tried not to be surprised. When he fed it back to her, it was tamped down a little: that she liked Frank Razzi, maybe was coming to love him, gave herself over to him. But, he wondered aloud, when did she know who he was?

Not until the end. Had no idea. None.

Today the commander has returned Dan's final things to her, the cards and photographs Frank carried in his pocket. She holds them and then puts them down on the table in front of her.

Across from her sits the commander with the kind eyes.

They sit here today with the problem of truth. All right, had some idea, some. Way down under, where she couldn't catch it.

"I was not . . . doing well," she says. "I had this feeling of *losing* Dan every hour in little ways. Suddenly I couldn't picture him or hear him anymore. That was worse than his dying."

Christie leans forward over his knees, says, "I hear you."

"I didn't think I could ever— Frank took me by surprise. I can't explain it beyond that. He gave me a lot of attention. But I also knew he needed me for something."

"I don't like to admit I'm wrong," Christie says. "One of my faults, so Marina tells me. But I didn't handle it right. I tried to solve it on my own. I didn't keep you in the loop. Although we might never have caught him if I had."

The word *caught* occupies her. Frank was caught. And he wasn't; he also got away.

Perhaps they both think about these things in the December afternoon. It's a gray day. Outside there are the cries of schoolchildren running home. There's a hint of snow to excite them, a flake here and there, swirling.

After a while, she says, "I wish I could talk to Dan."

Christie comes over to where she sits, surprising her, overwhelming her with the amount of feeling in his expression. He stoops awkwardly before her and takes her hands. "It's okay. You're human."

Then there he is, suddenly, there's Dan, right behind the detective's eyes. She hasn't been able to find him for such a long time and now he's one foot away from her, simple and himself.

Christie squeezes her hands for a long time. He must sense how hard it is for her to part with him, because he has admirable staying power. It can't be easy on his knees. "You're okay," he says. "Better than okay. You're true-blue. Able to love."

And then he stands. "I have to go."

She rises and walks him to the door.

"I'll call you from time to time," he says.

Elizabeth watches him turn from her, walk down the driveway to his car, stop, turn around. He doesn't wave. He just stands there, noting the snow coming down in large flakes, letting her look at him.

IT WAS EASY. SHE GOT THE JOB AT KINKO'S WITHOUT BREATHING. It's only temporary. Every day, if she has to, she will bug the office at Pitt until she gets a university job with tuition benefits. Next September she is going to be in school. Period.

Place to stay, too. She followed up six ads and chose an apartment.

It sounds passive to just stay where she landed and maybe it is, but she thinks not. She plumbs *what is* for the gold.

She thinks about Frank Razzi every day, every minute.

One thing she is sure of. Frank Razzi wanted her to figure it out. He gave her all that time in the house, he wanted her to know. He *chose* her. And in the end, he opened his hands and let her go. He knew. He *knew*.

She feels she is holding a big awkward something. A version of his ashes and bones. Knowledge. She asked the police if she could have his papers and they said no, it wasn't allowed, but Christie sounded as if, in time, with prodding, he might relent. Waste. Otherwise it's pure waste. What will they do, burn everything?

And if they do, it doesn't matter, she holds it anyway, with only the faintest glimmer of understanding, but that's okay, too, it will come.

ABOUT THE AUTHOR

KATHLEEN GEORGE, a director and theater professor at the University of Pittsburgh, is also the author of *The Man in the Buick*, a collection of short stories, and *Taken*, a novel. Her fiction has appeared in many publications, including *North American Review*, and *Mademoiselle*. She lives with her husband in Pittsburgh.